Memory Ranch

Marc Sercomb

Coyote Moon Press – Los Angeles, CA
ISBN: 979-8-218-73365-0
Library of Congress Control Number: 2025914460
Title: Memory Ranch
Author: Marc Sercomb
Digital distribution | 2025
Paperback | 2025

This story is based on an idea by Marc Sercomb and Tim Chandler.

Dedication

To the great Richard Farnsworth, the original inspiration for Dusty Bob, and to all the singing cowboys of yesteryear.

About the Author

A native son of the Golden State, Marc Sercomb spent a large part of his aimless youth wandering vast stretches of North America and Europe before becoming a teacher for twenty-eight years. He resides in the parched foothills of Los Angeles with his wife Robin, two cats, and a pair of horses named Ransom and Redemption. His hobbies include reading, music, motorcycles, food, and browsing in hardware stores. He spends a lot of time in his backyard staring at clouds.

He is also the author of the novels *Picasso's Motorcycle* and *Living in Cleveland with the Ghost of Joseph Stalin*.

"I write stories mostly to amuse myself," he once said, to no one in particular.

Chapter 1

Dusty Bob and his trusty sidekick and confidant, Jim Dupree, had engaged in the same daily ritual for the last thirty years: strong black coffee and one hand-rolled cigarette at 6:00 am. Neither one had missed a day, in sickness or in health, rain or fair weather. Change was not something looked upon in a favorable light around Memory Ranch, where the two had been meeting at sunrise for too many years now to count. Dusty Bob wore the same sweat-stained, cream-colored Stetson, well-worn, gold-stitched cowboy boots, and amply-waxed handlebar mustache that he always had, and, well into his ninth decade of life, saw no reason to change things now. Besides, it had taken him nearly twenty years to get the Stetson's shape and patina the way he wanted it.

"What are you up to today, Bob?" Jim drawled, taking a long, slow sip of coffee. They were sitting on the front porch of the diner, watching the sun rise.

Dusty Bob took his time responding. He didn't do anything much in a hurry these days, especially talking. "Nothin'. What are you up to, Jim?"

"Nothin'. Say, I've got an idear. Why don't we take the pickup truck and drive into Holbrook today?"

Dusty Bob hesitated, looking out over the Arizona desert sunrise through narrowed slits beneath bushy grey eyebrows. "Nah."

Jim Dupree considered Dusty Bob's response a good, long while. He smiled slightly, remarking to himself how their morning conversations had lately taken on all the pacing and excitement of a turtle race. "Well, what you got going on around here that's so pressin'?"

"Gotta get the place ready."

"Ready for *what*?" Jim challenged, with just a smidge of lethargic impatience.

"The guests."

"The guests? When, exactly, was the last time we had any guests?"

"We get 'em from time to time."

"Oh yeah? I bet you can't even remember the last time we got any guests."

"Sure I can," Dusty Bob said with confidence.

"Well, when was it?"

"A while back."

There was a longer pause than usual.

"Why don't we go into Holbrook today?" Jim finally demanded.

"I told you, someone's gotta be here to check the guests in."

"Sally can do that, if any poor lost souls happen to show up," Jim suggested. Sally Hawk was the plump middle-aged Indian woman who cooked in the diner and looked after the guest cabins in the motel. Sally's husband had been stricken suddenly with the wanderlust and left a long time ago, but she had a strong connection to the spirit world and was therefore able to track his wanderings through her telepathic and clairvoyant abilities, as well as being able to read minds and foretell future events around the ranch. Sally Hawk also had a special recipe for *mole* sauce that made people tell the truth when they ate it.

"I don't want Sally to be the first thing the guests see when they get here," Dusty Bob explained with an admirable amount of restraint. "I don't want them to be frightened off by that Devil Woman and her strange ministrations. I don't want her to be the visual representation of my honorable establishment. It's *Dusty Bob's* Memory Ranch, and I should be the one they first encounter after venturing this far out into the desert to see me."

Jim wasn't about to remind him, but the fans had stopped "venturing out to see him" long ago. They were lucky if they got someone stopping in for a Coke and asking directions to the Grand Canyon. Dusty Bob had been a big star in the western pictures in Hollywood, but that was a long time ago now and nobody really remembered him anymore. Now he was just another sad old drunk broke cowboy out in the middle of nowhere, living off bittersweet memories of lost love and hopeful delusions that people still remembered him.

"The way you talk about her, one might think you're anti-Injun or somethin'," Jim replied.

"Aw, I ain't anti-Injun, an' you know it," Dusty Bob scoffed, exhaling cigarette smoke. "The Red Man's got no better friend than me. I even hired a few of 'em for my pictures when the rest of Hollywood was paintin' up Filipinos an' Chinese to *look* like Injuns."

"You are a true humanitarian," Jim dead-panned. "I'm just surprised you haven't won one of them Nobel Prizes, or somethin'."

"Your tone is rather prickly this morning," Dusty Bob observed.

"Not particularly. I just don't like you talking about Sally that way. It's *unbecoming*."

"Looks to me like somebody's goin' all soft on Sally Hawk," Dusty Bob teased, like a schoolboy.

"Nothin' of the sort," Jim protested.

"The way you two always skinny-dippin' down at Resurrection Creek, it's hard to believe nothin's ever happened between you by now."

"Well, the water in Resurrection Creek is mighty *cold*," Jim responded slyly. "Besides, it ain't like that."

"Oh? Then why do you swim nekked with her?"

"We don't wanna get our clothes wet," Jim explained. "Besides, it ain't about the skinny dippin'. Our outings are purely platonic. We like to go on picnics. We enjoy each other's company, is all. We talk about worldly, sophisticated topics. Where else am I gonna find such stimulating, intelligent conversation?"

"Thank you very much."

Jim was right – he had no romantic inclinations toward Sally Hawk whatsoever. But he also knew that she pined for him with a mighty yearning – heretofore unrequited, as Jim's romantic thoughts, sadly for Sally, leaned towards another.

Such was the state of life on Memory Ranch.

"Speaking of topics, let's get back to Holbrook," Jim recommended. "It would be good for you to get away from this ranch – you know, see the world."

"I've been to Holbrook. It's over-rated."

"You sure are a boring son-of-a-bitch," Jim snapped.

"Yep."

"And stubborn, too."

"That's me. Now if you will allow me, I'd like to read a little of the Good Book in peace and quiet – that is, if you can keep your yammerin' mouth shut for two seconds." Dusty Bob picked an old worn leather Bible off an orange-crate table and opened it near the middle.

Jim laughed and did a spit-take of coffee. "The *Good Book*? Really. Since when did you get religion?"

"We're not gettin' any younger, Jim," Dusty Bob explained patiently. "Don't you think it's time we started contemplatin' more eternal matters? I mean, do you know where you're going when you sever these weighty chains of flesh and finally shed this mortal coil?"

"I hope to Holbrook," Jim replied. "That way I can get away from the Looney Tunes I'm hearin' around here."

"Seriously, Jim," Dusty Bob persisted. "If you could just stop the comedy routine for a minute and talk to me on a higher intellectual plane, I'm sure you would agree that Death, in all its macabre glory, beckons us with each passing moment."

"This has turned into a surprisingly uplifting conversation."

"Time is counted out in minutes, hours, days," Dusty Bob continued. "I feel a compelling sense of the clock runnin' out. I just want to be sure of the state of my eternal soul."

"Well, I for one can tell you that your eternal soul is *bonkers.*"

"I just wish you could be serious for once in your life," Dusty Bob opined. "Just once."

"All right, all right. What got you thinking about all this dyin' stuff, anyhow? What happened?"

Dusty Bob paused dramatically before answering. "Jim, I've seen my own death."

"Really?"

"No, but the character I played in *Dead Man's Hand* did, and I figure that's pretty much the same thing. See, he saw his own death, exactly when and where it would happen, but he still went ahead and did everything the same, even though it portentously led him, step by fateful step, to his ultimate doom. Now, why did he do that, Jim?"

"Because that's how the screenwriter, Sid Weisman, wrote the script," Jim answered.

Dusty Bob closed the Bible. "Sid Weisman didn't write *Dead Man's Hand.* That was Abe Fingerhut. Sid Weisman wrote *Dead Man in South Dakota.*"

"No, no, no," Jim shook his head. "Gabriel Levinson was the screenwriter of *Dead Man in South Dakota.*"

"You're wrong, as usual" Dusty Bob protested.

"No, I'm sure it was Gabriel Levinson," Jim said. "I remember because I dated his sister, Delilah, a few times – you remember her, the girl with the thick coke-bottle glasses and buck teeth –"

"That was *Sid Weisman's* sister," Dusty Bob insisted.

"No, it wasn't," Jim shook his head. "You're gettin' all mixed up. Sid Weisman's sister was the girl with the weak chin and underbite. I

4

only went out with her once, because she drank too much tequila and got sick on the seat of my brand-new Oldsmobile."

"No, it was Gabriel Levinson's sister who couldn't hold her liquor," Dusty Bob corrected him. "You see, this just proves my point, Jim: you're gettin' so old your memory's shot."

"You're older than *me*!"

"But at least my memory's still sharp as a tack!"

"What's all this about, Bob?" There was a graver tone in Jim's voice now.

"I don't want to die, Jim."

"Everybody dies, Bob."

"But I'm not ready to go yet."

"You're not dying, Bob."

"But I will someday."

"But you're not today, so why worry about it? Look, it's simple: don't worry about dyin', worry about *livin'*."

"Oh, I've screwed everything up, Jim" Dusty Bob moaned, burying his head in his hands.

"What?"

"My career, my movies, Olivia – everything."

"So this is about Olivia, again," Jim said, getting it. "You didn't screw anything up with Olivia. She died, Bob. She loved you, and she died. Twenty-five years ago. It wasn't your fault."

Olivia Del Monte. Beautiful Olivia. Dusty Bob's leading lady, paramour, soulmate. At the premiere of their last picture together, *Rendezvous in Reno*, she contracted a chill which resulted in her death from pneumonia three days later. It was just one of those things. Dusty Bob never recovered, crawling inside a whiskey bottle and letting his career slip through his fingers. Even the friendship of his long-time stuntman, Jim Dupree, couldn't pull him out of his tailspin. Long gone were the big house and swimming pool in Beverly Hills and the Texas-sized, gold-plated Cadillacs.

All that was left was Memory Ranch, where he eked out a desperate living coaxing tourists on their way to the Grand Canyon to stop and buy a few cheap trinkets, take a few snapshots with a fading star from yesteryear.

Dusty Bob was despondent the rest of the day. When he got like this – got on an Olivia kick – there was nothing anybody could do. Except ride it out.

They had become fewer and farther between in recent years, but when they hit, they hit with all the intensity and ferocity of the early years, after Olivia died, when Dusty Bob was a complete wreck. Showing up on location so drunk he couldn't stay in the saddle. Starting fist fights with crewmembers over perceived slights that never really happened, getting kicked out of swanky restaurants for disorderly conduct and brandishing his silver-plated revolvers in bars and diners. Eventually, his studio, Olympic Pictures, gave up and cancelled his contract, which he had breached countless times already.

And then the slide down really began.

By some miracle, he was just able to hold onto Memory Ranch, where he was able to pull himself together enough to keep the motel and diner barely running. He still talked of the glory days in Hollywood, but Jim always encouraged him to think of the future.

"Come on, Bob. Let's get this ranch up and workin' again," Jim would say, but Dusty Bob seemed content to put on his cowboy boots and Stetson every day and sign autographs and take snapshots with any stray tourists who happened by. So, loyal Jim Dupree was now the ranch handyman/foreman, and stayed around mostly to look after his dear old friend and try to help him keep things together around the place.

After reading the Good Book on the porch for a while, Dusty Bob took a bottle of whiskey and one of his silver-plated revolvers out back behind the diner and plinked away at empty bottles set atop a distant fence. Sally Hawk came outside to see what all the commotion was about.

"Better steer clear, he's in one of his *moods* today," Jim warned her. She glared at Dusty Bob for a while, then turned away, shaking her head in disgust. The gunfire continued from behind the diner at a steady pace. Then there was the sound of a car, and both of them turned to the road. A State Trooper patrol car pulled off the road and crossed the gravel parking lot toward the diner.

"What does *he* want?" Sally asked disdainfully.

"Bet I can guess," Jim replied with a knowing grin. Sally turned away in a huff and disappeared into the diner. The patrol car stopped and a heavy-set state trooper got out and approached the diner entrance.

"Mornin', Trooper Torres," Jim said in a friendly voice.

The trooper stopped in front of Jim and smiled nervously. Trooper Torres was vaguely soft and round and doughy and exhibited a strangely unbeguiling presence for a lawman. His uniform was slightly askew, and his shirt-tail wasn't completely tucked in in the back. He was forty-six years old and terminally single. He kept glancing nervously inside the diner as if expecting to catch a glimpse of something rare and beautiful.

"What brings you here on a pleasant morning such as this?" Jim casually asked. More loud gunfire from behind the diner punctuated his question. "Could it be Bob's morning shooting spree?"

Trooper Torres blinked in a distracted manner. "What? No, I hadn't even noticed that." He glanced inside the diner again, then looked away like a naughty schoolboy. "I, umm, just thought I'd stop by for a cup of coffee."

"Oh," Jim said.

Trooper Torres didn't move. "Is, umm, Sally around?"

"Right inside the diner," Jim replied. "Go on in."

Trooper Torres smiled nervously again, started to say something, then closed his mouth and slowly entered the diner. In truth, Trooper Torres was no stranger to Memory Ranch. He appeared almost every morning, sitting at a table alone drinking coffee and reading Keats and Byron, stealing longing glances at Sally when he could. Sally always put salt and chili pepper into his coffee to drive him away, but the more she sabotaged it the more he told her how good it was.

"Nobody makes better coffee than Sally!" He would declare loudly to the mostly-empty café.

He sat in his usual corner booth, waiting for Sally to bring him a cup of coffee. The diner had a lunch counter that could seat six, and four booths with old-fashioned tufted seats. The far end was made up to look like a western saloon, with a heavy dark mahogany bar and a large mirror behind it that read *Dusty Bob's World-Famous Memory Ranch* in faded, hand-painted lettering. Next to the bar stood Texas Pete, Dusty Bob's famous movie horse, decked out in his finest rhinestone saddle and bridle, the rhinestones now tarnished and dull beneath years of dust and time. Upon close inspection it soon became evident that Texas Pete had seen better days, and was, in fact, something of a taxidermist's nightmare. In this regard, and in order to retain at least a modest aura of dignity, the once-majestic steed was better viewed from a good distance.

The walls were covered with peeling, yellowed movie posters, representing Dusty Bob's greatest cinematic triumphs, with the star himself, as big as life, in the center of each, striking dramatic poses in and out of the saddle, his trusty silver-plated six-shooters in hand. They were all there: *Tuesday in Taos, Tombstone Two-Step, Sante Fe Senorita, Dying in Dodge City, Tucson Tryst, Dead Man's Hand, Requiem at Red Rock, Rio Grande Renegades, Double-Cross at Diablo Creek,* and, of course, his greatest masterpiece – *Rendezvous in Reno.*

What little wall-space that was not taken up by the posters was covered with gold records, for Dusty Bob had been a singing cowboy, after all, and his songs were quite popular on the radio in the old days. His theme song and biggest hit – "Lonesome Trails" – hung in the place of honor, right above an old jukebox filled with more of his songs. In a drunken fit of pique, Dusty Bob had removed all of Gene Autry's songs from the jukebox years before.

Dusty Bob was particularly proud of "Lonesome Trails," as he had composed the piece himself on his cherished 1932 rosewood Gibson guitar, which hung next to the Gold Record. The epic song was composed during a feverish night of drinking after meeting his paramour, the beautiful Olivia Del Monte, for the first time. Whenever he sang the song, he got goosebumps when he got to the line *"and I know these lonesome, lonesome trails will always lead me back to you,"* because it always made him think of Olivia. After all, he had written the song for *her.*

"Lonesome Trails" had gone straight to the top of the Hit Parade, edging Bing Crosby out of the number one spot, and was a staple on radio for years afterward. Nowadays, it went neglected and un-played on the radio, completely forgotten amid the clamor of "race music, jazz, and rock 'n' roll," as Dusty Bob put it. Hence, as a form of protest, Dusty Bob refused to listen to the radio anymore.

And Olivia was there, too. A lovely, framed publicity shot, all decked out in her cowgirl gear: soft, wide-brimmed hat, embroidered suede gauntlet gloves with fringe, red ranch shirt with yellow bandana tied around her feminine neck – a frontier Mona Lisa with pouty red lips, rouged round cheeks, and big, soft, innocent, brown eyes.

She was the most gorgeous woman Dusty Bob had ever seen.

Sally Hawk kept Trooper Torres waiting for his coffee extra long today. She generally did everything she could to discourage his amorous advances, as childlike as they were, and today was no exception. She even put extra chili pepper in it today, for good measure.

When she finally got around to serving him, you wouldn't have known that it took so long from the smile on his pudgy face. "Morning, Sally," he said reverently. She grunted and frowned.

He sipped coffee and smiled again. "As good as always," he beamed. He'd gotten used to the putrid taste long ago. She went back behind the counter and pretended to wipe some milkshake glasses with a grimy towel. Then Trooper Torres suddenly remembered something, and shook himself out of his reverie.

"Say, did you hear about the excitement down on the highway this morning?" he called to her. She went on wiping glasses, like he hadn't said a thing. "Some of the Zimmerman cows broke through the fence and got on the highway before sun-up. One of 'em got hit and killed by a truck. Yeah, it was a real mess for a while. And this is the best part, Sally. You know what kind of truck it was?" He waited for a response, which didn't come.

"Go on, take a guess," he prompted her.

"I don't know," she sighed, uninterested.

"A *meat* truck! That's right! Hey – what are the chances of that, huh?" He chuckled contentedly, replaying the scene in his mind. "Hey, Sally, what is that called, anyway?"

"What is what called?"

"You know, when something so unexpected happens, but somehow it really makes sense in a funny way – like a cow getting killed by a meat truck."

She knew, but she didn't answer. Right about this time, Jim moseyed in and refilled his coffee mug from the pot. He sniffed it first to make sure he wasn't getting any of Trooper Torres's special brew. Sally winked at him in reassurance.

"Hey, Jim," Trooper Torres called out to him. "What's it called when something unexpected happens, but somehow it really makes sense in a funny way – you know, like a cow getting killed by a meat truck?"

"Tuesday," Jim said without missing a beat.

"C'mon, Jim, I'm serious," Trooper Torres pleaded. "It happened down on the highway this morning. A cow got killed by a meat truck. I *know* there's a word for it."

9

The shooting out back had stopped now. A couple of minutes later Dusty Bob entered through the squeaky back screen door and Sally started right in.

"Run out of bullets so early?" she goaded.

"I'm savin' a few for a certain sassy-mouthed Injun squaw I know," he replied, pouring himself a mug of coffee.

"I didn't hear much glass breaking out there," she continued, without missing a beat. "Just a lot of bullets whistling through a lot of hot air."

"Uh-huh," Dusty Bob nodded, sipping coffee.

"And gas," she added.

"Gee, you're sure on a roll this mornin', Miss Sally," he retorted. "Say, where do you think your footloose husband is today?"

"He's in West Virginia, working in a coal mine," she said matter-of-factly.

"That's what I figured," Dusty Bob smiled. "Diggin' a hole to China, tryin' to get as far away from you as he can."

"I thought he was in Bakersfield, working on an oil rig," Jim piped up.

"That was last month," Sally clarified. Sally was right. She was connected to the spiritual world and could tell where her husband was at any given time, no matter how far away. Before that, he had worked on a garbage barge in New Orleans. And before that, a fishing boat off of Kodiak Island, Alaska. And a bellboy at the Ritz in New York City, and a short-order fry cook in a greasy spoon diner in Caspar, Wyoming...

"Hey, Dusty Bob," Trooper Torres called out. "What's it called when something unexpected happens, but somehow it really makes sense in a funny way – you know, like a cow getting killed by a meat truck?"

Dusty Bob pretended not to hear him. "Now Sally, I got an idea for you. Why don't you use your prodigious clairvoyant powers to go track him down an' bring him back home, where he belongs?"

"If you don't want me around here no more, you can just come right out and ask me to leave," Sally said calmly.

"Devil Woman, you can pack your bags and leave right now for all I care," Dusty Bob said.

"Maybe I will," she said. "But I wouldn't do that to even *you*, Mr. Dusty. This place would fall apart without me."

10

Dusty Bob looked around his tattered domain with a satisfied, regal air. "It *is* quite the paradise, isn't it?"

"Besides, he's not worth it," Sally said, referring to her husband. "Let him wander the world all alone for the rest of his life."

"Well, blessings come in many different packages, you could say," Dusty Bob mused. He loved giving her such a hard time because she loved giving him such a hard time. And he knew that was because she was jealous of his unusually close relationship with Jim. Even though all they ever did was argue.

"Hey, Dusty Bob," Trooper Torres called out again. "What's it called when something unexpected happens, but somehow it really makes sense in a funny way – you know, like a cow getting killed by a meat truck?"

"That's a cliché," Dusty Bob answered.

Jim laughed. "No, it's not. It's a *metaphor.*"

"You're *loco*, my friend," Dusty Bob countered professorially. "In the more literary days of my wild yet cultured youth, I knew all about such matters. And I'm tellin' you, the unfortunate, and some would even say tragic, situation just described by our esteemed law enforcement *amigo* here is clearly and indisputably a *cliché.*" He said it like two distinct words – *clee shay.*

"Metaphor," Jim argued.

"Clee-shay."

"Metaphor."

"Clee-*shay*!"

Sally Hawk couldn't take it anymore. "It's *irony.*"

"Iron-*what*?" Dusty Bob looked at her quizzically.

"It's an example of *irony*, you old fool," she repeated.

"How would *you* know?" Dusty Bob challenged. "You didn't get past the fourth grade in school."

"We learned what irony was in the fourth grade," she explained. "Any fourth grader knows what irony is."

"She may be right about that, come to think of it," Jim said. "I change my vote to *irony.*"

Dusty Bob turned his ire on Jim now. "Why don't *you* just get in the pickup truck and go to Holbrook, like you been talkin' about all mornin'," he said icily. "Or are you just all *talk*?"

"As a matter of fact, I think I will," Jim said. And that's just what he did. Only instead of going to Holbrook, he drove six miles in the

11

opposite direction and ended up at a small, crumbling white adobe house out in the middle of nowhere. Loud opera music blared through the open windows.

It was Trooper Torres's house, where he lived with his reclusive, socially awkward sister, Lucia. With Trooper Torres otherwise occupied back at the diner, Jim was quite pleased with the prospect of having Lucia all to himself for the rest of the morning.

Lucia fancied herself an artist, along the lines of Frida Kahlo. She even cultivated her eyebrows in such a fashion, which she felt bestowed great honor on her artistic idol. Lucia painted desert landscapes – fast and copiously. What her paintings lacked in quality was made up for in quantity.

Lucia was a nut-job, but for some inexplicable reason that remained a mystery to even him, Jim found her irresistible.

He found her out back, standing at an easel facing the open desert, discarded canvases scattered around her like leaves shaken from a giant tree. On each one was painted the same basic scene, with subtle differences. All had, for some reason or another, been rejected by the artist, and she was currently working on the latest attempt.

Jim edged closer, watching her every move, trying not to interrupt her work. She seemed to be having great difficulty with the shape of a cactus.

"The *saguaro* is mocking me today!" she suddenly exclaimed, in an exasperated tone. She was about five foot seven, had a slender boy's body wrapped in an oversized artist's smock, and had her long brown hair pinned up on top of her head. She was about thirty years younger than Jim, and had thick calves. Her fingers were covered with layers of paint. Despite all of this, the mere sight of her never failed to create an overwhelming desire within him.

"No, no, no, NO!!" She threw the canvas violently to the ground and replaced it with a blank one. "The energy from the rocks is the only thing sustaining me right now. The sun is overbearing, suffocating even. And the *saguaro* – well, very disappointing and uncooperative today." Lucia was obsessed with painting the perfect *saguaro* cactus, but they never came out to her satisfaction and she was existentially tortured by it. She was near tears.

"Why don't you take a little break?" Jim gently suggested.

"Take a *break*?" she said incredulously. "Did Frida take breaks? Did Diego take breaks? You are not an artist. You cannot possibly understand the burden I carry…"

"Painting seems to make you very unhappy," Jim observed.

"*Happy*?" she repeated. "Was Frida happy? Was Diego happy? What about Picasso – do you think *he* was happy?"

"I don't know."

"Artists do not create for such trite, inconsequential sentiments as *happiness*," she lectured him. "That is so pedestrian, Jim. I would have thought you could understand that. No, the artist's burden – the artist's *sacrifice* – is to forego such bourgeois concerns and aim for the sublime, the revelatory. It is the artist who peels back the truth like the layers of an onion. It is the artist who suffers for the senseless masses. It is the artist who sacrifices for all mankind."

This kind of talk always seemed to arouse Jim. Or maybe it was just her intense passion that got him going. "C'mon, girl – let's go inside for six or seven minutes," he said desperately.

"I cannot go inside now," she laughed scornfully. "I will not have this light all day. This is morning light – my *muse*. All night long I lie awake waiting for the morning light, so I can *live*."

"*Please.*"

"No, Jim. I don't have time to dally with your libido today. There is one *saguaro* in particular which will not allow me to capture its essence. This enigmatic cactus mocks me in my dreams. Don't you see? I must *subdue* it – I *must* unravel its ancient mysteries. You are just a sad old *gringo*. You cannot possibly understand my plight."

Disappointed, Jim randomly picked a discarded canvas off the ground. "This one's nice."

She glanced at it and sneered. "A failed attempt. Like all the others. They will haunt me in my grave."

"I like it."

"You would," she said with disdain. "The cactus is flaccid. It sags uselessly, like the *verga* of an old white man."

"I'd like to buy it." He picked up two more. "And these. Fifteen dollars?"

"You patronize me," she said condescendingly.

"I brought cash."

She held out her hand, palm up, without looking at him.

13

*   *   *

Back at the ranch, Dusty Bob was sitting on the diner porch, polishing one of his silver-plated revolvers, when the pickup truck pulled up. Jim got out with the three canvases stacked under his arm.

"You keep polishin' that thing, it might just go off unexpectedly," Jim drawled.

"How's the re-tard?"

"She's on a mission to capture the essence of a *saguaro*," Jim replied.

Dusty Bob saw the canvases under Jim's arm. "Adding to your collection, I see."

"I've got some extra wall-space I need to cover."

"Why don't you just open up your own gallery?" Dusty Bob smirked. "We could serve chardonnay and finger foods while you try to hawk her insane scribblings to the tourists. Or, I could take 'em out back an' use 'em for target practice."

"It makes her feel better about her art when I buy 'em."

"Is it gettin' you anywhere with her?"

"Not yet," Jim admitted. "She's a sensitive artist. She needs to be wooed and caressed, like a wild filly."

"I'm just afraid that's one filly you're never gonna get to ride, Jim."

"Now I'm takin' romantic advice from the likes of *you*?"

"I just don't want to see you get hurt."

"Why don't you just mind your own damn business, Casanova?"

"All right, partner," Dusty Bob softened. "Simmer down, now."

"Besides, what the hell do *you* know about matters of the heart, anyway?"

Dusty Bob stopped polishing the six-shooter and thought a moment. "Well, in any well-informed discussion of love, I reckon we got to start with Will Shakespeare. I seem to recall the Bard likened love to 'sunshine after the rain,' or 'sweet-seasoned showers to the dry ground.' On the other hand, he also called it a 'sea nourished by lovers' tears' and a 'madness and choking gall.' The Good Book says love is patient, kind, not jealous or arrogant, doesn't take into account a wrong suffered, bears all things, believes all things, hopes and endures all things. Plato reckoned that each human bein' is only half a person, and that we're all just wanderin' through life tryin' to stumble upon our other half. Aristotle believed love is composed of a

14

single soul inhabitin' two bodies. The poet George Sand called love the only happiness in life. But what did *she* know – she couldn't even figure out if she wanted to be a man or a woman. Victor Hugo said life is the flower for which love is the honey. Goethe said that love never dominates, just cultivates. Lao Tzu said that lovin' somebody with all your heart gives you strength and courage. Scott Fitzgerald called it the beginnin' an' end of everything. So you may be right, I may not know anythin' about affairs of the heart. But I <u>do</u> know that one day in 1932 I met a beautiful young siren named Olivia Del Monte, and we were never apart for a single day until the day she died. And if I hadn't met her and spent seven heavenly years with her, I don't think I ever would've existed in the first place. I can't imagine bein' alive and drawin' breath and walkin' this earth without havin' known her. And ever since that dreadful night she expired in my arms, I've felt like a dead man walkin', an' her memory is the only glimmer of hope that keeps me movin' forward. I'd give darn near anythin' to hold her in my arms one more time."

Jim stepped up onto the porch and leaned the paintings against the wall. He sat down in the chair next to Dusty Bob and silently started rolling a cigarette. Dusty Bob went back to polishing his gun.

"That was very movin'," Jim finally said, sticking the cigarette into his mouth and lighting it with a match. "I'm sorry about the Casanova crack."

"Aw, that's all right," Dusty Bob said quietly. "I reckon I deserved it, and then some."

Chapter 2

That night, Dusty Bob stayed up late, as was his custom. As owner and proprietor of Memory Ranch, his personal motto was "last to bed and first to rise." When it got nice and quiet around the diner, he turned out the lights and listened to music on the jukebox. He couldn't find the exact right song to match his pensive, melancholy mood. Then he finally got around to punching C17, "Lonesome Trails." That seemed to do the trick.

He listened carefully, hardly believing he'd penned these words nearly three decades ago:

> *I've got a restless soul and a one-track mind,*
> *Eyes lookin' for a place I can never find.*
> *Can't remember the last place I called home,*
> *When it comes to livin' I was born to roam.*
> *I was never one to settle down,*
> *Put down roots in any town.*
> *Crowded places keep me movin' on,*
> *You won't find me in a city long.*
> *I always ride alone, just seem to do better on my own*
> *I never get lonesome with the prairie wind a blowin'*
> *And wide-open places where the grass is growin'*
> *But sometimes when the stars are big and bright,*
> *And the crickets' song is just right,*
> *My thoughts turn back to you.*
>
> *No matter where my wanderin' heart takes me,*
> *I know these Lonesome Trails will always lead*
> *me back to you.*

As he listened, he cocked his head and thought back through the years. He remembered how he had been inspired to write it by the wide-open places he'd been to and the exquisite beauty of his new paramour, Olivia Del Monte. He remembered the musty smell of the old recording room at RCA studios in Burbank, California, and how he sang it in one take in a high, plaintive, dry-bones croon that would become his trademark vocal style and would set him apart from all the other singing cowboys. He had performed it on his trusty 1932 Gibson guitar, accompanied by little more than a fiddle, a standup bass, a pedal-steel guitar, and a harmonica played by none other than Studs Monahan, an old friend of his and the best campfire harmonica player in the west.

He remembered how the song had taken on a life of its own, something he hadn't expected. It got played on the radio and seemed to strike a nerve in the heart of Depression-era America. With so many jobless men hitting the rails and the Okies clogging Route 66 in their sputtering jalopies on their way to California and long soup-kitchen lines in every town and city, the song spoke to everyone's need to leave their cares behind and roam free and easy wherever they pleased. And if they couldn't, at least they could hear his song on the radio and dream about it.

He'd never intended to write an anthem of hope for a nation in despair – he was never that ambitious – but only a simple, heartfelt tune expressing every cowboy's feelings about being tied down to a job, woman, family, or what have you.

The song's closing lines – *"No matter where my wanderin' heart takes me, I know these Lonesome Trails will always lead me back to you"* – turned his thoughts to Olivia, and he began to pine for her something awful.

As if remembering something, he got up and walked to a small storage room behind the diner's kitchen and moved some boxes around looking for a trunk. When he found it, he was surprised at how beat up and aged it had become; he hadn't opened it or even laid eyes on it in twenty-five years, soon after Olivia had died.

He carefully unlatched the trunk and opened it. It was filled with old memories and trail dust. He rummaged around inside it and pulled out Olivia's soft, wide-brimmed hat, yellow bandana, and suede gauntlet gloves – the same ones she wore in the picture hanging in the diner. He sniffed the bandana and caught a faint, lingering trace of her expensive perfume. A thousand memories flooded back at once, overwhelming him.

He carefully placed the items back in the trunk, and pulled out a metal film canister. Wiping the dust from the yellowed label, he could read the title: *"Rendezvous in Reno."* He held the canister a long time, considering the weight and depth of the memories it contained. He had purposely avoided watching any of his old movies since Olivia

17

died, but something – the song, the faint smell of her perfume on the bandana – was compelling him to break his cinematic abstinence, open the canister, and watch it.

He grabbed the old film projector sitting on a shelf and carried it, and the film, back out to the diner. He draped an old bed sheet over the large mirror behind the saloon bar, set the projector on a table, and spooled his forgotten masterpiece up for viewing. The celluloid was brittle, but it just might hold. He plugged the projector in and was pleased to see it sputter to life when he turned it on. He poured two shot glasses of whiskey and sat them on the table. Then he sat down to watch the movie as the ghostly black and white images began to fill the bed sheet.

Everything flooded back to him in a rush. The plot was pretty simple: a young boy, Brian, becomes an orphan when his wealthy but loving parents die suddenly in a bizarre cattle stampede at midday through the streets of Reno, Nevada. An evil rancher pays off a corrupt judge to declare Brian too young to inherit his father's silver mine, and make the evil rancher the conservator until Brian reaches the age of eighteen. The boy is placed under the care of the rancher, who promptly trundles him off to an orphanage to be forgotten.

Olivia plays the evil rancher's beautiful saloon-owner daughter, Kate. Dusty Bob is a lone drifter named Jake Matson who wanders into Reno looking for a place to clean up, lay low, and possibly do some gambling for a while. The minute he lays eyes on Kate, he knows he's come to the right place. Then the corrupt town sheriff has a mental breakdown and confesses his part in the rancher and judge's plot to steal the silver mine to the full saloon on a Saturday night.

Hearing the truth, Kate begins to plot a way to thwart her father's wicked scheme and restore Brian's rightful claim to the silver mine. Meanwhile, looking for some poor sap he can control, the judge appoints Jake as the new sheriff, thinking a drunk drifter like him will be compliant.

For a while, Jake goes along with the corrupt judge and rancher, but Kate works on him and eventually turns him around to be on her side against her father. Hearing of this, the rancher sends his henchmen to ambush Jake, but he is able to fight them off in an epic, climactic gunfight scene.

After the fight, Jake walks into the saloon, orders a whiskey, and dances silently with Kate to "The Yellow Rose of Texas" played by a blind fiddle player in the corner. It is the film's romantic climax, and it becomes clear that Jake and Kate were made for each other. After the dance, Jake and Kate get word that the rancher is sending more henchmen to the orphanage to kill Brian, so they beat them there and try to fight them off. Seeing that their boss's daughter is there with a rifle, the henchmen are hesitant to attack, even though her father coldly orders them to kill her. "She's a traitor to her family and the town of Reno!" he tells them from atop his horse. "She's a traitor to everything we hold dear!"

Kate then gives an impassioned speech about the virtues of orphans and her father's wicked scheme to steal the silver mine from Brian. The henchmen, some in tears, are won over and spontaneously lynch the evil rancher right there on the spot.

The orphan children cheer and dance around the rancher's dangling corpse, and Kate and Jake get married, adopt Brian and all the orphans, sell the saloon and silver mine for a sizable profit, and move to Sausalito.

The film was praised at the time for its action-packed sequences and realistic gunfight scenes, terse, gritty dialogue, and the on-screen chemistry of its romantic leads. "Jake and Kate share a love for the ages," raved the *Los Angeles Times* review. "A love of almost Shakespearean proportions – a love so great that it destroys the greed and pettiness of the evilest of men."

All of these memories rushed through his mind as he watched his youthful past flicker across the bed sheet in blue projector light. Then, just after the big gunfight scene, something peculiar happened. When the grandfather clock in the corner struck midnight, the projector light turned off and the reels ground to a halt. The ceiling fan, which had been turning slowly, stopped dead. The neon glow from the jukebox died out. Dusty Bob sat there in complete darkness for a moment.

"Power must've gone out," he said to himself, with a chuckle. Then he looked at the grandfather clock and noticed in the pale moonlight from the window that the pendulum had stopped swinging and the hands were motionless. "But that clock's not electric," he murmured, confused. Suddenly, the projector came back on and the movie continued, but the jukebox and ceiling fan stayed dark and unmoving.

Perplexed, Dusty Bob watched the bed sheet screen as Jake Matson entered the saloon and looked around for Kate. The only one there was the blind fiddle player in the corner, playing a slow, somber rendition of "The Yellow Rose of Texas." Then, as Kate came down the staircase and walked toward Jake, Dusty Bob was aware of someone entering the diner from the kitchen.

"Jim?" There was no answer. "Sally?"

The figure emerged from the shadows into the moonlight. Dusty Bob turned and saw Olivia, dressed in her tight-waisted, frilly saloon-keeper's costume, walk to the table and pick up one of the shot glasses. Dusty Bob blinked, rubbed his eyes. She was still there. Smiling down at him, she drank the whiskey down in one shot, mimicking her image on the screen. Dusty Bob sat motionless.

"Go ahead, cowboy," both Olivias – the one on the screen and the one standing over him – urged in unison. In the movie, Jake picked up his shot glass and knocked it back. In the diner, Dusty Bob did the same. Then, on the screen, Kate reached out her hand and Jake took it. In the diner, Olivia reached out her hand, and Dusty Bob took it. And as the young couple on the screen began their quiet dance in the saloon, Dusty Bob and Olivia followed their every move in the diner, re-enacting the scene step-by-step, move-by-move, just as they had done twenty-five years before, just as it had been written in the script.

Dusty Bob held her in his arms, her soft face nestled in the crook of his neck, as young as she was the day they shot the movie scene, the same faded perfume scent from the bandana now fresh and vivid in his nostrils, and for a brief moment the twenty-five years evaporated into the ether and they were both one, and young, again.

Neither spoke, Dusty Bob unsure if it was even happening at all, wondering if it was merely a hallucination or a dream. And then the music began to fade out and the couple on the screen slowed their dance. Olivia began to pull away, but Dusty Bob held onto her. She shook her head "no," and languidly slid out of his embrace, receding into the shadows from which she had come. When she was gone, the neon on the jukebox lit up again and the ceiling fan resumed turning.

Still stunned, Dusty Bob glanced at the grandfather clock. It still said twelve o'clock. Then the pendulum began to swing again, and the hands began to move.

"This…must have been a dream, or somethin'." He looked down at the shot glasses – both empty. Then he turned off the projector and went to bed.

*   *   *

When Dusty Bob woke up the next morning, it didn't take him long to start doubting what had happened the night before. "Maybe it was just a dream," he told himself. Or maybe he was just one Joker short of a full deck. There was only one way to find out which was the case.

That night, after everyone else had turned in, he soberly set up his impromptu movie theater in the diner and started *Rendezvous* at about the same time as the night before, so that the saloon dance scene would begin precisely at midnight. Then he poured two shot glasses of whiskey and waited with growing impatience for the grandfather clock to strike midnight.

After the twelfth chime, it happened. The pendulum stopped dead and the clock hands stopped moving. The ceiling fan stopped turning and the neon glow from the jukebox went dark – just like the night before. The projector stopped momentarily, too, then re-started as if operated by a ghost.

The saloon dance scene started, and everything was as before: Olivia entered from the shadows in the kitchen and downed the shot of whiskey. "Go ahead, cowboy," she said. Dusty Bob drank his whiskey, and they began their strangely wonderful dance. Then Dusty Bob couldn't help himself, and said her name out loud.

"Olivia…" He immediately regretted it, for she instantly vanished in his arms. The ceiling fan began turning, and the jukebox lit back up. The grandfather clock came to life and the minute hand moved to one minute past midnight. Whatever magic spell there was had been broken when he spoke.

He would have to wait until the next night to try again.

The next night, he followed the same procedure to a "t," and everything worked like a charm until halfway through the dance. Caught up in the enchantment of holding her in his arms again, he couldn't help himself, and uttered, "My darling – is it *really* you?"

Instantly, the spell was broken again, and he cursed himself.

The next night, he forgot to drink the whiskey before standing up to dance, and she disappeared.

The night after that, he was so eager not to make the same mistake that he jumped the gun and drank the whiskey before she said her line, "Go ahead, cowboy." She disappeared again.

The next night, he got the timing of the whiskey right and was able to restrain his tongue, but couldn't help moving in to kiss her rosy-red lips during the dance.

She disappeared.

"Dag-nabbit, you sure are particular about this thing!" he grumbled in frustration.

The protocol was extremely unforgiving, he was beginning to realize. It had to be done with great care, a certain way, just as it was in the movie, with absolutely no deviation from the way the scene was written in the script. That meant no extra talking, for there was no dialogue during the dance. And every time he made a mistake, he would have to wait twenty-four hours to see her again.

But the good news was, no matter how many mistakes he made, he was always given a new chance the next night.

Over the next several nights, he began to get the procedure down pat, and got to where he hardly ever did anything to end the dance prematurely. For a long time, he kept it to himself – mostly because he wasn't quite sure if it was really happening, or just his imagination.

Then one morning over their 6 a.m. coffee, he spilled everything to Jim. He just couldn't keep it to himself any longer – he had to tell *someone*. And that someone was certainly not going to be *Sally*.

Jim listened to the whole story without interruption, quietly smoking his hand-rolled cigarette. He seemed non-plussed. When Dusty Bob had finished, Jim took a long drag and said as he exhaled smoke, "Well, that's a mighty wild tale, Bob."

"It ain't no tale, Jim. It happens every night. At midnight. Long as I follow the rules."

"The rules?"

"Yeah, see, it's got to be just the way it's written in the script," Dusty Bob explained. "If I do anything different – say anything, or forget to do something right – it breaks the spell and Olivia disappears. For example, one time I didn't start the movie on time, and the saloon scene didn't start right at midnight. Olivia never showed."

"Until the next midnight."

"That's right, partner."

Jim looked at Dusty Bob for a long time.

"You think I'm *loco*, don't ya?" Dusty Bob asked.

"Well, I know you're not lyin'," Jim said. "You've never lied to me in your life."

"That's right. But you think I'm missin' a few wheels on my buggy, don't ya?"

"I wouldn't say that," Jim replied.

"Well, I wouldn't blame ya, Jim," Dusty Bob admitted. "Sometimes I wonder about myself. Is it real, or is it all just some kind of hallucination?"

"I don't think anything's wrong up in your attic," Jim observed. "You seem to me as sharp as ever, Bob. No, somethin's definitely goin' on. Maybe it's Olivia's *ghost*."

"I'm tellin' ya, Jim, when I'm holdin' her in my arms, she feels just as real as can be," Dusty Bob testified. "Real flesh an' bone. I never heard of no ghost feels like *that*."

"No, from what you're tellin' me, this is surely somethin' *different*, all right." Then Jim got an idea. "What if I stay up with you tonight? If both of us see her, we'll know it's not a hallucination."

Dusty Bob shook his head. "Won't work. I'm tellin' ya, it's gotta be just me an' her, just like the scene in the movie."

Jim thought and smoked. "Well, I just don't know what to tell ya, then."

*　　　　　*　　　　　*

Dusty Bob repeated the ritual every night, and soon came to live for these brief, wordless encounters each day. Each encounter, each dance with Olivia, always left him wanting more, but he knew that if he didn't follow "the rules," he wouldn't have her at all. He quickly decided they had to suffice, they had to be enough to get him through each day. He was determined not to lose her again.

Then he began to notice something peculiar about the film. Every night he checked it carefully to make sure he wasn't imagining things. When he was sure he wasn't, he confided in Jim.

"Each time I watch the film, the images become a little bit fainter," he sadly explained.

"Are you sure?"

"Yep. I been checkin' each night," Dusty Bob said. "I'm sure of it. The celluloid is becoming more transparent with each viewing. Don't ya see? When it gets to be completely see-through, when there's nothing left, she'll stop appearin'. I don't know why or how, but it's happenin'."

"Isn't there anything you can do to stop it?" Jim asked.

"I found I can lay off watchin' it a night or two, but it doesn't stop the process," Dusty Bob explained. "The next time I watch it, they're still fainter. All it does is slow things down a bit."

"We'll find another print of the film," Jim suggested. "There's gotta be another one somewhere."

Dusty Bob shook his head. "That's the only one left. I don't know of another one anywhere."

"We'll go out to Hollywood. The studio's gotta have one."

"Olympic Pictures went out of business years ago," Dusty Bob reminded him. "Who knows what they did with all their old prints. Probably burned 'em."

"A TV station somewhere, then," Jim persisted. "We'll put the word out –"

"Thanks, old partner," Dusty Bob smiled weakly. "But it ain't no use. Why would anyone have held onto a print of *that* old movie? It's just as forgotten as *I* am."

"What are you gonna do?"

"Conjure her less often, I suppose," Dusty Bob reasoned. "Skip a few nights every now and then. Make it last as long as possible. But the fact is, I'm losin' her again, Jim. It's just a matter of time…"

Chapter 3

A day or two later, Jim asked Dusty Bob if he'd be needing the pickup truck that day. Dusty Bob informed him that he hadn't planned on using the pickup truck at all. "Why? Where you goin' anyway?" he asked Jim.

"Holbrook."

"Without me?" Dusty Bob asked.

"You said you didn't want to go to Holbrook."

"That was last week."

"Well, do you want to come with me today?"

"I don't reckon so, not bein' asked right off, an' all..."

"Well, fine then. Stay here."

"What you gonna do in Holbrook?" Dusty Bob asked after a spell.

"That's *my* business, ain't it?"

"Well, you don't have to get snippy about it," Dusty Bob said, defensively.

"That wasn't snippy. That was *curt*."

"Curt is a tad more polite than snippy. It goes by degrees. That was definitely *snippy*."

"No, it wasn't."

"You sayin' I don't know *snippy* when I hear it?" Dusty Bob demanded.

"Do you want to come to Holbrook, or not?"

"You go on. I got a busy day planned on the place."

"Doin' what, exactly? Shootin' empty whiskey bottles off the fence? Polishin' all the chrome off your little pea-shooter there?"

"I've got some readin' of the Good Book to do."

"Well, I think that's a fine idear," Jim nodded. "You need to do some character-buildin' for a change."

"Says the heathen who don't believe in the Good News contained within these sacred pages," Dusty Bob retorted.

"I got no quarrel with the ancient scriptures, per se. Read 'em in Sunday school when I was a kid. Probably what accounts for my superior moral character."

"That's bound to be it," Dusty Bob agreed, dryly.

"I just don't need to read 'em over and over again every day, like someone else I know."

"Well, I find it very calmin'," Dusty Bob explained. "It helps me cope with the frenetic pace of life around here."

"You are quite the whirlwind, aren't you?"

"Somebody has to make sure things don't fall apart around here."

"Uh-huh."

"Everyone can't be runnin' off to Holbrook whenever they feel like it. Nothin' would ever get done around here."

"That's right. Who would shoot all the empty whiskey bottles and drink all Sally's coffee and take four-hour naps every afternoon?"

"You know I need my beauty sleep, Jim. I have to maintain my rugged good looks for the guests."

"You mean Trooper Torres and the occasional road runner? Those are about the only guests we ever get around here."

"You see, it's just that kind of defeatist attitude that I have to counter-act with my natural cheerful and optimistic outlook."

"Your optimism sure does make a difference around here," Jim chuckled.

"You know, I keep waitin' to hear the pickup truck start up an' head out toward Holbrook, but all I hear is a lot of yapperin' an' yammerin'."

"Oh, I'm headed to Holbrook, all right – propelled by all the hot air comin' from your direction, no doubt."

"Glad to be of help getting' your long-awaited and much talked about journey started."

"Keep talkin'," Jim urged. "The tail-wind you're creatin' should save me a couple of gallons of gasoline, if I'm lucky."

"Well, drive careful, an' try not to get lost in Holbrook," Dusty Bob said. "I hear it's quite the metropolis these days."

"I know my way around Holbrook."

"The red-light district, maybe."

"That's *your* old stompin' grounds, if I remember correctly."

"Which reminds me, if you see any sweet young *senoritas*, tell 'em I haven't forgotten about 'em. Tell 'em I'll be around to see 'em directly."

"I will. As soon as they stop laughin', old man. Better yet, why don't you get off your duff an' put pen to paper an' tell 'em yourself, Valentino?"

"I could do that, I suppose. But that would spoil the mystery. Besides, I didn't want your trip to be a complete waste of time, is all."

"I'm fightin' back tears, contemplatin' the depths of your generosity," Jim said, finally rising from his chair. Dusty Bob watched as Jim walked to the tool shed and disappeared inside. A moment later he emerged with a shovel. He tossed it in the bed of the truck and climbed in the cab.

"Remember to be back by curfew, son!" Dusty Bob called as the truck drove away. "Now what's that boy gonna do with that shovel, I wonder?"

Dusty Bob sat on the diner porch wondering how he should begin his day. There was the Good Book that needed reading. There were some empty whiskey bottles that needed shooting, but there were also some *full* whiskey bottles that needed *emptying*. So many options to contemplate often had a way of rendering Dusty Bob immobile for a good, long spell.

When he'd just about decided, a car pulling off the highway toward the diner distracted him and he remained idle. It was a state trooper patrol car.

Trooper Torres parked in front of the diner and got out of his prowler. His uniform was tousled, his shirt-tail un-tucked in the same customary spot in the back. He looked especially anxious this morning.

"Trooper Torres."

"Dusty Bob."

There was a long pause. Finally, Dusty Bob spoke. "You look like you've got somethin' on your mind, son."

"It's, well, you know…"

"I assure you, I haven't the foggiest," Dusty Bob promised.

"It's about…*women*." He whispered the last part, like it was a four-letter word.

"What about 'em?"

"Well, you know, I been tryin' to get a *certain woman's* attention for years now, and it just ain't goin' nowhere."

"An all-too common story, I'm afraid," Dusty Bob commiserated.

"I just don't know what to do, Dusty Bob. I'm…I'm really at the end of my rope, here."

"Aw, buck up, son. It ain't impossible, ya know."

"It ain't?"

"Lookie here, son," Dusty Bob said with a wink. "Courtin' women is just like breakin' in a new horse. You can't just rush up an' throw a rope around their neck."

"You can't?"

"No. That'll make 'em bolt. You got to hang back, give 'em space. No sudden moves. Make eye contact. Talk to 'em in a quiet, soothin' voice."

"What do you say?"

"Just let 'em know you're not gonna hurt 'em," Dusty Bob counseled. "When they start to see that your friendly and gentle, *they'll* come to *you*."

"They will?"

"Sure, but you gotta be patient. Remember, all this time they're thinkin', they're sizin' you up."

"They are?"

"Yup. They're watchin' you to see what you're gonna do, to see if they can trust you or not."

"Really?"

"And when they start trustin' you, that's when you reach over nice and gentle, and slip the rope over their head, nice an' easy-like. Then they'll do whatever you ask."

"What if she runs away?"

"Well, when they do that, see, they're lookin' to see if you'll come after 'em or not."

"Do I?"

"Yes, sir, you surely do," Dusty Bob said. "That's just what they want you to do, see?"

"Gee, I don't know if I can remember all of that."

"Sure you can. Just remember: don't crowd her. Give her space. Talk to her in a calm voice, but don't say too much. An' make eye contact. That's very important. Let's 'em know you mean business."

"Okay. Eye contact. Slow movements. Got it."

"Now, go inside an' get started before her husband finds his way back home."

Trooper Torres adjusted his wide-brimmed trooper hat and walked inside the diner. He stopped and stood just inside the door. "Mornin' Sally," he said very quietly and calmly. Sally, who had the ears of a coyote, heard him just fine.

"What's wrong with your voice today?" she demanded gruffly.

28

"Nothin'." He just stood there, not crowding her.

"Your coffee's there on your table," she told him, motioning toward his booth. He didn't move. "Well, are you gonna sit down and drink it, or not?"

He finally edged over to his booth, very deliberately and slowly, giving her plenty of space. He sat down and slurped coffee, never taking his eyes off her.

"Nobody makes a cup of coffee like Sally!" he declared calmly. It was loaded up with salt and chili pepper, as usual.

"Why are you staring at me like that?" she asked.

"I'm making eye contact," he calmly explained.

"Well, it's giving me the willies."

He slurped coffee again. Everything he did was in slow-motion – no sudden movements.

"What's wrong with you? Did you lose the lid off your pickle jar, or somethin'?"

"Huh?"

"Are you feeling all right today?" she said very slowly and clearly.

"Uh-huh."

She shook her head and turned away, busying herself behind the counter.

Sensing it wasn't going well for Trooper Torres, Dusty Bob entered the diner and asked, "Well, what's going on in the dangerous and excitin' world of law enforcement, Trooper Torres?" He thought a change of subject just might distract Sally from the trooper's peculiar behavior.

"Oh, I almost forgot about what I was going to ask you," Trooper Torres admitted. "Have you seen any strange lights around here lately?"

"Strange lights?" Dusty Bob asked.

"Yeah, you know – in the sky, at night?"

"No, cain't say I've noticed any such thing." Dusty Bob went behind the counter and poured himself a mug of coffee.

"Well, there's been some trouble over at the Zimmerman place," Trooper Torres announced.

"Did his cows get out on the highway again?"

"No, but two nights ago three of his cows went missing. The fences were all fine, no holes or any places for them to escape. They just *vanished*."

"You don't say," Dusty Bob said.

"I do say. And just this morning, they reappeared – just like that. Only they had parts missing."

"What do you mean? What kind of parts?"

"One was missing her eyes. Another one was missing her tongue and liver. The third one was missing her brain and udders."

"You don't say," was all Dusty Bob could say.

"We had the vet from Holbrook out there, and he said the incisions looked like they'd been made by an expert surgeon – even cleaner. He said they were so clean and cauterized, that it must have been done with something sharper than a scalpel."

"What's sharper than a scalpel?"

"Think about it, Dusty Bob."

"I am a thinkin'."

"Don't you get it yet?" Trooper Torres asked excitedly. "Laser-beams. Like in the science fiction movies. They must've done it with laser-beams. It's the only way they could've made cuts like that."

"You mean, flyin' saucer people?"

"Yeah, only they ain't people at all – they're creatures from outer space." Trooper Torres pulled a magazine out of his jacket and showed Dusty Bob the cover. It was a garish illustration of flying saucers destroying the U.S. Capitol in Washington, D.C. The title blared, THEY'RE HERE! THE CREATURES FROM OUTER SPACE!

"That's what the strange lights were," Trooper Torres went on. "Flying saucers!"

"I don't believe in such poppycock," Dusty Bob declared.

"I saw the lights," a dry old voice piped up from the corner of the diner. "When I was just a boy. Strange lights in the night sky. Saw 'em all the time." Everyone turned to where the voice was coming from. It was Old Mr. Young, one of the long-time locals. He was about a hundred years old, and looked it. Nobody had even noticed he was there before he spoke up.

"Where did *you* come from?" Dusty Bob asked.

"One night when I was about nine," the old man continued, ignoring Dusty Bob, "there was a terrible electrical storm – dark clouds, thunder, lightnin' – but no rain. Then the clouds parted, an' it emerged: a huge metal disc, about a hundred yards wide. It wasn't all smooth and shiny, like the flying saucers in the pictures. It was kinda beat up an' dented, like a giant metal trash can lid. It came down low an' hovered over my house a while, and then mechanical metal arms reached down an' snatched up my dog, Skeeter, an' flew off with him. Nothing happened for days, an' then they brought old Skeeter back an' put him down in the yard like nothing ever happened. Only they must have experimented on him, because he just wasn't ever the same."

"What did they do to him?" Trooper Torres asked, thoroughly engrossed.

"Not sure," Old Mr. Young went on, "but I began to notice some mighty strange things about old Skeeter. First, I discovered he could communicate with me telepathically, an' he had quite a good vocabulary, for a dog. An' boy, did he have a lot to tell me about his trip in the flying saucer. He told me of worlds beyond our galaxy that I couldn't even imagine existed. He told me of advanced civilizations with technology that would make radios an' TV sets look like somethin' from the Stone Age. He vividly described the birth of new stars an' solar systems, an' the violent death throes of dying supernovas. He tried to explain black holes an' quantum mechanics an' the secrets of the universe to me, but my young brain was not capable of comprehending such advanced knowledge.

"Skeeter kept asking me to construct a special radio transmitter so he could send messages to his new friends in space, but our Earthly electronic parts were woefully inadequate for such a sophisticated device. He was able to play chess, an' once talked me through performing an emergency appendectomy on my younger brother, Bill. No sir, there never was a dog quite like Skeeter once the spacemen got a hold of 'im."

"What happened to him?" Trooper Torres asked.

"The government got wind of the whole deal an' confiscated him," Old Mr. Young said sadly. "Last I heard, they were studyin' him in a top-secret underground facility out in New Mexico somewheres."

"I find your story, as compellingly detailed as it is, just a might too fanciful to believe," Dusty Bob told him.

"The whole thing is a…is a…hey, Dusty Bob, what's the word for something that's mysterious, puzzling, or difficult to understand?" Trooper Torres asked.

"My people know of the lights," Sally Hawk interjected. "The Elders called them the Bright Ones, great spirits who came to this world to learn the ways of The People. In return, the legend says, the Bright Ones taught The People how to communicate with the buffalo and the bear."

"Clap-trap!" Dusty Bob scoffed.

"I *know* there's a word for it," Trooper Torres said. "Hey, Dusty Bob, what's the word for something that's mysterious, puzzling, or difficult to understand?"

"A conundrum," Dusty Bob replied.

"No, that's not the word I'm thinking of," Trooper Torres said.

"An anagram," Old Mr. Young said.

"An anagram is a word or phrase that says the same thing backwards an' forwards," Dusty Bob impatiently informed him. "He's talkin' about a *conundrum*."

"You're batty," Old Mr. Young replied. "It's an anagram."

"You call the ways of The People clap-trap?" Sally asked Dusty Bob, who, fortunately, was practiced in the art of carrying on several conversations at the same time.

"Superstitious clap-trap," Dusty Bob repeated.

"*Superstitious?*" Sally scoffed. "That, from the one who's been cavorting with spirits every night?"

"What are you talkin' about?" Dusty Bob asked Sally.

"It's anagram, plain and simple," Old Mr. Young argued.

"Oh, I know all about your ghost," Sally told Dusty Bob. "That's right: little happens on the spiritual plane around here that I don't pick up on, sooner or later."

Dusty Bob went white. "She ain't a *ghost*. Ghosts are not corporeal entities, such as I hold in my arms every night."

"An apparition, then," Sally said. "A specter."

"Not them, neither," Dusty Bob insisted. "She's flesh an' bone, all right."

"Does she have body heat?"

Dusty Bob thought a moment. "Now that you mention it, she *is* a might cold to the touch…"

"Aha. My people call them the Dead Walkers – half living, half dead," Sally triumphantly explained.

"That's a zombie," Trooper Torres interjected, trying to be helpful.

"Devil Woman, I don't truck with your voodoo magic," Dusty Bob said. "The Good Book says neither necromancers nor sorcerers shall inherit the Kingdom of Heaven."

"Indians don't have sorcerers," Sally clarified. "We call them *shaman*."

"It's all the same in the eyes of the Lord."

"Funny how white man's God thinks just like white man."

Dusty Bob was trying to think of a good retort when Trooper Torres said, "I just wish I could remember what that darn word is…"

"It's *enigma*," Sally said to Trooper Torres. "The word you're thinking of is *enigma*: a puzzling mystery, something difficult to unravel." Then she looked at Dusty Bob. "A *conundrum* – a problem that doesn't seem to have an obvious answer – has a slightly different shade of meaning. But don't listen to me, I never made it past the fourth grade."

For once, Dusty Bob was speechless.

Chapter 4

Jim drove around the desert for three days and two nights looking for the perfect *saguaro* cactus. When he returned to the ranch at sunset on the third day, Dusty Bob was sitting on the diner porch strumming his old guitar. He got up, leaned his guitar against the chair, and went over to see what was in the bed of the truck.

It was a *saguaro* cactus and a shovel.

"It's for Lucia," Jim said by way of explanation. "She couldn't find one worthy of paintin' at her place."

"You lied to me about Holbrook?" Dusty Bob asked, slightly perturbed.

"No, I didn't lie to you. I also went to Holbrook to get her some new canvases for the cactus." They were on the passenger seat in the cab.

"Is this woman really worth all this, Jim?"

"Yes."

"All right, then."

Jim waited until the middle of the night, then drove out to Trooper Torres and Lucia's little adobe house. He dug a hole and planted the *saguaro* out back where she was sure to see it in the morning. He wanted it to be a surprise.

While he was working, he saw some strange lights in the sky, over in the distance near the Henderson place. They were multi-colored and very beautiful. They moved in a slow, hypnotic pattern. He stopped and watched them a long time, wondering what they were. He also heard several cows lowing and mooing in distress over that way.

He arrived back at the ranch about sunrise. Dusty Bob was just stirring.

"How're you?" Jim asked.

"I think I just passed a kidney stone," Dusty Bob sighed.

"Say, I was just over there plantin' that cactus at Lucia's, an' I saw some strange lights in the sky over by the Henderson place. I watched them a long time, but never could figure out what they were. They were causin' a real commotion with his cattle, though."

They decided to drive over to the Henderson place to check it out. They pulled off the highway near the front entrance. The sun was up now. Trooper Torres was there, standing next to his car, looking intently at the cattle on the other side of the fence.

"What's goin' on?" Dusty Bob asked.

"Well, we got us a real mess here," Trooper Torres said. "Looks like they struck again. Seems they've transplanted Zimmerman cow parts into Henderson cows, and vice a versa."

Dusty Bob and Jim took a closer look at the cows. They just didn't look right. They were moving and acting in a very un-cowlike way – stunned, confused. You could even see where the new parts had been stitched in place on their bodies.

"Zimmerman and Henderson are both claiming the cows are theirs because the parts are all mixed up and it's impossible to tell them apart," Trooper Torres informed them. "It's a real mess."

"Looks like a case of cosmic pranksters, if you ask me," Dusty Bob said.

"I don't know how they're ever gonna sort this mess out," Jim commented. They watched the Frankenstein cows for a while, then Dusty Bob and Jim got back into the pickup and drove home. Jim dropped Dusty Bob off and stayed behind the wheel.

"I'm going over to Lucia's to see what she thinks of the cactus," Jim said, and drove off. When he got there, she was already out back painting up a storm.

"I love it, Jim!" she gushed when she saw him. "I'm so inspired! Where did you find it?"

"You don't wanna know." He had to shout over the opera music blaring from the house.

"It's perfect!" she chirped, returning to her work.

He'd never seen her so happy. He knew he'd just scored a lot of points with her, and decided to leave her alone with her new muse. So he drove back to the ranch and sat on the porch with Dusty Bob for a spell, pleased as punch.

A while later, a shiny new car they'd never seen before pulled off the highway and parked in front of the diner. Two men got out and started to look over the place. They wore suits and dark glasses. *Government men?*

"Are you Dusty Bob?" the taller man asked.

"That's me," Dusty Bob said, not getting up.

"Mike Hightower," the man said. "And this is Clive Watley. We came all the way from New York City to see you."

"Is that right?" Dusty Bob whistled in surprise. "That's a long ways, all right."

"Yes, but well worth the trip," Hightower smiled. "Well, I'll just get right to the point. You see, we want to do a feature on you, for *Life* magazine. You know: *Whatever Happened to Dusty Bob,* that kind of thing. For our older readers. We think there might be a lot of people out there who still remember you."

"Well, I'll be," Dusty Bob said, stunned. "I...I just reckon there might."

"So, you think it would be all right for us to interview you? You know, for the feature?"

"Well, young man, I don't see why not."

"Terrific! Say, this might take a day or two," Hightower said. "We hear you run a...motel, or something. We'd like to check in, if you don't mind."

"Not at all," Dusty Bob beamed. "Our guest cabins are very comfortable an' folksy. You all get your bags out an' step into the office, an' we'll get everything squared away."

"Terrific!" Hightower exclaimed.

While they were signing the register, Dusty Bob pulled Jim aside and said, "Listen, I don't want them to see Sally. Tell her to go to her trailer and stay there until they leave."

"But who'll do the cookin'?" Jim asked.

"*You* will. Now go tell her, Jim. I'm countin' on you to keep her under wraps. I don't want Memory Ranch to be represented by the likes of her in *Life* magazine."

"But, Bob..."

"Just do it!"

Hightower and Watley were all signed in and paid up. "By the way, this is my long-time associate and confidant, Jim Dupree. He's got some pressin' business to attend to at the moment, but after that, he'll be at your disposal for anything you need. Now, allow me to show you to your accommodations where you can relax an' freshen up from your long trip." Dusty Bob was in full hospitality mode, pouring on the folksy charm.

Sally wasn't happy with Dusty Bob's dictum, but she complied. She lived in a rusty old Airstream trailer out behind the diner and kept exactly a dozen mangy stray dogs. Dusty Bob called them "The Apostles."

"And try to keep them dogs quiet while the guests are here," Jim urged. The whole thing rubbed Sally the wrong way, but she bit her tongue and did it to make things easier for Jim.

Hightower and Watley didn't stay in their cabin for long. They were eager to get the story and head back to New York City as soon as possible. That was fine with Dusty Bob, who seldom passed up an opportunity to talk about himself to anyone who would listen.

They set up for the interview in the diner. Hightower, the writer, brought in his notebooks and a tape recorder. Watley was the photographer. "Clive, why don't you get some shots of the horse and the other memorabilia. Dusty Bob and I will get started with the interview."

Clive took his camera and went to "shoot" Texas Pete and the other stuff cluttering the walls.

"I'd like to start at the beginning, with how you got into show business, if you don't mind," Hightower announced, turning the tape recorder on.

"Well, I started out on the rodeo circuit as a youngster, you know, ridin' bulls an' ropin' an' such," Dusty Bob began. "Then Will Rogers saw me at a rodeo in Tulsa, an' when he discovered I could sing a little, he put me on his radio show. I sang 'Home on the Range' an' 'Bury Me Not on the Lone Prairie.' A fella who owned a record label called Tombstone Records heard it an' thought I was pretty good, so he put out a song I wrote called 'The Next Morning in New Mexico.' I guess I just always had a knack for makin' up my own songs. It did pretty well on western music stations, an' another fella from Olympic Studios heard it an' asked me to come out to Hollywood to do a screen test. He said all the studios were lookin' for western stars who could talk an' sing on account of the talkies had just come out an' a lot of them silent stars didn't sound too good when they tried to open their mouths an' say somethin'. Well, the screen test went well an' he wanted me to make a picture. I told him I'd never acted before, but he said, 'Don't worry, son. You don't need to be a good actor to make westerns. Just be yourself.' I always remembered that advice.

"So we made my first picture, *Six Bullets and a Badge*. But before they put it out, the head of Olympic Studios said I sounded like a rube an' he wanted them to over-dub all my parts with a professional actor. But the feller that brought me out to Hollywood an' the director, Doc

Blandings, both stood up for me so the head of the studio backed down an' they let me keep my own voice. So they put out *Six Bullets and a Badge* an' I guess it did all right, because they wanted me to make another picture, so I said yes an' they signed me to a contract. I made pictures for Olympic Studios my whole career, an' they done right by me so I done right by them, I reckon."

"What happened after your last movie, *Rendezvous in Reno*?" Hightower asked. "Why did you seem to just disappear overnight?"

"Well, it wasn't overnight, exactly," Dusty Bob replied thoughtfully. "See, I made another picture after *Rendezvous*, but it just didn't feel right because Olivia was gone. At the premiere for *Rendezvous in Reno*, Olivia caught a chill an' it turned into pneumonia. She died three days later. I was never the same after that. Never the same."

"I'm sorry. Can you tell me what happened?"

"Whiskey's what happened," Dusty Bob said forlornly. "And lots of it."

"I see," Hightower said, stopping the tape recorder. "Perhaps we should take a little break."

During the interview, Jim took the opportunity to slip off to Lucia's to see how the painting was coming. When he got there, there was already a pile of used canvases scattered at her feet. He could tell there was something wrong.

"I have painted many paintings, but none satisfy," she blurted in a frustrated tone.

"What's wrong?" Jim asked.

"There are no flaws in this *saguaro*," she replied.

"But I thought that's what you wanted – the perfect cactus."

"Flaws are what make it interesting," she lectured. "Flaws are what make it accessible. One can relate to flaws in a cactus, just as one can relate to the flaws in one's own character."

"I don't understand." Jim was lost.

"You say this is a perfect cactus, but it is not. A perfect cactus has flaws, to give it character. This cactus has no character." She painted a big X over her current canvas and tossed it to the ground with the others.

Jim was discouraged, but unwilling to give up. "Then I'll find you a cactus with just the right amount of flaws."

She turned to face him. "Forget about me, Jim. I will never make you happy. I will only make you miserable, like me."

"My dear, I would rather be miserable than without love."

*   *   *

Back at the ranch, Hightower had a new question for Dusty Bob. "From what I hear, you were something of a hell-raiser in Hollywood back in the day."

"I reckon there's some truth to that."

"I recall something about you brandishing a gun at Spencer Tracy in Chasen's?"

"That wasn't Spencer, that was Errol Flynn," Dusty Bob corrected. "There was somethin' I didn't like about the way he smiled and called me 'pardner.' No, Spencer was aces, we got on just fine. But Errol was a tights-wearin' fruit."

"Did that incident bring any bad press?"

"I reckon so, but the studio tried to smooth it over the next day – made it look like a publicity stunt for my next picture – even got Errol to say it was all in fun. Besides, the gun wasn't loaded. I never took loaded guns into Chasen's. I always took the bullets out before going inside."

"Wasn't there some bad blood between you and Gary Cooper?"

"Gary Cooper's a pussy," Dusty Bob replied. "You can print that."

"I think not," Hightower demurred. "How much did alcohol have to do with these public scuffles?"

"Umm, a lot," Dusty Bob admitted. "But things changed after meeting Olivia. She laid down the law. She straightened me out."

"Tell me about Olivia."

"Oh, sweet Olivia," Dusty Bob mused. "Before her, I was a ship lost at sea. She was the lighthouse, brought me into peaceful waters. She could ride, shoot, drink, and cuss every bit as good as me. Knew her way around a Winchester rifle, that one did. Oh, she had my number, all right. But there was a tenderness – she knew how to take the sting out of me."

"Now, I understand you and Gene Autry were once very close. What happened there? Was it over a woman?"

"Well, yes an' no," Dusty Bob replied. "Me an' Gene had been friends for a long time. He had been seein' Olivia romantically before

39

I ever met her. She even co-starred in a few of his pictures. Then I met her on a trail ride, an' that was it. The moment I laid eyes on her, I knew. So, I reckon you can say I stole Gene's girl, although he had a few young ladies waitin' in line an' he took it all pretty well. We were still good friends, anyway. But then, a few years later, something strange happened. One day I was over at Gene's place an' we were knockin' back a few an' playing each other some of our new tunes on guitar. We used to do that, you know, play our new tunes for each other an' give each other tips how to make 'em better an' such. Well, this time I played him a new one of mine called 'Amarillo Annie,' an' he said it wasn't one of my better compositions but I could tell he really liked it an' just didn't want me to know. I could tell he was down-playin' it, you know, hopin' I'd give up on it an' give it to him. So that's how I knew it was good, an' I decided to keep it for my next record. But before I could book a studio, I heard my song on the radio, with Gene singin' it! He stole my song! And it was a hit for him, too! When I confronted him, he acted like I should think of it as an honor for him to sing my song! I told him he had no right to do it, but what steamed me the most was he had changed all the best words. And you know what he said? 'Well, Bob, I needed a song to put out right away, an' I didn't think you'd mind.' Then I realized what it was *really* all about: I'd stolen his girl, see, so he stole my song. Tit for tat. Well, that was it between him an' me. We haven't spoken since."

Hightower turned the tape recorder off and said, "This is great material. Why don't we all go outside and take some exterior shots now. Dusty Bob, you can show us around the ranch."

"Don't mind if I do," Dusty Bob said cheerfully, rising from his chair.

Outside, the photographer took some shots of Dusty Bob and Jim standing in front of the diner, at the foot of the windmill, and under the water tower. Then they went over to the corral and took some pictures with a couple of swayback horses and a mule named Aristotle.

"Who's that?" Hightower asked, pointing back behind the diner. They all turned, and there was Sally, all done up in her Indian garb, chanting and doing a rain dance outside her trailer.

"Oh, that's just a crazy old woman we let live back there," Dusty Bob blustered. "Out of charity, so to speak."

"This is *terrific!*" Hightower exclaimed. "Some authentic Southwest color here, just what the story needs. Clive, you've gotta get some shots of *this!*" Watley immediately put his camera to work, getting shots of Sally's energetic dance from various angles. Sally was eating up the attention. Dusty Bob felt a sinking feeling in his belly.

"I *told* you to tell her to lay low," he hissed at Jim.

"I did," Jim shot back.

"Oh, this is just *terrific!*" the *Life* reporter kept saying. "I've never seen anything like this! I've got to interview her for the story!"

"I told you, she's a might touched in the head," Dusty Bob tried, but it was no use. Hightower was already on his way over to her.

"Excuse me! Can you please tell me the significance of this dance?" he asked Sally excitedly. "What are you doing? Communicating with your ancestors? Conjuring up spirits?"

She stopped dancing and stood motionless, her eyes closed, her hands raised dramatically over her head.

"What are you doing now? Are you in some kind of trance state?" Hightower asked, his eyes wide in wonder.

"Ssshhhh!" Sally hissed, and Hightower obediently covered his mouth with his fingers.

"Oh, brother..." Dusty Bob moaned, watching *his* story in *Life* magazine go down the drain.

"I am an eagle," Sally said, eyes still closed, arms still raised. "I am flying high above the Earth. I am watching The People below. The People are happy, the children play, the fathers hunt buffalo and fish in streams, the mothers grind *maize* and nurse their young. Everything fine. Then White Man come, make The People move far away, onto strange new land that is not theirs. Leave ancestors behind. No buffalo to hunt, no streams to fish in. But the White Man says stay here, this your land now."

Hightower was trying to scribble everything down in his reporter's notebook.

"Then White Man come back many years later. Take strange new land away from The People. Make Indian woman live in crappy old trailer behind diner with twelve smelly dogs. Make her cook food for strangers, clean cabins, do washing."

"You can leave anytime, Devil Woman," Dusty Bob said.

"Try pay her with old buttons and cheap beads," Sally went on.

"That's NOT true!" Dusty Bob blurted.

"Then strangers stop coming. White Man run out of money, say he pay Indian woman next month. Same thing every month."

"Well, things *have* slowed down a bit," Dusty Bob admitted. "We've all got to learn to make do."

"But Indian woman smart. She correct White Man grammar and diction. She put up with mistreatment because she has nowhere else to go. This her home now." And with that, Sally opened her eyes, lowered her arms, and, with great dignity, walked into her rusty trailer and closed the door behind her.

"This is *gold*!" Hightower enthused, scribbling the last of it down in his notebook. "Were you just going to hide her from us back here the whole time?"

"Well, that was the plan, anyway," Dusty Bob said.

*   *   *

That night after supper, there was more activity over near the Henderson place. "What are those strange lights in the sky?" Hightower asked, watching them intently.

"Some kind of phee-nom-enon," Dusty Bob replied. "Them lights been messin' with the Zimmerman cows and the Henderson stock. Got 'em all mixed up, nobody knows what's goin' on."

Dusty Bob and Jim drove Hightower and Watley over to the Henderson place to check things out. Trooper Torres was already there. On the other side of the fence, the cows were acting mighty peculiar. They were standing dead still, as if lobotomized, in perfectly even, straight rows, like soldiers on a military parade ground. And they were *glowing* – a bright, phosphorescent green color.

"Spooky, ain't it?" Trooper Torres said quietly.

"How long they been this way?" Jim asked.

"Ever since I got here," Trooper Torres replied.

"I ain't never seen cows stand so still before," Dusty Bob remarked.

"I ain't never seen cows glowing bright green, neither," Jim observed.

"It's kinda givin' me the willies," Dusty Bob confessed with a shiver.

The men watched the motionless, glowing cows in silence for a long time. Hightower quietly asked Watley to shoot a roll of film, and the photographer obliged him.   Then Hightower and Watley said goodbye and got into their car.

"Where you goin'?" Dusty Bob asked.

"Back to Phoenix," Hightower said, rummaging through the glove compartment for a notepad.   "We're gonna get this story to the Phoenix newspaper for tomorrow's edition."   He turned to Watley. "You drive, I'll write it on the way."   Watley got behind the wheel, and they were off in a cascade of gravel and dust.

Chapter 5

After reading the article in the Phoenix newspaper, the governor got right on it. He sent a professor and some graduate students from the University of Arizona to study the cows and figure out what the dickens was going on out there in the middle of the desert. Since Memory Ranch offered the only food and lodging for miles around, Dr. Lowbridge and his students were compelled to bed-down in one of the guest cabins.

"It'll be nice to have someone intelligent to talk to, for a change," Dusty Bob said when Dr. Lowbridge checked in. "You sure you're a *real* professor, son?"

"Yes, sir," Dr. Lowbridge assured him. He was younger than Dusty Bob expected, and had glasses and the kind of closely-trimmed beard that beatniks and other riff-raff were accustomed to wearing.

"Well, as soon as you get settled in, Jim an' me'll take you out an' show you where the Henderson place is," Dusty Bob said, leading him to his cabin.

When they got out to the Henderson place, Trooper Torres was there watching the cows. The governor had two National Guard airplanes constantly circling over the field, taking pictures of the glowing cows from the air in case they moved.

"I'm Dr. Lowbridge, from the University," the professor said, shaking Trooper Torres's hand. Trooper Torres looked him up and down. He looked out of place here, in his glasses, corduroy jacket with arm patches, and khaki slacks.

"Has anyone been in close contact with these cows in the last few hours, trooper?" Dr. Lowbridge asked in an authoritative tone.

"No, sir," Trooper Torres answered.

"Good. Make sure nobody approaches them until we can figure out what's going on here."

"Yes, sir."

"The governor made it very clear that he doesn't want any civilians accidentally contaminated by these cows," Dr. Lowbridge continued gravely. "We don't know what's making them behave this way – what's making them glow like this – and he doesn't want anybody hurt on his watch. Understand?"

"Yes, sir."

"Good. By the way, trooper, you're doing a marvelous job – a simply marvelous job," Dr. Lowbridge said. "Rest assured, your vigilance and valor and dedication to duty will be duly noted in my official report to the governor."

"The *governor*? Thank you, sir!" Trooper Torres positively beamed.

"You're quite welcome, trooper. And may I add, it's rather bracing to find a civil servant – a law enforcement officer – a servant of the public – of your caliber on the job here. It's quite inspirational, indeed."

The group of men stood in silence, watching the cows for a long time.

"Well, what's the first step, professor?" Dusty Bob finally asked.

"The first step," Dr. Lowbridge said blankly. "Yes, the first step...well...well, we've got to find out what's making these cows glow, don't we?" He didn't have a clue how to begin. But he immediately went into action, making a show about ordering his graduate students to retrieve the sensitive scientific equipment from the back of their station wagon and prepare for the impending investigation. After all, he represented the University of Arizona, at the behest of the governor, and whatever they needed to do needed to be done in an orderly and efficient manner. Once they succeeded in determining what needed to be done, that is.

Eventually, their sensitive scientific equipment now strewn on the ground all around their station wagon, Dr. Lowbridge and his students donned bulky white contamination suits, hoods, goggles, and thick rubber gloves, and painstakingly started to make their way through the barbed wire fence. This delicate operation took quite a while, but once on the other side, the professor and his team apprehensively approached the cows and began scanning their large glowing bodies with what looked like expensive Geiger counter-type instruments.

In the meantime, looky-loos who'd seen the newspaper article began to show up and watch the cows in wonder and take snapshots of them for hours on end. They were mostly city folk. After a while, the kids started getting antsy and the adults looked tired and hot. That gave Dusty Bob an idea.

"Folks, I'm Dusty Bob. If you're hungry, just follow me back to my ranch an' we'll fix you up with some good ol' home-cooked grub, *pronto!*"

So Dusty Bob and Jim got into the pickup and led a string of cars back to the diner. Sally and Jim whipped up some BBQ ribs and hamburgers, while Dusty Bob held court in the diner and told stories about the old days in Hollywood. Then he pulled his old guitar down off the wall and sang 'Lonesome Trails' and some other western favorites for them. After eating, he took the kids out to see Aristotle and the horses, and even let them play with some of the Apostles – Sally's stray dogs.

Dusty Bob was beside himself, being the center of attention once again. After the city folks packed up their kids and drove off, he told Jim, "I haven't had this much fun in years!"

"You sure haven't lost your touch with people," Jim observed.

"And look: we made almost seventy dollars!" Dusty Bob said proudly. "Now we can start fixin' some things up around here."

"And pay Sally," Jim added.

"I was gettin' to that," Dusty Bob insisted. "I think this is just the beginnin', Jim. Tomorrow mornin' you can go into Holbrook an' pick up some supplies, then we'll go out to the Henderson place an' pick up another batch of city folks."

The next day, there was another group of looky-loos gah-gahing over the Frankenstein cows and the men in the bulky white suits who were still avidly taking readings of them with their instruments, and after a few hours the kids were hot and hungry and in the mood for some down-home ranch hospitality, as well. With the growing crowds, the governor had stationed about a dozen National Guardsmen and State Troopers along the fence to keep order.

"Come on, Jim – let's get these folks back to the ranch and get 'em properly fed an' watered," Dusty Bob said.

Much later, after the last batch of city folks left the ranch, Dusty Bob and Jim sat on the diner porch rolling cigarettes.

"Well, I'm bushed," Dusty Bob proclaimed with a satisfied air.

"Me too, pardner," Jim agreed.

Dusty Bob counted out a roll of cash. "Eighty-three dollars and some change. Not bad for a day's labor, eh?"

"Have you paid Sally yet?" Jim asked.

"I'm gettin' around to it," Dusty Bob said, a might irritated.

"Boy, I'll tell you what: gettin' a nickel away from you is like tryin' to take that book away from that lady in New York."

"What the hell are you babblin' about now, Jim?"

"Aw, you know what I mean."

"I don't have the foggiest," Dusty Bob asserted.

"That lady in New York. You know, the big, green *lady*."

"Do you mean, by any chance, the *Statue of Liberty?*"

"The very same."

"I still don't see what you're gettin' at," Dusty Bob confessed.

"All right, let me spell it out for you: you hold onto a nickel the way that lady holds onto that book. And you're not gonna get it away from her, neither, 'cause it's *part* of the statue. Now am I clear enough to penetrate your thick skull?"

"I get it, now," Dusty Bob said. "Only it ain't no book she's holdin'. I believe it's a tablet."

"Now why would that lady be holdin' a *tablet?*" Jim argued. "You think she's plannin' on doin' some sketches of the New York City skyline?"

"The tablet represents law an' order, Jim," Dusty Bob patiently explained. "You know: the U.S. Constitution, an' the Declaration O' Independence, an' other such important documents our country was founded upon."

"I don't know where you're gettin' your information from," Jim scoffed. "But it's a book of French poetry she's holdin'."

"Why French poetry, in particular?"

"Because the whole deal's a gift from *France*."

"Well, I beg to differ with ya, partner."

"An' I return the favor an' beg to differ with *you*."

They sat and smoked in silence for a while. Then Dusty Bob broke it.

"You know what I have a hankerin' to do?"

"No. What?"

"Well, I noticed how them city folk sure like to take pictures of them cows out there," Dusty Bob said. "An' it got me to thinkin'. They gotta take that film to the drug store when they get back home an' get it developed into pictures, an' that might take a couple of weeks, an' by the time they get the pictures they might not even care about 'em no more."

"So?"

"Well, what if we was to take our *own* pictures of them cows, and sell 'em to those folks right there on the spot, so they can take 'em home with 'em right then and there to enjoy? Better yet, why can't

47

we put a picture of them cows right on a t-shirt, an' sell *that* to 'em, instead? An' we could even advertise the place: *Dusty Bob's Memory Ranch* right across the t-shirt, so they don't forget us. What do you think?"

"Oooh-wee. For bein' a whiz at industry, that fella Howard Hughes got nothin' on *you*, Bob."

"Do I detect a slight tone of sarcasm, Jim?"

"Not at all. We oughtta get on that right away. In fact, why stop at t-shirts? Why not put them pictures on pants, too? An' we can put a big picture of your smilin' face right on the part of the pants you sit on."

"That's the last time I share any brilliant idears with a troglodyte like you," Dusty Bob sniffed.

"What's a troglodyte?"

"It's someone who can't see the sense in a good idear when he hears it."

"Then I'm a *proud* troglodyte," Jim said.

"You're a wet blanket on everything I try to do to benefit mankind."

"Someone's gotta keep you in line."

Just then, they heard a car pull off the highway. Dr. Lowbridge's station wagon pulled up and parked in front of the diner. The professor and his students got out and approached the porch. They'd been out in the field with the glowing cows all day, and their appearance was alarming. They still wore the bulky contamination suits, but had their hoods off. Their faces looked clammy and splotchy and pale. Their eyes were watery and rimmed with red. They moved slowly and seemed to have difficulty thinking clearly and speaking. One of the graduate students looked around in confusion. Another one doubled over and vomited on the station wagon's fender.

"Gee, you fellas don't look so hot," Dusty Bob observed.

"The readings are…off the charts," Dr. Lowbridge said, blinking as if his eyes refused to focus on Dusty Bob and Jim.

"What readings?" Jim asked.

"Radiation…extremely high levels…like I've never seen before…" The professor squinted painfully, struggling to find the words. "Not of earthly…origin…"

One of the other graduate students looked like he was going to faint.

"You fellas like some supper?" Dusty Bob asked. "There's some leftover short ribs in the diner."

"Not hungry," Dr. Lowbridge shook his head slowly from side to side. "Just need rest...will be better in the morning..."

First thing in the morning, Dr. Lowbridge called the governor and told him about the radiation levels.

"It's out of my hands now, Towbridge," the governor told him. "The Feds are taking over."

Two hours later, a government car pulled up to the diner and two men in black suits and dark glasses got out. They stared ominously at Dusty Bob, who was sitting on the porch polishing his six-shooter.

"Dr. Towbridge?" one of the G-men asked.

"No, my name's Dusty Bob."

"We have orders to take Towbridge to Washington, D.C. Where can we find him?"

"Cabin number three."

The men rounded up Dr. Lowbridge and his graduate students, who were still pale and listless and confused, and told them to pack up immediately.

Jim stepped out of the diner to see what all the commotion was about. "He ain't in any kind of trouble, is he?" he asked.

"That's classified," one of the G-men said.

"He's an awful nice feller, is all."

"Would either of you fellas care to sit down for a cup of coffee?" Dusty Bob asked.

"No time. The president's waiting."

"The President of the United States?" Dusty Bob asked.

"That's classified."

"By the way, the Phoenix newspaper got the story all wrong," the other G-man said ominously. "They made a mistake. This whole thing has nothing to do with flying saucers or men from outer space."

"You don't say," Dusty Bob said.

"What about the glowing cows?" Jim asked.

"A crop-dusting mishap."

"A crop-dusting mishap?" Dusty Bob asked.

"That's right," the G-man confirmed. "A crop-dusting mishap. That's the official story now. From Washington. If anybody asks you about it, you tell them: a crop-dusting mishap."

"Well, how do you explain the lights in the sky?" Jim asked skeptically.

"Methane gas," the first G-man replied.

"Methane gas?"

"Methane gas. In the atmosphere. As simple as that."

"Say, since you fellas work for the government, maybe you could settle a little argument we got goin' here," Jim said. "Is Lady Liberty in New York Harbor holdin' a book, or a tablet?"

"That's classified."

The men got into the car and drove away, followed by Dr. Lowbridge's station wagon. Dusty Bob and Jim watched as the vehicles turned onto the highway and headed towards Phoenix.

They were quiet a good long time before Dusty Bob said, "Sure been a lot of excitement around here lately."

"You said it," Jim replied.

Trooper Torres's prowler pulled off the highway and parked in front of the diner. He got out and looked at Dusty Bob and Jim forlornly.

"What's got *your* chin on the ground?" Dusty Bob asked. "You look about as low as a pregnant sow's belly."

"They're gone," Trooper Torres said. "They're all gone."

"Who's all gone?" Jim asked.

"The cows. The Feds came this morning and loaded 'em up into big trucks and drove 'em off to Washington, D.C. Told all the people to go home and forget what they saw." Dusty Bob felt sorry for Trooper Torres. For a few days, at least, guarding those cows gave him a purpose.

"Well, that's it, I reckon," Jim said matter-of-factly. "Things oughta be gettin' back to normal around here now."

"To tell you the truth, I'm a might relieved," Dusty Bob yawned. "All that excitement kinda tuckered me out some."

*   *   *

In his spare time, Jim had been diligently searching for another, less-perfect, cactus for Lucia. While driving down an old dirt road he hadn't been on in a while, he spotted one that seemed to stand out from all the others. He stopped the pickup and got out to examine the cactus, and try to figure out what was so different about it. Then he realized all the other *saguaros* had two arms raised up towards the sky, but this one had one arm pointing to the ground.

Why was one arm pointing to the ground? Excited, he got back into the truck and drove straight to Lucia's house. "You've got to come with me *now*," he insisted.

"Don't be ridiculous," she laughed. He grabbed her easel and canvases and threw them in the back of the truck.

"Get your paints," he said firmly. "We're wastin' valuable time."

Somewhat surprised at his forcefulness, she complied. He drove her out to the dirt road and found the cactus. She got out of the truck and studied the cactus in silence for a very long time. Jim got out and waited beside her. He knew the risk he was taking; if she didn't fancy it, his chances with her were probably through.

"Don't you like it?" he finally asked nervously.

"I don't know yet," Lucia responded distractedly. "Be quiet while it tells me its story."

She "listened" to the cactus a good twenty minutes or so. Jim didn't hear anything. Finally, she turned around and said, "This *saguaro* has a very sad story. I can paint this *saguaro*'s story. Get my things out of the truck."

Jim got her easel out of the truck and set it up. Then he got her canvases and paints and brushes. But she didn't start painting.

"There is still something this *saguaro* is not telling me," she said, staring strangely at the plant. "Why is it holding back? Why? Never mind – I will coax it out of him."

And she began to paint. She painted until the sun went down and the stars came out, and then she painted by moonlight, all night, until the sun came up. Then she painted by sunrise light. Jim had fallen asleep in the truck. He woke up about an hour after sunrise. Lucia had painted a half-dozen canvases, many of them strewn on the ground around her feet.

Jim picked one up and examined it. "Hey, these are pretty good."

"*Good* is not acceptable," she said, still painting feverishly. "But this *saguaro* is less coy than the others, more forthcoming. There is a generosity of spirit in this one that my other *saguaros* lack. The wilted arm has captured my imagination. Why does it point to the earth? Is it a defect? Or is he trying to tell us something? That is what I must uncover."

She continued to paint all morning, without stopping. Jim watched her work with pleasure, and a certain amount of concern.

"Don't you wanna take a break?" he asked.

"I am not tired," she insisted. "I feel energized. I don't want to lose momentum."

"You need to eat."

"Food is trivial," she argued. "The artist must learn to master mundane distractions such as hunger."

"Still, you need your strength – for your work. I'll be back in a bit."

Jim got in the truck and drove back to the diner for food and coffee. When he got back, she was working on a new painting.

"Say, that's gettin' somewhere," he said.

"Yes, it is less objectionable than the others," she conceded in a brighter tone. This was Lucia being pleased.

"Coffee?" he asked.

"Hot coffee would not be unwelcome."

He unscrewed the thermos lid and poured coffee into it. He handed it to her and she tasted it. "That is not unpleasant," she admitted.

"I brought some sandwiches and key lime pie."

"Maybe later," she said. "I must capture this *saguaro*'s prodigious mirth before its mood changes."

Jim stayed quiet and watched her work. The tone of this painting was altogether different than her other ones. It was lighter, less harsh, more whimsical, even. Her other paintings were often bleak and hopeless, even when depicting the beauty of desert life. But this one had a new sense of life, light, and color that he hadn't seen in her work before. To Jim's untrained eye, it represented something of a breakthrough.

When she was finished, even Lucia seemed pleased with the results. "You have done well, Jim," she told him. "This *saguaro* was waiting for me to unlock its secrets – eager to share its story with the artist."

These words were music to Jim's ears, although part of him was still waiting for the other shoe to drop, for *something* to suddenly backfire on him.

"There's just one thing, though," Jim said. "Did you ever figure out why he's pointing at the ground?"

Lucia smiled enigmatically at him, wiping paint off her fingers with an old rag. "It's very simple, Jim. He is pointing to the ground because all of the other *saguaros* are *not*."

And this was what Lucia liked most about her new *saguaro*. In fact, she liked it so much that she had a dream about it that night. It was a dream so vivid that it woke her from a dead sleep. Unable to go back to sleep, she took a shovel and Trooper Torres's prowler and drove out to the cactus. She started frantically digging in the ground, right where the down-turned arm was pointing.

About a foot deep, the shovel hit something solid. Digging around it some more, she pulled out an ornate wooden box. It looked very ancient. She wiped the desert soil off of it with her slender fingers, then slowly opened the hinged lid. An eerie greenish light emanated from inside the box and illuminated her face. She stood transfixed for a moment, contemplating the contents of the box, then gasped loudly and closed the lid.

A pair of headlights pulled up behind her and stopped. Two men in black suits got out and approached her. They were the two government men who came to collect Dr. Lowbridge from Memory Ranch a few days earlier. Without a word, one of them reached out and gently started to take the box out of Lucia's hands. Still stunned at the revelation of its contents, Lucia loosened her grip and allowed him to take it.

The man in the black suit walked over to their car and carefully placed the box in the center of the back seat. Then he and his partner got in the front and drove away, leaving Lucia all alone in the middle of the desert, underneath the brilliant Milky Way.

The next morning, Trooper Torres didn't show up at the diner at his usual time for coffee. Puzzled, Jim got in the pickup and drove over to the little white adobe house to see what was up.

"She took the prowler and left in the middle of the night," Trooper Torres told him when he got there.

"I think I know where she is," Jim said. They got in the pickup and drove out to her *saguaro*. Sure enough, there she was, sitting on the ground next to the hole she had dug. When they got out and approached her, she didn't stir.

"Lucia? You all right?" Jim asked. She looked up at him, but did not speak. They reached down and pulled her to her feet.

"What happened? What did you find?" Jim asked.

She just shook her head. She couldn't talk. Jim drove her home, Trooper Torres following in the prowler. They put her to bed, where she fell into a deep sleep. Jim looked around the house, but couldn't find her last cactus painting – the masterpiece.

"Have you seen a painting – a really *good* one – of the cactus we just found her by?" Jim asked Trooper Torres.

"No," Lucia's brother replied.

"Well, I wonder what happened to it?" Jim asked.

In another part of the desert, the two government men were driving down a lonely highway. They both had their dark glasses on. "What's that sound?" the one in the passenger seat asked.

"What sound?" his partner asked.

"It's coming from the back seat."

"I don't hear anything."

"Pull over."

"What?"

"Just pull over."

The one behind the wheel complied. The passenger turned around and looked in the back seat. The box was there, emitting a strange greenish glow through the seam in the lid. Next to it was Lucia's painting of the cactus pointing at the ground. There was a faint hum coming from the box.

The passenger got out of the car and opened the back door. He took the box out and lifted the lid. His face was bathed in an eerie greenish light. His eyes glazed over.

"Oh, my God…" It was the last words he spoke.

*   *   *

A few hours later, Old Mr. Young showed up at the diner with the strange ornate box and Lucia's painting. "I found 'em out on the highway. Someone just off an' left 'em there."

"That's Lucia's painting," Jim said. He looked at the box closer and noticed dirt clumped on the outside. "Have you opened the box?"

"This box hums," Old Mr. Young replied. "I figure any box that hums probably contains something I shouldn't see."

"What are you gonna to do with it?" Jim asked.

"Well, I don't rightly know, young man. Any suggestions?"

"There was a fella here a while back from the university," Jim said. "A professor of some sort. He might know what to do with it."

"And you could put it in this professor fella's hands?"

"I reckon so."

"Then I'd be much obliged if you would do so, because to tell you the truth, it kinda gives me the willies."

"What about the painting?" Jim asked.

"I kinda wanted to keep that."

"I'll give ya fifty dollars for it," Jim offered.

Old Mr. Young handed him the painting.

Chapter 6

It had been four nights since Dusty Bob had conjured Olivia with *Rendezvous in Reno*. He'd been trying to go as long as he could without it, to make the brittle, fading print last as long as possible. But each time he played the film, its images became fainter and fainter – especially the saloon dance scene.

But on the fifth night, he just couldn't help himself; he set up the projector, spooled up the film, and poured two glasses of whiskey. Then he turned it on and waited impatiently for Olivia to appear. When she did, she was paler than ever, but still there.

They danced to the sad music like dozens of times before, and he tried to hold her especially close this night. But there was something different about her; she felt somehow lighter, less solid in his arms. Olivia was fading, along with the image on the celluloid. Everything went according to the script until the music faded out and it was time for Olivia to take her leave. But instead of pulling away, she hesitated slightly, then slyly reached into her cleavage and pulled out a shiny silver dollar. She gave it to Dusty Bob, winked mischievously, and then faded into the shadows of the dark kitchen.

Dusty Bob looked at the silver dollar a long time, wondering what he was supposed to do with it. Then the jukebox lit up and the grandfather clock came back to life, just like always. Dusty Bob looked at the jukebox and got an idea. He went over to it and put the silver dollar into the coin slot. Before he could push a button, the jukebox started playing "Lonesome Trails." Halfway through the song, he glanced over at Texas Pete and noticed he wasn't there in his place of honor in the corner – his platform was *empty*.

Then he heard a horse whinny outside – a familiar sound. He walked outside the diner and saw Texas Pete standing in the moonlight, as alive as could be. His rhinestone saddle and bridle were burnished to a glistening sheen. Seeing Dusty Bob, Texas Pete whinnied again and stamped his foot.

"Well, hello boy," Dusty Bob smiled. Texas Pete looked anxious to get going somewhere. Dusty Bob walked over and mounted him.

"Okay, fella – let's go."

Texas Pete left the diner and started walking out into the open desert, away from the ranch.

"Where we goin'?" Dusty Bob asked. Texas Pete whinnied impatiently. "Okay, fella – I'll just wait an' see." After a while, Dusty Bob saw something in the moonlight in the distance. As they got closer, he saw that it was an old western town. "I don't recall *this* bein' way out here."

They rode into the town and down the main street. They rode past silent shops and storefronts, then Texas Pete stopped in front of a saloon and whinnied again. Dusty Bob looked up and read the sign: "The Silver Dollar Hotel and Saloon."

"Well, I reckon I could use a libation to clear the dust from my throat," Dusty Bob said, dismounting. He went into the saloon and looked around. It was empty, but there was old-timey music coming from a player piano in the corner. The only soul in the place was a bald man with an eye patch behind the bar. Dusty Bob walked up to the bar and said, "Where is everybody, friend?"

"Everybody's here," the one-eyed bartender said, wiping a glass with a towel.

"Doesn't anybody live in this town?"

"*Live?* No," the bartender said cryptically.

"Then I suppose folks just sorta pass through, do they?"

"You could say that. What'll it be, sir?"

"I'm a whiskey man," Dusty Bob proclaimed.

The bartender picked up a strange-looking bottle without a label and poured a thick green fluid into a glass.

"That don't look much like whiskey to me," Dusty Bob observed.

"That's because it ain't whiskey."

"I'll take whiskey, please."

"This is all we serve here, sir."

"Well, what *is* it?"

"If I have to explain it, you wouldn't get it anyway."

"I don't know…" Dusty Bob hemmed, staring at the unappetizing beverage.

"It's on the house," the bartender smiled.

"Well, I don't want to drink it."

"Suit yourself. But most folks pass through here drink it."

Dusty Bob and the bartender fell into an uneasy silence for several minutes, as the player piano continued a jaunty tune.

"Supposin' I *do* drink it," Dusty Bob finally said. "What happens then?"

"Only one way to find out, friend."

Dusty Bob picked the glass up and drank it down quickly.

"Well, what do you think?" the bartender asked.

"It's sweet," Dusty Bob observed.

"Sure, it's sweet," the bartender winked with his good eye. "But doesn't it pack a wallop?"

"Yes, sir, that it does," Dusty Bob agreed, a little woozy. "I think I'll have another."

The bartender pointed to a sign on the wall behind him: "One Drink Per Customer."

"Why, I've never heard of a saloon with a rule like that," Dusty Bob complained. "What is this – a dream or somethin'?"

The bartender stopped wiping glasses, cocked his head, and thought about it a long time. "You know, I've never really thought about it before. But yeah – I reckon it could be a dream, at that." Then he shrugged his shoulders and continued wiping glasses.

Dusty Bob rubbed his forehead. "I feel small. I mean, *strange*. Dag-nabbit, I don't know *what* I'm tryin' to say…"

"Don't worry, friend. It has that effect on everybody. Why don't you go see Granny now?"

"Who?"

"Granny, at check-in," the bartender pointed across the room. "She'll give you your key."

"Key?"

"Yeah, only don't lose it," the bartender warned him, lowering his voice. "Or you'll never get to see what's behind the *door*."

Foggy-headed, Dusty Bob walked over to check-in. Behind the counter, an ancient white-haired woman wearing dark glasses sat in a rocking chair with a shotgun across her lap.

"Howdy, Ma'am," Dusty Bob said uncertainly. "Barkeep sent me over for a key of some sort."

The old blind woman spit a long brown stream of tobacco juice into a brass spittoon without getting any on the floor. "Name?"

"Dusty Bob, Ma'am."

"Sign the register."

Dusty Bob looked at the register. The page was completely blank. "Reckon you don't get many guests around here."

"You from the Census Bureau?"

"No."

"Then I'd be much obliged if you would keep your migratory observations to yourself and sign the register," the well-armed blind woman said, launching another stream into the spittoon.

"Yes, Ma'am," Dusty Bob said, picking up an ink pen and signing his name. The old woman listened intently to the scratch of the pen on the paper.

"And the waiver."

"The what?"

"The *waiver,*" she repeated. "That paper right next to the register."

"What's it say?" asked Dusty Bob.

"It says we're not liable," she answered.

"Liable for what?"

"*Anything.*" Another marksman-like shot at the spittoon. Dusty Bob signed the waiver.

"Now, where's the key?" he asked.

"Check your pocket."

Dusty Bob reached into his pocket and pulled out a shiny brass key. It was ornate and felt unusually heavy. "How'd you do that?"

"Room Twelve," Granny said. "You'll find it upstairs."

Dusty Bob walked up the creaky staircase to a long corridor lined with many doors. He couldn't see the end of it. The building was much bigger inside than it appeared from the outside. The rooms were randomly-numbered, and out of sequence. He finally found Room Twelve and inserted the key. The door opened and he walked into a nearly-empty room – no bed, no furniture. The only light came from an oil lamp burning in the corner.

In the middle of the room was an antique Kinetoscope machine with a small table next to it. Next to the table was a chair in which sat a rumpled, friendly-looking gray-haired man. He had a benign smile on his face and looked like everybody's lovable old grandpa.

"*Walter*?" Dusty Bob squinted in the dim light. "What are *you* doing in this dream?"

It was Walter Brennan, the famous character actor and perennial side-kick to western stars. In fact, he'd been Dusty Bob's sidekick in three pictures.

"It's not a dream, Bob," he said in that familiar, folksy cackle of his. "It's a *memory*. And I'll be here to guide you through all of 'em."

"*All* of 'em?" Dusty Bob asked. "You mean, there'll be others?"

"Why, of course," Walter chuckled good-naturedly. "They're *your* memories, son. There's a whole lifetime of 'em! Ready to get started?"

"I – I suppose..."

"Good. You see that nickel there?" Walter pointed to the small table next to the Kinetoscope. There was a doily on it with a buffalo nickel right in the middle. "Go ahead – pick it up. Put it in the machine there, and let's get started."

Dusty Bob picked up the nickel and examined it, then fed it into the Kinetoscope's slot. Light immediately began to flicker from the viewfinder. Dusty Bob leaned over and peered into the machine.

He saw a dry, rugged landscape with lots of sagebrush and open sky and a range of jagged majestic peaks in the distance. A group of riders on horseback approached along a trail, in no particular hurry. There was Dusty Bob and Jim Dupree, both thirty years younger, Dusty Bob mounted on good old Texas Pete. Then he looked at the other riders. It was the whole Hollywood bunch.

There was Harry Carey and Walter Huston. There was Hoot Gibson and Spade Cooley. There was Boots Mulligan and "Tumbleweed" McClane and Montie Montana, and an assortment of other rodeo trick riders and movie stuntmen with familiar faces but whose names had long ago fallen through the cracks of Dusty Bob's mind.

"Well, I'll be," Dusty Bob said out loud, it all coming back to him in a rush.

"Sure, you remember, Ace," Walter chuckled. "Ace" was his nickname for Dusty Bob, since it was Dusty Bob's habit to keep an extra ace of spades up his sleeve at all times in case any unexpected, impromptu poker games should come up. "The leisurely trail rides, a chance for like-minded souls to escape crowded Los Angeles and the Hollywood grind for a few precious days of freedom and sunshine and fresh desert air."

Dusty Bob smiled as the scene unfolded before his eyes and he recalled those days with great fondness.

"There were no luxuries out on the trails," Walter continued in his folksy narrator's voice. "No hotels or restaurants or drugstores. You cooked over a campfire and slept on the ground underneath the stars at night. No telephones or automobiles. Civilization was far away and the crickets and the lonesome call of the coyote were the only sounds at night."

Then Dusty Bob noticed the pretty blond girl, on an appaloosa pony behind him, her cowgirl's hat perched on the back of her head and tentatively held in place by the drawstring, struggling to stay balanced in the saddle and keep up with the group. It took Dusty Bob some time to match a name to the face.

"Yeah, you remember her, don't ya, Ace?" Walter asked. "Remember her name?"

"Veronica," Dusty Bob said.

"Try again, Ace."

"Victoria."

"Bingo."

"Can we stop for a while?" Victoria asked in a high, whiny voice. "I need to rest."

The line of riders stopped. Young Dusty Bob dismounted and helped Victoria down out of her saddle.

"Victoria was a pretty thing," Walter continued his narration. "And you were quite smitten with her, weren't you? But she was more of a city-girl, wasn't she? She had little aptitude or love for the outdoors, as I recall."

"These boots are *killing* me!" Victoria complained, sitting on the ground and raising a foot in the air. Young Dusty Bob pulled her boots off one at a time, then her socks, and stood watching Victoria as she massaged her delicate white feet. Dusty Bob handed her a canteen to drink from, but she poured water on her toes instead.

"Not too much now," Young Dusty Bob cautioned. "You're gonna need some of that for drinkin'."

"Those boots!" Walter said. "Very fashionable, but not made for riding. You tried to warn her, but she wouldn't listen, would she? She went for fashion over comfort, like always."

The other riders, still mounted, watched the proceedings impatiently. Harry Carey shot Dusty Bob a sharp look, and Dusty Bob just shrugged his shoulders sheepishly. Victoria pulled a cigarette out of her purse and waited for Dusty Bob to light it. Then she smoked quietly, looking miserable, hot, and uncomfortable while everyone waited.

"You remember how you met her?" Walter asked. "She was an extra on the set of *Tombstone Two-Step*, remember? With her golden

61

tresses and pretty girl-next-door looks, she caught your eye. You'd been seeing each other pretty regular for a couple of weeks when you made the mistake of inviting her on the trail ride."

"Can't we stop at a café somewhere to cool off and get something to drink?" Victoria asked miserably.

"There ain't a café for a hundred miles in any direction, Sweetheart," Young Dusty Bob replied helplessly.

"I can't believe I let you drag me all the way out here like this," she whined.

"I told you it was a trail ride," Dusty Bob replied, not wanting to get into a lover's spat in front of all his cronies. "What did you *think* it would be like?"

"I don't know," she admitted. "All I know is I'm hot and dusty and I need a bath and a highball and a clean hotel room to spread out in."

Young Dusty Bob stared down at Victoria like he didn't know what to do. She looked like she was going to pitch a fit any second.

"The horses are getting restless," one of the other riders said.

"Well, I can't go any further today," Victoria said emphatically.

"It's a might early," Young Dusty Bob finally said. "But I reckon we can stop and camp here for the night." Reluctantly, the riders dismounted and began setting up camp. By sundown, they had a good fire going and a kettle of stew cooking. Victoria sat off by herself on a rock, sulking. Dusty Bob brought her a plate of stew and sat by her while she picked at it.

"I guess she didn't have much to say to you at that point, Ace," Walter observed.

Young Jim Dupree walked over and sat down next to Young Dusty Bob. "You need to think about this, Bob. This girl's not right for you, and you know it."

"Maybe not, but she's mighty pretty to look at," Young Dusty Bob replied.

"After supper, everyone settled around the campfire to talk and tell stories," Walter narrated as Old Dusty Bob watched the scene unfold through the viewfinder. "Walt Huston pulled a bottle out of his saddlebag and filled everyone's cup with strong Irish whiskey. Harry Carey told about the first time he got drunk with John Ford and ended up at a racetrack in Mexico two days later not having the faintest idea how they got there. Then more whiskey was poured and the talk turned to rodeoin'. Hoot Gibson held court and everyone wanted to hear his stories from the old days."

"I've got one about our friend Dusty Bob here," Old Dusty Bob watched Hoot Gibson tell the riders gathered around the campfire. "The Greeley Stampede, 1929. Remember that one, Bob?"

"You can just put a cork in it right now, Hoot," Young Dusty Bob said, but it wouldn't do – everybody wanted to hear it now.

"See, Dusty Bob and I were both entered in the steer ropin' competition," Hoot continued in merry defiance of Dusty Bob. "Ten thousand rodeo fans waitin' to see some expert ropin', so I loosen the cinches on Dusty Bob's saddle while he isn't lookin', see, and so he gets out there and wraps one end of his rope around his saddle horn, and when he ropes that steer with the other end it yanks the saddle right out from under him!"

"You can just shut up right now, Hoot," Dusty Bob said through the laughter.

"Not just yet, Bob," Hoot said. "There's still more to come. Well, this minor setback isn't going to derail our hero Bob, so he gets down off his horse, grabs the loose end of the rope, and proceeds to wrassle that steer to the ground and tie him up good. But in the confusion, Bob here somehow gets one of the steer's legs tied to his own ankle, and when that steer gets up and takes off, there goes old Bob draggin' along right behind him."

"That ain't exactly how it transpired," Young Dusty Bob said sheepishly, but it was already too late seeing that most of the gang were either doubled over or laying on the ground in fits of laughter.

"Then, thinkin' quick-like, I get on the speaker system and say in an official-soundin' voice, 'We regret to inform you, Mr. Bob, that the position of rodeo clown has already been filled.' Yes sir, the crowd just loved that last bit, all right."

When things settled down a bit, Young Dusty Bob got out his guitar and Spade Cooley got out his fiddle and they played some old cowboy songs like "Sweet Betsy from Pike," "The Gal I Left Behind Me," and "Pecos Queen." Walt Huston pulled out a battered old harmonica and tried to play along, with everyone else singing along out of tune. Perking up a bit, Victoria squeezed herself in around the fire and sang a rousing version of "San Antonio Rose," more than happy to be the center of attention. Then everyone decided to get some shut-eye and bedded down for the night.

"What happened next sorta sealed the deal," Walter narrated, followed by a loud, shrill scream from Victoria.

"What's wrong now, Darlin'?" Young Dusty Bob asked, alarmed.

"There's some kind of *creature* in my sleeping bag!" Victoria screamed in reply. The whole camp was awake now, and not very happy about things.

"Will you *please* do something about your gal, Bob?" Harry Carey grumbled.

"Hold your horses, fellas," Dusty Bob said calmly, pulling his six-shooter out of its holster and shooting a full-sized, adult rattlesnake as it slithered out of Victoria's sleeping bag. He blew its head off with one shot.

"I am not staying in this crazy place one more night," Victoria screamed at Dusty Bob. "Take me home right now!"

"We ain't goin' nowheres 'til sun-up," Young Dusty Bob drawled, holstering his revolver. "So just climb back into your bag there and try to get some sleep."

"Oh, no – I'm not sleeping on the ground anymore!" Victoria vowed, climbing up onto the big rock and drawing her legs up under her.

"So, Victoria spent the night sitting on the rock while everyone else slept peacefully," Walter narrated. "And in the morning, she coldly informed you that you would be taking her to the nearest hotel – preferably one with an attached restaurant and hair salon."

After breakfast, Young Dusty Bob told the other riders. "I think we're gonna cut off to Tehachapi, so I can send her home. I'll catch up with you boys in Grass Valley."

"Good luck with that one," Walt Huston said, nodding in Victoria's direction.

"You want me to come with you?" Jim volunteered. Good ol' Jim.

"Naw, I reckon I can handle her," Young Dusty Bob winked. "You go on ahead with the fellas."

"So the gang said their goodbyes and continued down the trail without you, while you and the Dragon Lady headed to the nearest town with a telephone," Walter said.

"That's right," Old Dusty Bob remembered. "She called her sister to come pick her up. They were roommates."

"Olivia drove all the way from Los Angeles without battin' an eye," Walter cackled. "It was the first time you ever laid eyes on her. It was all over for you, wasn't it, boy?"

"I guess once I saw her, I couldn't take my eyes off her," Old Dusty Bob confessed. "Victoria was so jealous she could just spit, as I recall."

"It was Olivia's idea, wasn't it?" Walter asked. "You know, to take Victoria's place and finish the ride with you."

"I believe it was, at that."

"And she turned out to be a fine rider, as I recall."

"A mighty fine rider, indeed," Old Dusty Bob concurred. "She could hold her own in the saddle with any of the boys."

"So, Victoria, steaming-mad, drove the car back to Los Angeles alone while you and Olivia met up with the fellas further on down the trail," Walter mused. "You shoulda seen the looks on the boys' faces when you came ridin' up with another girl and introduced her as Victoria's sister."

"They were none too pleased, as I recall," Old Dusty Bob admitted.

"But they soon discovered Olivia and Victoria were as different as night and day," Walter said with a folksy grin.

The scene in the viewfinder faded to a nighttime campfire somewhere further down the trail. The boys were all gathered around Olivia, vying for her attention.

"Yes sir, she took to the trail like a duck to water," Walter continued. "When the boys all saw how outdoorsy she was, it really won 'em over, all right. She fit right in, rollin' her own smokes an' drinkin' Irish whiskey out of a tin cup. She never complained about the dirt an' dust and heat even once – a real trooper, she was. By the end of the ride, she had everyone's respect."

"That she did," remembered Old Dusty Bob. "At the end of the ride, Walt Huston came up to me an' said, 'Son, if you don't hold onto this one, you'll regret it the rest of your days.' That was the moment I realized she was The One."

"But wooin' her wasn't always a smooth ride, as I recall," Walter remarked. "Wasn't she your buddy Gene Autry's girl?"

"Yep. She really put me through it, sometimes," Old Dusty Bob chuckled, thinking back. "But I wasn't about to give up."

Then the campfire scene faded out and the Kinetoscope's viewfinder went dark.

"Is that it?" Dusty Bob asked.

"For now," Walter said. "There'll be more soon."

"Will I be seein' more of you?"

"Probably more than you ever wanted, pardner," Walter winked. "But it's time for you to go now." The lamp faded out and the room became dark. Dusty Bob left the room and closed the door behind him. He walked downstairs to where Granny was still sitting in her rocker with the shotgun across her lap.

"Leave the key," she said, expectorating into the spittoon. He placed the key on the counter and walked out of the hotel. Texas Pete, still very much alive, was waiting for him at the hitching post outside.

"Well, fella, it sure was good seein' the old gang again," Dusty Bob said, patting the horse's neck. Then he mounted up and rode him back to the ranch in silence.

The next morning, Texas Pete was back in his place on the platform in the diner, as ratty-looking as ever. Dusty Bob played "Lonesome Trails" on the jukebox, but the horse didn't stir. Then he got an idea and opened the change box on the jukebox, but all he found was two nickels, three pesos, and an assortment of washers. The silver dollar wasn't there.

*   *   *

During the next screening of *Rendezvous in Reno*, the same thing happened at the end of the saloon dance scene: Olivia produced the same shiny silver dollar from her cleavage and gave it to Dusty Bob before disappearing into the shadows. Into the jukebox it went, and "Lonesome Trails" started to play. Then Dusty Bob waited patiently for Texas Pete's familiar whinny.

When it came, he went outside and found his trusty horse once again very much alive and eager to hit the trail.

"Hey there, *amigo*," Dusty Bob said, climbing up into the saddle. "It's good to see you again." Texas Pete moved right out into the dark desert and kept up a steady pace until they reached the ghostly little western town in the middle of nowhere.

Inside the Silver Dollar Saloon, the bald, one-eyed bartender smiled when he saw Dusty Bob enter.

"Welcome back, sir," he said cheerfully. Nothing had changed. The player piano played the same jaunty saloon tune as before. Dusty

Bob made his way past empty tables and stopped at the bar. "It's very good to see you again, sir."

"I take it you haven't seen many new faces since my last visit," Dusty Bob said.

"Business has been quite slow, sir," the bartender acknowledged. Dusty Bob noticed the wall behind the bar was covered with several dozen portraits – old, yellowed photographs of mostly older men and women.

"Who are them folks?" Dusty Bob asked.

"Oh, them? Former guests, patrons who don't come around much anymore. Now, what'll it be? The usual?"

"I reckon so, seein' as that's the only drink you seem to serve around here."

"Excellent, sir." The bartender poured a glass of the same thick green fluid. Dusty Bob picked it up and knocked it back in a studied, western saloon fashion. The familiar movie-set ambience of the place almost made him feel like he was back in the pictures.

"It looks like you're taking more of a liking to it, sir."

"It's growin' on me," Dusty Bob replied, his head already spinning.

"Very good, sir. Granny's waiting at check-in."

Dusty Bob reflexively reached into his vest pocket for change.

"Still on the house, sir," the bartender said, holding up a hand.

"Much obliged." Dusty Bob turned and walked over to the check-in area.

"You again," Granny said, contributing another stream of warm brown juice to the spittoon.

"Does it ever get full?" Dusty Bob asked, indicating the spittoon.

"Your business here is to be conducted *upstairs*," Granny said sternly, shifting the position of the shotgun across her lap. "It doesn't include custodial issues or the maintenance of the premi—*sees*."

"Beg your pardon, Ma'am," Dusty Bob said, signing the register. Granny cocked her head and listened carefully to the scratching of the ink pen on the coarse paper. Then Dusty Bob signed the waiver, and Granny nodded her approval.

"Room Nine," she said. Dusty Bob felt in his pocket and pulled out a shiny brass key. Then he walked up the creaky stairs and, with some effort, managed to find Room Nine. It was located, logically enough, between Room Fifteen and Room Twenty-three.

He inserted the key and opened the door. The inside of the room was identical to the time before: a Kinetoscope machine, a small table, an oil lamp – and a chair with the hunched, lumpy physique of Walter Brennan in it.

"Hello again, Walter," Dusty Bob said warmly. It was good to see his old friend again.

"Howdy, Ace. Glad you came back for another trip down Memory Lane."

"I'm glad it's you, Walter – you know, takin' me back an' such."

"Wouldn't have it any other way, pardner. Just like the good old days, eh? Now, why don 't you pick up that buffalo nickel and let's get the show started."

Dusty Bob picked up the old nickel and fed in into the machine. It whirred to a start, yellow light flashing from the viewfinder. "What've we got on the bill today?"

"You'll remember this one, Ace," Walter assured him. "It was Olivia's birthday, and you took her riding in Griffith Park. It was exactly what she wanted."

Dusty Bob anxiously peered into the viewfinder and saw the scene: Him on Texas Pete, Olivia sitting lovely on her appaloosa pony, riding down a tree-and-brush-lined ravine in a bright splash of sunshine. They wound their way over a twisting trail, and rode out onto a high bluff with a vista of downtown Los Angeles. There were no skyscrapers – the iconic obelisk-shaped City Hall was the tallest building on the skyline. Behind them sprawled the giant "Hollywoodland" sign. Just below them there was a large construction site with workers laying the foundation of a long, odd-shaped building.

"What are they building?" Olivia asked.

"That's the new observatory," Young Dusty Bob proudly informed her. "It's gonna be a building where you can go an' look into outer space through telescopes an' see all the planets, up-close-like. They say there's gonna be a room where you can look up an' see the Milky Way Galaxy splattered all across the ceilin'."

"The world is changing so fast," Olivia marveled. "I can't wait to see it."

Old Dusty Bob watched the scene and smiled, too. "I remember that day. After that, we stopped for lunch at that little *tamale* stand in Los Feliz."

"Enrico's," Walter said.

"That's the one."

"I can still taste those *tamales*," Walter said, licking his chops.

"It was a beautiful day," Old Dusty Bob said wistfully.

"It was also your first quarrel."

"It was?"

"Watch." Walter whistled a little bit of "The Yellow Rose of Texas" and the scene in the viewfinder changed to the *tamale* stand. The horses were tied to a hitching post, Young Dusty Bob and Olivia sat at a small table in the shade of a spreading oak tree. A plump woman in a bright dress with red flowers on it brought them a plate of fresh *tamales*.

"That's Enrico's wife, Martina," Old Dusty Bob observed. "The *tamales* were her great-grandmother's recipe."

"You still have a great memory, Ace," Walter cackled.

In the memory, Young Dusty Bob called out to Martina's husband. "Hey, Enrico. You don't happen to have a bottle of *tequila* layin' around, do ya?"

Enrico, a short man with a thick black bottle-brush mustache brought a bottle and two glasses to the table.

"It's Olivia's birthday, and I feel like celebratin' a little," Young Dusty Bob told him.

"Okay, *Senor* Bobs," Enrico said. "But I don't have a liquor license, so don't tell nobody."

"Relax, *amigo*," Young Dusty Bob assured him. "Didn't you hear the news? The dry spell's over! Prohibition just got repealed! We're all free to drink once more!" The younger man in the memory spoke with a brashness and bravado that the Older Dusty Bob had long since lost. It made Old Dusty Bob cringe a little, like watching a precocious child over-step his bounds.

Young Dusty Bob poured two glasses and handed one to Olivia. "To your twenty-seventh birthday, and may there be more than twenty-seven more!" They clinked glasses and downed their shots, giggling like young people in love.

"Didn't you say something about a quarrel?" Old Dusty Bob asked Walter. "Looks like they're gettin' along pretty well to me."

"Wait for it," Walter said.

"This has been such a lovely day," Olivia beamed.

"And it ain't over yet," Young Dusty Bob assured her. "I've got some great news."

Olivia looked at him with mock sternness. "Just *what* have you been up to now, mister?"

"I've been workin' on a little deal," Young Dusty Bob said proudly. "Yours truly has arranged it so *my* studio, Olympic Pictures, is gonna buy out your contract with Republic. You're moving over to Olympic, starting first thing Monday mornin'."

Olivia's face fell. "Why would I want to do that?"

"So you can be in *my* pictures, Darlin'," Young Dusty Bob said enthusiastically.

"But I like working at Republic," Olivia protested. "I don't want to move to Olympic. Why didn't you think to ask me first?"

"I reckon I thought you'd recognize a good deal when you saw one," Young Dusty Bob explained. "You're gonna get more money now, and we get to work together more. I just wanted to help your career."

"Look, I don't *need* your help, Bub," Olivia said hotly. "I was doing just fine before I met you."

"Playin' shop girls an' school marms in Gene Autry pictures? You call that doin' just fine?"

"I like it at Republic. They've always been fair with me and they treat me with respect."

"But Darlin', they bury you in forgettable parts," Young Dusty Bob argued. "You're always in the background somewhere, sometimes it's hard to even pick out your name in the credits. I wanna bring you into focus, get your name up there at the top of the bill, where you belong." He swept his hand through the air grandly, as if reading a marquee. "'*Olivia Del Monte.*' The public's waitin' for ya!"

"Look, I know you meant well, but this is all very insulting, Bob," Olivia said. "I mean, what is this, the Victorian Era? Doesn't a girl have a say in her own career these days? What have women been fighting for all these years, anyway?"

"Girl's got spunk," Walter observed.

"That she did," Old Dusty Bob chuckled. "She always knew how to put a haughty young bronc in his place."

Back in the memory, Young Dusty Bob was trying to talk his way out of it, but Olivia wouldn't have any of it. "You can take me home now, Bob," she said, crossing her arms.

"But we're on the horses," Young Dusty Bob haplessly reminded her.

"In that case, I'll see myself home. Good day." And she got up and huffed off.

"That was rough to watch," Old Dusty Bob confessed. "But I smoothed it over the next day, as I recall, with some flowers and a box of chocolates – and two tickets to the premiere of *It Happened One Night,* with Clark Gable and Claudette Colbert. My old buddy Clark really came through for me on that one, I tell ya. She'd been talkin' about seein' that picture for weeks, so she couldn't rightly say no when I showed up at her doorstep with the tickets. It didn't have no horses in it, but I reckon it was still a pretty fair picture."

"And she finally did move over to Olympic, once the dust settled," Walter said.

"And lo and behold, she started gettin' more leadin' parts right away," Old Dusty Bob said. "But that was mostly on account of me pullin' the strings behind the scenes, which I didn't exactly tell *her* about, if you get my meanin'. Still, she held her own up there on the screen – even stole a scene or two from the likes of me, if you can believe it."

"And you *did* get to act together in three pictures," Walter pointed out.

"Yep. Let's see, that would be *Down to My Last Ace*, *Ticket to Purgatory*, and…"

"*Rendezvous in Reno*," Walter added.

"That was her best performance," Old Dusty Bob said. "The fans loved her in that. Lord, I miss her, Walter. I miss her somethin' awful…"

Chapter 7

The next time Dusty Bob found himself at the Silver Dollar Hotel and Saloon, he was surprised to see a photograph of himself had been added to the gallery of portraits on the wall. It was one of his eight-by-ten glossies – the kind he used to sign and hand out to fans back in his heyday. It bore the inscription: "To Maria Elena: Thanks for all the good times, especially that crazy night in Juarez. Sincerely, Bob."

"I see you hung my picture on your wall," Dusty Bob said to the bald, one-eyed bartender.

"Now that you're becoming something of a regular, we just thought it was time, sir."

"I don't remember writin' that inscription, though," Dusty Bob said. "Or Maria Elena, whoever she is. Must have been an acquaintance of my impetuous youth."

"No doubt, sir."

"Say, it just occurred to me that I don't know your name," Dusty Bob said. "If I'm going to be more of a regular around here from now on, maybe I should know what to call you."

"My name is Hieronymus, sir," the one-eyed bartender said. "Hieronymus Quinn."

"Glad to make your acquaintance, Mr. Quinn."

"You may call me Hieronymus, sir."

"Well now, that's quite a mouthful," Dusty Bob chuckled. "How 'bout *Harry?*"

"As you wish, sir."

"And how long have you been of service to this establishment?"

"Since before the war, sir."

"Which one? The first, or the second?"

"The war between the North and the South, sir."

"You don't say?" Dusty Bob looked surprised. "You look pretty good for your age."

"The Silver Dollar has been good to me, sir."

"I can see that," Dusty Bob said. "Say, who owns this place, anyhow?"

"Oh, the Silver Dollar has had many owners over the years, sir."

"Who owns it now?"

"The current owner is a man named Aloysius T. Barnabas, sir, of Cherub Falls, Wisconsin. A conjuror and illusionist by trade, he was a very popular and well-paid performer in the parlors and back rooms of the richest and most well-established Eastern families. Scandal and ill-advised financial investments drove him to abandon his career and seek a new path here in the West, where he has managed to turn things around and has done remarkably well."

"Where is this fellow?" Dusty Bob asked. "I'd like to meet him."

"Oh, I'm afraid that's quite impossible, sir. You see, Mr. Barnabas suffers from a severe disorder which renders him incapable of meeting new people, and he has never set foot on the premises. The only people he can associate with are the few familiar souls who knew him before the onset of the tragic disorder. They are the ones who care for him and administer his many business dealings, but, unfortunately, they also keep him completely isolated and under their firm control."

"Don't that beat all," Dusty Bob said.

"Yes sir, it does beat all."

"And what about this town?" Dusty Bob asked. "I've had my ranch for thirty years and never knew *any* of this was here."

"There is a book that may be of assistance in this matter, sir," Hieronymus said, rummaging around behind the counter. "Ah, here it is!" He produced a very large, heavy book and slammed it down on the thick oak bar. It was leather-bound and very ancient-looking, and looked as if it contained about a thousand pages. *The Curious Beginnings and Exhaustive History of the Town of Silver Dollar,* declared its title in impressive, gold-embossed letters.

"This looks promising," Dusty Bob said, opening the book and leafing through its pages. "Hey, some of these pages are *blank*."

"Oh, I think you'll find, upon further investigation, that *all* of the pages in that book are in fact blank, sir," Hieronymus told him.

"All of them?"

"That's right, sir."

"Why in blazes are all the pages *blank*?"

"Well, sir, I'm afraid that this particular book has yet to be written."

"I don't follow."

"In the fullness of time, sir, every endeavor, great and small, has its rightful season."

"Tell me, Harry: Does *anything* around here make sense?"

"Excellent question, sir."

73

"Well, *does* it?"

Hieronymus thought a long time before answering. "I'd like to be of further assistance in this matter, sir, but I'm afraid my duties begin and end with serving drinks, engaging in meaningless small-talk, and keeping a tidy bar."

"I feel like I'm losin' my mind."

"Perhaps you need a drink, sir."

"I reckon it couldn't hurt."

The bartender poured a glass of the thick green fluid, and Dusty Bob drank it down quickly.

"Feeling better now, sir?"

"That's the ticket, all right," Dusty Bob said, instantly floating.

"Rather makes you forget the cares and burdens of this world, doesn't it, sir?"

"And how," Dusty Bob concurred. "I reckon I better be gettin' along and pickin' up my key now, Harry."

"Always a pleasure talking to you, sir," Hieronymus smiled.

Upstairs, Walter was waiting for him in Room Seventeen. "I was wonderin' when you were gonna show up, Ace."

"I was engaged in a foolhardy conversation with Harry the one-eyed bartender, and the time just seemed to slip through my fingers."

"That's okay, Ace. I've got all the time in the world."

"Tell me the truth, Walter," Dusty Bob pleaded. "This is all just a figment of my imagination, isn't it? You, this hotel, Granny and her shotgun – none of it's real, is it? I'm, I'm just imaginin' it, or losin' my sanity, or just dreamin' it all up – right?"

"Oh, it's quite real, Ace," Walter assured him. "And there's nothing wrong with your mind. Your cheese is still sittin' right on top of your cracker, where it belongs."

"Then what's happenin' to me, Walter?"

"A *blessing*," Walter said kindly. "Most folks would give anything to be able to be with a lost loved-one again, to relive their most cherished memories one more time before they're gone forever. Sit back and enjoy the gift, *amigo*."

"Fine," Dusty Bob said. "You say you're here to take me back, help me relive my memories. Do I have to stick to the menu, or can I order up anything I want?"

"That's not how it works, Ace. The memories have been pre-selected, for maximum impact. I can't change that."

"So, you're just a puppet, like Charlie McCarthy."

"I just follow my orders, like everyone else," Walter explained with an impish grin. "The loyal sidekick, remember?"

"Okay, pardner. What've you got for me tonight?"

"A good one, Ace. Now drop the nickel in that slot and let's get started."

Dusty Bob complied. The ancient machine sputtered into action and he eagerly put his eyes to the viewfinder. He and Olivia were driving one of his Caddies along a lonely stretch of highway at night. The moonlight was shining on the ocean beside them.

"It was a weekend getaway, driving up the coast with no particular destination in mind," Walter said in his best side-kick narrator's voice.

As Dusty Bob watched, the night sky darkened as storm clouds gathered and blocked out the moon. It began to rain.

"A sudden storm rolled in and made a real mess of the road," Walter said.

"I remember that trip," Old Dusty Bob said. "It was raining so hard, I couldn't see where I was goin'. We had to find a place to stop, but there wasn't anything for miles. So I kept drivin', real slow-like, waitin' for somethin' to come up."

"Then Olivia saw a sign for the 'Valhalla Lodge,' and you turned off the road to find it," Walter continued.

"We drove on that little narrow road for miles lookin' for that place in the pitch dark," Old Dusty Bob remembered. "I was beginnin' to think there was nothin' there at all."

"Then you found it."

The car pulled up to a huge, rustic lodge built out of logs and covered with a sturdy roof of thick birchwood shingles. All the windows were lit up invitingly, and smoke poured from the stone chimney – signs of life inside.

"But there were no other cars in the parking lot," Old Dusty Bob pointed out. "I sure thought that was mighty strange."

Old Dusty Bob watched as Olivia and his younger self got out of the car and trundled into the lodge's warm, dry reception area. A huge stuffed grizzly bear dominated the foyer, and behind the desk sat a great fat man with mutton-chop sideburns and smoking a corn-cob pipe. He wore wire-rimmed glasses, a nineteenth-century admiral's coat with gold-braided epaulets, and a coonskin cap on his head. The fat man stared at them for a while, and then said "Can I help you?" in a thick Scandinavian accent.

"Yes sir, you sure can," Young Dusty Bob spoke up. "Do you have a room available for the night?"

"We have forty rooms. Which one would you like?"

Taken aback, Young Dusty Bob answered, "Any one will do, I reckon…"

With great effort, the fat man stood up and turned to face a massive board full of labeled room keys on the back wall. He picked one out randomly, in almost *eeny, meeny, miny, moe* fashion. "This one," he said with great satisfaction, handing Young Dusty Bob the key.

"How much do we owe you?" Young Dusty Bob asked.

The fat man pointed to a jar with some bills and coins in it sitting on the counter. "If the room is satisfactory, pay us what you like in the morning."

Young Dusty Bob saw a sign: NO ROOM SERVICE. "We haven't had any supper yet," Young Dusty Bob explained. "Is there any way to get something to eat?"

"The dining room is open all night," the fat man said. "Gustav will show you the way." A tall, straight man with black slicked-back hair and an impeccably neat waiter uniform appeared out of nowhere and led them to the dining room. The dining room was abuzz with people, noise, and activity.

"This way," Gustav said, leading them through the crowd to a table for two in the corner. They took their seats, and Gustav looked down at them sternly. He wore a monocle in his left eye and seemed to take his job very seriously. "You will wait here while I get your wine."

Gustav vanished into the kitchen and Young Dusty Bob and Olivia looked around the dining room. There was a blazing fire in the big rock fireplace, and live music blaring from a bandstand. Every table was full of revelers and diners enjoying sumptuous meals and decadent-looking desserts. An old-fashioned style cigarette girl milled around the crowded room. Then Gustav was back with the wine.

"I'm afraid all we have left is the house wine," he said, pouring two glasses. "Our sincerest apologies."

Olivia picked up the wine bottle and read the label. Her jaw dropped. "This is a 1904 Domaine Leroy Richebourg," she said in amazement.

"What does that mean?" asked Young Dusty Bob. "Is that good?"

"*Good*?" Olivia laughed out loud. "1904 was an extraordinary vintage."

"I hope the wine will be satisfactory for *madame* and *monsieur*," Gustav said with a worried look on his face. He now had the monocle in his right eye.

"It'll do," Young Dusty Bob assured him. "Can we see a menu?"

"There are no menus," Gustav informed them. "The meal is served in seven courses, continental-style. You will eat what is served."

"Sounds all right to me," Young Dusty Bob said.

"Very good, sir. Enjoy your wine. I shall return with the first course." Gustav shot away to the kitchen. Olivia picked her glass up and sipped wine.

"Oh, my God." A look of profound pleasure crossed her beautiful face.

"Is it good?" Young Dusty Bob asked.

"Oh, my *God*," was all she could say.

Young Dusty Bob took a drink. "Tastes all right to me." He took a good look around the room for the first time. "There's something mighty peculiar about this place."

"It was full of writers and artists and poets and celebrities and industrialists," Old Dusty Bob told Walter. "How did all those folks find that place, way out there in the middle of nowhere like that?"

Back in the dining room, Cab Calloway was leading his orchestra onstage while Billie Holiday sang a jazz song. At one nearby table, Rudy Vallee and T.S. Eliot were engaged in a heated discussion about FDR's New Deal policies and Hitler's rise to power in Germany. At another table, Ernest Hemingway was arm-wrestling World Heavyweight Champ Joe Louis. In the back, some hayseed in a cowboy hat was doing rope tricks for a fascinated Salvador Dali.

"Look at that sap over there trying to be Will Rogers with the rope," Young Dusty Bob laughed.

Olivia took a good look. "Dear, I think that *is* Will Rogers."

"What? Naw – it can't be." Young Dusty Bob looked closer. "Darn me, you're right. That's really him!"

Gustav was back with the first course – turtle soup. Olivia liked it, but Young Dusty Bob would have none of it. "I ain't eatin' no *turtle*, and that's that!"

"Suit yourself," Gustav sneered, the monocle back in his left eye.

"Is it just me, or does his little eyeglass keep changin' sides?" Young Dusty Bob asked Olivia.

The second course was more to Young Dusty Bob's liking: game hens. "Now that's somethin' I can get my lips around!" The courses kept coming, each one more tantalizing and decadent than the last: braised rabbit, hams, pheasants, poached salmon, oysters, duck in orange sauce – a sumptuous feast.

"I give up," Young Dusty Bob protested when Gustav brought the fifth or sixth course. "I can't eat anymore!"

Gustav glared at him disdainfully. The monocle was now in his right eye.

"Say, fella. Wasn't your little German eye-piece on the *other* side before?"

"I change it periodically, to keep my vision balanced," Gustav explained, switching it to the other eye.

"Why don't you just get yourself a pair of spectacles?" Young Dusty Bob inquired.

"Why does the Central American Montezuma Oropendola build its nest in the *pejibaye* palm trees of Eastern Costa Rica?" Gustav sniffed, adjusting his waiter uniform and scooting off to the kitchen.

"Odd fellow," Young Dusty Bob said.

The cigarette girl came up to their table. She was a cute platinum blonde with chubby cheeks and long, slender legs. "Hi, I'm Mimi. Cigarettes, anyone?"

"Oh, I'd like a pack of Lucky Strikes, please," Olivia said, reaching for her purse.

"Sorry, no Lucky Strikes," the girl smiled.

"No Lucky Strikes?" Olivia asked. "That's odd. All right, a pack of Chesterfields, then."

"Sorry."

"Camels?"

"Nope."

"Well, what kind of cigarettes *do* you have?" Olivia asked.

The girl reached into her tray and pulled a pack out. "Truth."

"Truth?" Olivia was confused. "I've never heard of that brand. What else do you have?"

Mimi pulled out several more packs. "Umm, Absolutism, Enlightenment, Minimalism, Existentialism…and oh, here's a pack of Absurd Realism – that's *my* brand!"

"I've never heard of any of these brands" Olivia confessed. "Why don't you sell the popular brands, like all the other cigarette girls?"

"Maybe I don't want to be like all the other cigarette girls," Mimi said emphatically. "Maybe I want to be different, unique – you know, have a voice of my own."

"I don't understand…"

"Listen, I'm a philosophy major, and I happen to believe that even a simple thing like selling cigarettes can help mankind. I want to sell cigarettes that help people understand what life is all about, okay? Anything wrong with that?"

"Not at all," Olivia said. "I'll take a pack of Absurd Realism and a pack of Absolutism, please."

"Good choice. The Absolutism will counter-act the Absurdism, giving you a nice balanced outlook. That'll be thirty cents."

Mimi sauntered off to another table and Olivia opened the pack and lit up an Absurd Realism.

"How is it?" Young Dusty Bob asked.

"All of my senses are heightened," Olivia said, exhaling a cloud of absurd smoke.

"That confused young lady is why I prefer to roll my own," Young Dusty Bob said. "I wish I brought some tobacco."

Gustav was suddenly at his elbow, holding a small pouch of tobacco and some rolling papers.

"Why, thank you, Gustav. I was just saying how I wished –"

"I *know*," Gustav said dismissively, turning and walking away quickly.

"They got everything you could want in this place," Young Dusty Bob said in wonder, commencing to roll himself a smoke. Billie Holiday and Cab finished up their set and left the stage. A very thin, dapper, well-dressed man smoking a cigarette came onstage and sat down at the piano. He warmed up the keyboard for a few minutes, and then very nonchalantly began to play "I Get a Kick Out of You."

"Is that Cole Porter?" Olivia asked.

"I've never met the man," Young Dusty Bob said.

"Yes, I'm sure that's him," Olivia said. She was a big fan of the Broadway musical *Anything Goes*.

Young Dusty Bob had just finished rolling his cigarette and was raising it to his lips to light it when someone lassoed his wrist with a rope and pulled it away.

"Dusty Bob, you old scrapyard dog!" It was Will Rogers on the other end of the rope. "I *thought* it was you! Why, I haven't set eyes on you since you moved yourself out to Hollywood and became a bigshot in the pictures!"

"Hello, Will," Young Dusty Bob said, un-snaring his wrist and lighting his cigarette. "I mighta known it was you – you never could tie a lasso worth a plug nickel."

"What have you been doin' with yourself all these years, besides swimmin' in swimmin' pools an' eatin' in fancy restaurants an' keepin' the Cadillac dealers in business?"

"I been busy workin'."

"*Workin'*? You call that workin'?" Will laughed.

"It pays the rent, and it's mostly honest."

"Does more than pay the rent, by the looks of it," Will said, rubbing the fabric of Dusty Bob's coat between his fingers. "These some mighty fancy duds, brother." Then he noticed Olivia. "Well, who's this fine *senorita* here, Bob? And don't tell me she's your sister."

"This is Olivia Del Monte," Young Dusty Bob said.

Will doffed his hat and took her hand with a chivalric flourish. "Enchanted, Ma'am. Have you tried the duck? I thought it was simply divine."

"It was very nice," Olivia agreed, taking a drag of her cigarette.

"Oh, are those Mimi's cigarettes?" Will asked earnestly, sniffing the smoke. "I've been dying to try a Minimalist."

"I didn't buy that brand," Olivia told him.

"Okay, then give me one of those Absurdists – in honor of my new friend Salvador Dali." He waved to Dali across the room. Olivia handed him a cigarette and he lit up. "Hmmm. Smooth. Maybe I'll understand his paintings now."

Will picked the half-empty wine bottle up and read the label. "Hmmmm. Nice. Drink up, kids. There's no hang-overs at the Valhalla Lodge."

Young Dusty Bob laughed at the joke.

"That's no joke," Will said, pointing to a sign on the wall: "No Hang-Overs at the Valhalla Lodge – signed, Management."

"Who owns this place, anyway?" Young Dusty Bob asked.

"A very wealthy Indian Prince from Calcutta," Will answered. "And several Swiss armaments manufacturers. And I hear Chaplin holds a special interest. He's got his own private suite upstairs, they say."

"Is that so?" Young Dusty Bob asked with little interest.

"Well, I gotta be shovin' off," Will said, draining Dusty Bob's wine glass and setting the empty glass back down on the table. "It was good seein' ya, Bob. Hey, we gotta pry you outta that soft Beverly Hills mansion and get you back on the rodeo circuit where you belong, brother. Get you back to that good, honest, character-buildin' work. Don't be a stranger, now!" And the legend walked off to find another table to hold court at for a while.

"Oh, Bob, they're playing some swing music now," Olivia said. "Let's dance a little!"

"I reckon I wouldn't mind stretchin' my legs for a spell," Young Dusty Bob said, and they made their way to the crowded dance floor. After a couple of turns, someone bumped into Dusty Bob, hard.

"Watch it there, fella!" Dusty Bob warned, turning around. It was Ernest Hemingway. His face was glistening with sweat and his hair hung down over his forehead.

"Would you like to take this *outside*, cowboy?" Hemingway challenged.

"Not particularly."

"Why not?"

"Because it's rainin' pretty heavy out there at the moment," Young Dusty Bob informed him.

"Well, in that case, may I cut in?" He grabbed Olivia and started spinning her around the room without waiting for an answer. Young Dusty Bob sat down at his table and watched them dance for a spell. When they were through, Hemingway escorted her back to the table and sat down with them.

"May I?" Hemingway asked, pointing at a wine glass.

"Be my guest," Young Dusty Bob said.

Hemingway grabbed the glass and chugged its contents. "I know who you are. Oh, yes. I admire Western literature. Western pictures, too. Rugged American Spirit. True, honest values. Courage. Discipline. It took grit to forge this country. Fortitude. It took man-sized balls to subjugate the frontier. The loneliness of the prairie. The big, open sky above us at night. These are American ideals. I've traveled the world, my friend. Gustav! More champagne! *Presto, amico!* Have you ever been to Italy? Your girl here doesn't say much, does she? But she's one hell of a dancer! Reminds me of Zelda Fitzgerald, only more reticent, more guarded. But a fire burns underneath, *n'est-ce pas?* Do you know the Fitzgeralds?"

"Can't say I've had the pleasure," Young Dusty Bob said. Gustav appeared with a bottle of champagne and poured glasses all around.

"Oh, when Zelda throws a bash, my friend, you'd better x-out a week in your calendar book! Simply for recovery purposes. Nutty as a squirrel in winter, but the lady knows how to entertain. Of course, Zelda never broke my heart. She's more like a sister to me. Gertrude Stein broke my heart. Many times. Broke it in two. Heartbreaker. Have you ever had your heart broken by an old lesbian? No, I don't suppose you have." Hemingway stopped long enough to drain his champagne glass, then continued without even taking a breath.

"But Scott is my friend. And friendship is one of the sacred virtues. Brotherhood. The Brotherhood of Man. Many ideals are conjured by friendship. Ideals like honor, loyalty, fidelity. But we do not speak them. They are intrinsic. Unspoken. Never speak of them. Talisman. Ideals lose their potency when spoken of too much."

The champagne was going to his head. He was rambling now, running out of steam. "Listen, I have this spectacular idea for a Western. You play a sheriff of a small town of, say, three hundred people or so. No, two hundred people. And one night, all the townspeople disappear. You wake up in the morning, and they're gone. Where did they go? You ride all over the desert, but do not find them. Demoralized, you don't go back to your empty town. Instead, you wander aimlessly in the desert for many days. Weeks, even. You forget everything, who you are, all about being a sheriff."

"Is that it?" Young Dusty Bob asked.

"No. You finally come to another town. Almost identical to your old town. The people there tell you that recently, two hundred strangers wandered into town and took up residence. You think you've found your people, but when you ask to see them, you don't recognize a soul. You see their faces. They are grotesque, haggard. They are not from your old town. They are from *another* town."

"What's the point?" asked Young Dusty Bob.

"Isolation," Hemingway said. "The treeless, windswept prairie. It drives people mad. They wander the countryside, searching for meaning. Searching for their *humanity*."

"What happens to the sheriff?"

"He wanders from town to town, searching for his lost people, for months, years. Finally, he marries a one-legged, alcoholic prostitute named Kate or Peggy or something and she slowly drives him to commit suicide."

"That sounds like one of them artsy French films," Young Dusty Bob commented.

"The days of the shoot-outs at the O.K. Corral and jumping horses over chasms are on their way out, my friend."

"But that's what folks want to see!" Young Dusty Bob argued.

"There's a more sophisticated audience out there, Bob," Hemingway argued. "*Existentialism*. You heard of it? They're looking for realism, irony – not the cliches and ready-made cardboard characters the studios have been shoving down their throats for decades."

"No studio would make a picture like that," Young Dusty Bob said.

"Then we'll make it ourselves," Hemingway suggested. "Pool our resources, take out a mortgage on that mansion of yours. I'm the idea man, you're the one with the assets and the connections. What do you say?"

"Well, the story needs some tinkerin'."

"Absolutely," Hemingway concurred. "That was just off the top of my head. I can bang out a treatment in a couple of days. If Faulkner and my buddy Scott can write screenplays, how hard can it be? I've already got a title: *Futility*."

"Well, I'll have to think about it, Hem."

"Grand. That's all I'm asking. There's my friend I met in Spain last summer. Hey, Salvador, I want you to come meet my new friends – tell them about the ants!"

"Maybe another time," Olivia said.

"Oh, here he comes now," Hemingway said, pulling out a chair for his Spanish friend.

Salvador Dali sat down and looked Young Dusty Bob and Olivia over with an artist's trained eye. "Albert Camus and I were just having the most enlightening conversation about birds."

"Birds?" Hemingway scoffed.

"Yes, birds," Dali said rather seriously.

"Forget about birds," Hemingway said. "I want you to tell them about your *ants*."

"No," Dali shook his head emphatically. "Tonight my mind is occupied with birds." He kept looking first at Olivia, then at Dusty Bob, then back at Olivia in a curious fashion.

"I like your mustache," Young Dusty Bob said to Dali. "What do you use to make it so shiny?"

"A special oil carefully extracted from the pineal gland of the Norwegian harbor seal," Dali replied without the slightest hesitation.

"You actually *kill* seals to get oil for your mustache?" Olivia asked in surprise.

"No, madame. The oil must be taken from *live* seals, or it loses its luster. That is why it must be so carefully extracted."

"Well, it gives it quite a sheen," Young Dusty Bob said with admiration.

"And *your* mustache is a robust specimen, as well," Dali admitted.

"Why, thank you," Young Dusty Bob said, a little embarrassed.

"Enough about facial hair," Hemingway said impatiently. "If you don't want to talk about ants, then tell us what's so interesting about birds."

"Not just *any* birds," Dali protested. "I am speaking of a very rare species of Spanish songbird that lives in a very remote region of the Pyrenees Mountains. I was visiting a small village there once when I happened upon a bird market. There I heard the most beautiful bird-song I'd ever heard in my life. Overcome, I asked the proprietor what made these birds sing so beautifully. He told me that decades before, the locals had discovered that these birds sang with more passion if they could not see. That's right, if they were blind. So, a custom developed in which the locals would capture these wild birds and puncture their pupils with needles, to make them sing more beautifully."

"How cruel," Olivia said.

"But why did they sing better when they were blind?" Young Dusty Bob asked.

"Those blind birds were living – and *singing* – solely from memory," Dali explained. "It made their song sadder – and much sweeter – than before. You see, that is the power of memories. Our memories can provide a rare kind of beauty, like the song of the blind birds. Without our memories, we are not fully alive. Without our memories, we do not *exist*."

"It would be sad to have nothing to live on but memories," Young Dusty Bob said.

"We live to *make* memories," Dali asserted. Then he suddenly looked distracted. "Are you a *real* cowboy?"

"I reckon I am," Dusty Bob replied.

"And is that a *real* Stetson hat you are wearing?"

"I wouldn't put anything else on my head," Young Dusty Bob said proudly.

"Would you mind turning your head a little to the right?"

"Sure thing."

"Now raise your chin a little."

Young Dusty Bob complied with the artist's request.

"Splendid," Dali said, looking wide-eyed and pleased. "I really *must* paint you sometime."

* * *

"Well, that was some night, Ace." Old Dusty Bob heard Walter's folksy cackle. It sounded faint and far away, but it pulled him out of the memory and back to the present.

"That it was. When we finally went upstairs to our room, it was huge – kind of a combination between a presidential and honeymoon suite. There was a big fruit basket brimmin' with pineapples and mangoes and other exotic fruits, and a box of Belgian chocolates and fragrant French soaps in the bathroom. We were tired, but Olivia wanted a hot bath. The bath was already drawn for her, with bubbles, just the way she liked it. Now, how did they know *that*? She told me the water was still hot, and started to undress right then and there. I told her that I might just join her, but she told me to stay out and let her freshen up, and closed the bathroom door in my face. And the bed that night was as soft as sleeping on feathers from the wings of angels.

"You know, I went back many times after Olivia died and tried to find that place, but I never could. I even asked some of the locals, but they'd never heard of it. It's like it just vanished, or it never even existed in the first place."

"Maybe it just existed for a moment – just for you and Olivia, in that moment," Walter suggested.

"I reckon you could be right."

"By the way, did you happen to hear what you said to Salvador Dali about memories?"

"Yeah, I heard it all right."

"You know, the part about having nothing to live on but memories…"

"Dag-nabbit, I said I *heard* it, Walter!"

"Well, all right then. I was just askin'."

Chapter 8

At exactly 6:13 the next morning, Dusty Bob and Jim were having their usual coffee, cigarettes, and stimulating conversation, when Trooper Torres pulled up to the diner and hastily exited his patrol car.

"It's here!" he exclaimed, waving a copy of *Life* magazine excitedly in the air. It was the new edition, the one with the story about Dusty Bob in it, and Trooper Torres looked about as excited as a little boy on Christmas morning.

"Let's see that!" Dusty Bob impatiently barked. Trooper Torres tossed it to him, and he perused the cover with unbridled anticipation. His countenance fell when he realized he hadn't made the cover, however. Instead, it was an iconic shot of John Wayne from his new John Ford western, *The Searchers*.

"The story's inside, on page twenty-three," Trooper Torres informed him. Dusty Bob quickly turned to page twenty-three, put his reading spectacles on, and started reading it to himself.

"Well, read it out <u>loud</u>, willya?" Jim said in his most exasperated tone.

"Read the title, Dusty Bob," Trooper Torres urged.

"All right, just hold your horses, the both of ya," Dusty Bob growled, adjusting his spectacles. "The title says, 'Old Memories Come to Life in the Arizona Desert.'"

"Isn't that a great title?" Trooper Torres couldn't help blurting.

"I reckon it is," said Dusty Bob, obviously pleased. "It says, 'For those who think the Old West died out with Wyatt Earp and Annie Oakley, don't write its epitaph just yet. There's a sweet little place called Memory Ranch somewhere out in the Arizona desert, and its proprietor, one Dusty Bob, is fighting hard to keep the dream alive. You may stumble upon it on your way to the Grand Canyon or Meteor Crater, that other great prehistoric hole in the ground near Winslow. If you're lucky enough to find it, you're in for a real old world-style treat. You may recall seeing one of Dusty Bob's old westerns on the Late-Late Show on TV. He's much older now, and a little worse for wear, but he's still got that recognizable handlebar mustache, sweat-stained Stetson hat, and affable charm that will entertain you and make you feel right at home. Memory Ranch is a family stop, with a diner serving BBQ ribs and burgers, and even a motel with several cozy guest cabins for those looking for a longer stay.'"

"So far, so good," Jim smiled. "That feller really hit the nail on the head, didn't he?"

"Let's see what it says on the next page," Dusty Bob said. He turned the page and his broad smile quickly became a frown. "'Entering the diner, one expects to be whisked away into a charming Old West saloon or family eatery, but what one finds instead is a cracked countertop, old, ripped, mismatched bar stools, and a few shabby booths. There is an attempt to recreate something of the Old West with a big oak bar in the back and a dozen or so yellowed, curling movie posters, but the feeling it evokes in the visitor is one of disappointment and sadness rather than wonder or excitement. Dusty Bob's trusty movie horse, Texas Pete, is there, but he's been rendered rather ratty with outdated taxidermy and dusty tack – his rhinestone-encrusted saddle needs a good polishing, for sure. All in all, Texas Pete is something you may want to keep your eyes away from if you want to keep that greasy plate of BBQ down.'"

"That's just awful!" Jim shook his head.

"I can take as much criticism as the next man," Dusty Bob seethed, "but you just don't talk that way about a man's *horse*!"

Then it got worse. "'Should you still decide to seek this unusual place out, the best part of your visit may just be an authentic rain dance by a real Indian Dusty Bob keeps living out back in a beat-up old trailer, where she takes care of his many dogs. Mr. Bob also puts the Indian squaw to work in his diner, where there seemed to be an issue with poor working conditions and unpaid back wages – '"

Dusty Bob threw the magazine down. "That's just about *enough*! 'Poor workin' conditions and unpaid back wages?' A man can only take so much abuse! I should sue them for, for – "

"Libel," Jim said. "Now, I'm not sayin' it wouldn't be warranted, mind you – but don't you think that big, fancy New York City magazine would have a passel of big, fancy, New York City lawyers workin' for 'em?"

"You're probably right, Jim," Dusty Bob agreed. "The little man – bein' _me_ – would seem to have little recourse in such a David and Goliath scenario, to be sure. But I'll tell you what: the whole thing just sticks in my craw, is what. Just sticks in my _craw_."

But in spite of the article's rather tepid endorsement, there was, in actuality, a noticeable trickle of curious tourists passing through over the next few days – taking family snapshots with Dusty Bob and asking him to autograph their copies of *Life* magazine. Dusty Bob, of course, played the gentleman rancher to the hilt, dispensing hospitality and homespun Old West wisdom in equal measure. In fact, a number of tourists asked to see "the Indian" mentioned in the article, prompting Dusty Bob to request that Sally don her Indian garb and perform a rain dance two times a day – at 10:00 in the morning and 2:00 in the afternoon.

"White Man ask Indian squaw to demean herself – and her culture – to entertain culturally-insensitive white people and try to get them to spend more money at White Man's tacky tourist trap?" Sally Hawk asked. Speaking in cliched "Indian-talk" was her favorite way of mocking Dusty Bob. "Not a chance."

Dusty Bob held out a wad of cash. "Of course, there are several back payments of wages involved."

Sally grabbed the cash and stuffed it into her cleavage. "Two shows a day, you say?"

But perhaps the most unexpected result of the article showed up a few days later in the form of Kitty O'Connell. Not a tourist or autograph seeker, Kitty was about thirty years old and very pregnant. A pretty brunette with a very pale complexion, she was dressed in somewhat grungy travel clothes and carried a single yellow suitcase. She had hitched a ride from Albuquerque with an Omaha family, and showed up at Memory Ranch with a copy of the *Life* article and asking for Dusty Bob.

"My Mama told me all about you when I was a little girl," she chirped to a confused Dusty Bob. "She described you to a 't.' Your long mustache, your silver-plated six-shooters, the way you played your own songs on that old guitar of yours. Yes sir, Mama told me all about you. I've seen most of your movies. But I thought you died a long time ago. I didn't know you were still alive 'til I saw this here article in *Life* magazine. Why, it couldn't have been easier. It told me right where to come and everything. And now, <u>here</u> I am."

Dusty Bob listened carefully. He still hadn't caught on, but Jim Dupree was already getting a queasy feeling in his stomach.

"And why exactly did you come all this way out here, darlin'?" Dusty Bob asked cluelessly.

"Why, to meet my Daddy, of course!"

Kitty told Dusty Bob and Jim that her mother, the late Daisy O'Connell, had been a wardrobe girl on *Dead Man in South Dakota* – and that was how she met Bob. It started out with typical workplace attraction and flirtation, then Bob and Daisy dallied for several weeks. Dusty Bob said he didn't recall Daisy O'Connell, or remember anything about the affair. There were so many attractive girls on the movie sets – wardrobe, makeup girls, script girls, catering – hundreds, really, over the years. How was Dusty Bob expected to remember *all* of them?

"I remember Daisy," Jim offered. "She had these real cute dimples, just like <u>this</u> girl."

"What, exactly, are you gettin' at, Jim?" Dusty Bob asked, still not understanding.

"I believe this girl is tellin' the truth, Bob."

"About what?"

Jim Dupree got real patient with his old friend. "This girl – Kitty here – she's your *daughter*, Bob. I remember her mother, Daisy, an' you two carryin' on together for a spell."

"My *daughter*?"

Kitty opened the suitcase and pulled out an old, faded red bandana. "Mama gave this to me before she died. She said you gave it to her." She handed it to Dusty Bob, who examined it blankly.

"See there – your initials, D.B. – embroidered right here on this bandana," Jim said. "This proves it."

"But, I don't *have* a daughter," Dusty Bob protested weakly.

"You're just bein' thick as molasses, pardner. This is *Daisy's* girl, Bob. And you're her <u>father</u> – plain an' simple."

Kitty's condition – about eight months along, by the looks of it – seemed to doubly confuse Dusty Bob, so she decided she'd better explain. She told them she was fleeing an abusive relationship with an auto mechanic and part-time jazz musician in Albuquerque, and raised her sunglasses to show them a purple-tinted shiner under her left eye.

"I've left him for good," she said with conviction. "But he may be comin' after me. I don't want him hurtin' me again, or my baby." She held her belly gently with both hands. "Please, Daddy – I need a place to lay low, so he don't find me."

"I think we oughta let her stay, Bob," Jim suggested softly.

"I'm real handy with tools an' such," Kitty promised. "I could help you fix this place up real nice."

The shock was starting to wear off now – Dusty Bob was finally beginning to grasp the situation. "Well, I reckon it'd be all right," he finally said. "We could always use an extra set of hands around here, what with the sudden influx of guests."

When Sally Hawk was informed that Dusty Bob's new daughter would not only be staying at the ranch indefinitely, but would also be helping out around the place, she was less than pleased. The diner and the guest cabins were *her* territory – her domain – and she wasn't about to have any upstart pregnant girl pulling rank on her just because she was Dusty Bob's daughter. Bob may have been the owner and proprietor of Memory Ranch, but, in Sally's book, she was the one who made the establishment <u>*hum*</u>. Still, the girl <u>was</u> with child and had just traveled hundreds of miles to get there, so Sally momentarily set aside her territorial instincts and whipped up a hot meal for Kitty.

Kitty sat at the diner counter and wolfed the food. Sally stood on the other side of the counter, watching her in disapproval.

"When was the last time you ate anything?" Sally asked her coldly.

"Umm, Gallup, I think," Kitty answered between bites. "Three days ago."

"How'd you get that baby in you?"

"The usual way."

"Who's the daddy?"

"Guy name Vince," Kitty replied, inhaling mashed potatoes. "Fixes cars at a garage in Albuquerque. Does body work, too."

"Looks like he worked on <u>your</u> body pretty good," Sally said.

Kitty stopped eating. She was still wearing the shades. "How'd you know?"

"I know things," Sally replied with satisfaction. "I don't have to *see* things to know."

"That an Indian thing?"

"It's a *psychic* thing."

"Okay."

Sally leaned in over the counter, closer to Kitty. "Just what are your intentions?"

"My intentions?"

"Why did you come here?"

91

"I found out my Daddy's still alive. I never knew him. I wanna get to know him."

"Your daddy and I have never liked each other."

"That so?"

"We've never spoken a civil word to each other."

"Why's that?"

"Jim."

"What does *that* mean?"

"Son of a bitch has never done right by Jim," Sally said. "All he thinks about is himself. Jim gave up everything – his whole life – to come out here with Bob when Bob ran his life off the cliff. And for what? Jim is three times the man your father is. Bob's never truly *appreciated* Jim Dupree."

"Why're you telling me this?" Kitty asked.

"Because, you need to know. As much as I despise your father, this is still *his* place. I *never* forgot that. *He* built it. And it's <u>all</u> he has left. And I'm not about to stand by and watch a child he never knew he had come in and take it away from him."

"That's not why I'm here."

"It's not?"

"No."

Sally looked Kitty in the eye a long time, studying her. "All right."

"We good, then?"

Sally continued to eyeball her. "I don't know yet."

They watched each other uneasily. Finally, Sally spoke. "That baby you got in you. It's a boy."

"Is that something you '*know*?'"

"Uh-huh," Sally nodded. "He's not like his father. He's special...*different*..."

"In what way?"

"I don't know yet," Sally admitted. "Just...*special*..."

*   *   *

The two government men drove their car through the desert until it finally ran out of gas. They abandoned it and continued to walk through the arid terrain for many days. Eventually, they emerged from the desert and arrived at Lucia's house with beards and soiled, torn clothes. They found the still-mute Lucia behind her little white adobe house obsessively painting night-time desert scenes with strange lights in the sky.

She was so engrossed with painting the strange lights that she didn't even notice them. Wordlessly, they watched her paint for many hours. Then, they slowly picked up canvasses and paintbrushes, and began to paint the strange lights, too.

Chapter 9

That night as Dusty Bob and Texas Pete sauntered up to the Silver Dollar Hotel, Bob could tell something was different. As he got down off of Texas Pete and tied him up, he could hear what sounded like a loud, boisterous group of people inside the saloon. Curious, he stepped inside and saw that the place was full of noise and people and clinking glasses and card games and jaunty frontier piano playing. He stood there a few minutes taking it all in, and slowly began to recognize the revelers.

At one table sat all his rodeo-in' cronies from the bad old days, playing poker. There was Bill Pickett, Tad Lucas, Hoot Gibson, and Freckles Brown. At another table, all the old Hollywood gang: Clark Gable, Doug Fairbanks, Jimmy Cagney, Gary Cooper, Howard Hawks, and Montie Montana. At another table, all his old trail ridin' buddies – Walt Huston, Harry Carey, "Tumbleweed" McClane. And over at a table in the corner sat all the musicians he'd sat in and picked with over the years. Extras from his western movies sat at the bar, mingled, and played darts to add authentic atmosphere.

Shaking his head in wonder, Dusty Bob walked over to the bar where Hieronymus Quinn stood behind the counter. "Say – what's with the party, Harry?"

"Why, hello sir. We've been waiting for you. This is a very special occasion." Hieronymus reached down behind the bar and pulled up an ancient scatter gun. He casually discharged two rounds into the ceiling to quiet everybody down.

"Gentlemen, PLEASE!" Hieronymus shouted. "Our guest of honor has arrived. Without further ado, I hereby award our old friend, Dusty Bob, full membership in the Golden Memories Club, with all the rights, privileges, and honors it carries with it." He regally presented Dusty Bob with a plaque and a bronze statue of him astride Texas Pete, who was majestically rearing up on his hind legs. The statue was in the exact style of Frederick Remington, and would have made a dandy mantelpiece over anyone's hearth.

"Speech! Speech!" someone called out from the crowd.

"Aww, naww..." Dusty Bob shook his head, a little embarrassed.

"Speech! Speech!" others chanted in unison.

"Oh, all right, then," Dusty Bob raised his hand to quiet them. "If you insist. Just remember – you asked for it."

"Don't worry, Bob – we'll tell ya when to shut up – like we always do!" Hoot Gibson hollered.

"I know you will," Dusty Bob chuckled. "I could always count on you pack of hyenas for that. But seriously now – I don't know how Harry here got you all together in one place like this, most of you bein' released from your corporeal bodies an' cut loose o' this mortal coil an' such, but I'd like to thank each an' every one of you for bein' here to share this special moment with the likes of me. Shoot, as I look around this room an' see all your ugly old mugs starin' back at me, a flood of memories comes over me like the grand ol' Mississippi overspillin' its banks in spring. With some of you, we rode the circuit together in them bad ol' days, sharin' the broken bones an' dust an' rough accommodations an' whiskey an' the women – all the stuff that goes along with rodeo-in' in the minor leagues. An' I'm mighty proud to say fellas, you're my brothers, and always will inhabit a special place in my heart. Others of you have experienced the highs an' lows of life right alongside me, and for that I'm mighty grateful for your friendship and companionship all these years. Other faces I see remind me of the scrapes we been through together – an' some of you really pulled me outta the fire a time or two, I can tell ya – an' the pictures we made together an' the trail rides we took together in God's great glory an' the music we made together to help life go down a might easier when times was hard. Seein' you all here together an' thinkin' what we all been through together over the years makes me stop an' appreciate the wonders of life –"

"Yeah, yeah, we get it, Bob," Old Walt Huston growled. "Always were somethin' of a windbag, weren't ya?"

"An' you were always somethin' of a pain in the ass if I recollect rightly, Walt," Dusty Bob winked. "But I forgive ya, seein' it's such a solemn occasion an all."

Then Dusty Bob went from table to table, shaking hands, slapping backs, and exchanging pleasantries with everyone in the room. When he was finished, he looked around the room forlornly, as if he'd missed someone.

"She's not here," Hieronymus told him, pouring a shot glass of the thick green liquid. "Why don't you get your key from Granny now and go on upstairs."

Upstairs, Walter Brennan was waiting for him in his chair next to the old Kinetoscope.

"I thought you'd never get up here, Ace," Walter wheezed.

"Quite a party goin' on downstairs."

"I heard it," Walter nodded. "Some gatherin', all right."

"Well, what's on the bill o' fare tonight, *amigo*?" Dusty Bob asked, still in a good mood.

"Dusty Bob's Lonesome Trails Christmas Eve Radio Special," Walter replied. "And the controversy surrounding it."

"Oh." Dusty Bob lowered his head. "Is there any way we can just skip that one?"

"I'm afraid not, Ace. You don't get to pick and choose the memories. It doesn't work that way. No, it's all or nothin', I'm afraid."

"Not my finest hour," Dusty Bob admitted sheepishly.

"The night before the radio special, you and Olivia were having dinner at Chasen's, and <u>somebody</u> had a little too much to drink."

"I remember."

"Sometime after your fourth whiskey, you saw Errol Flynn at the next table and…well…questioned his manhood."

"Well, he was always makin' them fruity pictures with a bunch of fellas in tights," Dusty Bob said defensively. "An' you heard the rumors goin' around, Walter…"

"But you wouldn't let up on him, would you, Ace? Sometimes the whiskey could really bring out the bully in you."

"As much as your words pierce me, Walter, I won't quibble with the truth."

"You ended up brandishing your pistol –"

"It wasn't *loaded* –"

"Diners started leavin', the police were called," Walter recounted sadly. "Olivia was mortified at your boorish behavior. The fracas appeared in the papers the next day – Christmas Eve – the studio tried to spin it as a publicity stunt to promote your next picture, but Olivia told you she was through with you 'til you got your drinkin' under control."

"*That* got my attention, all right."

"The day of the radio special, you were in pretty bad shape, Ace – hung over and in a rotten mood. Maurice Chevalier and Benny Goodman were booked for the special, but they both pulled out at the last minute over the Chasen's debacle. Scrambling to fill their spots, the studio managed to scrape together Bela Lugosi an' Rin Tin Tin. The writers scrambled to rewrite the script an' somehow fit a bloodthirsty vampire an' a dog into the Christmas theme. It looked like the broadcast was going to be a complete disaster."

"It was somethin' of a low-point in my otherwise esteemed career," Dusty Bob admitted.

"And, as I recall, it all turned out to have something of a silver linin' in the end," Walter brightened a bit. "Let's take a look, shall we?"

Dusty Bob picked up the Indian head nickel and slipped it into the Kinetoscope. The machine lit up and whirred to life. Dusty Bob looked into the viewfinder, and he was back in that dreary old radio studio on a Christmas Eve so many years ago. Someone had tried to inject some Holiday spirit with the addition of a scrawny Christmas tree and a few strands of colored lights stapled to the walls, but, somehow, these hitherto cheerful efforts managed to miss the mark.

The announcer, a very corpulent man in round spectacles and a red bowtie, stood at the center microphone waiting for the red light on the wall to come on. When it did, he swung into action immediately with one of those ultra-professional radio voices – helium high and caffeine coffee fast. "This is the Tantamount Broadcasting Corporation, coming to you live from beautiful Hollywood, California!"

"Actually, it was *Burbank*, as I recall," Dusty Bob interjected.

"It's the Dusty Bob Lonesome Trails Christmas Eve Radio Special," the announcer continued. "With music by Don Bland and his orchestra, featuring the Hormel Foods Company Singers! This Holiday season, let Hormel set your table with a delicious variety of sodium-laced processed meats!"

The meager studio audience applauded apathetically.

The announcer went on: "With special appearances by Bela Lugosi and Rin Tin Tin! Our show tonight is brought to you by Old Gold Cigarettes with the new zip-top package – the last smoke is as fresh as the first! And X-Ray brand double-edged razor blades – for that close shave she'll *reward* you for later, fellas! And, Spam – it's ham in a can – what *more* do we need to say?"

"So far, so good," Dusty Bob observed drily.

"And now, here's our host for the evening, the steely-eyed man who's looked down a thousand gun barrels and stared down a thousand outlaws, renegades, and desperados, Olympic Pictures film star, Dusty Bob!"

The applause sign blinked – more tepid applause.

"I thought I heard a 'boo' in there somewhere, Ace," Walter cackled.

"You need to have your hearin' checked, old man," Dusty Bob retorted without a beat.

In the viewfinder, Young Dusty Bob stepped up to the microphone.

"Well, I don't look so hot," Old Dusty Bob shook his head and clicked his tongue.

"Good thing it was only radio in them days," Walter observed.

It was true, though. Young Dusty Bob's shoulders slumped and his famous handlebar mustache seemed to droop. But he still gave it his good old movie star try. "Good evenin' folks! I wanna thank ya'll for listenin' tonight. Well, I reckon it's Christmas Eve, an' we got a great show for ya, so keep it right here on TBC – The Tantamount Broadcastin' Corporation. We're gonna start things off with an excitin' musical number, with the Pasadena Ladies Booster Club playin' Handel's 'Messiah' on water glasses. Let's hear it for the gals, now!"

Old Dusty Bob watched the performance in the viewfinder blankly. "Yup – that's Handel's 'Messiah' on water glasses, all right."

Next up was a twelve-year old boy scout who had saved a nun from a stuck elevator. The boy scout and the rescued nun stood side-by-side at the microphone while Young Dusty Bob attempted to conduct an interview.

Young Dusty Bob: "Tell us about your ordeal."

Nun: "It was very frightening. I was on my way up to the fourth floor of the hospital to pray with the sick children. There I was riding along, thinking about all the terrible diseases the children might be suffering from – polio, typhoid, leprosy, lupus, tuberculosis, ichthyosis, pleurisy, gangrene, gonorrhea – they just kept going around and around in my mind – hideous, oozing sores, pustulant abscesses, septic lesions, festering boils, jagged, amputated stumps, third degree burns covering their precious little arms and legs – and I kept thinking, 'Lord, why me?' And then a great wave of doubt overtook me, and I began to wonder why I had ever become a nun. Did I really believe in God, after all? Or was I just deluding myself? If there really was a God, why was there so much suffering in the world? Why were the hospitals full of so many children suffering from the most horrible diseases? It was during this great crisis of faith that the elevator just suddenly stopped."

Boy Scout: "I heard the nun screamin' inside the elevator. I just thought, 'Hey, you're a boy scout – you gotta do somethin'!'"

Nun: "So he rescued me using nothing more than a penknife and his boy scout neckerchief."

Young Dusty Bob: "Can you explain to the folks at home how you did that, son?"

Boy Scout: "Sure, Dusty Bob. (Holding up the penknife and boy scout neckerchief) I just got her outta there quick with this here penknife and my boy scout neckerchief. Before she ran outta oxygen an' turned all blue."

Young Dusty Bob: "Well, let's hear it for this brave young fella, folks! A real hero, in Dusty Bob's book!"

The applause sign blinked.

"Tell us, Sister," Dusty Bob said to the nun. "Did you ever make it up to see the children?"

"Yes, I did," the nun replied. "That ten minutes in the dark, stalled elevator turned out to be a blessing. The Supreme Being spoke to me – He told me He really did exist, although He was very busy and hard to reach sometimes, so He understood why people wondered about it. He said my question about why there was so much suffering in the world was a good one, but that it was quite complicated and He didn't really feel like getting into it right then. Then He said that He wanted me to stay a nun and that I was doing a cracker-jack job, and not to be afraid to go bring comfort to those sick children on the fourth floor. So, my faith restored, I did go up and visit those kids – but this time I took the stairs!"

Next up was a skit with Dusty Bob and the show's guest stars. The writers managed to pull together a last-minute skit about a vampire (Bela Lugosi) who terrorizes a western town on Christmas Eve.

Announcer: "It was Christmas Eve in the town of Rocky Butte, but all the thirsty vampire could think of was where he could find his next drink – of human blood! Then, he stumbled into the saloon where Miss Belle, the lovely town lady of the night, was singing a lovely, heart-breaking Christmas carol…"

(Old-timey Christmas music on the piano)

Miss Belle: (singing) "I'll be home for Christmas…" (she sees the vampire and stops singing) "Say, you're not from around here, are you?"

Lugosi: (heavy accent) "I'm from Transylvania."

Miss Belle: "Oh. Isn't that near Tombstone?"

Lugosi: "A little farther away than that."

Miss Belle: "Well, what brings you to Rocky Butte, stranger?"

Lugosi: "I'm very thirsty…

Miss Belle: "Well, we got just what the doctor ordered. What's your poison?"

Lugosi: "Something full-bodied…and RED…(lunges at Miss Belle's neck. She SCREAMS)

Announcer: "And then the blind sheriff, Dusty Bob, and his trusty seeing eye dog, heroic Rin Tin Tin, burst in just in time to save the lady in distress."

Rin Tin Tin: "Arf! Arf!"

Young Dusty Bob: "Get 'im, boy!

Rin Tin Tin: "Grrrrr!

(Exciting music builds)

Announcer: "And the brave dog chased the bloody vampire and bit him on the calf."

Lugosi: "Owww! Hey! What did you do that for?"

Young Dusty Bob: "I don't know how things are in Transylvania, but folks around these parts don't take kindly to this type of anti-social behavior. In fact, some would say it's downright rude!"

Lugosi: "I didn't mean to be rude, it's just what a vampire does."

The skit ended with a corny homily about forgiveness and the vampire receiving "Christmas Spirit."

Next, Lugosi insisted on doing a dramatic reading of "The Night Before Christmas."

Lugosi: (heavy accent) "It was the night before Christmas and all through the house, not a creature was stirring, not even a mouse…the nylons were hung in the graveyard with care, in hopes that the Big Red Guy would soon be there…the children were nestled all snug in their beds, while visions of Death danced in their heads…"

"That's when we discovered Bela had been nippin' from a flask he kept hidden in a secret pocket of his cape," Old Dusty Bob explained.

"The radio station received several calls from parents complaining that their kids were too scared to go to sleep that night," Walter remembered.

"Halfway through the poem we got him to stop," Old Dusty Bob recalled. "An' me an' him did a duet of 'White Christmas,' which was almost as scary as the poem. After the song, I had a few thoughts of my own to share."

Young Dusty Bob: (into microphone) "You know, that song puts me in mind of a fella who had just about everything in the world, but didn't recognize his most valued treasure until it was gone. It was one lonesome Christmas Eve, much like this one, that this foolish fella threw away the best thing that ever happened to him, with his loutish and undignified behavior. And as the clock slowly ticked away towards midnight, this fella started to see the error of his ways and started gettin' downright angry and disappointed with himself. You see, he had embarrassed and hurt the person he cared about most in the world, and it got so he just couldn't look at himself in the mirror anymore. Long about the sixth chime of midnight, this fella was so miserable that he got down on his knees next to his sad, lonely Christmas tree with no presents under it, kneeling in the pale moonlight streaming through the window, watching the slow, silent snowflakes fall past the frosted windowpanes outside.

"And for each perfect little snowflake this fella said a little prayer, askin' for forgiveness from the one he'd hurt, 'til a little past midnight the Spirit of Christmas came upon him and he knew no matter what happened next, everything was gonna turn out all right in the end. And from that day forward, that poor fella knew what Christmas was all about: keepin' the ones you love close to you and never lettin' 'em go again."

"You could hear a pin drop in the studio after that," Walter remembered. "Bela Lugosi could be seen discreetly wipin' a tear from his eye with a corner of his long black cape."

Young Dusty Bob: (into microphone) "Well, I reckon we should all sing 'Silent Night' now an' get on home to be with our loved ones."

During the song, Old Dusty Bob watched with misty eyes as Olivia walked into the studio and his younger self locked eyes with her through the glass window in the control room. He waved her into the studio proper and she joined the group gathered around the microphones to finish the song.

"She'd been listening to the radio at home," Walter explained. "When she heard how sorry you were for bein' such an ass, she rushed down to the studio before the broadcast was over."

"Her forgiveness meant more'n anything to me, Walter," Dusty Bob reminisced. "When I saw her walk into that studio, I just knew everything was gonna be all right."

When the song was over, Young Dusty Bob said, "Well, I reckon that's it for tonight, folks. Here's wishin' you all a merry, merry Christmas with your families and friends! Remember to stay on the trail you started on, that's your one true path through life, and we'll see you all someday, God willin', back at a magical place called Memory Ranch. Good night, now!"

"Memory Ranch," Walter said, somewhat amused. "You didn't have the ranch yet back then. Where did *that* come from?"

"I have no idear, pardner," Old Dusty Bob replied. "I reckon it just sorta popped into my head."

"And now for one more memory before the Silver Dollar Hotel closes up for the season," Walter said, motioning for Dusty Bob to look into the viewfinder again.

It was a graveside funeral scene.

"No – not *this*," Dusty Bob said in sudden desperation.

"After Olivia died, you lost interest in making the kind of popular pictures you were known for. So you wrote, directed, and bank-rolled your own picture, *Dry River*."

On the Kinetoscope screen: Young Dusty Bob on a movie set, directing his picture.

"It was a dark, brooding story of loss and vengeance with an unhappy ending," Walter remembered. "Can you recall the story?"

"You *know* I can."

"Tell it."

"No."

"*Tell* it."

In a slight reversal of protocol, the Kinetoscope showed everything as Dusty Bob spoke it. "It's about – it was about – a proud, successful rancher."

"Go on."

A pause. "Who – who loses his wife to a terrible disease."

Walter, like a therapist: "Keep goin'."

"Decimated by grief, the wealthy rancher falls in love with the pretty young wife of his neighbor," Dusty Bob recounted, as the Kinetoscope "showed" his movie. "Driven by rage an' jealousy, he uses his wealth and influence to sabotage the neighbor's ranch in order to drive a wedge between the couple an' steal her away for himself. All the while, the old rancher – played by me – pretends to be the young rancher's friend an' mentor while he is actually underminin' him at every turn and workin' to take away everything he loves."

"Ironically, the older rancher's obsession with the younger woman leads him to ruin as he stubbornly tries to destroy his neighbor's livelihood and life," Walter reminded him.

"*Dry River* was a box office flop," Dusty Bob admitted.

"Your audience didn't go for it," Walter said. "They were confused because you didn't smile like a hayseed and sing corny western songs. You didn't even <u>touch</u> a guitar in that picture, Ace. And, most of all, they refused to accept you as the villain. They stayed away in *droves*."

"Thanks for remindin' me, pard. Everybody told me not to make that picture, but I wouldn't listen. I mortgaged my house in Beverly Hills – I gave everything I had – to make it. And lost everything – everything but my little Arizona ranch."

"Memory Ranch."

"Memory Ranch."

"Where you retired – *withdrew* – to lick your wounds."

"Where I've been ever since."

*　　　　*　　　　*

The next morning, the ranch was abuzz with activity. Kitty O'Connell had got it in her mind to redecorate, renovate, and fix up the place, and now Dusty Bob and Jim sat lethargically on the shady porch, half asleep, watching Kitty paint the guest cabins a cheerful yellow. She was quite a sight, with her big belly and her hair tied up in Dusty Bob's old bandana, slapping paint on the cabin walls with a roller on a long pole.

"She's been goin' at it all mornin'," Dusty Bob remarked with a measure of fatherly admiration.

"That girl sure has a lot of energy, all right," Jim said.

"She sure is an enterprisin' young lady," Dusty Bob concurred with a yawn.

Sally came out on the porch and eyed Kitty suspiciously for a while, then shook her head in disapproval and went back into the diner.

"Yep – that girl like about never stops," Jim said, putting his feet up on a barrel.

Kitty stopped working a moment and called over to Dusty Bob. "Hey, Daddy – how you like the yellow?"

"Looks mighty fine from over here, sweetheart!" he called back. "Mighty fine!"

Smiling, she went right back to work, twice as hard. Trooper Torres drove up for his morning coffee, got out of his patrol car, and lumbered up onto the porch. He watched Kitty work for a spell, then said, "New paint looks nice."

"You bet it does," Dusty Bob said proudly. "We're fixin' this place up to get ready for tourist season."

Trooper Torres nodded absently, keeping his eyes on Kitty working. "Do you think she should be doing work like that, you know, in *her* condition?"

Dusty Bob and Jim watched her work in silence a moment, as if giving serious consideration to Trooper Torres's question.

"Naw, she's fine," Dusty Bob scoffed.

"That kinda work is *good* for the baby," Jim said with authority. "Worst thing a pregnant woman can do is sit idle – health-wise, that is."

"She's young, and anyone can see that's a healthy child she's carryin'" Dusty Bob added.

"Yep – I'll wager that baby'll be an eight-pounder easy, when it finally launches," Jim predicted.

Trooper Torres shrugged his shoulders and dropped it. He peered through the screen door at Sally, who was trying to look busy wiping down the counter but still frowning. "What's wrong with Sally today?"

"You best watch your step around her today," Jim cautioned.

"Seems some people don't like change," Dusty Bob opined. "The more territorial of the species tend to see competition as a threat, rather than the natural motivation to spur us on to greater heights of industry and achievement that the Good Lord intended it to be."

Trooper Torres shrugged again. "I don't mind moody women." Then he opened the squeaky screen door and went inside for his coffee.

"Remind me to ask Kitty to do somethin' about that squeak when she has a chance," Dusty Bob said off-handedly. "Gets on a man's nerves after a while."

"Will do, boss," Jim said.

Kitty stopped painting now and was planting flowers in front of the guest cabins with a garden trowel.

"Yesterday, she fixed a clogged toilet in Number Three, and got the old ceilin' fan in the diner workin' again," Dusty Bob noted.

"I vote we keep her on, how 'bout you?" Jim asked.

"That goes without sayin'," Dusty Bob replied. "But the nagging question remains: with Kitty willin' an' able to handle the handyman duties around here, what do I need *you* for?"

"Well, *somebody* needs to keep your ego in check," Jim shot back. "An' that's a full-time job. No, sir – I submit I'm more than useful around here, keepin' your head from gettin' so big it won't fit through doorways, an' such."

"Well, I don't know about that, Jim. But I *will* admit you're mighty useful makin' sure we never have a dangerous food surplus situation around here."

"As *you* are at keepin' the whiskey supply from gettin' too cumbersome."

"I do what I can."

"*That's* an understatement."

They sat in silence for a while, neither one able to come up with a snappy enough retort.

Finally, Jim spoke. "Well, I guess I'll go on over an' check on Lucia."

"Your sideways *senorita*."

"I don't know what that even means."

"Just a figure of speech," Dusty Bob chuckled. "She still not talkin'?"

"Nope. Not a word."

Dusty Bob shook his head. "First, a re-tard. Now she's a mute, as an added bonus. I'll say one thing, Jim: you sure can pick 'em."

When he got to Lucia's, Jim was puzzled to find her little adobe house surrounded by tents and old camper trucks and trailers. Grey smoke rose from a few scattered campfires. A couple dozen scraggly-looking characters of various ages and genders were painting along with Lucia. As always, opera music blared from the house. Nobody spoke. They all just painted and painted – the same strange lights they'd seen in the night sky over the Henderson place. It was as if Lucia had somehow *drawn* them to her – had somehow become the unintentional leader of a strange light-painting cult.

"My-oh-my," was all Jim could say.

Chapter 10

The next time Dusty Bob tried to find the Silver Dollar Hotel, it wasn't there. In fact, the entire western town was gone. There was no trace of it left – just barren, empty desert.

"Well, I'll be…I know this is where it was…where it *used* to be," he said out loud. Then he remembered Walter Brennan saying something about the hotel "closing for the season" last time they were together.

Texas Pete whinnied and stamped his right hoof. That always meant he wanted to move out. Dusty Bob hesitated, still trying to figure out what was going on. Texas Pete whinnied and pawed at the ground again.

"All right, boy. Let's get movin'."

Texas Pete started walking in a very intentional straight line across the desert. "Well, at least one of us knows where we're goin'," Dusty Bob said, letting him have his way. After a few miles, a mountain started to appear in the distance.

"I never seen that mountain there before," Dusty Bob noted. Texas Pete whinnied, and kept on course straight for the mountain. Before long, they had reached the foot of the mountain, where the moonlight revealed an entrance to an abandoned mine. There was a wooden sign over the entrance that read "LOST MOUNTAIN MINE. CLOSED UP ON ACCOUNT OF NO MORE GOLD."

"I've owned my ranch for thirty years, an' never heard of this mine before," Dusty Bob said. Looking closer, he noticed a mining cart sitting on a track which led right into the dark mineshaft. Texas Pete whinnied and pawed the ground. Dusty Bob dismounted and walked over to the cart. Texas Pete whinnied and pawed the ground again.

"You want me to go in?" Dusty Bob asked. Texas Pete whinnied and nodded. "Okay, partner." Dusty Bob climbed into the cart and sat down. As soon as he did so, the cart started to move slowly toward the opening of the shaft. Dusty Bob looked back at Texas Pete. "You sure about this, boy?"

Texas Pete whinnied and nodded again.

"All right, I reckon I gotta trust you now," Dusty Bob said, as the cart disappeared into the hole in the side of the mountain. It was pitch-black inside the shaft, but a few yards in he noticed candles mounted on the walls that flickered to light just as he passed them. This provided just enough light to see the shadows of the rough-hewn walls of the shaft, but not enough to see very far ahead. At this point, the cart began to descend into the earth, and as he went down Dusty Bob could feel the air grow thicker and noticeably warmer.

"I don't know about this," he worried, but there was little he could do at this point. As he descended deeper into the earth, he began to hear loud explosions and see bright flashes of light, as well as voices shouting commands and the sounds of many men digging and hammering rock.

About five hundred feet down, the narrow shaft opened up into a larger chamber. It was hot and steamy, with a red molten glow on the walls and ceiling – like a scene out of Dante's *Inferno*. Dusty Bob could just make out dark figures – like men – blasting away and picking at the hard rock walls of the chamber, in a frenzied attempt to uncover some type of valuable treasure.

The cart came to a slow stop near the center of the chamber. Dusty Bob made no move to get out – he stayed put, gawking in disbelief at all the noisy activity going on around him. He began to realize that the miners all around him were singing as they worked. He recognized the song – it was "John Henry." *"This hammer's gonna be the death of me, Oh Lord, this hammer's gonna be the death of me…"* they sang, keeping rhythm with the heavy clanging of their steel hammers and picks. These were surely no ordinary men, he thought – they seemed to work with super-human strength and stamina.

Dusty Bob looked to his right and saw one of them attacking the solid rock wall heroically with a pick-axe. "What are you digging for?" he asked the miner. "The sign out front says there's no more gold."

The miner stopped working and turned slowly to look at Dusty Bob. He was about six feet tall and powerfully built, wearing denim overalls and a dented metal hardhat. He was completely covered in grey soot – even his face, which made the whites of his eyes shine like high-beam headlights on a car. He had a long, wispy beard that nearly reached his waistline, and a silver earring in his left lobe, like a pirate.

"We're not diggin' for gold," he growled in a fearful, rumbling Irish brogue. "We're diggin' for *memories*. _Lost_ memories."

"Well, whose memories, exactly, you diggin' for?"

"*Yours*," the miner grinned. His teeth – what there were left of them – were somewhat less white than his eyes.

"Mine?"

"These are the memories you've stuffed way deep down there somewhere an' forgotten about. Our job is to dig 'em out for ya."

Dusty Bob looked around at the hopeless, foreboding scene around him: the dark, soot-covered miners, feverishly working in the heat and noise and darkness of the deep underground chamber.

"Well, maybe I don't wanna see 'em," Dusty Bob told the miner. "Maybe there's a *reason* I stuffed 'em down so deep."

"Oh, see them you will," the miner promised with a nod of his head. "You didn't come all this way for nothin'. Besides, each lost memory buys you one more dance with your beloved. Now, don't tell me you still wanna leave after hearin' that!"

"Do – do you have a name?" Dusty Bob asked.

"Virgil."

"How long have you been down here?"

"How *long*?" Virgil looked at Dusty Bob, puzzled. "What an odd question. This ain't the surface. There is no *time* down here. The work never stops. It's all just one endless, repeating cycle. Like a sixteen-ton wheel, slowly turnin', an' turnin', an' –"

He was cut off by another deafening explosion. The chamber shook and heavy dust fell from the ceiling. Loud, excited voices shouted "WE'VE GOT SOMETHING! OVER HERE!"

"Get out of that cart and come with me!" Virgil grabbed him and lifted him out like a rag doll. They rushed over to where a group of phantom miners were frantically sifting through the debris of the blast. From among the large chunks of rock, Virgil pulled a fist-sized emerald and examined it carefully. The smooth rock glowed with a soft green luster, and Virgil turned it over in his hands until he was satisfied.

"Aye, we've really got somethin' here," he finally announced, handing it to Dusty Bob. "This little beauty's been buried deep for a long, long time."

Dusty Bob looked it over. "It sure is pretty, but – what do I *do* with it?"

"Look into it," Virgil instructed him.

Dusty Bob looked into it. "I don't see nothin'."

"*Concentrate*," Virgil insisted. "It'll come."

Dusty Bob concentrated. Slowly, a picture began to form, deep within the emerald. "I see somethin'!" As he continued to peer into the emerald, the picture slowly came into focus: a forlorn boy in ragged clothes. "That's *me*..."

As Dusty Bob watched, a small "movie" began to unfold inside the emerald. The boy stood next to a bed, where a woman lay dying. "When I was thirteen, my mother died of typhoid. My father couldn't deal with it an' took off drinkin' and cowboyin', leavin' me an' my sister Emaline on our own."

All the work had stopped; Virgil and the other miners gathered in close around Dusty Bob, listening intently.

The scene switched to Young Dusty Bob and Emaline getting off a train, being met at the station by a striking woman in western-style clothes. "Our Aunt Adelia took us in at her place, the Muddy Creek Ranch, outside Winnemucca, Nevada, where I grew up workin'."

Now the emerald showed Emaline with a dark-skinned, long-haired boy. "Emaline went an' took up with an Indian boy from the nearby reservation. They met in secret. I noticed a change in her behavior, a distance between us that wasn't there before. We always used to be close, but that was all gone now, an' I didn't understand why. Now I realize she just reckoned I'd disapprove of their relationship – which may have been true."

The emerald showed several men discovering Emaline and the boy together, and tying him up with ropes. "One night, the ranch hands brought Emaline an' the Indian boy back to the ranch to show me what she'd been up to. Just to scare the boy, they started tyin' a noose like they was fixin' to lynch him. I shoulda tried to stop 'em, but I didn't. They was all older n' bigger'n me. Mixed relationships just wasn't allowed back in them days, you know."

A shadow fell over Dusty Bob's face, but he continued to narrate as the action unfolded inside the emerald.

"When they put the noose around the boy's neck, he was so scared that he collapsed dead on the ground. I knew he was dead because I saw his spirit fly away into the darkness of the night. It was a black crow, an' it just peeled off him an' ascended straight up to heaven. The boys took his body back to the reservation an' gave him back to his people, an' ol' Emaline just went inside the bunkhouse, sat down in her rockin' chair, an' never spoke another word ever again. She was unresponsive from that moment on, 'til the day she died.

Couldn't communicate with her at all. I think they call it cat-a-tonic. But sometimes a black crow would come and sit outside her window all night, just like he was keepin' watch over her. It's true, I seen it with my own peepers. We eventually had to commit her to an institution in Reno, where she died in silence many years later. I asked them folks at the institution once if they ever seen a black crow sittin' outside her window, but they said they hadn't. I reckon Reno was just a little too far for that ol' bird to fly to."

The emerald went dim. "Well, I hadn't thought about that – about Emaline – in many a year," Dusty Bob said quietly, wiping a tear from his eye.

Virgil put his hand on Dusty Bob's shoulder, comfortingly. "Well, back to work, boys! We've got more lost memories to dig out!"

The phantom miners worked furiously for another hour or so, until someone called out, "OVER HERE!" This time it was a ruby – the largest ruby Dusty Bob had ever seen, about the size of a cantaloupe. Dusty Bob peered deeply into the beautiful glowing stone, again narrating what he saw.

"One day a mysterious drifter named Kansas Jack showed up lookin' for work, an' Aunt Adelia hired him on at the ranch. Kansas Jack kept to himself most of the time, but soon proved himself a valuable addition to the Muddy Creek through his unique skill at tamin' horses: by playin' the fiddle. Ol' Kansas Jack didn't play the usual fiddle tunes we was all used to, though. He played that long-hair stuff from Yoo-rup – Bach, Bay-toven, an' the like.

"He'd play those sad, slow fiddle tunes to the horses an' it worked like a charm. Even the meanest bronc would calm right down an' let ol' Kansas Jack come up real close-like an' play that fiddle right into his ear. Before ya knew it, Jack was up on its back a gettin' it to do whatever he wanted it to.

"One time, I asked him how he learned to play the fiddle so high and lonesome like he did, an' he told me he heard all them songs played in a concert by a Vee-in-eez feller in St. Louis, an' remembered 'em note for note on only one hearin'. I reckon Kansas Jack was some kind of a musical genius or somethin'.

"Well, it weren't long before Kansas Jack became somethin' of a mentor to me, teachin' me all about horses, cards, an' women. 'All three takes a steady hand,' he'd say to me with a sparkle in his eye an' a wink. 'A steady hand, lad.' He patiently taught me how to rope a steer. He taught me it takes two men to do the job right – one man ropes the head, then the other man ropes the back legs. Once you got the beast on the ground, you tie your rope off on the saddle horn an' get off an' help your partner finish tyin' the animal up while your horse holds the rope just taut enough to keep the steer's head straight an' slightly elevated. See, what most cowhands didn't know was how important it was for the horse to keep that rope just the right tautness while you're down there in the dust a wrasslin' that animal. Kansas Jack had his horse, Cracker, tamed to hold that rope taut, but not so tight that it cuts off the steer's wind, ya see? That was the trick, an' ol' Kansas Jack was the master.

"He never slept. He would stay up all night on the bunkhouse porch in a rockin' chair, whittlin' away on his little pieces of wood. He said he was makin' a chess set. The white pieces he cut from pine, an' they were the Confederacy – Stonewall Jackson, Robert E. Lee, an' ol' Jeff Davis was the king. The black pieces he cut out of ebony, an' they was the Union – William Tecumseh Sherman, Ulysses S. Grant, an' Abe Lincoln was the black king. An' they was the exact spittin' image of the real historical figures! When he was finished with the whole set, he commenced to teach me how to play chess."

All the miners were now quiet and huddled around Dusty Bob, enraptured by the vividness of his memories.

"Kansas Jack liked the ladies, all right, an' I'll tell you what: they sure did return the favor. It wasn't long before he'd even charmed Aunt Adelia into a romance of sorts – it was the smell of his lilac mustache pomade that did it, Aunt Adelia confessed after too much sherry one night. Any-hoo, the two of 'em carried on like they was sure to get hitched before too long. But there was a problem: it seems ol' Kansas Jack was already married to a woman in Boulder, Colorado. An' another one in Wichita. An' one in Ft. Worth – an' oh, I believe he had one stashed in Reno, as well.

"It all came to a head when one of his wives came to town an' promptly installed herself in the hotel. Well, of course Kansas Jack had to go pay his respects. Aunt Adelia got wind of it an' followed him into town an' burst in on 'em an' shot Kansas Jack clean dead right there in his Boulder wife's arms.

"'Well, what on earth did you go an' do <u>that</u> for?' the wife asked in surprise.

112

"'I don't take kindly to bein' sweet-talked an' womanized by no second-rate Casanova,' Aunt Adelia replied, an' calmly left the room. Then she walked straight to the sheriff's office an' turned herself in. Two days later, the judge let her go on account of ol' Kansas Jack bein' a polygamist an' such, which was illegal ever-wheres 'cept U-tall in them days. An' since we wasn't in U-tall, the judge let Aunt Adelia go with a warnin'. I have to say, I missed ol' Kansas Jack somethin' awful, an' was quite put out with Aunt Adelia for a spell, I can assure you."

With that, the memory faded and the ruby went dark. At Virgil's direction, the phantom miners went back to work blasting and chipping away at the hard rock until another memory was unearthed. This time it was a violet sapphire, and it was roughly the size and weight of a Christmas fruitcake.

All the sweaty, soot-covered miners gathered around Dusty Bob again to hear the next lost memory. Dusty Bob peered into the sapphire's soft glow and wasted no time launching in.

"Well. After the sudden and violent death of Kansas Jack, Aunt Adelia bagan actin' mighty peculiar-like. She stopped bathin' an' took to long spells readin' the Old Testament and Herman Melville. She lived off molasses an' whiskey, an' talked mystically of Isaiah an' Ezekiel an' Captain Ahab an' monstrous white whales, an' God's covenant with the Children of Iz-rul. It wasn't unusual to find her strikin' rocks with her walkin' stick, tryin' to bring forth water like Moses did at Horeb for the thirsty Iz-ruh-lites.

"Then she took up with an old beau named Bob Kingfisher, who had one eye, and brought him on at the ranch as we were short a man after she up an' shot Kansas Jack dead an' all. There were several accounts as to how Bob Kingfisher lost his eye, but the most reliable one involved a Romanian dentist who became convinced Bob had stolen his dog an' therefore took his eye out while Bob was under chloroform during the removal of an infected bicuspid. Ol' Bob Kingfisher was glad to get rid of that rotten tooth sure enough, but admitted to missin' that eye from time to time.

"Any-hoo, now there were *two* Bobs on the place, you see – him an' *me*. So the boys took to callin' him One-Eyed Bob an' me Dusty Bob, on account of I was always walkin' 'round in a cloud o' dust from wranglin' them horses an' cows all day. An' that's how I got my name. I guess it just sorta stuck, an' I reckon it suits me, anyway.

"Well, just as fate would have it, turns out ol' One-Eyed Bob wasn't as blind as you'd a thought on account of when he'd taken his fill of whiskey he could actually *see* out of that empty socket. It's true! The boys an' I even tested him many times, coverin' up his good eye nice an' tight with bandanas an' handkerchiefs an' what-not, then holdin' up playin' cards an' postcards an' magazine advertisements in front of his empty socket an' he was able to read every one just like any man with two good eyes. An' I'm here to tell ya, that socket was as empty as Jesus' tomb on resurrection mornin'! I cain't rightly 'splain it, but I seen it with my own two peepers.

"But One-Eyed Bob could also 'see' the future when he'd had a good measure of liquor and covered his good eye. Oh, he prophesied many marvelous an' miraculous wonders – children swingin' hoops o' plastic 'round their waists like deranged banshees, telephones with no 'lectric cords attached to 'em, men walkin' on the moon like they was strollin' through downtown New Orleans on a Sunday afternoon. But the biggest prophecy One-Eyed Bob had was for <u>me</u>. That's right, he told me my future wasn't in ranchin' at all. No, my future was to be a *showman*. One-Eyed Bob told me to go to Tulsa an' bust my way into the rodeo. 'If you heed my words and do this, you will be a BIG star someday,' he told me.

"So I worked the Muddy Creek Ranch hard and learned my trade well 'til I was grown enough to get into rodeo-in' an' took to it real quick-like. Before I knew it, I started makin' a name for myself on the circuit. But I sure miss those days on Aunt Adelia's ranch sometimes, I don't mind admittin'."

Chapter 11

Blanch Faith Constance Goodreau was a former cheerleader, beauty queen (Miss Yorba Linda), and underwear model in the Montgomery Ward catalog. She had so much vivacious personality from the get-go that her parents, a successful Orange County chiropractor and his manic depressive, gambling-addicted dental hygienist wife, were convinced she was worthy of at least four official names.

After the catalog work, Blanch went on to advertisements. She was the girl in the convertible lighting the driver's Lucky Strike for him while he drove so he could keep both hands on the wheel. The ad said, "It's always good to have a pretty girl and a pack of Lucky Strikes along to make any road trip safe and fun!" Her big break came when she landed a Frigidaire TV commercial, in which she had to operate the automatic ice-maker while wearing a pearl necklace and evening gown as the voice-over declared, "Frigidaire makes it easier than ever for the little lady to freshen up her hubby's drink after a long day at the office."

But after a stint hand modeling diamond rings, women's watches, cookware, and Chesterfield cigarettes, during which she made a bucket full of money but became addicted to Mars bars and Eskimo pies, Blanch had gained so much weight that she was no longer the "pretty" young girl, and the advertisement offers started to dry up.

So she decided to become a professional tennis player, and caught the eye of Ed Munley, the Southern California used car king ("Save lots of MONEY with Ed MUNLEY!" – Ed came up with that little gem all by himself) by hanging out at his country club in tight tennis skirts and sweaters. He gave her a job managing one of his car lots just to keep her close, and the two began a not-so-secret affair.

It all blew up when several cars were reported "stolen" from the lot so Ed could collect the insurance money to pay for a trip to Hawaii for the two of them and the FBI got involved and began a fraud investigation and Ed's wife hired a private dick to follow them and take pictures of them checking into the Surfside Inn in Huntington Beach. On the day the FBI frog-marched Ed off one of his car lots in handcuffs, Blanch cashed in the tickets to Hawaii and skipped town in the lovely baby blue convertible that broke down at Memory Ranch.

"That sure is a pretty-lookin' car you got there, miss," Dusty Bob said, looking over Blanch's immobilized convertible. The hood was up and steam was pouring out of the radiator and engine compartment.

"Yeah, it's pretty all right," Blanch agreed with a frown. "But it's not running right now, and I'm stuck _here_. Can you fix it?"

"Well, I'm afraid this is just a little ol' desert ranch, miss," Dusty Bob said, shaking his head. "I know horses pretty well, but I cain't say as I know how automobiles work, much."

"Well, what am I supposed to _do_?" Blanch demanded.

Trooper Torres stepped forward. "Well, miss, I can radio for the tow truck from Holbrook. They can come out and tow it back to the garage in the morning."

"In the _morning_?" Blanch grimaced. "You mean, I'm stuck here all _night_?"

"We've got some lovely guest cabins that happen to be uninhabited at the moment, miss," Dusty Bob informed her. "You can take your pick. The rates are reasonable, and the cookin' in the diner ain't too bad, most nights."

Blanch looked at the freshly-painted guest cabins, with the colorful flowers planted in front. "Well, I guess that'll have to do."

There was loud hammering from on top of the diner. Kitty was up there fixing the roof.

"Why do you have a pregnant girl fixing your _roof_?" Blanch asked.

"That's my daughter, Kitty," Dusty Bob replied.

"Should she be up there?"

"Well now, I don't see any other way for her to fix the roof without bein' up there, do you?"

"Who owns this place?" Blanch asked brashly.

"I do," Dusty Bob replied proudly.

Trooper Torres went to his patrol car and retrieved the copy of _Life_ magazine. He turned to page twenty-three and handed it to Blanch. She scanned a few lines of the article and looked up at Dusty Bob.

"You were in the _movies_?" she asked, impressed.

"That's right – _westerns_, to be precise."

Blanch looked interested, for the first time. "But this place is in the middle of nowhere. Do you get many tourists?"

"Yeah, we get a few folks on their way to the Grand Canyon."

"How many?"

"Oh, about two or three families a week."

"How many people visit the Grand Canyon in a week?"

"I reckon a lot."

You could see Blanch doing the math in her head. "*Hundreds*, that's how many. You should be doing a lot better than two or three families a week. Do you advertise?"

"That there article helped, a bit."

"There should be more," Blanch insisted. "Look, I know a little bit about running a business."

"You do?"

"Sure. I was the manager of one of the biggest used car lots in Southern California. Ever heard of Ed Munley?"

"Cain't says as I have."

"Good – I mean, it was one of his lots," Blanch said quickly. "We did 'good' business – maybe fifteen hundred, two thousand dollars a week."

Dusty Bob whistled. "That sure is a lot of *wampum*, all right."

"How much do you clear in a week, here?" she asked.

"Not even close to that much," he admitted.

"Well, you *could*," she said. You could see the wheels turning. "Say, I could take a look at your books – you know, give you some pointers, some sound business guidance."

"Books?"

"Yes, your balances – your records…"

Dusty Bob gave her a blank look.

"You don't keep *books*? Oh, no – that just won't do. What will you do when the IRS drops in, wanting to take a look at your taxes?"

"Taxes?"

"You don't pay _taxes_?" Blanch asked in disbelief.

"We're just a little operation here, miss," Jim interjected. "The IRS never *drops in*. Nobody ever notices us out here."

"And who are *you*?" Blanch asked with disdain.

"This is my colleague and associate, Jim Dupree," Dusty Bob clarified.

"Well, *Jim,* they're cracking down on businesses like this," Blanch warned. "We've got to get your books in order, *pronto* – you could go to prison for shoddy book-keeping!"

"*Prison*?" Dusty Bob looked alarmed.

"Now, ain't nobody goin' to no prison," Jim scoffed.

"Oh, the Feds are quite serious about this kind of thing," Blanch insisted. "Believe me – I've seen first-hand what they can do."

"The IRS don't even know we're out here," Jim argued.

"They will when the interstate comes through," Blanch countered.

"The interstate?" Dusty Bob blinked.

"That's right," Trooper Torres verified. "They're startin' construction on it next month."

"It's a *Federal* highway system," Blanch explained with calculated patience. "All the way across the country. When it's finished, you're gonna see *thousands* of tourists through here every year. And when *that* happens, the Feds are gonna know all about you…"

"You see?" Dusty Bob asked. "There's no getting' around it – they're gonna *know*, Jim."

"Sounds like a load of hogwash to me," Jim groused.

Blanch ignored him. "You've got to start getting ready now, Robert. When the interstate comes though, every cabin you have will be full every night. Your lovely diner here will be overflowing with hungry tourists – there won't be an empty seat in sight. There won't be room around here for all the tourists – tourists with dollars to spend – tourists looking to buy knick-knacks and Navajo blankets and turquoise jewelry and genuine fake Indian arrowheads. But before all that, you've got to get your books in order, Robert!"

"Well, I don't know, miss…" Dusty Bob balked.

"Well, I *do* know," Blanch smiled, taking Dusty Bob by the arm. "Trust me – I know all about this stuff. And I happen to be between engagements at the moment. I've been looking for something worthy of my talents, something with potential, and I think this is it. You've got the *brand* – the western movie star – I've got the business smarts to make it happen. We'll make a great team! But the first thing we've got to do is get together all the receipts and business expenses you've got and come up with a system to keep track of sales and income from now on. You know what? You're kinda lucky I broke down here today."

Blanch Goodreau spent the night in Cabin Four, but didn't get much sleep. Her head was positively reeling at the potential goldmine she'd stumbled upon by breaking down at Memory Ranch. It wasn't random chance – surely it was fate, *kismet*. She knew she had been *born* for this moment. Was she the only one who could see the potential this place had for making tons and tons of cash once the new interstate came through? Oh, never the way it was now – dirty, rundown, unappealing squalor. But she had vision – vision to see what Memory Ranch could really be – with a woman's touch and the application of some sound business acumen. The pregnant girl – Kitty? – seemed industrious and capable and would probably prove beneficial in getting the place in shape. A little muscle and elbow grease would always come in handy, and if she was really Dusty Bob's daughter she'd be more likely to work cheap.

But Jim Dupree and the Indian – Sally – were dead weight and would have to go. Perhaps Sally could be transitioned out of the diner and into the new trading post – who knows, a *real* Indian might just boost sales of the kind of cheap trinkets tourists just couldn't get enough of.

But Jim was gone – Blanch knew she would have to have complete control of Dusty Bob to make the dream happen. Besides, even with the great profits she envisioned, there wouldn't be enough pie to cut it so many ways – at least to *her* way of thinking.

Dusty Bob, of course, would have to stay. He would be the figure-head – roll him out for the tourists to take pictures with – "Look, Ma: a *real* cowboy star!" – and then put him away out of sight until the next group of tourists show up. He would be like the Queen of England – a symbol, an image that carried no real power of her own, but made people feel good seeing her from time to time and just knowing she was there. Dusty Bob would be that: the Queen of Memory Ranch. Or king – it didn't much matter, as long as Blanch Goodreau had all the *real* control.

Additionally, she felt Memory Ranch was the perfect place to lay low until the Ed Munley fraud fiasco back in California died down.

By morning, a rough plan of action had begun to take shape:

Step One: Seduce Dusty Bob into marrying her.

Step Two: Sideline Jim and Sally and manipulate Dusty Bob into firing them (unless Sally's heritage could be suitably exploited to make more money).

Step Three: Assume complete control of Memory Ranch and begin to transition into an all-out Indian trading post/tourist trap before the completion of the new interstate.

She closed her eyes and went over the outline of the plan again in her mind. It was a solid plan – once again, Blanch was pleased with herself in that special way she believed every genius feels when they realize with a sudden rush of adrenaline and joy the true superiority and sagacity of their own mental prowess.

She went into the cabin's tiny bathroom to freshen up for the day, determined to implement the initial stages of her plan immediately. She emerged from the cabin a few minutes later wearing her tightest deep-cleavage sweater, a red bandana tied rakishly around her neck, and a pair of Capri pants that had to be squeezed into and, therefore, perfectly accentuated her ample curves. She found Dusty Bob and Jim where they were every morning, on the diner porch with their coffee and cigarettes. Trooper Torres was standing on the porch, pretending to talk to them and shooting periodic, furtively desperate glances inside at Sally Hawk.

"Well, good mornin' ma'am," Dusty Bob said to Blanch.

"It's miss," Blanch said demurely.

"How did you sleep?" Dusty Bob asked. "I hope you found the accommodations to your likin'."

"Just fine, thank you, Robert," she replied with a smile. "Very...pleasant."

"Oh, miss," Trooper Torres said. "Tow truck'll be by any time now to take your car into Holbrook. Driver said you can ride up front with him in the cab."

"Oh, I'd like to stay *here* while they fix the car," Blanch said, shooting a meaningful look at Dusty Bob.

"You might be more comfortable waiting in Holbrook," Jim said bluntly. "City gal like yourself might find town more to your likin'."

"Oh, I like it here – at Memory Ranch," Blanch protested. "I find it absolutely *charming*."

"You *do*?" Dusty Bob asked in surprise.

"Oh, yes! As a matter of fact, I did a lot of thinking last night. Remember how I said I was between engagements at the moment? Well, I've decided I'd like to stay around here and offer my services."

"Doin' *what*?" Jim blurted.

"As a CPA."

"A C-P-*What*?" Jim asked.

"A *bookkeeper*," Blanch clarified. "You know, like we talked about yesterday. Getting your books in order, preparing this place for the *thousands* of tourists the new interstate's going to bring. I've already got *millions* of ideas!"

120

"Lady, we hardly make enough to take care of ourselves," Jim said impatiently. "And now there's a little 'un on the way. We just cain't hire anyone on at the moment."

"Who am I talking to here?" Blanch smiled, looking at Dusty Bob. "I was under the impression _you_ were the owner of this establishment."

"You can talk to _me_," Dusty Bob said.

"That's what I thought," Blanch said calmly. She shot Jim a quick smirk and then said to Dusty Bob, "With the understanding that business, at the moment, is more a trickle than a flow, I am willing to defer my salary and work for room and board until things pick up around here after the interstate comes through."

"Now, miss, I cain't rightly ask you to do that – to work for nothin'." Dusty Bob shook his head.

"It wouldn't be for nothing," Blanch smiled. "It would be an investment in the future, to show my good faith. I'd have my basic needs met – a place to sleep, and meals – a girl doesn't really need much more than that."

"Well, I reckon I cain't afford _not_ to hire you on those terms," Dusty Bob said.

"Wonderful!" Blanch gushed. "I'd like to get started right away, if that's all right with you."

Jim just glared at her, but Dusty Bob took her back to the office behind the kitchen and flipped the light switch. A bare bulb hanging from the ceiling illuminated a real mess: dusty cardboard boxes full of old tools, movie memorabilia, and stacks of papers and magazines everywhere.

"I'm afraid I don't use this office much," Dusty Bob apologized.

"Oh, I'll have it cleaned up and organized in a _jiffy_," Blanch said brightly. She touched his arm and flashed that smile again. "And thank you for this opportunity, Robert."

"Aww, now you can just call me Bob, like everybody else."

"I prefer Robert," she said, and gave his arm a little squeeze.

"Well, I reckon I'll leave you to it, then," Dusty Bob said self-consciously. "Let me know if there's anything you need. And don't mind the old bat in the kitchen – she's a bit _loco_, but she's more bark than bite."

Dusty Bob went back out to the porch and sat down next to Jim. Trooper Torres was still there, trying to get up the nerve to go inside and face Sally, who had been in a rotten mood since Kitty O'Connell's arrival.

"Why don't you just go on in?" Dusty Bob asked.

"She keeps throwin' pots and pans around everywhere," Trooper Torres said, a bit spooked.

"Just go on in, she'll be fine."

Trooper Torres took a long look inside, then straightened his hat and jacket and walked into the diner. Dusty Bob and Jim immediately heard Sally's loud, shrill voice: "JUST SIT DOWN OVER THERE IN YOUR SPOT AND BE QUIET!" Trooper Torres sheepishly did as he was told.

"That's one intrepid lad," Jim said.

"True love knows no fear," Dusty Bob opined.

"Say, Bob – I don't have a very good feelin' about takin' on this new gal right now," Jim said. "After all, we really don't know anything about her – where she's from, what she mighta done –"

"Relax, Jim," Dusty Bob said reassuringly. "I have an excellent sense about these things."

"But, what's a gal like her doin' all the way out here all alone, anyway? What's she runnin' away from?"

"Why do you always assume the worst about people?" Dusty Bob asked. "See, that's just the difference between you an' me, Jim. I'm willin' to take a person's word for somethin' an' trust 'em when they says they on the up an' up. I'm always willin' to give 'em a hand up, when all you can do is think the *worst* about folks."

"Yeah, yeah," Jim scoffed. "I hear the Pope's gonna up an' declare you a saint any day now. All I'm sayin' is, there's somethin' off about that gal, Bob. Mark my words – she's _up_ to somethin'."

Once Blanch got the office organized, she implemented a new guest registration system and bookkeeping process. "Every cent is going to be accounted for around here from now on," she told Jim and Sally. "From now on, there's no more dipping into the till whenever you need spending money. If you need to buy something for the ranch, make sure you get a receipt or you're not getting reimbursed."

"Everything that gal does just sticks in my <u>craw</u>," Jim complained to Sally out of Blanch's earshot.

One day, Blanch called Dusty Bob and Jim out to the corral. "These mangy, flea-bitten, sway-backed horses have got to go," she said firmly.

"But, this is a *ranch*," Jim protested weakly.

"All they do is eat hay and use up resources," Blanch explained. "They don't contribute anything."

"Maybe you don't understand the concept of a *ranch*," Jim suggested.

"I'll handle this if you don't mind, Jim," Dusty Bob said, turning to Blanch. "The guests like to bring their kids out to pet 'em," he told her gently.

"And how do we make any money out of kids petting horses?" Blanch demanded. "Let's offer horseback riding, then. That's something people will pay for. Twenty minutes in the saddle for, say, two dollars. Three dollars for adults. Jim, you can take the groups out. Give them a little talk, show them around the place, and collect the money. That's the only way we can afford to keep these horses."

"*Me*?" Jim asked. "What makes you think *I* have the time to do that?"

Blanch looked at him with daggers in her eyes. "Cut into your vital porch time, would it?"

"I reckon we could manage that," Dusty Bob said, trying to smooth things over.

"Good, then," Blanch smiled, touching Dusty Bob's arm. "From now on, there's nothing on this place that doesn't generate profit. No more *dead weight*." Then she turned and walked back to the diner.

Jim looked at Dusty Bob.

"Why so serious, partner?" Dusty Bob asked.

"I don't like bein' bossed around by no *woman*."

"Aww, shoot, Jim – she ain't *that* bad."

"Tellin' me what I'm gonna do and not gonna do, an' you just standin' there like you forgot how to *talk*."

"I'll talk to her," Dusty Bob promised. "Ask her to just put a little more *sugar* on things."

"An' always talkin' 'bout *money*," Jim continued. "We never cared so much for money like that before, Bob. It takes all the *fun* outtta things!"

"She's just lookin' out for us, is all," Dusty Bob said. "I think she's right. We won't survive ten minutes when that interstate comes through if we ain't runnin' a tight ship."

But that wasn't all that was bothering Jim.

"I don't like the way she's always touchin' him," he told Sally later. "Makes me think she's tryin' to use her feminine wiles to get him on her rope."

"I'd like to rope *her*," Sally said. "Put her in the back of the truck an' drive her out to the middle of the desert."

"An' the way he acts around her, like a lovestruck little boy," Jim went on. "An' her less than *half* his age!"

"He's actin' like a fool," Sally agreed.

"Flatterin' him all the time, 'Oh, *you're* the attraction, Robert. They're comin' to see <u>you</u>, never forget that.' Robert – she actually calls him <u>*Robert*</u>! Woman rubs me the wrong way..."

"We could bury her in an anthill. With only her head above ground," Sally fantasized.

"She's up to somethin', all right, or I don't know what I'm talkin' about," Jim said with conviction. "An' Bob just as unaware and innocent as a new-born chick!"

"He's an idiot," Sally declared. "I *never* liked him."

But Jim did like he said he would, and started taking the guests out for horseback rides – 'baby-sittin',' he called it. It became a popular attraction at the ranch, and the city slicker tourists were more than happy to cough up the money in exchange for real time in the saddle. And Jim actually felt relieved that they'd be able to keep the horses, for, as he often asked nobody in particular, "What's a ranch without horses?"

But about a week later, Blanch came to Dusty Bob with a problem. "He's skimming off the top," she told him.

"What are you talkin' 'bout, darlin'?" Dusty Bob asked.

"The numbers aren't adding up," she explained. "The number of riders versus the money collected. They don't add up."

"Just what are you sayin'?"

"I think Jim's skimming off the top," she repeated. "He's pocketing some of the money, before he turns it in to me. That's the only explanation."

"<u>Jim</u>?" Dusty Bob scoffed. "Naww, he wouldn't do that."

"He's been caught with his hand in the till before, Robert – and you know it," she said. "They both have. Meaning, Sally, too."

"I cain't believe it," Dusty Bob shook his head. "Jim don't need money. He's never been like that..."

"You're such a good man – a *strong* man – and I admire your trust and loyalty to your friends," Blanch said, squeezing his arm in her usual touchy fashion. "But you just don't see how they're taking advantage of you. You can't see it or believe it in others because *you're* not like that, Robert. But it's happening, and I will do everything I can to take care of you – I promise." Then she kissed him on the cheek.

Later, Dusty Bob went and found Jim. "Here," he said, handing him some cash.

"What's this?"

"If you need money, take it," Dusty Bob said. "All you gotta do is ask, Jim. You know that."

"This have anything to do with Blanch?"

"Look, Jim –"

"I don't need your damn money," Jim said, throwing it on the ground and walking away.

*   *   *

Blanch spent the rest of the day laying out rocks on the ground in the shape of a long rectangle. Dusty Bob watched her working in the sun from his shady porch, wondering what the devil she was up to. Finally, she stopped and was standing back carefully surveying her work when he decided to mosey on over to get the low-down.

"What's this supposed to be?" he asked lethargically.

"This will be where the new trading post goes," Blanch said, admiring her work with satisfaction.

"Tradin' post?"

"That's right," Blanch explained. "All those tourists from the interstate are going to want to buy some Indian souvenirs – Navajo blankets, turquoise jewelry, genuine fake Indian arrowheads. We'll make a fortune on that kind of junk."

"But, I don't have the money to build no tradin' post," Dusty Bob pointed out.

"Oh, we'll get the money from a bank," Blanch said matter-of-factly. "That's how *everybody* does it, silly."

"The bank will give us enough money to build a tradin' post?"

125

"Well, not *give*, exactly," she clarified. "We'll get a loan. Against your land. You've got land here to put up for collateral – enough to pay for a trading post, and then some."

"Like what?"

"Well, over there we'll put in some gas pumps," Blanch pointed over by the diner. "People from the interstate will need to buy gas. And we'll put a swimming pool over here by the cabins."

"A *swimmin'* pool?"

"Of course, silly," Blanch smiled. "Kids are going to want to cool off and have some fun after a long day stuck in the car. And there's even room for six more cabins and a miniature golf course right over *there*."

"The bank'll loan us enough to build all that?" Dusty Bob asked, incredulously.

"Sure! With the new interstate coming through soon, they <u>know</u> we'll be able to pay it all back, with interest. Plus, with all the improvements I have in mind, we'll be able to raise the rates on the cabins several dollars a night."

Dusty Bob looked around the place, scratching his stubbly chin. "Well, I just don't know, darlin'."

"You don't have to know," Blanch said confidently. "You just leave it all up to me. You don't have to worry at all, I'll take care of *everything*."

Next, Blanch wanted to check on Kitty, who was doing some repairs in the diner. They found Kitty underneath the kitchen sink, wrenching on a rusty pipe. Dusty Bob thought she looked like a tick just about ready to pop.

"How is it going?" Blanch wanted to know.

"Well, I can patch it up for now," Kitty said, wiping her brow with her bandana. "But these old pipes are so rotten they'll have to be replaced sooner or later."

"Can <u>you</u> do it?" Blanch asked hopefully. She knew Kitty would be a lot cheaper than a real plumber who would have to come all the way from Holbrook.

"Yeah, but not *today*," Kitty said, dropping the wrench and holding her swollen belly with both hands. "I think…it's *ti-ime…*"

"What's the matter," Dusty Bob asked. "Is she sick or somethin'?"

"No, Robert," Blanch said calmly, helping Kitty to her feet. "She's going to give birth to your grandchild now."

"What – right _here_?" Dusty Bob asked, confused. Kitty's water broke and spilled out all over the floor.

"It appears so," Blanch said.

"In the _kitchen_?" Dusty Bob asked again.

"I don't think the baby much cares _where_ we are right now, Daddy," Kitty gasped, riding a huge contraction. "He just wants out – NOW!"

"Well, what should we do?"

"Put her in the old washtub out back, with her feet up," Sally Hawk ordered. "Get a pile of sheets – clean ones – and I'll boil some water."

"Do you know anything about childbirth?" Blanch asked anxiously.

"Enough to know _she'll_ be doing most of the work," Sally replied, starting a pot of water on the stove.

Dusty Bob and Blanch took Kitty out back and put her in the washtub. Blanch helped her out of her shorts while Dusty Bob went for sheets.

Sally came out and wiped Kitty's brow with a damp cloth. "It's going to feel like you're trying to pass a baby buffalo, but you've got to keep _pushing_," she told Kitty. "Trust your body – it'll stretch."

Dusty Bob came out with the sheets. He looked down at Kitty and looked like he was going to be sick.

"Stop gawking and go get the water off the stove!" Sally barked.

Kitty was puffing, panting, and groaning – but Sally stayed right with her. Then Kitty began to dilate. "Something's not right," Sally said, reaching down there and feeling around with her hand. "The baby's facing the wrong way." She placed her other hand on Kitty's belly and started singing an Indian song. She slowly moved her hand up and down the round, taut belly as she sang.

Dusty Bob took his hat off and placed it over his heart. "Heavenly Father, I never been one to bother you much seein' as you're so busy keepin' the world goin' an' all, but if you could just see fit to get this young 'un turned around the right way so's he can come out and get on with his life, I'd be much obliged. I reckon that's all for now, 'cept just to thank you for this wondrous miracle we're all beholdin' right now, and let us not soon forget it. Amen." He put his hat back on as Sally continued singing in Indian and massaging Kitty's belly.

"Something's happening now," Sally announced, as Kitty's pain seemed to intensify. Sally put her ear to Kitty's belly and listened intently. With a great push from Kitty, the baby crowned.

"VINCENT ARCHULETA, I'M GOING TO HUNT YOU DOWN AND MAKE YOU _PAY_ FOR THIS!" Kitty screamed as the baby's head and shoulders appeared. Then he was out, and Sally was wiping him down and wrapping him in a sheet.

"I admit to feelin' a might green around the gills right about now," Dusty Bob said, relieved.

"Is he _breathing_?" Blanch asked, concerned. "You've got to make sure the baby's _breathing_, you know."

"He's breathing," Sally said, cradling the baby in her arms. Kitty looked pale and exhausted.

Sally held the baby in the air and gave him a traditional Indian blessing. "Winds, Clouds, Rain, Mist, all you that move in the air, hear us! Into your midst has come a new life. Make his path smooth, that he may reach the brow of the second hill! Hills, Valleys, Rivers, Lakes, Trees, Grasses, all you of the earth, hear us! Into your midst has come a new life. Make his path smooth, that he may reach the brow of the third hill!"

"How many hills _are_ there?" Dusty Bob asked impatiently.

Sally lowered the baby and looked at him with fiery eyes. "Child of the earth, your Spirit Animal is the Owl, the quiet watcher of the night, whose steely eyes survey the world of darkness and the night-moon, and hunts his prey at the break of dawn. I will call you, Running Owl."

"Running Owl?" Dusty Bob asked. "That don't even make no sense."

"His name is Sigmund," Kitty said weakly from the washtub.

Sally continued to bounce the baby gently in her arms, cooing over him.

"Don't you think he should meet his _mother_ now?" Blanch asked.

Sally shot Blanch a dirty look, then bent down and carefully placed the bundle into Kitty's arms.

"You'll _always_ be my little Running Owl," she whispered before letting him go.

Chapter 12

A noticeable change came over Sally Hawk after Sigmund – or Siggy, as he quickly came to be known – was born. She took to the little guy like apple butter to bread. And, in an unexpected turn, Sally and Kitty even bonded a little over him. Kitty recuperated for a day, then was up and back to work on the place. Sally ran the diner and looked after Siggy between feeding times, until Kitty knocked off work in the afternoon and he took his place on his mother's hip or breast for the rest of the day.

Being thus passed back and forth like a football, young Siggy may not have been exactly sure which one his mother was. Regardless, his needs were met around the clock by whoever was on watch, and it quickly became apparent that Siggy was a happy, healthy, curious, and energetic tyke.

Dusty Bob took to being a grandpa quicker than he took to being a father, seeing the two events were mere weeks apart. Even Jim, who was still a little sore at being accused of embezzlement, brightened up somewhat when Siggy was around. Siggy himself was a good baby who rarely cried, as every need was pretty much met before he himself was even aware of it, and he seemed sufficiently entertained by the daily goings on of Memory Ranch. He even slept through most nights, as if he knew how hard Kitty worked and how much she needed her rest. And he was a real hit with the guests, who loved having their pictures taken with Dusty Bob's new grandbaby.

Siggy was scarcely a week old when one day as Dusty Bob and Blanch stood out where the new swimming pool was going to go and Blanch was making drawings in a sketchbook of how the pool would be shaped and just where the cabanas were going to be built around it, Trooper Torres came driving up from the highway in his patrol car. He got out of the car, along with a rather turned-around looking man and a very young-looking female.

"Picked up these two just walkin' along the highway," Trooper Torres announced. "Said they were lookin' for <u>your</u> place."

The man had a beatnik look about him – black goatee, bowling shirt, cool shades and a porkpie hat – and held a battered saxophone case in his hand. The girl was very young and very pregnant. She held a tattered suitcase in one hand and had a rolled-up canvas tent under her other arm.

"Well, welcome folks!" Dusty Bob went right into his jocular host spiel. "I'm Dusty Bob! Come on up to the diner, an' we'll get you checked into a nice cabin, *pronto*!"

"We didn't come here to check in, Pops," the beatnik said.

Dusty Bob's face fell. "Well, in that case, what can I do you for?"

"My name's Vince," the young man said. "I came here to see Kitty."

Dusty Bob looked him up and down, putting it together. "Well now, just what makes you think she wants to see you?"

"She has something of mine," Vince said. "And I want it."

"I think you ought to get back in the car and let Trooper Torres take you someplace else," Dusty Bob said in a measured voice.

"You're the old cowboy star, aren't you?" Vince asked.

"I'm Kitty's *father*."

"A few weeks ago, you didn't even know she existed," Vince scoffed.

"Considering the condition she was in when she got here, you'd best just leave before I commence to teachin' you some manners," Dusty Bob said, looking him straight in the eye.

"I can't believe you actually had the *nerve* to show your face here." It was Kitty – she had come out of the diner and was standing behind Blanch and Dusty Bob.

"Good to see you too, baby," Vince lifted his shades and smiled.

"What the hell are you doing here?" Kitty demanded coldly.

"I quit my job at the garage," he said. "I want my two hundred dollars – the two hundred dollars you stole from me when you left."

"Well, I want my mama's gold bracelet back that you pawned to buy your saxophone with," Kitty shot back.

"I wasn't *buying* it, honey," Vince snarled. "I was getting it out of hock after you pawned it to pay the rent that time after I spent all our rent money on that pretty dress you said you had to have for your stupid cousin's wedding!"

"Well, I wouldn't have had to pawn your saxophone to pay the rent if you hadn't stolen all my tips from waiting tables at Arnie's to take all your musician friends out to the track and bet on all the losing horses!"

Vince held up his hand. "Stop, sweetie – you're making me dizzy with all this right now. I just want my money back."

"No!" Kitty said defiantly. Then she noticed the silent pregnant girl. "Who's *this*?"

"That's Debra Lynn."

"How old is she?"

"Eighteen."

"How _old_ is she, Vince?"

Vince hung his head. "Sixteen."

"Oh, you are something else, mister," Kitty shook her head in disbelief. "You *really* are something else…"

"I see you had the baby," Vince said. "Was it a boy, or a girl?"

"A boy."

"What'd you name him?"

"Sigmund."

Vince almost crumpled in disappointment. "Now, why'd you go and do a thing like *that* for?"

"I like it," Kitty said. "And so does he."

"That's ridiculous," Vince said. "He's only a few days old."

"Yeah, but he's smart already – and that didn't come from _you_."

Sally came out of the diner to see what all the ruckus was about. She stood on the porch, holding Siggy.

"Is that him?" Vince asked, pointing.

"Uh-huh."

"Well, who's that Indian holding him?"

"That's Sally."

"Well, what if I don't *want* an Indian holding my son?"

"I suppose you really don't have any say in the matter."

"I wanna see him," Vince demanded.

"No."

"He's *my* son, dammit," Vince said. "I have a right to _see_ him."

"You're lookin' at him right now."

"Up close – so I can see which one of us he looks like."

"He looks like _me_, thank God."

"Well, I'm not leaving until I see my son."

"This is private property," Kitty said. "If my Daddy says so, Trooper Torres will escort you two right off the place." Kitty looked at Debra Lynn. She looked meek and pale and beaten down. "She ever talk? Or is she not old enough to?"

"You leave her out of this," Vince said. "I want my money, and I want to see my son. I know my rights. I'm setting up camp right here until I get what I want."

"You don't have the right to camp on private property," Trooper Torres informed him.

"Then I'll set up camp on <u>public</u> property," Vince vowed – and that's just what he did. He and Debra Lynn pitched their shabby little tent just outside Dusty Bob's property line. Then Vince drew up a sign on a piece of cardboard that said, "THEY WON'T LET ME SEE MY SON" and stood facing the highway, showing it to each passing car.

"My, he is somethin', ain't he?" Dusty Bob asked, watching Vince's demonstration from afar.

"You don't know the *half* of it," Kitty rolled her eyes in frustration.

When he got tired, Vince turned the cardboard over and wrote "THEY WON'T LET *HIM* SEE *HIS* SON" and had Debra Lynn, with her big pregnant belly, stand by the highway while he sat in the entryway of the tent and played his saxophone.

"I don't claim to be no authority on jazz," Dusty Bob said, "but he really isn't any good, is he?"

"That's why he had to work at the garage," Kitty replied.

To everyone's surprise, they were still there the next morning.

"He's a might more tenacious than I'd expected," Dusty Bob said with studied understatement. "Maybe they'll fold up their tent an' *vamoose* if you just let him get a gander at the young 'un."

"That's not happening," Kitty said firmly. "They can just stay there until they dry up and blow away, for all I care."

"That girl don't look too strong," Dusty Bob observed. "They're gonna need some water today, don't you reckon?"

"I suppose so," Kitty said reluctantly. "But only for *her* sake…"

Dusty Bob took over a canteen of water and threw in a couple of biscuits that he snuck out of the diner without Kitty seeing. Surprised, the couple accepted the supplies, but Vince's pride wouldn't allow him to thank Dusty Bob. For his part, having successfully completed his mission of mercy, Dusty Bob felt an instructive sermon was in order.

"This is a fool's errand, son. You failed to do right by Kitty, and now you've done the same for this one." He indicated Debra Lynn, who was already hungrily devouring one of the biscuits. "It's time to stand up, gird yourself, pull your boots on, an' join the rodeo."

"Huh?"

"I say, it's time to stop pussy-footin' around like a little boy, an' be a MAN!" Dusty Bob clarified. "Now, it's too late to make things right with Kitty, and you'll just have to learn to live with that. But this here little gal, you still got time to do right by her. She needs a husband who knows how to be a man, and who'll be a father to that young 'un she's a carryin'. That's right: you need to go into Holbrook an' find the first justice o' the peace you can, an' get yourselves hitched up good n' tight so that young 'un will have a family to belong to when he fights his way outta there. Then you need to go back to Albuquerque an' get your old job at the garage back, throw away that saxy-phone, an' provide for your family. An' all that nonsense about hittin' women – son, you gotta put all that behind ya an' walk *right*. Now, what do ya think about *that*?"

Vince looked up at Dusty Bob a moment. "You got any more of those biscuits?"

Dusty Bob sighed. "I'll see what I can do."

*   *   *

There were more camping trailers parked and tents set up around Lucia's house now. Jim had to leave the truck a good distance away and walk the rest on foot. When he got to the house, he saw that there were a lot more people, too. Most of them were painting at easels – still painting the strange lights in the sky – all by memory, since it was still broad daylight.

Others were off in a group, on their knees, facing the Henderson place. It looked like they were silently praying. Another group looked like they were meditating to the opera music always blaring from the little white adobe house, blissful looks plastered on their faces.

But there was more organization now: they had set up a field kitchen, like the Army, serving a line of people holding trays. There was a first aid tent with a large red cross painted on it. A couple of medics were applying braces to strained wrists so people could keep obsessively painting. There was a visitor's center, with racks of pamphlets and an information booth.

Jim looked around for Lucia. He spotted her in the distance, up higher than everyone else, draped in a striking yellow robe. He made his way through the throng of people towards her.

When he got closer, he could see that her followers had built a riser for her, on which she painted the strange lights, in her yellow robe, above everyone else. It was surrounded by other, shorter risers on which people painted – these were the "First Adherents," the first people who joined Lucia after she first started painting the strange lights. Among the "First Adherents," who were accorded a great amount of honor and respect by those who came after, there were the two men who had once worked for the government in Washington, D.C. They were now unrecognizable, dressed in long robes with flowing beards and long, bushy hair like Moses.

These two men, along with Lucia herself, of course, constituted the elite echelon of the order, for they were the only ones to have peered into "The Box" – the box with the eerie green light emanating from it which they had once possessed, but had since mysteriously disappeared. The whereabouts of "The Box" remained unknown, but remained of the highest order of interest to Lucia's followers.

Jim tried to make his way up onto the riser to talk to Lucia, but her bodyguards – the men in the powder blue robes – denied him access. Jim tried to explain to them that he merely wanted to talk to his friend, Lucia – but the men just smiled and smiled, and would not let him pass. Jim began to become frightened. He called out to Lucia, but she acted like she couldn't hear him. She just kept painting and painting.

Everybody just kept painting and painting, as the opera music blared. Hundreds of silent, colorfully-robed people, blissfully painting pictures of the lights that held some kind of talismanic significance for only them.

It was like a nightmare.

When Jim got back to the ranch, he was still shaken and confused. He was in no way prepared for the news Dusty Bob had for him.

"Jim, I've decided to ask Blanch to marry me."

"You _what_?"

"Now, I know this is a lot to drop on you so sudden-like, but I been thinkin' about it a long time," Dusty Bob explained with a great deal of patience. "It's time to move on. Me an' her already have such a good partnership business-wise, an' I'm just sure as Moses it'll carry on over into holy matrimony real smooth-like."

The news hit Jim like a twister in a trailer park – he never saw it coming. "Are you out of your whiskey-soaked mind?"

"Now look, she's real smart, an' she's had a lot of good ideas for the place already," Dusty Bob argued. "An' in case you haven't noticed, she's right pleasant to take a gander at every now and again."

"Don't you see? She's just tryin' to get her hooks in you to get ahold o' this *place*."

"I hoped you'd a took the news better n' this, Jim," Dusty Bob said sadly. "I hoped you'd a been happy for me, for once."

"What about Olivia?"

"Olivia's a _ghost_, Jim. An' she's fadin' fast, by the way. Soon, I won't even have her. Meanwhile, Blanch is a real, live woman – in the flesh, so to speak, an' I aim to make an honest woman out of her."

"An honest woman?" Jim scoffed. "In-deed. Well, you sure got your work cut out for you in that department, partner."

"*Jim…*"

"You blind old fool," Jim said. "You go right ahead. Try to make an 'honest' woman outta that Jezebel. Go right ahead an' hand everything we worked so hard to build over to *her*. You're the boss – for _now_, that is."

"I wish you could see her the way I do, Jim."

"Can't you see: she's turned this place upside down," Jim said.

"The guests are happy, we're startin' to make money – I think she's been a blessin'."

"She means to have me an' Sally off this place – you realize that, don't you?"

"Now, you know I won't let that happen, Jim," Dusty Bob promised.

"I'm not sure you'll have much say over the matter, once the two of you are hitched an' she takes over."

"He's gonna ask her to marry him," Jim confided to Sally and Kitty later. He'd called a secret meeting in the barn – the one place he knew Blanch wouldn't likely walk in on them.

"That *floozy*," Sally hissed. "I knew she'd be trouble the minute she showed up here."

"She's been workin' her spell on him since the moment she realized this place was right where the new interstate would be comin' through," Jim said. "She aims to have this place, an' if he's married to her, I'm afraid she'll have her way."

"What about us?" Sally asked.

"You see her keepin' us around?" Jim asked. "The only ones likely to be able to talk some sense into Bob? But it's not just about us gettin' kicked off the place. We'd all land on our feet all right. I'm worried about <u>him</u>. She'll have him on a leash so tight, he won't know which way to turn. Then she'll be able to take everything he has left. I just cain't stand by an' watch her do that to him."

"We need to come up with a plan to sabotage her," Kitty said. She was holding Siggy, who was starting to get fussy. She handed him off to Sally, and he quieted down again.

"How do we do that, when he won't even *listen* to us?" Jim asked in frustration.

"He may not listen to us," Sally said. "But maybe he'd listen to Olivia."

"What – how'd you know about *that*?" Jim asked.

"Nothing happens on a spiritual plane on this place that I don't know about," Sally explained. "She's been haunting this place for a long time."

"Olivia – Daddy's one true love," Kitty said. They both looked at her, surprised. "Oh, Mama told me about Olivia. She knew she never meant as much to Daddy as Olivia did, and she was all right with that."

"So, Olivia's presence here goes beyond the midnight dances?" Jim asked Sally.

Sally nodded. "I've felt her presence at…other times."

This information got Jim's mind to working on a different level. "Could – could you talk to her, do you think?" he asked Sally, feeling a bit silly. "I mean, bein' Indian an' all –"

"Not all of my people have the gift," Sally said. "But many do. I do. This little one –" she hefted Siggy "—he's not even Indian, but he's got it in *spades*."

"Oh, my gosh…" Kitty said, putting her hand to her mouth. "You mean he's…"

"I told you he was special, before he was born," Sally reminded her.

Jim attempted to steer the train back on the track. "That's nice about the young 'un, but let's get back to Olivia. If there was a way we could communicate with her, it might be possible to have *her* warn Bob about Blanch."

"I don't know her well, but the other spirits could be helpful," Sally said. "I'll ask around and see what I can do. In the meantime, I'll need some of her personal items. Spiritual proximity depends on that – something she wore, or owned."

"I think I can handle that," Jim said.

Jim waited until Blanch and Dusty Bob were off on another part of the ranch planning where the miniature golf course or children's arcade would go, and then he went into the storage room behind the kitchen where he knew Dusty Bob kept his most cherished memorabilia in an old trunk. He opened the trunk and began to rummage around in it. There were some old movie scripts, and the print of *Rendezvous in Reno* that Dusty Bob used for his midnight dances with Olivia. Then he found what he was looking for: Olivia's leather gauntlet gloves, her red bandana, and her floppy-brimmed hat. There was also a hairbrush with some of her hair in it. He took all of the items out and closed the trunk. He stuffed them into a large leather pouch and left the storeroom.

Sally was pleased with the selection of items. "Her hair in this brush is *gold*," she smiled – and Sally seldom smiled. She told Jim the other spirits on the place – some Indian, some white settlers from way back – indicated a willingness to "introduce" her to Olivia.

"When can we try this?" Jim asked anxiously.

"Tonight at midnight."

That night, Sally, Jim, Kitty and Siggy gathered around a firepit far enough away from the diner to keep their activities secret. Jim built a small fire, while Sally spread Olivia's things out on a blanket on the ground. Then they all sat cross-legged on the ground around the fire.

"Oh Great Spirit," Sally began solemnly. "Whose voice I hear in the wind, whose breath gives life to all the world. Hear me: we need your help and permission to speak with the spirit of the beautiful white lady. Please accept this offering of tobacco as a gift." Sally lit an Indian pipe and puffed on it in silence a while.

"Please accept this offering of *maize* as a gift." She threw an ear of corn on the fire. "Please accept this offering of strong water as a gift." She downed a shot of whiskey from the bottle. Then she chanted some Indian words that sounded like some kind of incantation.

"The white lady's personal things are ready, Great Spirit," Sally continued. "Allow her spirit to approach and speak with us now."

Nothing happened for a few minutes. Jim and Kitty sat in respectful silence.

Then a change came over Sally. Her posture, mannerisms – even her countenance changed, as if she were now possessed by another person. She looked down at Olivia's things admiringly, picking each one up and examining it carefully, as if rediscovering long-lost treasures.

There was something about her mannerisms and body language that Jim recognized.

"Olivia…" he whispered.

Sally/Olivia tried on the leather gloves. "Oh, I'd forgotten how soft they were," she said in delight. It was Sally's voice, but higher, with a different inflection – Olivia's inflection. Then she picked up the hairbrush and brushed her hair, giggling like a young girl.

"Hello, Jim," Sally/Olivia said. "It's been a long time."

"That it has," Jim replied. Sally/Olivia looked at Kitty and Siggy.

"This is Bob's daughter, Kitty, and new grandson, Siggy," Jim told her.

"I know, Jim," she said pleasantly.

"Then you – you see everything here – in the *real* world, I mean?"

"Yes."

"Then you know what a fix Bob's gone and gotten himself into with Blanch."

"I do," Sally/Olivia replied. "I'm quite worried about it, Jim."

"We are, too," Jim assured her. It was still kind of strange hearing Olivia speak through Sally, but Jim was starting to get used to it. "In fact, we're tryin' to figure out what we can do about it."

"Have you come up with anything?"

"As a matter of fact, that's why we wanted to talk to you," Jim explained. "Bob, bein' as stubborn as he is – well, you know all about _that_ – just won't listen to us. So, we were hopin' that, well, maybe you could warn him about Blanch."

Sally/Olivia thought about it for a moment. "Well, all I can do when I manifest myself to him is re-enact the saloon dance scene from *Rendezvous in Reno* just as it was written for the movie. If he – or I – try to add something or change the scene in any way, it doesn't work."

"That's just what Bob said," Jim sighed. "Could you do other scenes from the picture?"

"Well, I don't know," Sally/Olivia said thoughtfully. "I'll see what I can do."

The next time Dusty Bob conjured Olivia with the film projector, he was surprised when she appeared during the scene where the two of them run into each other in the general store and Olivia's character, Kate, finds out Dusty Bob's character, Jake, has a sweet tooth when he buys a bag of hard candy. It was a cute scene, although less romantic than the usual saloon dance scene. Still, it was something of a breath of fresh air for Dusty Bob, by its sheer novelty if nothing else.

Olivia informed the others of the minor breakthrough at the next 'séance.' "The problem is, we still have to follow the script verbatim. There was nothing in that cute candy counter scene that could be used to warn him about Blanch. So we're still back to square one."

"I think I may have another idear," Jim said. The next chance he got, he went back to the old trunk and pulled out the *Rendezvous in Reno* script for the next meeting with Olivia.

Jim found Sally in the kitchen. "I gotta talk to Olivia – *now*."

Fortunately, it was getting to where Olivia could speak through Sally almost any time now, without all the rigmarole and Indian pipe-smoking they had to go through at first.

"Go ahead," Sally told him, preparing herself with a quick shot of whiskey. Then she slipped into Olivia effortlessly.

"I've got the original script right here," Jim told Sally/Olivia. "If we go through it scene-by- scene, we might find something you could use to warn Bob. Comin' from you, he'd listen a whole lot better n' from us."

They started going through the script, carefully evaluating each scene to determine if the dialog could be used as a message to Dusty Bob. The only promising scene they could find was the one when Kate talks her father's henchmen into going against his orders to kill the orphans in the orphanage so he can take over Brian's silver mine. The scene's central theme – it's wrong to take advantage of the weak in order to steal what doesn't belong to you – roughly paralleled the situation between Dusty Bob and Blanch.

As luck would have it, Dusty Bob conjured Olivia that very midnight. Instead of the usual saloon dance scene, she threw him a curveball and didn't appear until her climactic speech near the end:

"In the Good Book, our Lord and Savior tells us to rescue orphans in their hour of distress. Orphans – poor, defenseless, unloved – the forgotten ones, and yet, they are humanity's only hope for the future! Men, I implore you: leave not the orphan Brian in the rapacious hands of my father. My father – yes, the man who pays your wages, but also the man who would have you mercilessly kill the orphan Brian before he turns eighteen, so he can take his father's silver mine. Men, my father – the man you work for – built his ranching empire on the backs of poor, defenseless folks like Brian – stealing whatever he could – taking what he wanted from others – and now he wants Brian's inheritance from his dead parents, killed so tragically in that random cattle stampede down the main street of Reno – he wants Brian's silver mine, all that he has left of his poor, deceased parents – a mine my father didn't build himself – a mine he didn't pour his blood, sweat, and money into – a mine that doesn't belong to him – something he wants to snatch up and add to his empire like a collector adds a China plate or a crystal goblet to his collection. Men, in the name of decency, I ask you to stop this crime! Take your guns and turn them on the real criminal, the man who wants to take what isn't his – that's right, my *father*, Calvin T. Redstone IV!"

It was a speech delivered with all the passion of a Salvation Army sermon, and one that won Olivia an academy award nomination back in the day.

Visibly moved, Dusty Bob recalled his lines word for word: "Kate, your tender love of the orphans and your fiery thirst for righteousness compels me to lay aside my solitary, wanderin' ways – somethin' no other woman has been able to do. I pledge myself to you, an' you *only*, for the rest of my days, if you'll have me."

"Of course I'll have you, you sassy old cowpuncher!" Olivia cried. Then they kissed passionately.

For his part, Dusty Bob was caught up in the passion of the scene. But by the next morning, the passion of his words – "I pledge myself to you, an' you *only*, for the rest of my days" – had worn off, and he was back in the 'real' world of Blanch and her plans of expansion for the ranch. The scene did nothing to reveal Blanch's calculating machinations to Dusty Bob. He really didn't see Blanch as a betrayal of Olivia. He even felt a little bit proud of himself for being able to compartmentalize his life so efficiently. That's what a sophisticated man – to his way of thinking – did to juggle the myriad demands placed upon the successful man in the modern age.

Thus, what happened with Olivia at midnight was nice, but it was merely a dream – and a quickly fading one at that. And what happened in the light of day was *real* and *urgent* and *meaningful* – he had to do everything Blanch could think of to get the place ready for the interstate coming through soon.

Jim and the others were deflated by the plan's failure. "Well, I reckon that's it," Jim said with humble resignation. "We gave it our best shot, and it just wasn't good enough."

As if the failure weren't discouraging enough, Dickie Kaminsky showed up later in the day asking for Blanch Goodreau. Dickie was six feet tall, with thick black hair Bryl-creamed straight back, and a lazy eye. He chain-smoked Camel cigarettes, dressed like a wise-guy, always wore an impassive expression, and answered most questions with "You don't really wanna know."

Blanch quickly introduced him to Dusty Bob as her "brother." She didn't kiss him like a brother, though.

"Dickie's interested in horses," she told Dusty Bob. This did not mean Dickie liked ranches; he liked places like Santa Anita and Hollywood Park. But what Dickie was really good at was helping people with a particular kind of problem: so much money that they didn't want the IRS to know about it all.

"Dickie'll be very useful when we're up and running after the interstate comes through," Blanch assured Dusty Bob. Blanch said Dickie would be bunking in her cabin – they had a lot of "family" stuff to catch up on.

Everybody except Dusty Bob could see what was going on.

"What gets me is she's so *blatant* about it," Jim confided to Sally. "It's right under his nose."

"A foolish man thinks his corral is getting bigger when someone is stealing his horses," Sally replied sagely.

"Is that something your people say?" Jim asked.

"No. I just made it up."

As if to prove their point, Dusty Bob proposed to Blanch that very night.

She said, "Yes."

Chapter 13

The co-parenthood of his grandson by Kitty and Sally was something that just didn't sit right with Dusty Bob. He bit his tongue for as long as he could, but seeing Siggy passed back and forth between the two women like some kind of overgrown hot potato eventually compelled him to speak up.

"I don't want the Devil's Concubine doin' any of her Indian voodoo on my grandson," he told Kitty.

"Well, I appreciate Sally's help," Kitty said calmly. "Besides, Siggy really likes her."

"I don't think it's right for a boy to be raised by two *women*," Dusty Bob pontificated. "It ain't natural. It'll just confuse the boy."

"It's *1957*, Daddy," Kitty reminded him. "You're thinking like a caveman. You've got to adjust to the Twentieth Century."

"Well, it ain't *Godly*."

"Then God shouldn't have created a world where men are all little boys who are incapable of raising their sons," Kitty replied sharply.

Dusty Bob went to find Jim, who was at the stables brushing down the horses. "I'm afraid my daughter is...well, you *know*..."

"Is what?" Jim asked, confused.

"Is startin' to like women instead of men," Dusty Bob blurted out quickly, as if the words tasted like castor oil.

"Why on earth do you think *that*?" Jim asked.

"She's lettin' Satan's Mistress co-raise Siggy. It's like the young 'un has two mamas."

Jim stopped brushing the horse and looked at Dusty Bob. "You continually astound me with your uncanny ability to be wrong," he said. "Haven't you noticed her around Trooper Torres?"

"Trooper Torres?"

"Just watch her when he's around."

"Why?"

"Just watch her."

Dusty Bob did. And Jim was right: Kitty doted on Trooper Torres, getting him more coffee, hanging on his every word, asking about his law enforcement work, and sneaking him pieces of blueberry pie on the house when Sally wasn't looking.

For his part, Trooper Torres humored her, but still mooned after Sally.

"Well, I'll be," Dusty Bob mused to himself, somewhat relieved. "This _is_ a cozy little triangle: Kitty, Trooper Torres, and the Bride of Beelzebub…"

Kitty refilled Trooper Torres's coffee cup. "This doesn't taste like Sally's coffee," he said quickly, loud enough for Sally to hear. That's because Kitty didn't put chili powder in it like Sally always did. Trooper Torres had gotten used to Sally's secret formula.

"Tell me about your day," Kitty smiled, scooting into the booth opposite him. "Your work must be so exciting – and _dangerous_."

"Well, sometimes, I guess," Trooper Torres responded, glancing nervously over at Sally. He didn't want to incur her wrath for paying too much attention to Kitty, but, on the other hand, he suspected doing so might arouse some jealousy in her. "Take yesterday, for instance. I had four big calls."

"Four? Tell me about them," Kitty demanded eagerly.

"Well, three of them were from ninety-year-old Miss Abigail out on Gila Springs Road. She lives on her own and suffers from dementia. She keeps moving things or losing things or imagining things she hasn't had in years are missing, so she calls me. The first call, she tells me, '_That chair was over there. Somebody moved it._' I ask her who would want to break into her house and rearrange her furniture, and she just says, '_I have my suspicions._' Sometimes it's the government. Sometimes it's the Chinese. I tell her, in either case, there's not much I can do about it. The second time she calls, she tells me, '_I can't find my diamond necklace. Somebody stole it._' The third time, she says, '_I can't find my opera tickets. Someone's hiding them from me._' See, sometimes she believes she's a rich Manhattan socialite."

"Why do you keep going out there when she calls?" Kitty asked.

Trooper Torres shrugged his shoulders. "It's my job."

"I admire your dedication," Kitty said.

"Then there was Old Mr. Young. His goat busted into his shed and ate six sticks of blasting dynamite and got the hiccups real bad."

"What did you do?" Kitty asked.

"I filled out a report and told Mr. Young to tie him up outside away from the house and watch him real good for a while. How's he doin', Mr. Young?"

Old Mr. Young was sitting a few feet away, in the corner booth. "Got heartburn somethin' awful," he replied. "But I believe he's on the mend."

Trooper Torres continued his story to Kitty. "The dynamite was really old and probably defective, but I didn't want to take any chances, on account of there was a case of exploding sheep over in Greasewood a few years back. That was a real mess."

"How exciting," Kitty commented.

"You never know what each day brings in this line of work," Trooper Torres nodded, sipping coffee.

One morning, Kitty woke up to find Siggy missing. A window was open, the chiffon curtain flapping quietly in the breeze. There was a note on the dresser: "YOU SHOULDA LET ME SEE MY SON."

Vince was also gone, leaving Debra Lynn alone in the tent out by the highway.

"Where did he go?" Kitty demanded frantically.

"Wouldn't say," Debra Lynn replied, quiet as a mouse.

In reality, Vince hitchhiked with Siggy to Holbrook where they boarded a Greyhound bus to Las Vegas, where his cousin worked the roulette table at the Sands Casino. By the time he got to his cousin's shabby apartment, Vince was already regretting his hasty abduction because Siggy, usually a quiet, happy baby, was crying continually, and Vince didn't know how to stop it.

"Why don't you just take him back?" his cousin, who was named Preston Shoe, asked casually.

"I can't," Vince replied. "There's always this state trooper hanging around there. He'll arrest me for kidnapping or something."

"It ain't kidnapping if he's your son," Preston pointed out.

"It's reassuring you're such an expert on Arizona state law," Vince said sarcastically.

"Well, just put the kid back on the bus home by himself," Preston suggested.

"He's three weeks old," Vince told him. "I can't send him by himself."

They talked more about Vince's options. When Preston found out Siggy was Dusty Bob's grandson, he suddenly became interested.

"The cowboy star from the old movies? That old coot must be *loaded*." Preston quickly convinced Vince to hold Siggy for ransom. "Don't just give him back – make them *pay*."

They wrote a ransom note and sent it off to Dusty Bob at Memory Ranch.

When Dusty Bob received the ransom note, everyone gathered around him in the diner. He read the note out loud: "'To whom it may concern, chiefly Dusty Bob. Send one thousand dollars cash to this P.O. Box by tomorrow or thereabouts, or you will never see little Siggy again.' Then they crossed out the 'one thousand dollars' and wrote 'one thousand two hundred and fifty dollars,'" Dusty Bob informed them.

Dickie Kaminsky noticed it was written on the back of a Sands Casino flyer. "I know guys in Vegas," he said. "Don't pay the ransom. I'll have your grandkid back for you tomorrow."

"Maybe we should have the police handle this," Dusty Bob suggested.

"Trust me – my guys will do it better," Dickie insisted.

Kitty pulled Sally aside. "Vince was always talking about his cousin in Vegas. He works at the Sands – I *know* we can find him."

"I'm in," Sally said.

Without telling a soul, Kitty and Sally took the pickup truck and headed for Las Vegas.

Back in Vegas, Vince and Preston were in Preston's apartment engaged in a heated debate.

"We should've asked for more," Vince said. "We probably could've gotten – I don't know – maybe thirteen hundred!"

"Relax, cuz," Preston urged. "Let's not get too greedy, now…"

Two large, thuggish-looking men walked into Preston's apartment without knocking. They were not Dickie Kaminsky's guys. They were Preston's bookies.

"You're three weeks overdue, Preston," one of them said. "Where's the money?"

"I've had a bad run of luck lately," Preston gulped, trying to look unafraid. "I just need a little more time, to turn things around. I'll have the money by Friday."

"You work a roulette table at the Sands, don't you?" the other one asked. "Why don't you just pocket a few extra chips now and then – no one will notice."

"Oh, no," Preston said. "You guys know who runs that place. I'm not stealing a *dime* from them. I *like* my arms and legs – they're very useful. I wanna keep them attached to my body."

145

"Well, Friday's no good," the first one said. "We need the money _now_."

"I don't have it."

The bookie looked at Vince holding Siggy. "Then we'll take the baby."

"This is my son," Vince protested.

"Take the baby from the beatnik, Neil," the first bookie instructed the second calmly. Then he pulled his jacket back just enough to show a revolver stuck in his belt.

Vince handed Siggy over without a fight.

"When we get our money, you get the baby back," the first bookie said, then they left Preston's apartment and took Siggy back to their office.

"How much do you owe them?" Vince asked Preston.

"Twelve-hundred."

Vince visibly crumpled in disappointment. "That's almost all the ransom money! We're only gonna get…" he stopped and counted on his fingers. "Fifty bucks!"

An hour later, the bookies were raided by the police and taken into custody.

One of the cops picked Siggy up and held him. "What were bookies doing with a baby?"

"I don't know," the sergeant said. "Bring him back to the station and we'll try to find his parents."

The cops took Siggy back to the station and began trying to find out if there were any missing baby reports. They put Siggy in a cardboard box and left it on the counter while they worked. Then, over the loudspeaker there was a call about a bank robbery, and all the cops hustled out of the station. "Keep an eye on that baby!" the sergeant called to the desk officer on his way out.

The desk officer had a bad bladder infection and had to use the bathroom a lot. In fact, he had to use the bathroom right now. There was no one in the place, so he went back to the men's room and was in there a very long time, in great agony. While he was gone, a homeless woman wandered into the station and looked around. Seeing no one was there, she walked around the station pocketing things off of desks, looking at pictures of the officers' families, and sitting in their chairs. She typed gibberish on a typewriter for a while, then got bored and started rifling through desk drawers for valuables.

Then she looked up and saw the box sitting on the counter. She got up and went over to it. She saw Siggy inside. She picked up the box and left the station.

A few blocks from the police station, she stopped and made a sign that said, "HELP ME FEED MY BABY." Then she sat down on the sidewalk with Siggy and a cup and started begging. Everyone who passed her took one look at Siggy and emptied their pockets of change. A few minutes later, she saw a cop walking his beat who looked like he was coming her way. She left Siggy on the sidewalk and high-tailed it with the cup of change. The cop decided to cross the street before he got there, and never saw Siggy on the sidewalk.

A man who had recently received a head injury on his construction job was leaving a doctor's office after an appointment about his short-term memory loss saw Siggy on the sidewalk and picked him up. He took Siggy and got on the bus to go home. On the bus, he noticed a newspaper on the seat in front of him. He laid Siggy down on the seat next to him and reached for the newspaper. It was the sports section – his favorite section. He got so engrossed in it that he almost missed his stop. He got off the bus just in time, taking the sports section with him to finish at home over lunch but leaving Siggy behind on the bus seat.

Siggy rode unnoticed for six stops until a woman who had desperately been trying to have a baby with her husband for months with no success got on the bus and picked him up. Holding Siggy in her arms, she felt just like all the other mothers holding their babies on the bus – wonderfully normal.

She got off the bus with Siggy at a department store and went inside. A beautiful dress with flowers on it immediately caught her eye. It would be perfect to wear to her sister's upcoming wedding, she thought. She sat Siggy down for a moment to hold the dress up in front of her in front of the mirror. She struck several attractive poses – the dress looked fabulous! Pleased, she put it back on the rack, behind all the other dresses. She would come back for it later, after hitting her hubby up for some cash. Then she started to reach for Siggy, but on an impulse grabbed a lovely pair of white gloves instead and shoved them into her purse.

A store detective who'd been watching her from behind the lingerie rack came out of nowhere and grabbed her arm. He pulled her away and locked her in a room until the police arrived. He never saw Siggy lying on the floor. Siggy was found a few minutes later by a little girl who had stopped into the department store to buy some candy. She carried him outside to the park to show all her friends: "Look, I have a baby!"

"It's not your baby, you're only nine years old!" a jealous girl told her. Another kid called to a nearby cop, "Hey, that's not really her baby! She probably stole it!"

Panicking, the girl ran away to another part of the park and stashed Siggy in a baby carriage that already had a baby in it, while the mother wasn't looking. Failing to notice Siggy, the mother continued pushing the carriage right past the cop, who was too busy looking for the little girl with the baby to notice what was in the carriage. The mother left the park and pushed the carriage into a church, where she stopped to light a candle and pray. Then she looked into the carriage to check on her baby and saw _two_ babies instead of one and didn't know what to do. Her husband would _kill_ her if she brought home another baby. Panicking, she left Siggy on a pew and took her own baby home.

An hour later, a priest found him and took him to some nuns, who took him to their orphanage. The desperate woman who was arrested for shoplifting had been released on bail and was now hanging around the orphanage fantasizing about all the babies. While no one was looking, she grabbed Siggy. Recognizing him, she exclaimed, "OH, THIS WAS MEANT TO BE!" The orphanage nuns heard her, and started towards her to take Siggy back. The desperate lady ran outside with Siggy, the orphanage nuns chasing her down the street in broad daylight, their habits flapping in the breeze.

She ducked into a movie theater to hide in the dark. The teenage ticket taker said "Hey lady, you have to buy a ticket!" as she passed by with Siggy. She found a seat in the theater and it was dark because the movie had already started. She stuffed Siggy under her seat to keep him quiet, and pretended to watch the movie. It was Doris Day, her favorite entertainer. An usher came up to her and shined a flashlight in her face. "Lady, you didn't buy a ticket!" He grabbed her and hauled her out of her seat.

"Wait! My baby's under the seat!" she cried.

"Sure, sure, lady," the usher said, dragging her out of the theater.

Back at Preston Shoe's apartment, Dickie Kaminsky's Vegas associates finally showed up.

"Who're _you_?" Preston asked.

"We came for the baby," one of them said.

"Well, take a number and get in line," Preston said.

After the Doris Day movie, everyone left the theater. The usher who kicked the desperate woman out was sweeping up popcorn when he discovered Siggy under the seat. He took Siggy outside, looking up and down the street for a cop. He saw a cop and handed the baby to him.

"Some lady left her baby in the theater," he told the cop. The cop took Siggy and started to walk to the police station. The cop saw a man trying to snatch a lady's purse and said to a man standing there in a suit and tie, "Here, hold this baby a second." Then he chased the mugger around the block. The man in the suit waited and waited for the cop, but he never came back.

The man was late for an important job interview. It was his dream job, and if he didn't get it, he didn't know what he would do. So he decided to take Siggy to the interview with him and drop him off at the police station later. When he was called in for the interview, he left Siggy with the office secretary. She took Siggy around to show all the other secretaries how cute he was, and while she was gone from her desk, the man came out from the interview. He didn't get his dream job. He was determined to go straight home and put his head in the oven. Naturally, he forgot all about Siggy.

After work, the secretaries had a birthday celebration for one of the girls that involved a lot of bourbon. Before they realized it, they were smashed out of their minds and all went home floating on a cloud – leaving Siggy alone in the office.

In the middle of the night, the cleaning lady found Siggy and decided to take him to her daughter in the morning. Her daughter wanted a baby something awful but her husband suffered from a rare disorder in which he could not be naked in the presence of another human being so she felt like she'd never be able to conceive (by him, at least). At the end of her shift, the cleaning lady started to take Siggy home but the elevator got stuck on the way down and the fire department had to come and get her out. While they were working, she had a stroke. When they finally got the doors open, the firefighters sent her to the hospital in an ambulance. They took Siggy back to the fire station to wait for the police to come pick him up.

Eleven minutes later they got an emergency call about a high-rise fire and rushed off thinking the police would be there any minute to pick Siggy up. But after they left, a thief broke into the fire station and found the baby. He picked him up to take a good look at him. Just then, the police entered to pick up Siggy and the thief panicked and ran out, still holding Siggy. He ran down the street and stuffed Siggy into a trash can on the sidewalk in front of a bank. Then he ran off.

Then two men and a woman walked up and put masks on to rob the bank. The men drew guns and went inside, but the woman heard baby sounds coming from the trash can and looked inside. Surprised, she pulled Siggy out. She took him inside and held him under one arm as she and her two male accomplices robbed the bank and tried to make their getaway.

Outside the bank, the cops pulled up with sirens blaring. The woman robber stuffed Siggy into a bag with twenty-two thousand dollars in it. The robbers then split up, with cops chasing and shooting at each of them. The woman ran down an alley and threw the bag into a trash dumpster, intending to come back for it later when the heat was off.

Twenty minutes later, the homeless woman who had taken Siggy from the police station earlier wandered up and started digging around in the dumpster and found the bag with Siggy and the twenty-two thousand dollars in it. She took Siggy and the bag and went to the same department store where the desperate woman had tried to steal the white gloves the day before. There, the homeless woman bought herself the pretty dress with the flowers on it that the desperate woman had hidden behind the other dresses. She also bought gloves, shoes, and a hat. Then she went to an expensive French restaurant and ordered a five-course meal. Then she put Siggy back into the bag full of money and left the restaurant. She intended to find a cab and ask to be taken to the finest hotel in town, where she would indulge in a luxurious bubble bath, drink champagne and eat expensive Belgian chocolates from room service, and have the best sleep of her life. But the same mugger the cop was chasing before came up from behind her and grabbed the bag right out of her hands and ran away with it.

Ducking into an alley, he opened it and saw Siggy and all the cash inside. He closed the bag again and exited the alley back onto the street. He saw a political street rally and walked up to the crowd. He took Siggy out of the bag and handed him to someone, then ran off quickly with the bag of cash.

The person handed Siggy to another, and another, and another – Siggy slowly making his way to the front of the crowd. Then someone handed him to the politician at the podium, who smiled broadly. "What a beautiful baby!" the politician exclaimed, making a big show of kissing Siggy on the cheek. When he realized there was nobody to hand Siggy back to, he turned to his campaign manager and hissed, "Get rid of this kid, willya?"

Not having the slightest idea what to do with the baby, the campaign manager hailed a cab, put him in the back seat, and threw a five-dollar bill at the cabbie.

"Where to?" the cabbie asked.

"Anywhere," the campaign manager said.

The cabbie drove around a while, trying to find a policeman to give Siggy to. Then a man hailed him, so he stopped. The man got in the back – we'll call him the gambler.

"The Sands," the gambler said. They drove for several minutes. "Hey, mac – someone left a baby back here."

"I know," the cabbie replied. "I'll give you five bucks to take him with you."

"Five bucks? Sure thing, mac."

At the Sands, the gambler took Siggy into the casino and put the five dollars down on the roulette table. He won five hundred dollars and walked away gleefully counting his money, leaving Siggy behind.

On his way out of the casino, he passed Kitty and Sally coming in.

"Vince said his cousin works the roulette table," Kitty was telling Sally. They walked right up to the roulette table.

"Are you Preston Shoe?" Kitty asked.

"No, I'm filling in for him while he's in the hospital with two broken legs," the roulette table guy said. Then Kitty saw Siggy. Relieved, she picked him up and kissed him.

"Hey, buddy – Mama's been _looking_ for you!"

Chapter 14

Bud Silverman was a fifty-six-year-old former high school shop teacher who cashed in his retirement savings in the early 1950s to go into the movie business. He established Limelight Pictures and promptly began churning out the type of low-budget, B movie drivel that served the dubious purpose of filling out matinee and late-night movie theater schedules before and after the main features. He specialized in digging up washed-up old horror movie stars and hiring them for pennies to star in subpar, bottom of the barrel epics like *Frankenstein Discovers Mary Jane* and *Dracula's Cross-Dressing Vampire Cousin*. He also churned out cheesy science fiction flying saucer movies that looked like they were made by high school students using pie tins and fishing line. That's because they were. Bud Silverman knew kids had pretty creative ideas and they always worked cheap. And if you were willing to work cheap, you could always find a place on a Bud Silverman production.

When Bud caught a gander at the *Life* magazine article about Dusty Bob, he got an idea: he would produce his first western. Dusty Bob hadn't made a movie in decades – surely he'd be a good fit for Bud Silverman's budget. So he sent Dusty Bob two bus tickets and a telegram offering him one thousand U.S. dollars to come out to Hollywood and star in Limelight Pictures' first western.

When Dusty Bob received the telegram, he went straight to Jim for advice.

"Well, what do you think, Jim? Should I go?"

Jim immediately saw a couple of opportunities in the offer. "If we could get out to Hollywood and find Max Hoffman, we could get him to write some extra scenes for *Rendezvous in Reno* – scenes with you an' Olivia. Don't you see – if the original writer tinkers with the script, it just might reverse the fadin' process an' give you more time with Olivia." Of course, the other opportunity Jim kept to himself: maybe Max Hoffman could write new scenes in which Olivia could explicitly warn Dusty Bob about Blanch's true motives.

Dusty Bob thought it over. "Sounds like a long-shot to me, but I reckon a thousand dollars and a chance to make one more picture before they plant me in the ground makes it worth a try."

"They sent two bus tickets," Jim pointed out. "Who you gonna take with you?"

"Well, I cain't rightly make a picture without my trusty, long-time stuntman, now can I? Besides, I cain't just leave you behind with nobody to keep you in line, you know…"

When Blanch Goodreau heard about it, she was at first strongly opposed to the idea. But the more she thought about it, the better it sounded.

"All right, Robert," she finally relented. "You go make your picture. A new Dusty Bob movie would only be good for business around here, anyway. Dickie and I can hold the fort down here while you're gone. Some tourists may be disappointed to not find you here, but I'll tell them you're out in Hollywood making a new movie. That'll create some buzz."

"That's my girl – always thinkin' about business," Dusty Bob said.

"But you be sure and bring all of that one thousand dollars back here with you, you hear?" Blanch said firmly. "Every cent. And don't forget: the minute you get back, we're tying the knot. And I'm not about to let you wriggle out of that." She squeezed his arm and brushed his cheek with a half-hearted kiss.

"All right, darlin'" Dusty Bob drawled, a little embarrassed. "Whatever you say…"

The next morning, Dusty Bob and Jim boarded a Greyhound bus for Los Angeles. On the long, hot, cramped ride, Dusty Bob's spirits actually began to brighten.

"I tell ya, Jim – I feel ten years younger already!" he chirped. "Ya know, I just got to thinkin'. Who says this'll be my last picture? Why, if everything goes right, this could be my _comeback_."

"Now, don't go gettin' too far ahead of yourself, partner," Jim cautioned. "We don't know anything about this Silverman fella. We don't even know if he's on the up an' up or not."

"Leave it to you to be a damp cloud over my jubilee, Jim. I don't know why I even brought you along, to tell ya the truth."

"Because you wouldn't even know how to find Los Angeles if I wasn't here," Jim shot back. "Probably end up in Baltimore, or somethin'."

"I know Los Ange-leez like the back of my hand," Dusty Bob declared. "That was _my_ town back when my pictures was rakin' it in at the box office an' fillin' up all those big ol' movie houses from

Santee Monica to Pasadena, an' don't you forget it!" Dusty Bob smiled to himself and thought back to the days when it was not uncommon for him to ride Texas Pete through Laurel Canyon and right down Hollywood Boulevard, stopping in front of Grauman's Chinese Theater to sign autographs for surprised fans.

"I cain't forget it," Jim deadpanned. "You won't let me. Just don't be surprised if it's changed a lot over the last twenty or so years."

"Oh, fiddle-faddle! Limelight Pictures sounds like a classy organization," Dusty Bob mused. "I 'spect they'll be rollin' out the red carpet for me when we get there."

A little boy in the seat in front of him turned around and looked at Dusty Bob. "Were you a _real_ cowboy, mister?"

"I still *am*, son!" Dusty Bob declared proudly.

When they arrived in L.A., they were met at the bus terminal by a gum-chewing teenage boy with acne named Alvin. He was holding a hastily-fashioned cardboard sign with Dusty Bob's name scrawled on it.

"I'm Dusty Bob. This is my associate, Jim Dupree."

The kid just stared at them. "You're Dusty Bob – the _actor_?"

"That's right, son."

"But you're so _old_..."

Alvin took them to an old, beat-up car in the parking lot and opened the trunk for them. He made no move to take their bags, so Dusty Bob and Jim loaded their own suitcases. Dusty Bob looked the car over.

"Shouldn't you put some air in those tires?" he asked.

"You're a funny old man, aren't you?" Alvin remarked, vigorously chewing his gum. "Regular Bob Hope."

They climbed in the back and Alvin started the car. Thick black smoke poured out of the tail pipe and enveloped them in a dense cloud as they pulled out of the bus terminal parking lot.

Instead of taking them to Hollywood as Dusty Bob had expected, Alvin drove them to the Van Nuys Airport in the Valley. He pulled up in front of a rusty old corrugated airplane hangar with a sign over the entrance reading: LIMELIGHT PICTURES. Several of the letters were askew.

"This is it?" Dusty Bob asked.

"Yeah, Mr. Silverman's waiting for you inside," Alvin said. He took them into the hangar, where several old men, some Mexican laborers, and a few high school students were working on some Old

West sets. There was a saloon set, a sheriff's office with a jail, and some hotel room and church interiors in various stages of completion.

"This is the soundstage," Alvin said. Then he directed them to a small office that had been walled off in the corner of the hangar. They walked inside, and Bud Silverman was on the phone at his desk. The office was filled with movie props, mannequins wearing space helmets and costumes, a life-sized figure of the Creature from the Black Lagoon, old movie posters, and cigar smoke.

Bud was screaming into the receiver: "Now I want you to hear me, Mel – every print I make costs me _money_! Three theaters should be able to make do with <u>one</u> print…How? Simple: after the five o' clock showing at the Searchlight, they have a runner take it over to the Landmark in time for the seven o' clock show. Then I'll have Alvin or some other snot-nosed rug-rat pick it up and take it to the Avalon for the nine o' clock showing. Got it? Well, tell them they gotta make it _work_." He slammed the phone down and wiped sweat off his brow with a handkerchief.

Then he grabbed a lit cigar from an ashtray and shoved it between his greasy lips. He looked up at them, puffing furiously on the cigar.

"Those idiots with the prints," he rolled his eyes. "They're gonna give me a stroke. I gotta figure out _everything_ around here." Then he shot up out of his chair and came around to the front of the desk.

"I bet I know who <u>you</u> are," Bud beamed, the cigar now wedged tightly in the corner of his mouth. "Dusty Bob, am I right?" He grabbed Dusty Bob's hand with both of his and pumped it vigorously up and down.

"Pleased to meet you," Dusty Bob said politely.

"Oh, I'm a big fan," Bud enthused. "BIG fan. Saw all your pictures when I was a kid. You were my hero, Dusty – may I call you Dusty? – my _hero_!"

"Well, that's mighty flatterin'," Dusty Bob said humbly. "This is my associate, Jim Dupree."

Bud grabbed Jim's hand and pumped it up and down. "A real pleasure, Jim. How was the trip over, gentlemen?"

"Real comfortable," Dusty Bob lied. "Those Greyhound buses have the nicest seats."

"Good, good," Bud beamed between cigar puffs. "You know, on behalf of Limelight Pictures, I'd like to welcome you to the Limelight family of artists and say that it's a real honor to be able to create cinematic art with such an esteemed star as yourself!"

"Aww, that's mighty generous of you, Mr. Silverman," Dusty Bob said.

"*Bud*," Silverman insisted. "Please call me Bud. My door is always open – I'm a twenty-four-hour-a-day creative person, Dusty – may I call you *Dusty*? – so if there's anything you ever need, all you have to do is *ask*."

"Well, that's mighty neighborly of you, Bud," Dusty Bob said. "I'll be sure to do that."

"Well, let's get down to business, shall we?" Bud picked up some loose papers from his desk and gave them to Dusty Bob. "Here's the script. Memorize it tonight. We start shooting – on location – first thing in the morning."

"But there's only six pages here."

"Don't worry about that," Bud assured him. "I've got my top writer chained to his desk in the next room working on it now." He held up a key to prove it. "I give him a hamburger every time he finishes a scene. And every ten pages, he gets to use the bathroom."

"The writer's union is okay with that?" Jim asked.

"Union-shmunion," Bud laughed. "We make movies under the radar around here. Guerrilla style filmmaking! But, for the first time, in honor of Dusty Bob, the legend himself, I have hired a *real* director with actual *directing* _experience._ My philosophy is simple, gentlemen: nothing is too good for a Dusty Bob movie!"

"What about the thousand dollars upfront?" Jim asked skeptically.

"Oh, I've got your fee right here," Bud said, handing Dusty Bob an envelope full of greasy money. Dusty Bob fingered through it quickly.

"There's only five hundred here."

"Oh, you'll get the other five when we wrap," Bud promised. "You fellas have had a long trip and I'm sure you're bushed. Alvin, why don't you take our esteemed guests to their accommodations where they can clean up and relax. And remember: we start shooting bright and early in the morning!"

As they walked out of the hangar, they could hear Silverman screaming at the crew to work faster. They got in the car and Alvin started driving.

"How long you been workin' for Mr. Silverman?" Dusty Bob asked Alvin.

"Almost six months," Alvin replied. "I'm gonna be a writer-director, maybe do some acting someday. It's good experience."

"What kinda boss is he?"

"Oh, Mr. Silverman's swell," Alvin said. "He pays regular – that is, when he has the money. He hires a lot of young people, like me. You know, non-union. Saves us payin' dues. That's strictly on the QT, though, so keep it under your hat."

"Sure thing," Dusty Bob said, tipping his Stetson.

"Uh, Bob," Jim nudged him. "You realize this isn't a real studio, don't you? I mean, it's an airplane hangar in Van Nuys."

"Well, as I recall, Mack Sennett started in Echo Park," Dusty Bob reminded him. "Hollywood is a state of mind, not a location on a map, Jim."

"I'll keep that in mind," Jim said.

Alvin dropped them off at a crummy motel in a seedy part of Hollywood. They got out and looked it over. It had a bright neon sign: THE NIGHT-TIMER. A sign below it read: LOUNGE – POOL – AIR CONDITIONING – TV – HOURLY RATES – FREE PHONES (LOCAL CALLS ONLY!)

Alvin went inside the office to check them in.

Dusty Bob looked at the swimming pool. It was half full of brown water, trash, and leaves. It could have had a body floating in it. It was surrounded by broken patio furniture.

Alvin came out of the office and handed Dusty Bob a key.

"One room?" Jim asked.

"Oh, don't worry – I made sure it has two beds," Alvin said cheerfully. He opened the trunk for them to take their luggage out. "There's a taco stand on the corner if you get hungry, and a liquor store if you need anything else. I'll pick you up at five-thirty sharp. It's quite a drive out to the location."

"We'll be ready," Dusty Bob assured him. Alvin got in and drove away, leaving a cloud of black smoke. They picked up their bags and found the room. Dusty Bob unlocked it and they went inside. He turned on the light and cockroaches scurried under the bed. There were cigarette burns on the floor, the bedspread, the lampshades, and on the furniture.

"Well, it's not so bad, Jim." It was Dusty Bob's attempt to preempt any negativity from Jim. Jim just looked at him in disbelief.

"Well, at least the neighborhood's not so bad," Dusty Bob continued. "Those ladies feel safe enough to stand on the sidewalk out front."

"Those are workin' gals, Bob," Jim informed him.

"What?"

"Prostitutes."

"Now, how do you know that?"

Jim gave him another look. Then he saw the second "bed:" a folding roller bed. "Aww, now…"

"Don't fret, Jim," Dusty Bob said brightly. "We'll switch off with the good bed, so we'll each be gettin' a good rest half the time."

They decided to go down to the stand on the corner for a greasy taco. They stood out a bit in the crowd for their cowboy hats and boots.

"You buckaroos lookin' for a ride tonight?" one of the ladies on the corner asked them.

"No, Ma'am," Dusty Bob blushed. "We're just lookin' to go back to our room for a little shut-eye."

"That's a shame, cowboy," the hooker winked. "You look like you gotta lotta miles left in you yet…"

Walking back to their room, Dusty Bob said, "I could use a night cap before turning in."

They went into the motel lounge and looked around. The place failed to disappoint in its grimy seediness. A fat guy with long greasy hair sat alone at one of the tables. A sixty-year-old woman with dyed blond hair was passed out over the bar, snoring loudly. A group of bikers drank beer and played pool. A man in a wrinkled suit and loosened tie sweated profusely and chain-smoked cigarettes while talking nervously on the payphone by the men's room.

Then Dusty Bob froze. "Look, Jim – over there in the corner. It's _her_."

Jim looked and saw only an empty table.

"It was _her_." Dusty Bob looked like he'd seen a ghost.

"Who?"

"Olivia."

"What would she be doin' here, partner?" Jim asked gently.

"Maybe I'm just seein' things," Dusty Bob conceded. "But I coulda _swore_."

"It's been a long day," Jim said. "Let's get a drink."

They sat at the bar and ordered whiskeys. The bartender poured their shots and said, "You two aren't from around here, are you?"

"Ari-zonee," Dusty Bob said, picking up his glass.

"Gee, I never woulda guessed," the bartender said sardonically. "So, what brings you to the City of Angels?"

"I'm here to shoot a movie," Dusty Bob said.

"A movie? You don't say!" the bartender looked impressed. "Say, you know John Wayne?"

"Met 'im a few times," Dusty Bob replied. "He was a young, pretty-faced up an' comer in my day. Doin' bit parts here an' there, even in a couple of my pictures. Then John Ford found 'im. Ford put 'im in a picture called _Stagecoach_, an' it made 'im a star overnight. Yessiree, _Stagecoach_ was a mighty fine picture, all right. Wish I'd made that one, myself. In fact, I begged Ford to cast me in it, but he said he wanted someone younger – a fresh, unknown face – can you beat that?"

"Hey, gramps – what studio you working for now – MGM, Fox?" the bartender asked.

"Limelight Pictures," Dusty Bob said proudly.

The bartender's brow furrowed. "Never heard of that one." Then he wandered off and started wiping down some glasses.

"Hmmm..._saucy_ fellow," Dusty Bob groused, downing his shot and smoothing down his handlebar mustache in one deft motion.

Jim was staring at his whiskey. "These glasses are _dirty_."

"Never you mind that, Jim. The rot-gut'll sanitize 'em, all right."

Jim looked at Dusty Bob. "Aren't you disappointed?"

"With what?"

"With _everything_," Jim replied. "Limelight Pictures. Alvin. That death-trap of an automobile. The motel room. Them greasy tacos. This here saloon. _Everything_."

"Jim, this here's my last chance," Dusty Bob explained. "Louis B. Mayer didn't send for me, but Bud Silverman _did_. An' I aim to make the best of it. So, let's look at it like an _adventure_ – you know, like the old days – what do you say, partner?"

"I reckon I can try to do that," Jim conceded.

They went back to the motel room and tried to get some shut-eye, which was difficult on account of the ladies from the corner taking men in and out of the surrounding rooms most of the night.

Jim woke up early the next morning. Dusty Bob was already awake, sitting up in bed, staring at a chair in the corner.

"What are you looking at?" Jim asked.

"I saw her again, Jim. Sittin' right there in that chair – just as full as life."

Jim didn't know what to say. So he got out of his squeaky roller bed, stretched his achy back, and started getting dressed.

A few minutes later, Alvin was there to drive them to the location. "I brought donuts and coffee," he said. "Sit back and enjoy, fellas."

They got in the back seat and Alvin drove north through the Valley. The set was a broken-down ranch in Newhall, with a few sway-backed horses and a couple of flea-bitten donkeys standing around. The "crew" – the old men, young students, and Mexican laborers from the day before – were setting things up for the day's shoot.

"Let me introduce you to the director," Alvin said, and led them over to where a short, white-haired man with a patch over his right eye was instructing a crew member how to set up the camera. "Fellas, say hello to Gus Fleming."

The white-haired man turned around quickly and gave them the once-over with his good eye. "We've got to get started right away," Gus Fleming told them in a thick German accent, wiping sweat from his face and brow. He looked very stressed-out and had obviously been drinking heavily. "Ze owner's daughter's *quinceanera* is tonight und vee haff to be packed up and out of here by four o' clock."

Gus sent them to wardrobe, which was essentially an eighty-year-old woman working out of the back of an old woody wagon. "Who's who here?" she demanded, spitting tobacco juice into the dirt.

"I'm Dusty Bob, and this is my associate, Jim Dupree," Dusty Bob offered.

She looked them up and down. "Which one plays the sheriff?"

"I reckon that would be me, ma'am," Dusty Bob said.

"What's _he_ do?"

"He's my stunt double."

"Then I'll have to dress you up the same, as much as I can," she said slowly. "But you'll have to give him some of your costume when it's time for him to do the stunts."

She fixed Dusty Bob up with a sheriff's get-up – low budget, but passable.

"I'd like to wear my own hat, if you don't mind," Dusty Bob politely requested. "Took me years to break it in, an' it's my trademark – along with my mustache."

"Suit yourself," she shrugged, tossing the hat she'd picked – which wasn't Dusty Bob's style at all – into the back of the woody. "The costumes are on loan from *Gunsmoke*, so be careful not to rip anything or you've <u>bought</u> it," she warned with a glare, spitting into the dirt again.

The assistant director – a fifteen-year-old kid with red hair and freckles – called for everyone to take their places: shooting was about to begin.

"I haff zis little ritual I do before shooting starts on my pictures," Gus announced in his German accent. He pulled a large metal flask out of his pocket and took a very long drag. Then he snapped the top back on and put it away. "Ah, now I'm ready!"

"What is this picture about?" Dusty Bob asked suddenly. "I read the first six pages, but it didn't seem to make no sense."

"Don't worry about it," Gus assured him. "All westerns haff ze same plot, anyway."

"Umm, have you ever directed a western before?" Dusty Bob asked.

"No, but I've *seen* a few."

In actuality, Gus Fleming had directed a number of dark, brooding, European psychological dramas – existential, tortured – but Bud Silverman had snatched him up because he was available, worked cheap, and had at least a modicum of experience behind the camera – when he wasn't experiencing or recovering from a heart attack, that is.

Gus told the AD to fill Dusty Bob in on what they knew about the plot while he set up the first shot with the cameraman.

The AD said the movie was about an outlaw gang who terrorize a town because the sheriff (Dusty Bob) put the gang leader's father in prison many years before for robbing a bank, and he was murdered by another inmate, so they blame the sheriff and want revenge against him.

The sheriff's daughter, who runs the town's café, falls in love with one of the outlaws. The town-folks' support of the sheriff begins to waiver when the banker asks him to evict a poor family from their ranch and he does so, making the poor family into homeless beggars. In the end, the sheriff reverses himself, tears up the eviction notice, and lets the family move back onto their ranch. Feeling betrayed, the banker throws in with the outlaws and plots revenge against the good-hearted sheriff.

"We're doing the eviction scene today," the AD informed Dusty Bob. "So go over your lines, we start in five minutes."

When Gus called out "ACTION!", Dusty Bob was ready. Knowing the camera was rolling, he felt a powerful surge of adrenaline and cinematic passion he hadn't felt in decades. It was good to know he hadn't lost it, he thought.

Dusty Bob came riding up to the modest ranch house, where the poor family stood out front in their dirty, ragged clothes.

"What do you want, sheriff?" the father asked coldly. He looked tired but determined, and held a shotgun in his hands.

"You know full well why I'm here, Clem," Dusty Bob drawled in his best Old West accent. "You an' your kin have always been right friendly-like to me, so I don't have to tell you how hard it is for me to serve this here notice." He held out the eviction notice. "Why, I think I'd just about rather eat nails soaked in turpentine, I really do, Clem."

"How 'bout this, sheriff," Clem proposed. "We could just stay on our ranch an' you could see fit to just ride off back to town an' forget all about it."

"Well, you know I cain't do that, Clem. Bank's foreclosin' on your ranch. It's my job. There ain't nothin' I can do about it."

"I used to respect you, sheriff," Clem said sadly. "My kids – they looked up to you an' everything law n' order represents. You done a lot for this town, its people – but this, this is just plain wrong, an' you know it."

Dusty Bob hung his head slightly. "Now, you buck up an' be a man, Clem. You be a daddy to them young 'uns there, an' take this here paper."

Clem reached out, took the paper, dropped it in the dirt, stepped on it, and, finally, spat on it.

"Now, you ought not a' done that, Clem," Dusty Bob drawled, disappointed. "I think you best pick up that paper, dust it off, an' put that gum up before someone gets hurt."

"CUT!" Gus shouted, and the camera stopped rolling.

"I'm sorry everybody," Dusty Bob said sheepishly. "That was on *me*."

"Vat in ze world are you talking about?" Gus asked, sweat pouring down his face. "Zat vas *perfection!* We're going on to the next shot now."

"Don't you think we oughta reshoot that scene?" Dusty Bob asked in astonishment. "I said 'gum' instead of 'gun.' Let's do another take – I know I can do better."

"Nobody will even notice," Gus said. "COME ON EVERYBODY – SET UP THE NEXT SHOT!"

They did a few reaction shots of the poor kids and pick-up shots of the family working on the ranch, then Gus told the AD to have everyone break for a thirty-minute lunch.

"We shot all six pages already," Dusty Bob told the AD. "What are we doin' the rest of the day?"

"Mr. Silverman's on his way with the new pages," the AD said. "He'll be here any minute."

Dusty Bob and Jim moseyed over to the catering table to see what was for lunch. It was dry baloney sandwiches on stiff white bread, sweaty cocktail wienies, sardines that had been in the sun too long, stale donuts, and thick, black coffee. Flies swarmed over the rickety table.

"You better steer clear of that stuff," Alvin advised them. "Here, I brought *these* for you." He handed each of them a Mars bar.

"Thank you very kindly, son," Dusty Bob said.

"Don't mention it. You can always count on me, Mr. Bob."

Just then, Bud Silverman arrived with the new pages. "My writer escaped – I mean, *quit* – but don't worry. I've got some very talented kids who are taking a creative writing course in school, and they've got some fantastic ideas!" He quickly distributed copies of the new scene to the actors and director. Dusty Bob scanned them eagerly.

It was a dramatic cave rescue scene, in which a boy and his dog get caught in the middle of a shootout between Dusty Bob and his men and the outlaw gang. Seeking safety, the boy hides in an abandoned mine and falls into a deep pit. His dog alerts the sheriff, who calls a time out with the outlaws and works together with them to rescue the boy.

They had to pack up all the equipment and move everything to another part of the ranch where there was a large hole in the side of a hill that would serve as the mineshaft. It was a complicated scene to shoot: Dusty Bob and his deputies are riding through a pass when they get ambushed by the outlaws hiding in the rocks above. The sheriff's posse dismounts and returns fire, while the boy and the dog are caught in the middle of all the action.

The other actors were all Bud Silverman regulars, and appeared in all his movies. Lou Abelman, who played Clem, the poor rancher, was Bud's dentist. Art Spiegle and Hal Blum, who played Dusty Bob's trusty deputies, were his brothers-in-law. The third deputy was played by a used car salesman named Paulie. Davis Bower, the outlaw gang leader, was a butcher – literally. He had a little meat shop on Pico Boulevard. The rest of the outlaw gang consisted of a barber, a cab driver, two house painters, and an out of work short order cook. The rest of the cast and extras was rounded out with high school students, street bums, retired people from an old folks' home, and Mexican laborers Bud picked up on the street corner at the rate of fifty cents an hour.

Gus Fleming, in a panic over losing the light, allowed only one rehearsal, which came together quite well, with each part of the menagerie of men and horses and boys and dogs doing exactly (or about) what it was supposed to do exactly (or about) when it was supposed to do it. But when Gus shouted "ACTION!" and the camera was rolling, nothing seemed to go right. The posse rode through the pass with their guns drawn, as if anticipating the ambush. The outlaws started firing their blanks at *each other* instead of the sheriff and his posse. The dog was running around barking at the outlaws and then nipping at the heels of the posse's horses. It was complete chaos.

But Gus seemed pleased. "We'll fix it in ze editing room!" he announced cheerfully.

The riskiest shot was of the boy, played by the son of Bud Silverman's tax accountant, falling into the pit, but Gus did it without the use of a stand-in by having several Mexicans lowered into the pit on ropes until they were just out of sight of the camera, and catching the boy when he fell backwards into the gaping hole. Everyone on the set gave a cheer of relief and a round of applause when the boy was caught safely.

Next, the dog was supposed to run to Dusty Bob and alert him about the boy, but he kept running to one of the outlaws – the out of work short order cook. After three takes, it was discovered that the short order cook had one of the gamey baloney sandwiches from the catering table in his pocket. Gus Fleming ordered the cook to give the sandwich to Dusty Bob to put in *his* pocket, and the scene went much better after that. With cameras rolling, the dog ran up to Dusty Bob and started barking for the sandwich.

"What's that, boy?" Dusty Bob asked the dog. The dog continued barking for the sandwich. "I think he's tryin' to tell us somethin'!" The dog kept barking. "I think he's tryin' to tell us the Riley boy needs help!" Thinking fast, Dusty Bob took out a white handkerchief and tied it to a tree branch he found on the ground. He held it up for the outlaws to stop firing.

"Say, what gives, sheriff?" the outlaw leader called out suspiciously.

"This ain't a trick," Dusty Bob promised. "Have your men hold their fire. There's a boy trapped in the mine, an' we all need to work together to get 'im out!"

"Are you sure this ain't a trick?" the outlaw asked.

"I swear on my saintly mother's grave!"

"Well, all right, then," the outlaw said, holstering his gun. "C'mon boys! Let's get this boy out!"

They had to put a baloney sandwich in the boy's pocket to get the dog to lead Dusty Bob and the others to the pit, where the sheriff's men and the outlaws did an exemplary job working together to lower Dusty Bob down on a rope and rescue the boy.

"CUT!" Gus yelled. He stood silent a moment, looking at the ground. Everyone waited to hear what was wrong. Then: "Zat brought a tear to mine eye – and I don't cry easily!"

Dusty Bob thought Gus Fleming was by far the easiest-to-please director he'd ever worked with.

After that, Gus announced there was one more scene to be shot that day, and it involved a dangerous stunt. The crew packed everything up again and everyone drove east a few miles to Vasquez Rocks, a garden of exquisitely gargantuan sedimentary rock formations.

"We need a shot of the sheriff getting shot off his horse und tumbling down one of zeez big rocks," Gus announced. "I like *zis* rock. Set up the camera _here_."

This was where Jim stepped in. The wardrobe lady did him up in Dusty Bob's vest and hat while the crew built a micky-mouse series of steps and ramps to get the horse way up there on top of the rock.

165

After a series of refusals and false starts on the horse's part, they finally coaxed the animal up on top of the rock with a couple of carrots.

"Good, good – now *you* climb up zere und get on ze horse," Gus ordered Jim, who manfully climbed up the apparatus and took his place in the saddle.

"Are we rehearsin' this?" Jim called down to Gus.

"No, no – no rehearsals," Gus called back. "Vee do zis in *one* shot. If you break something, that's it – so be sure und do it right ze _first_ time!"

"Roger that!" Jim called down.

"Make sure ze ramps are out of ze shot," Gus instructed the camera operator. "We don't want to see any ramps. All right: everyone ready?"

"Let's do it!" Jim shouted, a little apprehensively.

"ROLL CAMERA! ACTION!" Gus called out. A prop man fired a blank into the air. "You're hit!" Gus called up to Jim. Jim grabbed his shoulder. "Now fall off ze horse!" Jim slid out of the saddle and fell off the horse. "Now, roll off ze rock!"

Jim started rolling. He rolled, and tumbled, and rolled again down the steep, steep side of the rock. Somewhere along the way, Dusty Bob's Stetson flew off. At the bottom, he hit the ground hard and lay very still.

Everyone held their breath a moment, watching Jim. He didn't move.

"CUT!" Gus shouted, wiping sweat off his face. Dusty Bob, Alvin, and the AD high-tailed it over to Jim. Dusty Bob knelt in the dirt beside him.

"Jim," he said quietly. "Jim, ol' buddy…"

Jim began to moan and stir.

"Are you all right, partner?"

"How's your hat?" Jim asked.

"Oh, I think it's just fine," Dusty Bob smiled.

They got him to his feet.

"Now move your arms and legs," Alvin suggested.

Jim did. "They're all movin'," he said.

He was all right. He had some scrapes on his face, and his clothes were shredded at the elbows and knees – but he was all right.

"That was a mighty fine tumble, partner," Dusty Bob said, brushing the dust off Jim's shoulders.

"All right, let's get zat horse down!" Gus Fleming shouted, obviously pleased. "Zat's it for today, everyone! Now I can go home und haff my heart attack!"

Chapter 15

Dusty Bob was a real trooper on the shoot, doing everything they asked with no complaints. In fact, you would've thought he was making a big-budget feature for Columbia or 20th Century Fox, the way he walked onto the set with a whistle and a smile, a happy "Howdy, how're *you* today?" for every crew member and extra he saw. In his mind, he was still a big star, with an image to uphold. To everyone else, he was just the nice old man who worked harder and took the whole thing more seriously than just about anyone else involved with the movie.

For his part, Dusty Bob soon began to notice that the script didn't actually seem to be all that important to Bud Silverman – or even to Gus Fleming, for that matter. As shooting progressed, they didn't seem to care – or even notice – if he stuck to the script or not. He'd acted in so many westerns that he could pretty much walk his way through each scene with little difficulty. He even got really good at being able to work lines from some of his old movies into this one, without anyone even noticing. Sometimes he just all-out ad-libbed his lines.

When it came right down to it, he ended up just pretty much playing himself in the end. And everyone seemed to be okay with it.

Between shots, he would sit in the shade drinking the bitter black sludge from catering, holding court and regaling cast members and extras with stories of Old Hollywood.

"Ain't you just Falstaff, though," Jim quipped after one such session.

"While I appreciate, and in some ways even admire, your astute nod to the Bard, Jim, I must ask you to remember I don't get out of Arizonee much. Please allow me to enjoy it."

The whole production had moved to Spahn Ranch, where most of the shooting would take place on the Old Western town set. As always, Gus Fleming showed up completely toasted. But, on the positive side of the ledger, he was never a mean drunk.

The first scene Gus wanted to shoot was the outlaw gang terrorizing the townsfolk. The townsfolk were played by an amalgamation of retired people from an old folks' home in Granada Hills, a few street bums, and children on loan from St. Evangeline's Catholic Parochial School in Chatsworth.

The script called for typical scenes of random western terror and violence. The morning was spent capturing these shots in a quick but efficient manner:

- The outlaws sending crank telegrams to the mayor about getting audited, and signing them "President Ulysses S. Grant."
- Tying the general store clerk's apron over his head, and laughing while they watch him run around bumping into things.
- Herding cows into the church during Sunday morning hymn-singing, then putting old washers and Canadian nickels into the collection plate.
- Taking the mayor's toupee off his head, setting it on fire, and using it as a frisbee.
- Lassoing and roping children in the school yard like calves while holding the school marm and making her watch.
- Crossing out the word "Sheriff's" on the Sheriff's Office sign and writing in "Clown's."

At the end of their spree, Dusty Bob confronted them in the saloon, which they had taken over as their new headquarters.

"All right, you've had your fun, now it's time to drag your sorry carcasses out of this establishment an' GIT!"

"Not so fast, Sheriff," the outlaw leader said. He had a barmaid sitting on his lap and was drinking from his own bottle of whiskey. Each outlaw also had his own bottle. "We kinda like it 'round here. This a *real* nice town – folks here got a real sense of humor."

"I'm not about to let you varmints use my town as your own private personal country club an' resort," Dusty Bob swore.

"Well, it isn't these nice townsfolk we got a problem with, Sheriff," the leader said. "It's _you_."

"Me?"

"The name Clayton ring a bell?"

"Cain't says it does."

"Think real hard, Sheriff."

"I'm a thinkin'."

"*Harder.*"

"I said, I'm a THINKIN'."

"I'm Chase Clayton," the outlaw leader declared. "My daddy was named Bartholomew."

"Still don't hear no bells a ringin'," Dusty Bob said.

"*Bart* Clayton."

"*Bart*?"

"Yessiree, Sheriff," Chase Clayton affirmed. "Bart Calyton was my *daddy*."

Dusty Bob's face showed the impact of this information.

"Twenty years ago, you sent him to prison – for robbin' a bank," Chase said. "All the man did was rob a silly ol' bank. An' you had to up and send him to *prison*."

"An' proud to do so, son," Dusty Bob said defiantly.

"Do you know what happened to him in prison, Sheriff?"

"Cain't says I do."

"He was *murdered*. By another inmate. Over a hidden ace of spades he was about to play."

"Ain't it *his* fault, for cheatin' at cards?" Dusty Bob asked.

"No, Sheriff," Chase Clayton grinned. "It's *your* fault – for puttin' him in prison. We don't hold nothin' against these nice townsfolk of yours – this is about *you*."

"Well, what do you propose?"

"You surrender yourself to us – right here, right now," Chase Clayton said in a reasonable tone. "You come with us as our prisoner, an' we'll leave this town peacefully and do no more harm to these fine folks. The decision is yours, Sheriff. You can end this nightmare, right *now*."

"I don't reckon I'll be doin' that, Clayton," Dusty Bob said. "You an' your like cain't just walk in here an' start dictatin' orders to a representative of the law like that."

"Why not?"

"Because it would set a dangerous precedent," Dusty Bob explained patiently. "Law an' order would break down all over the West. Nobody would feel safe. It would be *chaos*."

"It's like that now, Sheriff – that's why they call it the *Wild* West," Clayton argued.

"Well, I'm not takin' orders from no upstart gang of outlaws an' cut-throats," Dusty Bob said. "So I'm givin' you three an' a half hours to pack up an' get out of town – or *else*."

"Or else *what*?"

"Well, you'll just have to wait an' *see*, that's what."

"No, no, no – it don't work that way, Sheriff," Clayton said, shaking his head emphatically. "The outlaws always get to know the 'or else' before they capitulate."

"Not so."

"Is too."

"Is not."

"Says so in the Outlaw Rulebook."

"Oh yeah? Show me."

"Well, as it happens, I haven't got it on me right at the moment, Sheriff. But take my word for it: that's what it says."

"I gotta see it in black an' white."

Clayton looked around the room in exasperation. "Anybody got a copy of the rulebook? This guy's bein' a real stickler, here..."

The other outlaws patted their pockets and shook their heads.

"No one?" Clayton asked in disappointment. "Well then, looks like we find ourselves at somethin' of an impasse, Sheriff..."

"If you an' your gang ain't gone in three an' a half hours, the '*or else*' goes into effect," Dusty Bob threatened, turning to go. Then he thought of something and turned back around. "Oh, an' I'd sure appreciate it if you fellas would tidy up a might an' bus your own tables before you go."

In the next scene, the Sheriff's daughter, Jane – played by Mary Ellen Holcomb, a former high school cheerleading squad captain and current second-year student at the Beautician and Cosmetics Institute of San Fernando Valley, who got the part because her daddy, a podiatrist, was one of Limelight Pictures' financial backers – is horrified to find the poor rancher and his family begging in the streets of the town. Clem, the father, holds a sign that says, "THE SHERIFF TOOK OUR LAND." Jane goes to the café – which she owns and operates – and comes back with lemonade and a slice of chocolate cake, each on its own little plate, for each family member.

"Thank you kindly for the chocolate cake, miss," Clem says respectfully, as his wife and children break down crying out of gratitude but also out of shame that they have been brought to this lowly state of begging in the streets for chocolate cake.

In the following scene, Jane calls a contentious town meeting in the church building to confront her father, the Sheriff.

Jane stood up front with the poor family, heads bowed in shame, hats in hands.

"Well, I 'spect you all know the Evans family," Jane said to the crowd of townsfolk. "Today I found them begging in the streets – that's right, in the streets of _our_ sweet little town, folks. They hadn't eaten in days. If I hadn't brought them chocolate cake, I don't know what would have happened to them. And all because my father – our Sheriff – evicted them from their ranch." The crowd booed.

"That's not true," Dusty Bob protested. "It was the _bank_. I was just doin' my job."

"_Just doing your job_," Jane mocked him. "I suppose, in the holy scriptures, Judas Iscariot was just doing his job…Pontius Pilate was just doing his job…"

"It isn't that way at all, folks," Dusty Bob said. "I actually _like_ the Evans family."

"…Benedict Arnold was only doing his job…" Jane continued.

"I think we get the point, honey," Dusty Bob said to Jane.

"And what about the Clayton Gang, Sheriff?" someone in the mob called out. "What are you gonna do about _them_?"

"I give 'em three an' a half hours to skedaddle, or else," Dusty Bob replied proudly.

"Or else _what_?" someone else demanded.

"I am under no obligation to tell them the '_or what_,'" Dusty Bob maintained. A loud groan went up in the room.

"That's not what the rulebook says!" someone else shouted.

"Hang the rulebook!" Dusty Bob exploded. "If any of you people think the job of Sheriff'n is easy, just come on up here an' give it a try!" He took his badge off and held it over his head. "C'mon – any takers?"

The mob quieted down. "That's what I thought," Dusty Bob said, pinning his star back on. "Now listen, folks, I'm not your enemy. It's the Clayton Gang, an' you best not forget that. We gotta hang together on this thing, an' I promise you I will not rest until every last outlaw has been ousted from our peaceful municipality an' safety has been restored. But I need your support."

"What about the Evans family?" someone called out.

"We'll all come together as a community," Dusty Bob promised. "Every family will take turns housin' an' feedin' 'em 'til they're back on their feet!"

It was dead silent a moment. There seemed to be no enthusiasm for Dusty Bob's idea. "Can't they stay in the hotel?" someone asked sheepishly.

"Yeah – an' eat in the café?" someone else asked.

"Well, we'll work somethin' out," Dusty Bob said. "The point is, we gotta learn how to work together an' take care o' each other, just the way the Good Lord intended."

"CUT!" Gus Fleming shouted. His Teutonic accent seemed to be getting thicker and thicker as filming progressed. "Zat vas beautiful, everyone! I vas deeply moved! It's been a long day, und vee haff accomplished much, my friends. Und now, I think I'm haffing a heart attack – could somebody please drive me to the hospital?"

Gus looked extra pale and sweat poured off his face. He was holding his upper left arm, as if in pain.

Alvin, Dusty Bob, and Jim took him to the nearest hospital in the cloudmobile. Gus was half-delirious, laughing strangely and babbling in German. In the emergency room, the admitting nurse took one look at him and yelled for the orderlies. Two of them came bursting through the swinging doors with a gurney, laid Gus out on it on his back, and disappeared back through the doors.

Alvin, Dusty Bob, and Jim waited, drinking coffee and smoking cigarettes in the ER waiting room. Everyone was smoking – even patients waiting to be seen. The admitting nurse had run out of cigarettes and had to ask Dusty Bob for one. He rolled her one, and she lit up and happily puffed away as she admitted a car accident victim with multiple head injuries that an ambulance had just brought in.

The ER was filling up with a dense cloud of second-hand cigarette smoke. No one even noticed.

Forty-five minutes later, the doctor came out. He was in his late sixties, overweight, and breathing heavily. "You with the kraut?" he asked them.

"That's right, doctor," Dusty Bob said.

The doctor looked at Dusty Bob. He was still wearing his sheriff get-up. "You a *real* sheriff?"

"No, I'm an actor," Dusty Bob chuckled. "We're shootin' a western. This is my associate, Jim Dupree, stuntman *par excellence*, and the young 'un there is Alvin, my driver. The German fella you got in there is the director."

"Hmmm…" the doctor nodded slightly, taking it all in. Then he lit up a cigarette and took a long drag, exhaling the smoke slowly and with perceptible pleasure. "The kraut – he under a lot of stress?"

"As I said, he's the director, so I reckon he's under a good bit o' stress."

"Well, he's suffered a major heart attack," the doctor exhaled more smoke. "I mean *major*. It was really touch and go for a while there."

"Will be pull through, Doc?" Jim asked hesitantly.

"Who?"

"The German fella."

"Oh, yeah – he'll be fine," the doctor said cheerfully, taking another puff. "Gee, I sure like these knew menthols! Really smooth!"

"How long will he be down for?" Dusty Bob asked.

"I want to keep him in the hospital for three days to monitor his progress."

"Three days, huh?" Dusty Bob asked, thinking about the shooting schedule.

"At the minimum," the doctor said. He held the cigarette away from his mouth so he wouldn't blow it out with a protracted, rattling coughing spell that seemed to last minutes. "Excuse me," he said when he'd finally recovered and resumed smoking. "As I said, at the minimum. But it could be *weeks*."

They left the emergency room and drove back to Spahn Ranch. The cast and crew were still there, milling around eating stale donuts. Bud Silverman was there, watching two moving men load the movie camera into a big equipment truck and drive off.

"Gus had a heart attack, boss," Alvin informed Bud.

"Oh, yeah?" Bud asked, as if Alvin had told him it was going to rain tomorrow.

"He's gonna be in the hospital a spell," Dusty Bob added.

"Well, boys, we've got bigger fish to fry," Bud said gravely, watching the equipment truck drive away.

"Where are they takin' the camera?" Jim asked.

"Back to the rental shop," Bud answered, his cigar clamped tightly between his teeth.

"Why's that?" Dusty Bob asked.

"Because I can't pay 'em for the next week," Bud replied.

"But, without a camera, we can't finish the picture," Dusty Bob pointed out.

"Bingo," Bud said.

Bud calmly explained how they would have to shut down production and send everyone home because his main financial backer, an investment broker in Manhattan, had just been indicted by a federal grand jury on charges of perjury, mail fraud, embezzlement, tax evasion, violating sixty-seven Securities and Exchange Commission statutes, and transporting live mammals across state lines for unethical purposes.

"All I knew was, he was some kind of high roller on Wall Street," Bud said. "He never told me he was defrauding every bank in New York City!"

"So that's it, then," Jim said matter-of-factly.

"That's it," Bud agreed. "No camera, no money, no director – no *movie*. I'm really sorry, fellas."

"We got half a picture," Dusty Bob said, not ready to give up.

"We can't release half a movie," Bud said.

"All we need is enough money to finish it," Dusty Bob insisted. "How much you reckon it'll take?"

"Eight – ten – thousand," Bud replied.

"Hell, boys – we can find *that*," Dusty Bob said. "We'll all pitch in an' help!"

"Well, my brother's a talent agent," Bud said. "Van Heflin and Van Johnson are his clients. He's got a lot of contacts. Let me see what I can do."

They drove to the Van Nuys airplane hangar, where Bud worked the phone all night. By six the next morning, he had a list.

"Gentlemen," he said, holding up a piece of paper. "This list represents some of the richest people in L.A. – and they all want to get into the movie business!"

At the top of the list was Dr. Blinkman, who owned a chain of optometry stores throughout southern California. According to Bud, he was mega-wealthy, but very eccentric. "Whatever you do, don't mention his eyes," Bud warned Dusty Bob and Jim. Alvin drove them all out to Dr. Blinkman's palatial Brentwood estate and waited in the car. The three were shown by an immaculately-dressed butler to a veranda at the back of the house, over-looking a large, European-style garden.

A man in his mid-fifties who was just beginning to manifest the ravages of middle-age spread stood on the balcony, dressed in safari gear and holding a shotgun. "PULL!" he shouted, and an Asian servant girl dressed in traditional Thai garb operating a skeet catapult released a gleaming white disk into the air. The man fired the shotgun and missed. The disk landed and shattered somewhere on the grounds.

"Bud Silverman and associates to see you, sir," the butler announced, then turned and disappeared into the mansion.

The man with the shotgun looked at them and said, "Oh. Are you here about the giraffes?"

"Umm, no, Dr. Blinkman," Bud spoke up. "We're here about an investment opportunity. In our movie. I spoke to your secretary on the phone..."

"Oh. I've been waiting to hear from the people about the giraffes," Dr. Blinkman said. It was then that Dusty Bob and Jim both realized Dr. Blinkman was cross-eyed. Once they noticed, it was almost impossible not to stare. "Well, help yourself to some Danish and root beer," the doctor said, indicating a table to the side with platters stacked high with Danish and an elaborate root beer fountain. Two identical four-foot-tall Filipino serving men dressed in tropical shorts, calf socks, and pith helmets flanked the table.

"Uh, thank you," Bud stammered. "That's very kind of you..."

"PULL!" Blinkman shouted, and fired at another white disk as it spiraled through the air. Another miss.

"I use my ex-wife's China for skeet," Dr. Blinkman announced. "I had my lawyers make sure I got it all in the d-i-v-o-r-c-e. It's my little payback." He spelled the word out as if there were young children present. "So – you say you're making a movie?"

"That's right, a western," Bud said eagerly. "Half in the can. Just having some trouble scraping together the money to finish shooting it."

"What studio is this for?" Dr. Blinkman squinted at him.

"Limelight Pictures."

"Never heard of it."

"It's my own company."

"What movies of yours would I know?"

"Well, you may have seen *The Transvestite from Transylvania*," Bud said. "It did quite well at the box office. Or, maybe *Seven Virgins from Venus*. That was kind of a sexy flying saucer movie."

"I've never heard of those movies," Dr. Blinkman said with a shrug. "The kinky stuff – not my style. PULL!" He aimed a long time before firing, but it was another miss. He looked at the barrel of his shotgun as if it were bent or something.

"As I said, this new one's a western," Bud said, attempting to redirect him back to the topic at hand.

"I like westerns," Dr. Blinkman said. "Gary Cooper. John Wayne. Randolph Scott. The Old West. Good stories. Solid American values."

"I couldn't agree with you more," Bud smiled, sensing some progress. "And we just happen to have our own Hollywood legend as the star. Dr. Blinkman, meet Dusty Bob, leading man and star of some of the greatest western movies ever made."

Dr. Blinkman slung the shotgun over his shoulder and reached out to shake Jim's hand.

"No, doctor – _this_ is Dusty Bob!" Bud said.

"Oh, my mistake," Dr. Blinkman said, shaking Dusty Bob's hand. "Oh, I do remember! I used to watch your movies when I was a kid. You sang and played the guitar a little, as I recall."

"That's me, all right," Dusty Bob said proudly.

"Why, I haven't seen one of your movies in years," Blinkman said. "It's like you just disappeared off the face of the earth, or something."

"Well, I run a little ranch out in Ari-zonee now, on the way to the Grand Canyon."

"You don't say."

"This movie could be Dusty Bob's big comeback," Bud said, ready to reel the cross-eyed optometrist in. "A real dark horse, if you'll pardon the pun. It's quite an investment opportunity, and that's why I wanted to give you first crack at it before someone else swoops in and scoops it up."

"Well, you've got to admit he's been out of the movies a long time," Dr. Blinkman observed. "What makes you think today's audience wants to see an old, washed-up, forgotten star again?"

"Oh, he's been getting a lot of buzz lately," Bud lied. "He was featured in a recent *Life* magazine article – you didn't see that?"

"I guess I missed it."

"Well, we'll get you a copy right away," Bud promised.

"*Life* magazine, huh?" Dr. Blinkman asked. "That's a big readership, for sure."

"It doesn't get any bigger," Bud agreed.

"Well, some fellas pitched me a safari movie idea the other day," Dr. Blinkman scratched his chin thoughtfully. "I sure do like safari movies…"

"Safari movies don't do as well at the box office these days," Bud scoffed. "No, this is the 1950s – the decade of the western. Our movie's a sure bet, if you're looking for a good return on your money."

"Who isn't?" Dr. Blinkman laughed.

"You ain't just whistlin' Dixie there," Bud agreed.

"How much are we talking about here?" Blinkman asked.

"Ten – er, *twelve* thousand would be a reasonable number," Bud replied.

"Ten might be *more* reasonable," Blinkman said.

"Absolutely," Bud said quickly. "Ten is a *very* reasonable number."

"And the terms?"

"Your investment back in full – *guaranteed* – plus, let's say five percent of the box office."

"Hmmm." Blinkman thought it over. "Ten percent of the box office sounds better to me."

"How does eight percent sound?"

"I could do eight," Blinkman nodded.

"Great! I'll have my lawyer draw up the contract today," Bud chirped. "I could have it back here this afternoon for you to look over and sign – if that's convenient for you."

Dr. Blinkman looked at Bud oddly – even for a cross-eyed man. "Are you a charlatan, Mr. Silverman? Are you a grifter? A con man, perhaps?"

Bud was taken-aback. "Why, no…not at all, doctor…"

"Then what you're telling me is that you're a man of honor?"

"Well – I like to think so –"

"A dignified, upstanding man of your word? A man of untarnished, unparalleled integrity?"

"Dr. Blinkman, I can assure you –"

"Then why do we need a written contract?' Dr. Blinkman asked suddenly.

"Well, er – it's the standard way of doing –"

"I like to do business on a _handshake_, sir," Dr. Blinkman regally declared. "Two honorable gentlemen, making an agreement, pressing the flesh, as it were, in a bond of brotherhood and trust. Do you find that disagreeable in any way, Mr. Silverman?"

"Well, no – I suppose not," Bud stammered.

"Good," Dr. Blinkman said, extending his hand. Bud shook it. "Now let's get you your money!" He led them inside to his ornate, wood-paneled office, and sat down behind his large oak desk. He fished a key out of his pocket and unlocked a desk drawer. He pulled a strongbox out and carefully entered the combination to open it. He took out two stacks of five thousand dollars and pushed them across the desk to Bud.

Bud just stared at it. "Uh, that's – that's Monopoly money, doctor."

Nonplussed, Dr. Blinkman smiled and added another stack to the pile.

"Actually, that's, um…that's just more Monopoly money," Bud said.

Dr. Blinkman smiled up at them like a cross-eyed loon. Bud, Dusty Bob, and Jim turned and silently filed out of his office.

"Fellas – where are you going?" Blinkman called after them. "Don't you want your money?"

The second name on the list was Al Toledo. Al owned a string of seedy adult theaters all over the southland and the Inland Empire. Bud, Dusty Bob, and Jim met him at his office above one of his theaters on Vermont Avenue. When they walked into his office, it was like stepping back in time. It was done up like a Turkish harem. Al met them wearing a fez hat and a velvet smoking jacket with no shirt underneath. A large, gold Isis medallion hung around his neck and nestled gleamingly in the shrubbery of thick black fur on his chest.

He had a pencil mustache and wore sunglasses, even in the dimly-lit Mediterranean-style office.

He welcomed his visitors and motioned for them to sit on an exotically plush sofa opposite his desk. Then he sat down behind his desk, opened a drawer, and shouted, "MAYMUN – GELMEK, GELMEK!" into it. A rhesus monkey wearing a tiny fez and a red

Aladdin vest popped out of the drawer, climbed up his arm, and perched on his shoulder for the duration of the meeting.

"Before business, we must enjoy refreshments," Al said, clapping his hands twice. A side door opened and a six-foot-three-inch Jane Russell look-alike wearing a tight meter maid uniform entered with a serving tray. She put the tray down on his desk. It had strong, aromatic Turkish coffee and a bowl of dates on it.

"CEKIP GITMEK!" Al barked, and the busty Amazon quickly left the room. "You like Ophelia?" he asked them, smiling.

"Sure," Dusty Bob said. The others nodded.

"I found her waiting tables at Cantor's Deli," Al confided, pouring coffee for everyone – except the monkey. "I just couldn't leave her in such a place! I doubled her salary and brought her here. Life in this town isn't easy – especially for a girl with her type of...*impediment*. She has turned out to be surprisingly talented, however – even with the hunched back. I just couldn't get along without her, I'm afraid." He lifted his dark glasses a fraction of a second and winked knowingly.

Dusty Bob, Bud, and Jim all looked at each other – none of them had noticed a hunched back on the girl.

They sipped coffee quietly. Dusty Bob had had plenty of dark, sludgy trail coffee in his day, but this Turkish stuff really took the cake.

"It's an acquired taste," Al said, mock apologetically. "Please try the dates. I import them fresh from Marrakesh every week on their own chartered flight."

Jim reached for a date. "I've never had one of these before."

"I think I'll pass," Dusty Bob said; Al looked slightly offended. He sulkingly picked up a date and handed it to the monkey on his shoulder. "Siddhartha likes them well enough," he said, lovingly stroking the monkey's fur.

"Are you familiar with the mysteries of the Tantra?" Al asked, out of the blue.

"Cain't says I am," Dusty Bob answered quite honestly.

"Look into it, my friend," Al smiled. "My personal energy and stamina have increased six-fold since my discovery of tantric yoga. Its benefits far exceed simply making love-making more pleasurable. No, it's a spiritual journey, my friend. A journey of enlightenment. I highly recommend it."

"Well, I'll hafta do some readin' up on it," Dusty Bob said.

For some reason, Al was focused solely on Dusty Bob, almost ignoring the others.

"What about ancient Babylonian poetry? Have you read any, cowboy?"

"I reckon not," Dusty Bob replied.

"It's a passion of mine," Al confessed with a shy smile. "Gilgamesh and his trusted companion Enkidu make a six-day journey to the legendary Cedar Forest, where they defeat its guardian, Humbaba, and cut down the Sacred Cedar. When they kill the sacred Bull of Heaven in combat, the goddess Ishtar punishes Enkidu with a fatal illness, and Gilgamesh begins a sacred journey to discover all knowledge and the secret of eternal life. At the end of his quest, he meets the Akkadian goddess of carnal love, Shamhat, who teaches him that life has no real meaning beyond changing your underwear daily and keeping on good terms with your neighbors."

"Sounds mighty interestin'," Dusty Bob observed.

Al Toledo clapped his hands again, this time *three* times. A smaller door in the wall flew open and a midget wearing a *commedia dell'arte* clown costume with a white-painted face entered carrying a hookah apparatus. He left it on Al's desk and scurried back through the little door in the wall.

"Will you smoke, gentlemen?" Al asked, picking up the hookah mouthpiece and taking a drag.

"Don't mind if I do," Dusty Bob said, taking the makings out of his shirt pocket and starting to roll a cigarette. Bud chomped down and puffed away on his cigar. Jim just sat there chewing on a date.

"Like Gilgamesh, I am on such a quest," Al finally declared. "I am on a similar journey to discover the meaning of life and eternal enlightenment. Why are _you_ here, cowboy?"

"Well now, that's a weighty question, Al," Dusty Bob confessed. "I've never really been inclined to ponderin' the meanin' of life an' eternity an' enlightenment an' such. I've always left that to the clever fellas – the philosophers, an' professors an' the like –"

"No, I mean – why are you _here_, in my office?"

"Well, me an' these fellas here is makin' a western picture about a sheriff who's on his own kinda journey, I reckon you could say. See, he's tryin' to save his town from a violent gang of outlaws, but the townsfolk – an' even the sheriff himself, in a way – have lost faith in him."

"And he must, in some way, gain back their confidence so he can save them," Al added.

"That's about it right there, mister," Dusty Bob said.

"Intriguing," Al Toledo said, again stroking his monkey absent-mindedly. "And you play this sheriff?"

"I do, sir."

"You have spoken well," Al said pleasantly. "I will be your partner in this venture, cowboy. I want to help you make this movie."

He wrote them a check on the spot for ten thousand dollars. Bud took it to his bank and deposited it that afternoon. The next day his bank told him the check had bounced. Bud took the check to Al Toledo's bank to straighten things out.

"There's no mistake, sir," the teller told him. "This account only has thirty-four dollars and sixty-three cents in it."

They went back to Al's office and told him the check had bounced.

"I am so embarrassed," Al apologized sincerely. "That damned bank does this all the time. This is it! I'm going to close out my account with them and take my business somewhere else! I will write you a new check out of one of my other accounts, right this moment. And again, my sincerest apologies…"

He wrote a check from a different bank. *That* check bounced. "This account only has twenty-seven dollars and eighty-three cents in it," the teller at that bank told Bud. They went back to Al Toledo, who was very apologetic. After three more checks bounced, they gave up and went to the next name on Bud's list.

Sid Kaufman had a very nice little office tucked between a men's clothing store and an upscale antique shop on Santa Monica Boulevard.

Sid was a small, thin, well-groomed, quiet-spoken man with glasses. The kind of man you probably wouldn't take a second look at on the bus or in a crowded restaurant, but who, upon further inspection, could very well be quite wealthy.

He looked impeccably business-like in an expensive tailored blazer and tasteful red tie. "I invest money for a number of clients who, for various reasons, prefer to remain anonymous," he told Bud Silverman and his two cowboy companions. He went on to explain that among his many clients were several titans of industry, a Belgian arms dealer, an Arab sheik, and the ruler of a small European duchy.

Bud explained to him why they were there, and Sid listened carefully without interrupting. He seemed very knowledgeable and serious during the ensuing discussion, throwing out important-sounding business terms like "back-end disposable capital" and "cash-flow accruals" with an expert's flair. The language of business and commerce seemed to roll quite effortlessly off his tongue, as it were.

Furthermore, he said he liked the idea of the movie and thought it made good business sense to have a star of Dusty Bob's caliber on board. All things considered, everything seemed to be going their way, especially when Sid agreed to finance the rest of the movie out of his own personal resources.

"Let's meet tonight at The Brown Derby to iron out the details," Sid cheerfully suggested. "I'll bring the check. Shall we say, seven-thirty?"

Then, it happened. Sid Kaufman stood up to shake hands, and they saw that he wasn't wearing any pants. Just a very nice pair of expensive silk paisley boxers.

Sid gave no indication that anything was amiss. They all shook hands with him, as if the situation were completely normal.

They got to The Brown Derby at six forty-five and waited until eight-thirty.

Sid never showed.

That was because half an hour after their meeting that day, Sid got into his car – without pants – and drove himself to a nearby psychiatric facility, where he calmly committed himself for a nice, long rest.

Next up was a trio of well-dressed men in their fifties. Their names were Carmine, Tony, and Rocco, and they insisted on meeting in a warehouse just southeast of downtown. Eschewing the usual pleasantries and polite small talk, they got right down to business, telling their guests that their many enterprises included docks, trucking, cargo, municipal contracting, some light union connections, and ladies' apparel.

"I like ladies' apparel," Carmine said with affection.

"Me, too," Tony said.

"Give me a nice, satiny chiffon frock," Rocco said. "Goosebumps."

"Or a taffeta evening gown with pumps," Carmine said.

"Ooooh, tell me about it!" Tony cooed, rubbing his hands together.

Next on the list was Dick Fishman, owner of a chain of low-priced seafood restaurants called "Dick's Crab Shack." He wanted them to work a plug for seafood into the movie.

"Er – it's a *western*," Bud said.

"Yeah, yeah – but maybe they see something in the movie, you know – like a Maine lobster, or a nice halibut – and after the show they feel like stopping off at a Crab Shack on the way home for a nice dinner. See what I mean?"

Cornelius Meeks owned a chain of budget mortuaries called "Rest Nicely." Their most affordable plan – "Eternal Austerity" – featured a plain pine box lined with cotton batting and a wreath of whatever flowers the local florist was throwing out that day, for a mere two hundred twenty-five dollars. "Rustic Rest" was also a very popular option at two seventy-five.

Bud, exhausted with the process, threw all caution to the wind and asked for ten thousand dollars.

"I bet if you really tried, you could do it for five thousand," Cornelius countered.

Bud knew they couldn't finish the movie for five thousand, but he took the offer. At this point, *something* was better than nothing.

Always the shrewd bargainer, Cornelius said he would give them the five thousand – in cash – if Dusty Bob would agree to do a TV commercial for his mortuaries. And if they found a part in the movie for his niece, Iris.

"Done!" Bud said, desperate to walk away with some cash in his pocket.

Cornelius handed Bud the cash, and Dusty Bob shot the commercial the next day. It was simple, direct, sincere, philosophical – leaning heavily on ethos and pathos to get its point across. Dusty Bob wrote the copy himself, and he even called in an old friend for a cameo appearance.

The set was Old West in theme, with a Conestoga wagon in the background. "Hello folks, Dusty Bob here. In the Old West, life could be cut short in a heartbeat. Today, the Grim Reaper doesn't always strike so fast. That gives us more time to plan an' prepare just how we wanna send our loved ones off to that Big Cattle Drive in the Sky. Eternity – it's a long time, isn't it? Don't you want the security an' peace o' mind of knowin' your loved one's are gonna be taken care of by kind, carin', gentle professionals when their time comes?

And, all at a cost most honest workin' folks can afford. So, if you wanna be able to send Granny off with dignity an' style, without takin' a mortgage out on your homestead, come on down an' see the fine folks at Rest Nicely. You won't regret it. Right, Bela?"

Bela Lugosi sat up in an open coffin, all decked out in his cheesy vampire getup. "That's right, Dusty Bob!" he said in his unintelligible Hungarian accent. "Rest Nicely gets the Count's official Transylvania seal of approval!" Then he tried to smile, but it was real creepy.

The day after the commercial aired on three Los Angeles TV stations, Rest Nicely Funeral Homes, Incorporated, reported a thirty-six percent increase in walk-in business. Cornelius Meeks quickly signed Dusty Bob up to do three more commercials.

"Well, this'll get the camera back and pay for a couple of weeks of shooting," Bud said, waving the wad of cash around. "But we still need more to finish the movie." There was one more name on the list: Mrs. Lovelace, a rich widow who hadn't left her home in Los Feliz in over twenty years.

"Her hubby owned half of San Fernando Valley when he kicked the bucket," Bud told Dusty Bob and Jim. "She's gotta be *loaded*."

Alvin drove them to Mrs. Lovelace's home adjacent to Griffith Park – a huge, crumbling mansion with unkempt grounds and overgrown gardens. A mousy, middle-aged woman in a long dress and little round glasses – Mrs. Lovelace's personal secretary – answered the door. The secretary – Miss Minnie – let them in and showed them to a once-opulent parlor that immediately transported them several decades back in time. The curtains were drawn. There were cobwebs everywhere. The dust was stifling. The yellow light emanating from the ancient Craftsman lampshades was barely sufficient to see.

"Maybe the old bat's not as rich as you thought," Jim said to Bud.

"These gentlemen wish to speak with you, Ma'am," Miss Minnie said in a barely audible voice.

"Very well." The voice came from a plush, high-backed chair in the middle of the room. "And Miss Minnie: bring coffee for everyone."

"Yes, Ma'am." Miss Minnie curtsied, leaving the room.

As their eyes adjusted to the dim light, they could just begin to make out a small, gray-haired woman sitting in the huge chair, with what looked like a large rodent in her lap.

Dusty Bob was just about to call out, "*Watch out, lady – there's a big ol' rat in your lap"* when the diminutive widow ordered them to sit down on an ancient settee. The no-compromise tone in her voice compelled them to do so.

"I don't get many visitors anymore," Mrs. Lovelace said, stroking the rodent in her lap affectionately. "At one time, during the Golden Age, this house entertained the likes of Charlie Chaplin. William Randolph Hearst. Douglas Fairbanks, Jr. Mary Pickford. Gloria Swanson. William Mulholland. Louis B. Mayer –"

"I knew most of them folks you're talkin' about, Ma'am," Dusty Bob said.

"Oh? And just _who_ might you be, my good sir?"

"My name's Dusty Bob, Ma'am. I was in the pictures – the _westerns_ – back in them days you're talkin' about."

"I didn't care for *westerns*," the widow said disdainfully. "The sophisticated screwball comedies of Ernst Lubitsch and Preston Sturges – King Vidor and George Cukor – were more my cup of tea."

"I knew them fellas, too, Ma'am," Dusty Bob said wistfully. "I remember talkin' horses with that Vidor feller – an' George Cukor actually asked me to teach 'im some rope tricks! I reckon Hollywood was a smaller town back in them days. It sure has grown some, though."

Miss Minnie came in with a tray of coffee. She poured a cup for each of them, and then left. Dusty Bob sipped the coffee – it was cold, and tasted like it had been brewed days ago. Mrs. Lovelace drank it like there was nothing wrong with it. Then she opened a candy box on a table next to her and took out a bon-bon. Instead of eating it herself, she placed it between her lips and allowed the rodent to snatch it out of her mouth with its teeth.

The three men watched this unpleasant display in disbelief. Dusty Bob could hear Bud retching a little.

"Agamemnon has such a sweet tooth," Mrs. Lovelace laughed obliviously. "He certainly loves his treats…"

"Excuse me for askin', Ma'am," Dusty Bob said, setting his coffee cup on a table. "But why are you holdin' that big ol' rat on your lap like that?"

"This is not a rat, sir," the widow declared. "It's a _marmot_."

"Didn't mean no offense, Ma'am," Dusty Bob apologized.

"Oh, I'm not offended in the least," Mrs. Lovelace said brightly. "I find your simple-minded country rubisms and rustic charm quite refreshing and entertaining, I assure you."

"Well, thank you kindly, Ma'am," Dusty Bob said.

"Please, tell me more about your experiences in Hollywood," the widow instructed him. "It's so difficult to find *anyone* suitable to reminisce with these days."

"Well, I'd sure like that, Ma'am," Dusty Bob smiled. While they continued their trip down memory lane, Bud managed to sneak away to take a look around the house. The old lady was so caught up in Dusty Bob's stories that she didn't even notice him leave.

The first room Bud went into was full of taxidermied marmots in various poses – previous Agamemnons going back decades – no doubt poisoned into early deaths by too much sugar. With a shudder, he left the room and closed the door.

What he found in the next room truly astounded him. There were shopping bags, duffle bags, old chocolate boxes, Quaker Oats cartons – even suitcases – all stuffed to the brim and overflowing with *cash*.

In shock, he left the room and closed the door. He went to the next room and opened the door. It was the same thing – all manner of containers, bags, and suitcases – all stuffed with cash. He tried the next three rooms and found the same thing.

He froze, his mind racing – *an entire mansion, with rooms and rooms full of cash!*

"There must be millions," Bud whispered. "Millions and millions and *millions…*"

All he needed was five, ten thousand more to finish the movie. *She wouldn't even miss it!* She was about ninety years old – how long was she going to *live*, anyway?

He'd made up his mind. He went back into the last room, closed the door, and started stuffing cash into his pockets. Fifties, hundreds – into his blazer pockets, into his trouser pockets, into his socks. When he'd filled every possible space, he looked around and realized he hadn't even made a dent in the piles and piles of cash.

And this was only one room!

Flush from his exertions and sweating profusely, he left the room and closed the door behind him. He turned around and jumped when he saw Miss Minnie standing there in the hall.

"Can I help you?" she asked, in her mousey voice.

"I-I-I," he stammered, trying desperately to compose himself. "Umm, bathroom?"

"Down the hall to the left."

He walked down the hall and ducked into the bathroom. He locked the door behind him and went to the sink and splashed water on his face.

"Oh, my God," he said to his reflection in the mirror. Then he started laughing uncontrollably. He couldn't stop laughing. There was a mousey knock at the door.

"You all right in there?" It was Miss Minnie.

"Uh, yeah. Yeah, I'm fine." Bud looked in the mirror again and tried to compose himself. Fifties and hundreds were sticking out of his blazer pockets. He quickly stuffed the bills back down and left the bathroom.

When he rejoined the others in the parlor, they were still talking. The old lady had even engaged Jim in some of the conversation.

"Let's go," Bud said tightly, chomping nervously on his cigar. "We gotta _go_."

No one noticed how stiffly he was standing, how padded his blazer had suddenly become.

Dusty Bob looked up at him. "But we haven't asked her about –"

"I'm good," Bud said. "I mean, _we're_ good. Let's go now –" his eyes kept involuntarily darting toward the doorway.

"Well, we'll have to continue our conversation another time," the old lady said, petting Agamemnon, who was now sleeping curled up in her lap like a cat. "I thoroughly enjoyed talking with you, Dusty Bob and Jim Dupree. I'll have Miss Minnie see you out."

"That won't be necessary," Bud said, a little too forcefully. "I mean, we can find our way out. Ourselves. C'mon, fellas – I know the way. Out of the house and back to the car. Just follow me, now."

They left the mansion and got back in the car, where Alvin was waiting. "Drive. Fast. _Now_." Bud said nervously.

"Why didn't you ask her about the money?" Dusty Bob asked Bud.

"It wasn't necessary," Bud said as they pulled away from the Lovelace mansion. "I have it now. The money. Don't ask _how_. I've got enough to finish the movie _and_ promote it with style. Boys, we are back in business!"

188

Chapter 16

The next morning, Gus Fleming was released from the hospital and Alvin drove the whole gang over to pick him up. They brought a cake and some flowers and champagne to celebrate. But just as the orderly was wheeling him out in the chair, Gus suddenly went pale and clasped his chest dramatically.

"I think I'm haffing another heart attack," he gasped breathlessly. The orderly calmly turned him around and wheeled him back inside the hospital.

They all got back in the clunker and Alvin drove them out to the location at Spahn Ranch. The camera was paid up and the rental shop had just delivered it that morning. There was a whole day of shooting ahead of them, but no director.

"Why don't you do it?" Bud asked Dusty Bob. "Just 'til Gus gets out of the hospital."

Dusty Bob thought about it a while. "Well, I reckon I could, at that." He certainly had a lot of experience on movie sets over the years, and he'd directed *Dry River* himself, after all. He was already making up most of his dialog, anyway. Wearing one more hat at this point in the production shouldn't be that difficult, he reasoned.

Dusty Bob took to directing like a duck to Echo Park. It was a simple, no-frills western, and he was able to pick up right where Gus left off pretty seamlessly. The cast and crew liked his folksy ways, and did whatever he asked. Before too long, things were humming along like a well-oiled machine, and it looked like the picture would come in only slightly over schedule and over budget. Dusty Bob knew that was almost to be expected in the movie business.

During breaks in the shooting, Jim suggested they try to track down Max Hoffman. He had convinced Dusty Bob that Max could try to write new scenes for *Rendezvous in Reno* to try to prolong his precious encounters with Olivia.

"Don't you see?" Jim asked. "It has to be *his* words, or the whole thing doesn't work."

"Where do you reckon we start?" Dusty Bob asked.

"Haze MacAffrey," Jim replied. Dusty Bob hadn't heard that name in ages.

Haze MacAffrey was a buddy from the old Hollywood days, a character actor known for playing the comical but ultimately wise sidekick in westerns. Jim had heard he owned a bar on Western Avenue called "The End of the Rope." They had Alvin drive them over and found it pretty easily. Inside, the place was done up in an old saloon theme, although a bit on the shabby side. Headshots of old western actors lined the walls – including Dusty Bob – and kitschy movie memorabilia cluttered the place. A single old man nursed a beer at one of the rickety tables.

"Well, looky-here what the polecat done drug in," a familiar voice from behind the bar said. Haze MacAffrey sat in a wheelchair on a raised platform behind the bar, allowing him to tend bar from his sitting position. Both of his legs were gone. "Last I heard, you boys was out in – Ari-zonee, was it?"

"That's right, Haze," Jim said.

"What brings you back to your ol' stompin' grounds? Couldn't be the weather…"

"We're out here temporarily, shootin' a picture," Dusty Bob replied. "What happened to your legs, Haze?"

"Diabetes," Haze said, pouring three shots of whiskey. "Doctor took 'em about ten years ago."

"That's a shame," Jim said.

"I wasn't really usin' 'em for much, anyway," Haze shrugged, downing his whiskey. "Just gettin' around, an' such."

"Nice place you got here," Dusty Bob said. He and Jim sat at the bar and downed their shots. Haze poured three more. "These better be on the house."

"For old time's sake, boys," Haze laughed. "For old time's sake."

"I see you're still pourin' the cheap stuff," Dusty Bob said.

"No reason to get fancy at my age," Haze replied.

"How'd you end up in the saloon business, anyways?" Jim asked.

"Well, when I couldn't get around like before an' the parts started dryin' up, I took all my movie money – what my ex-wife left me with, anyway – an' bought this place."

"Is it always this busy?" Jim asked.

"All the regulars keep dyin' off," Haze answered. "You know how it is."

"Not a very healthy lifestyle, is my guess," Jim quipped.

"Tell me about this picture," Haze said. "Is it a _real_ movie?"

"Well, it ain't *imaginary*, if that's what you mean," Dusty Bob replied, a might prickly. "Fella's payin' real money, but I'll tellya, Haze – it just ain't nothin' like the old days."

"No, it ain't, boys," Haze agreed ruefully. "I'm here to tell ya. Everything's changed. This whole town. They got this method actin' now – Brando, James Dean. This new fella – Paul *Newman*. Pretty faces, but so vulgar – no class, no *style*. There's no *movie stars* no more. And TV – just turned this town upside down. Even the neighborhood's goin' to hell, with the Koreans an' the Filipinos an' the Mexicans movin' in everywhere. No, you boys did right leavin' this dump an' movin' to Ari-zonee."

"Listen, Haze: we wanted to ask you about a fella we're lookin' for," Jim said.

"Well, I'm afraid David O. Selznick hasn't been in here in a while, boys," Haze joked.

"The fella we're lookin' for is Max Hoffman," Jim said.

"Max Hoffman," Haze repeated, thinking. "You mean the writer?"

"That's the one," Jim replied. "You know if he's still kickin'?"

"Cain't says I do," Haze answered, rubbing the gray stubble on his chin.

"Somebody's gotta know," Dusty Bob posited.

"There ain't that many of us left," Haze observed sadly. "Say, you know who might be able to help you? Andy."

"Devine?" Jim asked.

"The same," Haze nodded. "I seem to remember Max doin' some writin' for a TV show Andy was workin' on a while back – oh, about six or seven years ago, now."

"Well, thanks a heap, Haze," Dusty Bob drawled, knocking back his second pour. "You been mighty helpful."

"Take care, Haze," Jim said, getting up to leave. "Don't work too hard, now. Slow down some an' take a rest every once in a while. This break-neck pace'll kill ya."

"Stop by anytime, boys," Haze grinned. "You know where to find me. I cain't get too far in this contraption."

They knew right where to find Andy Devine: at the Bob's Big Boy restaurant on Van Nuys Boulevard, eating pancakes. They walked right up to his favorite booth by the big window looking out on the busy street.

"Well, some things never change, do they?" Dusty Bob said. "Still like them flapjacks, I see."

Andy looked up at them, maple syrup dripping down his chin. "Well, I'll be! Sit down, boys – I'll buy you a stack."

"I'll pass on the flapjacks," Dusty Bob said, sliding into the seat opposite Andy. "But I reckon my tank *is* a might empty." Jim sat down next to him.

"How long has it been, fellas?" Andy asked, in his familiar wheezy rasp. Dusty Bob always thought it sounded like a squeaky hinge flapping in a windstorm.

"Oh, I'd say at least a lifetime," Dusty Bob guessed. The waitress came by, and Dusty Bob ordered a single egg, poached for exactly two and a half minutes, and a cup of black coffee. Jim ordered hashbrowns and lots of ketchup.

"Gee, I was so sorry to hear about Olivia, Bob," Andy said.

"Well, what's done is done, and the sands o' time have one helluva way of fillin' in old fissures," Dusty Bob rhapsodized.

"I'm not sure what that means, but you're sure lookin' good, *amigo*."

"I reckon I should be grateful for the youthful essence that clings to me like a spring mist," Dusty Bob said. "I could sure look a whole lot worse, at my advanced age."

"You been keepin' yourself busy, I hear," Jim said to Andy.

"I been workin'," Andy said, tucking into another multi-layered forkful of hotcakes. "What can I do? The offers just keep rollin' in. Mostly television."

"That's just mighty fine, Andrew." That's what Dusty Bob always called him. "Take it while you can get it, is what I always say."

"You do?" Jim challenged. "I've never heard you say that before."

"Don't be so literal, Jim," Dusty Bob said. "It's just a figure of speech."

"We just came from ol' Haze," Jim said to Andy, ignoring Dusty Bob now.

"Oh yeah?" Andy's face lit up. "What the dickens is *he* up to these days?"

"Oh, you know," Jim said. "Runs a little saloon over on Western. Don't have no legs no more."

"Aw, that's a shame."

"Seems to be adjustin' to it, all right," Dusty Bob said. "What's the laziest man alive need legs for, anyway?"

"That's just what I was thinkin'," Andy wheezed.

The food came. Dusty Bob investigated the temperature and consistency of his poached egg with his index finger and thumb, then pushed it away in disappointment. "Dagnabbit. I told her two an' a half minutes!"

"You can tell how long it was cooked with your index finger and thumb?" Jim asked skeptically.

"You doubt my acumen?" Dusty Bob bristled.

"Heaven forbid," Jim said. "I'm just sayin' there's no way to tell how long an egg was cooked by fingerin' it."

"With the pedestrian digits of the common man, no," Dusty Bob said, visibly riled. "My fingers have always had an uncanny sensitivity to temperature, texture, pressure, and consistency."

"Since _when_?" Jim was almost apoplectic at Dusty Bob's shameless bravado.

"Since all my _life_!" Dusty Bob snapped.

"Simmer down, now," Jim said. "It's just a poached egg…"

"You dare to question my well-documented, highly-attuned senses, and then tell me to '_simmer down_?'" Dusty Bob asked incredulously. His voice was getting noticeably louder. A few diners turned to look.

"_Documented_?" Jim challenged. "I must've missed that."

"Well, takin' a man's word for it ought to be enough," Dusty Bob huffed. "I swear, Jim – you'd argue with a gnat if it landed on your shoulder an' told you it was a fly."

"I just value truthfulness, is all," Jim said.

"That's rich, comin' from a man who drowns his hashbrowns in a sea of ketchup," Dusty Bob retorted. "Would you like some taters with your ketchup, Jim?"

The waitress came back. "Is there something wrong with the egg, sir? I can send it back and bring you another one."

"I'm not hungry anymore," Dusty Bob pouted.

Andy laughed. "You two sound just like an old married couple!"

"Speakin' of Haze," Jim said, remembering why they were there in the first place, "he's the one told us to look you up."

"Oh?"

"We're lookin' for Max Hoffman," Jim continued. "Haze said he might've written somethin' for one of your TV shows."

Andy put his fork down and thought about it. "Come to think of it, he wrote an episode or two for *Wild Bill Hickok* – back in, oh, fifty-one, or fifty-two. But I haven't even seen him since then."

"Can you give us any kind of clue where to find him?" Dusty Bob asked.

"Let's see…yeah, I remember somethin' about Max's son gettin' hitched to Smiley Burnette's daughter a while back."

"Does Smiley still own that coffee shop on Hollywood Boulevard?" Jim asked.

"Sure does," Andy replied. "If you hurry, you might be able to catch him there. He likes to help out with the noon-time rush."

The place was called "The Checkered Shirt." Dusty Bob and Jim walked in and saw Smiley right away, in the kitchen in the back cooking over a hot grill.

"You're a BIG star now, Smiley," Dusty Bob called out. "What you back there cookin' scrambled eggs for?"

"I like to cook, Bob," Smiley called back, without missing a beat. "Don't you remember?"

"That I do, partner," Dusty Bob said. "There was a venison stew seasoned with oregano an' chili peppers that stands out in my mind, if I'm not mistaken."

"That trail ride in the Sierras – what was it – thirty-eight, thirty-nine?" Smiley asked.

"Somethin' like that."

"Weren't them the days, though?" Smiley reminisced. "Well, sit down, boys. Want some scrambled eggs?"

"Well, *one* of us just ate," Jim said, looking at Dusty Bob.

"Can you make me a two an' a half minute poached egg?" Dusty Bob asked. "Apparently, it was too complicated for the culinary experts at Big Boy to handle."

"That's my specialty!"

They sat down at the counter, and a middle-aged waitress poured coffee for them. "So, you know the old man, huh?"

"We go a ways back," Dusty Bob admitted.

"Say, can you get him to raise my salary?" the waitress said loud enough for Smiley to hear. "The old geezer's a real cheapskate!"

"Nothing I can do about that," Dusty Bob said. "Ol' Smiley's always been tight-fisted with a nickel."

"He's not the only one," Jim said.

"I heard that," Dusty Bob said.

"I was countin' on it."

Two and a half minutes later, Smiley brought Dusty Bob his egg. He squeezed it delicately between his forefinger and thumb, and smiled. "Ah! Smiley, you're a genius!"

"So, how's life been treatin' you, Bob?" Smiley inquired.

"Life's treatin' me pretty good, these days," Dusty Bob beamed. "I'm livin' in Ari-zonee an' engaged to be married, as a matter of fact."

"Congratulations, you ol' coot!" Smiley exclaimed. "Who's the lucky gal?"

"Blanch Goodreau," Jim said dismissively.

"Now Jim, don't start," Dusty Bob gently cautioned. "Jim don't like my new fee-ance. He thinks she's too bossy."

"She *is* mighty bossy," Jim said. "An' schemin', an connivin', an' –"

"Now don't ruin this nice little visit, Jim," Dusty Bob said. "Smiley don't wanna hear all this juicy gossip an' dirty laundry an' such –"

"Who says?" Smiley asked, with a wink.

"Let's just put it this way," Dusty Bob said. "Jim seems to think my new fee-ance doesn't want me for my dazzlin' wit, intellectual brilliance, social graces, an' natural good looks."

"She wants him for his money," Jim said.

"No offense, Bob, but – _you_ have money?" Smiley asked.

"Will have, as soon as that new interstate comes through by my place," Dusty Bob explained.

"That's what she's bankin' on," Jim added. "Pun intended."

"Not to change the subject, but it's time to change the subject," Dusty Bob declared. "Jim an' me are on a manhunt for Max Hoffman. Now, we just been with Andrew Dee-vine, an' he told us Max's son is hitched to your daughter. Is that true?"

"Not no more," Smiley said. "They broke up two years ago. Divorced. She caught him cheatin' with a twenty-year-old cigarette girl from the Stork Club. Caught him in the very act, so to speak."

"Sorry to hear that," Dusty Bob said. "Do you know how we could reach him?"

"They don't talk. She cut off all communication. I don't even know where he lives. All I know is, he's an entertainment reporter at *Variety* – if that helps."

195

They left Smiley's coffee shop and stepped out onto Hollywood Boulevard. Dusty Bob looked down and saw Tom Mix's star in the sidewalk. Something hit him – *hard*. All the nostalgia, the fancy cars, fine dinners, big house in Beverly Hills – *Olivia* – it all swept over him like a tidal wave.

"We can go to *Variety* later," he told Jim. "I wanna find my star." They started to walk east, then Dusty Bob turned around and looked west. Confused, he looked at the nearby street signs.

"Darned if I can remember where it was," he said, feeling old. "I thought it was near the corner of Wilcox. Or was it Schrader?" They walked to both corners, but couldn't find his star.

"I think it was Cherokee," Jim said. They checked that corner, but it wasn't there.

While they were walking around like fools looking for it, a huge, gleaming, brand-new Cadillac pulled up to the curb and honked at them.

"Well, I'll be darned: if it isn't Dusty Bob!" a familiar man's voice bellowed out the driver's window. "An' Big Jim Dupree, too!"

They peered inside the massive automobile and saw a couple – a man and a woman – both dressed in stylishly expensive leisure wear. The man wore a tailored tan blazer over a white silk shirt, open wide at the collar.

It was Roy Rogers. "You fellas lost? I've got a map of the stars somewhere in the glovebox here, if you need it."

"Just stretchin' our legs a little bit – that's all," Dusty Bob said. "Say, mister: that little filly in the seat next to you better be Dale!"

It was. She winked and waved.

"Hey, I saw your mortuary commercial on TV, Bob," Roy smiled. "It's good to be workin' at your age, isn't it?"

"You take it where you can get it, these days," Dusty Bob said weakly.

"I couldn't agree more. Speakin' of work, we got to get to a big meeting at NBC now," Roy said. "Good seein' you boys. Keep hawkin' them caskets, Bob! Rest Nicely, now!" He revved the Caddy's big engine and squealed off down the street.

"Did it ever occur to you that Roy looks like a Chinaman?" Dusty Bob asked.

"Yep," Jim said.

They looked for Dusty Bob's star a little longer, with no success.

"You don't think they took it back, do ya?" Dusty Bob finally asked.

"I don't think they do that – unless you murder someone," Jim replied.

"Aw, it's gettin' mighty hot," Dusty Bob said, taking his Stetson off and wiping his brow. "Let's go get a chocolate soda."

They walked to Schwab's and ordered two chocolate sodas at the counter. Dusty Bob took one sip and felt like he was being watched. He turned around and saw Olivia sitting in a corner booth.

"She's here, Jim. Sittin' right over there in that booth."

"Where? I don't see nobody."

"Right over there, in _our_ booth," Dusty Bob insisted. "That was the booth we used to sit in, to drink our chocolate sodas."

And then she was gone.

"Let's go," Dusty Bob said, bolting from the drugstore.

That night, they laid on their beds in the motel room watching TV. Dusty Bob was especially quiet, after the Olivia sighting. His TV commercial played twice, and he still didn't say anything.

"Don't you think we should talk about it?" Jim finally asked.

"About what?"

"Olivia. You keep seein' her everywhere. Why do you think it keeps happening?"

"I don't know."

"I think you _do_ know."

"I don't know what you're talkin' about, Jim."

"Okay, I'm just gonna come right out an' say it: it's your _conscience_, Bob."

"My conscience? You're _loco_."

"It's your conscience, tellin' you to break it off with Blanch when we get back home."

"You don't know what you're talkin' about, Jim."

"You stubborn fool," Jim said. "You _know_ I'm right – but you'll never admit it."

"Just drop it, partner," Dusty Bob warned, a barb in his voice.

"Okay, Bob. I'll drop it. If that's what you want, I'll drop it. But I know _you_ know I'm right. An' I know it."

"I'm still waitin' for the part where you drop it," Dusty Bob said.

"Well, here it is."

"Good."

"I'm droppin' it now."

"Well, okay then."

Jim impatiently adjusted his position on the squeaky roller bed. "I just cain't seem to get comfortable in this thing. What happened to tradin' off every other night, anyway?"

Dusty Bob sighed. "I just got comfortable myself. But if you want me to get up an' trade beds with you right now when I'm already half asleep, I will…"

Jim waited. Dusty Bob made no move to do so. "Aww, never mind," Jim said. "One more night of torture won't make any difference, I reckon."

A special news report by Edward R. Murrow came on the TV. "A little white adobe house in the Arizona desert is ground zero for an unlikely revolution in art and science fiction – or is it science *fact?*" Murrow said dramatically, smoking a cigarette while he spoke. The report was all about Lucia and her followers in Arizona – and their paintings, which were gaining attention all over the country.

"Art lovers, flying saucer enthusiasts, and even curious tourists are flocking to the little house in the desert to buy the paintings in the latest wacky craze to hit the art world." Footage showed more people, tourists, stuffy art critics, and souvenir stands than Jim had seen the last time he was out there. "Among the art collectors who have paid top dollar for these strange, other-worldly paintings are Bing Crosby, Orson Welles, billionaire Howard Hughes, and Vice President Richard Nixon," Murrow intoned. "The artist mainly responsible for the much-sought-after paintings seems to be one Lucia Torres, a shy, reclusive genius whom we know very little about. Efforts to interview Miss Torres were derailed by a determined phalanx of her fanatical blue-robed followers, who would not allow our reporter access to the mysterious artist."

"Hmmm. Imagine that," was all Dusty Bob had to say.

Immediately after the newscast, the Rest Nicely commercial played again. "Hello folks, Dusty Bob here," ending the evening on a slightly surreal note.

"Well, you're hawkin' caskets an' seein' your dead wife all over Hollywood, an' my girlfriend's a cult leader," Jim said matter-of-factly. Then he turned the lamp off and nestled down into his uncomfortable roller bed.

"'Night, Bob."

"'Night, Jim."

Chapter 17

The next morning, Dusty Bob and Jim went to *Variety's* offices and asked the receptionist where they could find Max Hoffman's son. The receptionist, a young blond wearing an exorbitant amount of cherry red lipstick, picked up the phone and dialed a number. She talked to somebody in a hushed voice for a few seconds, and hung up.

"Mr. Hoffman no longer works here," she told them. "He was fired last week for making up a story about Cary Grant's secret children."

"Can you tell us where he lives?" Dusty Bob asked.

"I'm sorry sir, that's against company policy."

"Well, that's too bad, doll," Jim stepped forward. "You see, he had us make a bet for him at the track, an' his horse won real big. All we wanna do is make sure he gets his money." He reached into his pocket and pulled out a five-dollar bill. "And I'm sure he wouldn't mind us usin' a little bit of his winnings to make sure he gets it." He dropped the bill on her desk. The receptionist quickly covered it up with an ashtray, then looked around to make sure nobody had seen.

"Well, I sure wouldn't want him to miss out on his winnings," the receptionist said. Then she leaned toward Jim and whispered, "I heard he lives at the Hollywood Grove Apartments on Vine."

"Thanks, doll," Jim said. "I'm sure he'll appreciate it."

They went to the Hollywood Grove building and checked the names on the mailboxes. There it was: Harold Hoffman, apartment 2B. They walked up to the second floor and knocked on Harold's door. An unshaven man in his thirties, wearing a dirty undershirt and boxers, answered.

"Are you Max Hoffman's son?" Jim blurted out quickly.

Harold looked confused and scared. "Yeah. _No_ – all right, say I am?"

"Relax, son," Jim said reassuringly. "You're not in any trouble."

"All right. I _am_ his son, okay? What's he done _now_?"

"We're old friends of his from his movie-writin' days," Dusty Bob chimed in. "We just want to talk to him."

"You don't want any *money*?" Harold asked.

"No, we just happen to be in town and wanna catch up on ol' times," Jim said. Harold looked relieved. Dusty Bob peered inside the apartment. A Bugs Bunny cartoon was on TV, a half-eaten bowl of cereal sat on an end table next to a worn easy chair.

"Well, I don't know where he is," Harold said. "I haven't talked to him in years."

"Well, you must have a telephone number or an address," Dusty Bob insisted.

"You can try the Regal Apartments, in Reseda," Harold said. "But like I said, we haven't spoken in years so I don't know if the old geezer's still there or not."

Alvin drove them to the Regal Apartments, which was a real dump. They saw a middle-aged woman in a house dress with curlers in her hair watering the flowers in front of her apartment.

"Excuse me ma'am," Dusty Bob said, removing his hat in a chivalrous manner. "We're lookin' for Max Hoffman. He's about our age – we were told he lives in this building."

"Not no more, he don't," the woman said in an argumentative tone. "I remember Max. Always lookin' out his window at me when I was gardening in my house dress."

"Do you know where he lives now?" Dusty Bob asked.

"He couldn't afford to stay here," the woman replied, continuing to water her flowers. "Had to move to a motel – you know, one of those places with weekly rates. I think it was the Balboa Meadows – somethin' about plants, or flowers – somethin' like that."

They drove to a donut shop with a payphone out front and looked through the phone book – no Balboa Meadows motel.

"Well, another dead end, I reckon," Dusty Bob sighed. Alvin drove them over to the Limelight Pictures hangar, where Bud Silverman was engaged in a whirlwind of post-production activity. The movie had wrapped, and Bud was trying to come up with a title.

"*Untitled Western* won't do," he said. "We need a real grabber!"

They started kicking around ideas. "How about *Death Wears a Big Hat*?" Dusty Bob asked. It came from a speech in the film that he'd improvised during the funeral scene for several miners who were tragically killed when their shaft caved in on them. The townsfolk were in mourning, and it fell to Dusty Bob's sheriff character to give the eulogy in an attempt to comfort everyone. "I don't have no answers for you folks as to why this happened," he told the grieving crowd gathered around the miners' graves. "The Good Lord has His ways an' I've never been one to question the Supreme Bein'. These was good men, all around – good church-attendin' family men. I reckon all I got to say is that sometimes Death wears a mighty big hat."

"Hmmm. *Death Wears a Big Hat...*" Bud chewed on the words a while, then smiled. "I like it!"

And it was settled.

"Oh, by the way: here's the rest of your fee," Bud said, handing Dusty Bob a thick envelope of cash.

"Why, thank you kindly," Dusty Bob said while counting the bills in the envelope. "It was a pleasure doin' business with you."

"Likewise."

"When is the premiere?" Dusty Bob casually asked.

"We make B movies – second features – we don't have premieres," Bud informed him. "Don't worry, it'll be playing as the second feature after the main feature – Gene Autry or Roy Rogers – all over the country."

That wasn't exactly the most comforting news to Dusty Bob. He went back to the cheap motel room and locked himself inside with a bottle of whiskey.

"Would you let me in?" Jim asked, pounding on the door.

"Go away!" Dusty Bob called from within.

"This is about bein' second-billed to Gene an' Roy, ain't it?" Jim called through the door. "Look, Bob – you *knew* this wasn't gonna be *Gone with the Wind* – I mean, _Limelight_ _Pictures_?"

"Just leave me be for a while, Jim."

"All right, go ahead an' drink yourself into a coma, then," Jim said, and left. He had Alvin drive him back to Van Nuys to see Bud.

"Bob's in a tailspin," Jim told him. "He's locked himself in the room with a bottle of whiskey. It just...wasn't the experience he expected, I reckon."

"I understand," Bud said, rifling through a desk drawer and producing a business card. "Go see my brother, Gabe. He's a talent agent. He might be able to scrounge something up for Dusty."

On the way back to the motel, Jim asked Alvin to pause in front of a diner. "I wanna get somethin' strong an' black to sober him up with." He went inside and ordered two large coffees to go. When he came back out, he froze in his tracks, looking down.

"I'll be damned..."

It was Dusty Bob's star, nearly unrecognizable, covered with dirt and grime and wads of chewing gum. He put the coffees in the car and went back inside the diner.

"Forget somethin', mister?" the cashier asked. He was an old man with a walker and a bow tie.

"I was wonderin' if you could spare a little cleanser," Jim said. "An' a brush, an' some hot water."

"What you want them things for?"

"I wanna clean up your sidewalk out front."

The old man looked at Jim funny. "You feelin' all right, mister?"

"That's my friend's star out there," Jim explained. "We been lookin' for it everywhere. I cain't let him see it like *that*."

The old man gave him sone cleanser. And a brush, and a bucket of hot water. Alvin got out of the car and helped Jim scrape and scrub the star until it gleamed brightly.

"Just like new," Jim said, pleased. "Now we gotta get him here without lettin' on."

They went back to the motel, where Jim got a second key from the office clerk. He unlocked the door and found Dusty Bob sprawled on the bed, snoring like a twister in a hurricane. The whiskey bottle sat almost empty on the night stand.

"Why don't you go on home an' get some rest," Jim said to Alvin. "Looks like he'll be out all night."

Dusty Bob stopped snoring and stirred at about six fifteen the next morning. He got both legs over the side of the bed, held his head in both hands down between his knees, and moaned loudly – waking Jim.

Jim sat up and stretched, as chipper as spring. "I slept like a baby! How 'bout you?"

"Could you do me a favor an' keep your voice down, partner?"

"That bad, huh?" Jim asked, picking up the whiskey bottle and swishing around the little that was left. "You used to be able to drink more an' this, an' get up the next mornin' an' rope a calf before breakfast."

"I'm fixin' to come over there an' smash that bottle upside your ugly ol' head if you don't lower your voice," Dusty Bob promised.

"All right, all right," Jim said. "When did you go an' get so grumpy in the mornin'? Get up an' splash some water on your face. We gotta go out an' find you some coffee."

"Sounds about right to me," Dusty Bob moaned.

After dressing, Jim led Dusty Bob the two blocks from their motel to Hollywood Boulevard.

"Where we goin'?" Dusty Bob demanded.

"Oh, I think I saw a place up here we can find some coffee."

"We already passed two coffee shops."

"I hear the coffee's better at this place."

When they got to the diner, Jim stopped, but Dusty Bob would not look down.

"Well, we goin' in, or not?" Dusty Bob asked, irritated now.

Jim got an idea. He fumbled a nickel out of his pocket and dropped it on the sidewalk. Dusty Bob heard it, and bent down to pick it up.

Jim laughed. "I never knew you to pass up a nickel on the ground."

"Well, that's why I'm so rich an' you're headed straight for the poor –" Dusty Bob stopped in mid-sentence. "Jim, look –"

"What is that?" Jim asked in mock surprise. "Why, that ain't your _star_, is it?"

"It appears so," Dusty Bob said in wonder.

"Well, you just never know, now do ya?" Jim asked.

"Why, it's the cleanest star on the boulevard," Dusty Bob marveled proudly. "Cleaner than Tom Mix's – or even Doug Fairbanks!"

"Must be all the fans," Jim said. "See – they haven't forgotten you, after all."

Jim just stood there, watching his friend bask in the warmth of his star – it was worth the whole trip to California. It was the perfect hangover remedy, and Dusty Bob was almost back to his old self again by the time they finished breakfast. His poached egg, according to Dusty Bob, was "a tad runny – I'd say about two minutes an' nineteen seconds."

At the right time, Jim pulled the business card out of his pocket. "I think we ought to go see this Gabe feller – Bud's brother. He's a talent agent. Bud said he might be able to get you some work before we head home."

Dusty Bob was in a good mood now, so they headed over to Gabe Silverman's office on Sunset. It was above a men's tailor shop and was a little cramped, but he handled two pretty big stars – Van Heflin and Van Johnson – so he must've known what he was doing.

"Would you consider handlin' someone not named 'Van'?" Dusty Bob asked.

"It's a pretty hard rule of mine," Gabe said seriously. "But I'll tell you what: since my brother referred you, I'll make an exception." Gabe was the opposite of his brother, Bud: neat, tidy, well-groomed, with an air of sophistication.

Gabe got work for Dusty Bob almost immediately. After a week of personal appearances at supermarket openings, car dealerships, and kids' parties for chump change, Dusty Bob confronted his new agent.

"Cain't you find me any actin' jobs?"

"There isn't much demand for washed-up octogenarian former cowboy stars these days," Gabe said. "But hold on, I think I may have something." He rifled through some papers on his desk. "Aha, here it is: Captain Billy had a stroke and they need someone to do a new kiddie show on KTLA. I think it may be right up your alley."

Gabe called the station manager at KTLA, Buzz Atwood, and told him about Dusty Bob.

"Is he breathing?" Buzz asked. "Does he have a _pulse_? Send him right over."

Gabe hung up and smiled at Dusty Bob. "They're _very_ excited about meeting you, Bob. I think working with the little tykes is going to be a great look on you."

Dusty Bob and Jim high-tailed it over to the KTLA studios on Sunset, not far from Gabe's office. Buzz Atwood was a round-faced, doughy man with horn-rimmed glasses and a toupee that didn't quite adhere to his scalp in a convincing manner. He wore a bright red cardigan sweater over a conservative shirt and tie and always seemed to have a look of disappointment on his face.

This was especially true when he first saw Dusty Bob. In fact, it could more accurately be described as a look of unqualified panic.

"Oh, dear. Gabe didn't tell me how _old_ you were!" he said in horror, then quickly composed himself. "Still, I've got the Glendale Senior Ladies' Choir and a cub scout troop from Pacoima filling all this dead airtime, and I need a kiddie show right _now_." Buzz also had this peculiar habit of thinking out loud. "And, you do have this hard-bitten western charm about you – Grandpa on the Prairie, Old Uncle Bob's Wagon Train – I'm just brainstorming right now."

"My name's Dusty Bob, an' I've never used another," Dusty Bob declared firmly.

"Oh, all right – Dusty Bob it is, then," Buzz capitulated. "We can build a show around that. What are your skills?"

205

"Ridin', ropin', card playin', romancin' the ladies, shootin' pistols, an' dispensin' with outlaws, desperados, an' varmints – all with a certain rogue-ish flair an' devil-may-care sense of *panache*."

"And what does *he* do?" Buzz asked, indicating Jim.

"Falls offa things, mostly."

Buzz looked slightly less disappointed. "Gentlemen, I think we just might have ourselves a show, here!"

Buzz had his writers get right on it, and in twenty-four hours they had a script written for the very first show. It was called "Dusty Bob's Rodeo Roundup," and it was sponsored by Hasbro Toys – featuring Mr. Potato Head – and Jell-O – "the slimy, jiggly treat that's good to eat!"

It was live TV, airing in the choice afternoon slot of 3:30. Dusty Bob had no experience in television, but he had plenty in radio. "Don't worry about it," Buzz assured him. "The only difference is, on TV you've got to look as good as you sound." Dusty Bob was sure he could do that.

The set was a simple Old West backdrop. Dusty Bob started the first show by introducing himself and presenting a lesson on children in the Old West. "At times, the Old West could be a wild, dangerous place. But for young 'uns like you, it could be a whole lot of fun, too. In them days, pioneer families had to all pitch in together to get all the work done. Even children were expected to do their share of chores."

Then he had kids from the live audience come onstage to try their hand at typical pioneer chores, such as churning butter, washing dirty clothes on a washboard, and chopping and stacking firewood with a real ax. Dusty Bob went from group to group, giving pointers and praising the teams that did well.

"As you can see, pioneer chores took a whole lotta elbow grease an' teamwork," Dusty Bob commented.

"When can we stop?" a girl who was churning butter whined.

"Oh, not 'til it's good an' thick," Dusty Bob replied. "Keep churnin', now."

"I'm getting a blister!" a kid who was washing clothes on the washboard said.

"You really gotta scrub _hard_ to get all the dirt out," Dusty Bob said.

Another kid got a splinter stacking firewood.

"Blisters an' splinters' an' broken bones an' severed fingers an' limbs was all part of prairie life!" Dusty Bob informed them cheerfully. "That's why the Good Lord give us ten fingers – so we could afford to lose a few doin' chores!"

Only when a boy started chasing a girl with the ax did Dusty Bob call an end to the chores. The kids were exhausted.

"I think we learned a lot about pioneer life today," Dusty Bob chirped. "Only when the chores were done were the kids able to take a break an' play some fun games, like three-legged races an' kick the can full of rusty nails."

There were a number of minor injuries, but no lawsuits. In fact, the father of the girl with the blister came up to Dusty Bob after the show and said, "Aw, it's all part of growing up. When I was a kid, I cut off my hand trying to skin a catfish." He held the stump up for Dusty Bob to see. "Kids need to learn about life."

In competitive form, another parent pointed to his eye patch. "I lost an eye roller skating with a big iron spike. You don't see *me* complaining about it the rest of my life!"

The next segment introduced a number of puppet characters. There was Miss Daisy Mae, a very friendly sheep saloon maid, Bart the Vulture, who was obsessed with thinking about death, Spike the Turtle, who had an inferiority complex and retreated into his shell when threatened, Barney the horse, who was sheriff of the fictional town and wore a hat and badge, and the socially inept Red Dog.

In this skit, each character came to Dusty Bob, complaining that Red Dog was gossiping and spreading rumors about them.

"He's telling everyone I have bad breath," Bart the Vulture said.

"He's telling everyone I don't have any friends," Spike the Turtle said.

"He's telling everyone I have *too many* friends," Miss Daisy Mae said.

Finally, Red Dog himself entered and gossiped to Dusty Bob.

"Daisy Mae has three beaus at the same time. And she curses under her breath in church. Spike wets his shell at night. And did you know that Barney's parents were never married?"

"Now just hold on a minute, Red Dog," Dusty Bob stopped him. "I don't wanna hear no more. Do you know what you're doin'?"

"No, what?" Red Dog asked.

"You're gossipin'."

"What's that?"

"It's goin' around talkin' about people behind their back," Dusty Bob explained patiently. "It's makin' up stories about people that ain't true."

"Why is that bad?" Red Dog asked.

"Because it's just the same as lyin'," Dusty Bob told him. "It hurts people's feelin's when you say things that ain't true about 'em."

"It does?" Red Dog asked. "Gee, I didn't mean to hurt anybody's feelings, Dusty Bob."

"I know you didn't, Red Dog," Dusty Bob said. "You weren't thinkin' about what you were doin', or the consequences of your actions."

"I promise I won't do it anymore."

"I think you ought to apologize to each an' every one of 'em. Here they come now."

The other puppet characters came back on stage and Red Dog apologized to them.

"Friends, gossip is somethin' the Good Lord don't look kindly upon," Dusty Bob said to the live audience. "It makes Him mighty sad to see his own creations a fussin' an' malignin' each other like that. So, I wrote a song called 'Gossip is the Devil's Jukebox,' an' I'm gonna sing it for ya right now."

The puppets brought Dusty Bob's guitar to him, and he sang his new song.

I don't wanna hear no more songs from the Devil's Jukebox,
If you got nothin' good to say, then keep it to yourself, Boss.
You're just buildin' yourself up by makin' others look bad,
But you're givin' me the blues an' makin' everyone sad.

So, who's gonna unplug the Devil's Jukebox?
I'd like to wrap it in chains an' silver padlocks.
Don't put another dime in that wicked machine tonight,
'Cause tellin' lies about your friends just don't sit right.

Next came "Safety Tips from Deputy Dave" – Buzz Atwood's brother-in-law, and a real auxiliary deputy sheriff. Dusty Bob and all the puppets were gathered around, admiring the deputy's uniform and gun.

"Is that a real gun?" Spike the Turtle asked in wonder.

"Yes it is!" Deputy Dave said proudly.

"Can I hold it?" Spike asked.

"I'm afraid that's against department regulations," Deputy Dave said.

"I won't tell anyone," Spike promised.

"We're on *TV*, stupid!" Miss Daisy Mae said to Spike.

"We are?" Spike looked around as if noticing the camera and audience for the first time.

"Folks, Deputy Dave's here to share some important safety tips with us, so let's listen up, now," Dusty Bob said.

"Thanks, Dusty Bob," Deputy Dave said. "Kids, remember when you're riding in the back of an open pickup truck – hold on TIGHT! When you're lighting a barbecue, always pour the gasoline on the charcoal *before* you light the match.   When you're working underneath a jacked-up car, always place cement blocks under the chassis in case the jack fails. When you're storing oily rags in the garage, spread them out, never wad them up in a bunch – and keep them away from the water heater pilot light. If you have to run with scissors, keep the pointed end down. Your legs are more expendable than your eyes. When you're experimenting with matches, keep them at least three feet away from gasoline, kerosene, propane, hairspray cans, nail polish remover, old newspapers, and straw. Now, the hairspray cans are especially important, as holding a match in front of the can and then releasing the hairspray creates an exciting – but VERY DANGEROUS – flamethrower effect. Also, matches should never be experimented with indoors. Find a nice, safe place like a secluded alley or behind an old garage. Finally, when you're lighting a cigarette with a zippo lighter –"

"Them's some mighty important reminders, Deputy Dave," Dusty Bob cut him off quickly. "It's too bad we're out of time today. But, comin' up next week: fire cracker safety with Deputy Dave."

The show went to a Mr. Potato Head commercial, and when it came back on, Dusty Bob was sitting on a barrel in front of the audience. STORY TIME WITH DUSTY BOB was printed across the bottom of the screen.

"This is the story of the most unusual train robbery in the Old West," Dusty Bob said in his best around-the-campfire storytelling voice. "It's called 'The Disappearin' Train Car of Devil's Point.' It all started when two cowpokes named Bill Chase an' Frank Lands got tired of bustin' broncs an' punchin' cows for a livin' an' decided one big score was what they needed to set them up for life. So they set their sights on the Northern Pacific Railroad line through North Dakota, after findin' out that was the line that carried freshly-minted gold pieces to the banks out west. By gamblin' profusely in the saloons of Fargo for several weeks, they picked up a lot of idle chatter about the train schedules an' how much gold they carried, an' wrote everything down in leather-bound notebooks they kept hid under their mattresses in the hotel. Chase an' Lands was patient men, see, an' very meticulous in their plannin', an' they didn't mind waitin' to find out just when the biggest shipment of gold yet would be comin' through. Then they finally heard the date: June 17th, 1886, an' they wrote that date down in their little leather-bound books, too.

"In the meantime, they both knew they would need at least another man to help them pull the robbery off, but they just didn't know who they could trust. Now, Frank Lands had been seein' this woman around town an' finally got up the nerve to talk to her a bit, an' he found out she was a school teacher who kept to herself most of the time on account of she was mighty self-conscious about a slight hump she had on her back that was barely noticeable, but it was there as sure as Mount Rushmore. Now, she was a real purty thing in every other respect, but she never had no suitors on account of the hump an' all, which Frank Lands didn't mind much on account of his own dear sister Elizabeth had a similar hump in a similar place on her back an' Louise Pennington – that was the school teacher's name – kinda reminded him of Elizabeth in that way. So Lands got to talkin' to her one day an' found out she could ride an' shoot real good for a school teacher because she grew up on a ranch with three brothers. Now, it came about that when they grew up, two of those brothers turned to robbin' banks. So Lands went to Chase an' said, 'Say, Bill, we ought to throw in with this Louise Pennington, the school teacher, because she can ride an' shoot just like a man.' An' ol' Bill Chase said back, 'We cain't do that, Frank. There's no outlaw gangs with wimmin in 'em.'

"'Well, I never heard of no rule against it,' Lands replied, an' I reckon that got Chase to thinkin' 'cause he said, 'All right, why not? But will she do it?'

"An' Lands said, 'Sure she will – she got two brothers who are bank robbers already.' Now, this fact really impressed Chase. 'Well, all right, then. Let's ask her,' Chase said, an' that's just what they done.

An' you know what Louise Pennington said? She said she'd join the gang. So they told her all about the plan an' on June 17th they all three rode out to a lonely piece of the line an' waited for that train to show up.

"An' when they saw the smoke comin' out of the stack at a distance, they all three rode their horses up onto the track an' waited. Now, there had never been a robbery on this part of the line before, an' that was to the robbers' advantage, see, because the last thing on that engineer's mind was gettin' robbed, so he stopped that train when he saw them three riders an' their horses a standin' on the track.

"'Hey! This here track's the property of the Northern Pacific Railroad!' the engineer called out to them. 'You ought not be a standin' on it thattaway!'

"All three of the robbers pulled up their bandanas to cover their faces before the engineer got too good a look at 'em. Louise's bandana was a purty yeller one with her initials on it – L.P.

"'Well, we're not movin' 'cause we're set on robbin' this here train, mister,' Chase called back to the engineer. 'An' there ain't nothin' nor nobody can move us off that!'

"'But you got a woman right there,' the engineer called out. 'Ain't no woman ever robbed a train before!'

"'Well, we looked an' looked, an' we couldn't find no rule against it!' Chase said, drawin' his gun on the engineer fella. 'Besides, that's what makes *this* train robbery so interestin'. Yessiree, you'll have quite a story to tell your grandchildren someday. Now you just put your hands up in the air, mister – an' keep 'em there.'

Lands an' Louise pulled their revolvers, too. She kept hers trained on the engineer, while her male counterparts rode back to the mail car. This was where they kept the gold, see. Its door was heavily fortified with thick metal straps an' rivets the size of silver dollars. Chase fired his gun in the air. 'You in the mail car. This here train's bein' robbed! Open up that door!' Chase called out.

"'No, sir,' the railroad agent inside shouted. 'Company tol' me not to do that.'

"'I say once more: OPEN THE DOOR!' Chase shouted back.

"'No, sir – on account of the company's instructions.'

"'All right,' Chase said. 'That's the way it plays out, then.'

The bandits ordered everyone off the train at gunpoint. They told the crew to disconnect all the cars from the engine except the mail car and an empty cattle car.

"'Now, if you wait here for two hours until we get back, you won't have to walk thirty miles back to Fargo,' Chase told the crew. Then they put their horses in the cattle car, climbed onto the engine, an' drove the train five miles west to where another track split off north from there. They took that detour for about five miles, an' stopped over a deep ravine – *Devil's Point*. They got out an' unhooked the mail car from the engine an' the other car.

Chase called out to the agent inside: "This your last chance, mister! Open the door!'

"'No, sir. I won't do it, I say!'

"'Fine, then,' Chase said. They got the horses out of the cattle car an' tied 'em with long ropes to the mail car. Then they had the horses pull, an' release, an' pull an' release, while they pushed the mail car the other way, 'til they got the whole thing rockin' back an' forth. They finally got it rockin' so hard that they got it tipped over the side of the track, an' the whole thing went tumblin' down into that ravine – with the loyal railroad agent and all the gold inside.

"Then they got four sticks of dynamite out of their saddlebags an' blasted the big rocks at the top of Devil's Point down so they covered the mail car over completely. When the dust cleared, you would never know there was a mail car down there under all them rocks.

"You see, them robbers had a plan to bury the mail car with all the gold in it so it would never be found by the railroad, the Pinkertons, or anybody. They would remember where it was buried – fifty thousand dollars worth – an' come back a year later when the heat was off, to dig it out.

"Then Bill Chase did a surprisin' thing. He up an' shot Louise Pennington in the head.

"'Now, Bill, why'd you go an' do a thing like that for?' Lands asked in disbelief.

"'We don't need her now,' Chase said. 'Besides, now we can split the gold two ways instead of three – that's a bigger share for each of us.'

"Lands saw the reasoning behind Chase's actions, but he was still mighty sore about it. They buried her in the dirt off to the side of the tracks, but before they covered her up, Lands took off her purty yeller bandana an' stuffed it into his pocket for somethin' to remember her by. Then they loaded the horses back up an' drove the train back to where the crew was waitin'. They unloaded the horses, an' Chase said to the engineer, 'Y'all can be on your way, now. Hope we didn't inconvenience you too much.'

"Then they rode back to town, ponying Louise's horse behind 'em. Back in Fargo, they did their best to lay low and try to be inconspicuous. They had a year to wait to get the gold. It wasn't long before Frank Lands started havin' trouble sleepin' nights. It got to where Louise Pennington was hauntin' him in his dreams. Every night she appeared to him, begging him to avenge her murder by killin' Chase. 'You can keep all the gold for yourself,' she told Lands. 'Just kill him!' This went on night after night, to where poor ol' Frank Lands began to question his own sanity.

"Meanwhile, Louise's third brother came to town lookin' for her. An' he was a U.S. Marshal. He started lookin' around town, askin' questions of everybody, an' it made the two train robbers mighty nervous. 'You said her brothers was bank robbers,' Chase said to Lands. 'The others are – but this one's a marshal!' Lands replied. 'Well, we mighta known that before we hired her on to the gang, then,' Chase groused. But there was nothing they could do about it now.

"Every night, Louise's ghost asked Lands to kill Chase, until one night he snapped and did it. He buried him where no one would find him. Finally free from his murderous partner, Frank Lands started wearin' Louise's bandana around his neck, even though it had her blood on it.

"One day he was sittin' in the saloon mindin' his own business, when in walked Louise's brother, the marshal. He came right up and sat down at Lands' table. Then he just stared right at the man, until sweat started dripping down from under Frank Lands' hat. Finally, the marshal said, 'I talked to the owner at the stables. He said two men sold him a horse on June 18th. He took me back to see the horse – it was my sister Louise's. You know anything about that, mister?'

"'Why would I?' Lands asked, tryin' not to panic. 'Well, I also interviewed the Northern Pacific employees about the train robbery the day before,' the marshal calmly informed Lands. 'They tol' me somethin' very interestin' – very interestin' indeed.' 'Oh, yeah?' asked Lands. 'Yessir,' said the marshal. 'They tol' me all three robbers – two men and a woman – left with the engine and the mail car for two hours. And when they came back, it was just the two men – the woman wasn't with 'em. Now, what do you reckon happened to that woman robber?'

"'I'm here to say, I just couldn't tell ya, marshal,' Frank lands said, none too convincingly. Then the marshal noticed the yeller bandana, and saw the blood on it. 'I gave Louise that bandana.' Then he pulled his gun out an' aimed it right at Frank Lands' head. 'You killed her.'

"Lands told him the whole story. He even took the marshal out to Devil's Point, where they buried the mail car. 'Fifty thousand dollars in gold is buried in that ravine,' he told the marshal. 'An' Louise is buried right over there.'

"The marshal raised his gun to Lands' head. 'I did not kill your sister,' Lands said. 'But for what I've done, I surely do deserve what's comin'.'

"'Well, I'm mighty cheered to see you're takin' it so well,' the marshal told Lands. 'No hard feelin's, then?'

"'None on my part,' Lands told him. 'It's nothin' but my own poor choices what's brought this hell down upon me. The path I've taken has led me straight to perdition. I see it now. But it's been an instructive journey, and I'm lookin' forward to layin' down this burdensome guilt I been carryin' since my partner Bill Chase put a gun to your sister's sweet, innocent head, an' attainin' some modicum of peace and rest in the hereafter. I'll be holdin' no grudge against you in eternity, to be sure.'

"'I'm relieved to hear it,' the marshal said.

"Then the marshal shot him an' buried him next to Louise. On the way back to town, the marshal got to thinkin' about all that gold buried in the ravine. Maybe he wouldn't tell the railroad about it, after all. He could come back an' dig out a little at a time without arousin' suspicion – make it last the rest of his life. Yep, that sounded like a pretty good plan to the marshal.

"Just then, a rattlesnake spooked his horse. The horse reared back, throwin' the marshal to the ground, where his head splattered against a rock an' his brains spilled out all over the ground. An' all that gold sittin' up there at Devil's Point was never found! An' that's the end of the story, I reckon."

It was time for the second commercial – this time for Jell-O. During the break, Jim asked Dusty Bob, "Wasn't that the plot to *Dead Man in South Dakota*?"

"Well, I reckon it just coulda been, at that…"

Wrapping up the show, a boy scout troop was there to demonstrate first aid and the proper way to light a campfire. The first aid segment consisted of a copious over-use of splints and gauze, with volunteers with even the most minor complaints all ending up like stiff mummies. The campfire demonstration escalated into a minor panic when a lighting rig went up in flames like a six-week-old Christmas tree, resulting in the evacuation of the studio when nobody could figure out how to operate the building's fire hose.

"A decidedly rough start," Buzz Atwood said after the fire department got the blaze under control and the last of the children were picked up by their parents. "But I heard some of the comments from the kids – and a few parents – things like, 'This wasn't just another crummy TV show – this was an *adventure!*' So, given that response – and the fact that I have no other options or ideas – I'm prepared to offer you a tentative contract for six weeks of shows, at one hundred and fifty dollars per week."

"Well, I reckon you got yourself a deal," Dusty Bob said.

The next morning, there was a review in the TV section of the *Los Angeles Examiner*: "It's impossible to accurately describe *Dusty Bob's Rodeo Roundup* – it's part Tom Mix, part Marx Brothers lunacy, with a dash of absurd humor thrown in for good measure. One minute legendary cowboy host Dusty Bob is dispensing homespun western wisdom to youngsters during a lesson on pioneer life, the next minute he's singing a goofy song about gossip or telling a violent and bloody tall tale about train robberies in the Old West. In between are puppets with severe personality disorders and a truly clueless auxiliary deputy sharing some decidedly dangerous safety tips for children. One thing is for certain, though: you never know what's going to happen next – including studio fires and impromptu visits by the fire department!"

Chapter 18

Not long after the TV show's premiere, a group of film students showed up at KTLA studios asking for Dusty Bob.

"There's some beatniks looking for you," Buzz Atwood informed Dusty Bob, as casually as he might say, "Your coffee's ready." Dusty Bob and Jim went down to the lobby, where a group of young men with a decidedly "coffee house" look waited.

"Look – it's _him_," one of them said, pointing at Dusty Bob in awe.

"What can I do for you fellas?" Dusty Bob calmly inquired.

The star-struck students stared at him a while, speechless. Finally, one of them spoke up. His name was Leo, and he seemed to be their de facto leader.

"I, uh – we, uh, wanted to tell you, man," Leo stammered, "we really dig your show, man."

"You do?" Dusty Bob asked in surprise. "I'm not sure you're the intended audience. We were goin' for the smaller tykes an' such."

"But we _get_ what you're doing, man," Leo said reverently. "You know – the bizarre, surreal humor – the whole Samuel Beckett, Alfred Jarry scene. We think it's a real hoot."

"Well, I don't know who them fellas are," Dusty Bob admitted. "But I thank you for the compliment."

Leo fell silent again, gazing at Dusty Bob in admiration. One of his friends nudged him hard with his elbow.

"Oh, yeah," Leo remembered. "As film students – that is, aspiring filmmakers, like yourself – we wanted to express our admiration for _Dry River_ – you know, the one _you_ directed."

"Your last film," Leo's friend reminded him.

"Second to last, as of a few weeks ago," Dusty Bob corrected. "You've seen _Dry River_? As I recall, only about fifteen tickets were sold before it was swallowed up into a black hole of oblivion forever."

"Oh, that's because it was so far ahead of its time!" Leo said. "Now, it's just starting to get the recognition it deserves. Here – take a look at <u>this</u>." He handed Dusty Bob a cinema magazine with his picture on the cover. Dusty Bob looked it over, puzzled.

"I'm afraid I don't read no French."

"Oh, it's just calling you the inventor of the 'post-modern' western," Leo explained. "They also say you invented a new genre: 'western noir.'"

"Well, I just don't know what to say, fellers," Dusty Bob admitted. It was a first.

"There's a screening of *Dry River* at a theater in Silver Lake tonight," Leo said. "We were hoping you would – you know – be our guest of honor."

"Well, since I'm not doin' nothin' else tonight, I reckon I could manage that."

The theater was well-used and in pretty poor condition, but it was filled with a large crowd of hipsters, college kids, and artsy bohemian-types when Dusty Bob, Jim, and Alvin arrived.

"We saved you the best seats, man," Leo told them excitedly. "And the tickets are on us."

"Well, that's mighty nice of you fellas," Dusty Bob said.

He hadn't seen *Dry River* since its premiere twenty years earlier. It seemed bleak, desolate, dark, and hopeless – made by a man who had just lost the love of his life and was about to lose everything else.

And the kids loved it. They gave him a standing ovation. He was mobbed in the lobby by kids wanting to take pictures with him and get his autograph.

He felt a little bit like a star again.

Leo told him colleges all over the country were screening *Dry River*. Somebody was making cheap, low-quality copies of the one or two surviving original prints.

"You should get on top of this right away," Leo suggested. "Somebody's making a lotta money off you."

Dusty Bob and Jim went to see Bud Silverman. They explained the situation to him.

"Well, who owns *Dry River* now?" Bud asked.

"Olympic Studios went out of business," Dusty Bob said. "Since I paid for it, I reckon *I* do."

"Okay, I'll see if I can track down the existing prints, establish a copyright in your name, and issue a cease-and-desist order on these illegal prints," Bud said. "It could take some time, though..."

"Thanks, *amigo*," Dusty Bob said.

When he wasn't basking in the adulation of his new-found cult status or shooting *Dusty Bob's Roundup*, he and Jim were still trying to track down Max Hoffman. They'd hit something of a dead end with trying to find the Balboa Meadows Motel, which didn't seem to exist. They had checked six or seven motels in the Valley with no luck, when on the next try the manager they talked to said, "No, no – you've got the wrong name. It's the Balboa *Gardens*, on Balboa and Burbank."

They drove straight over and went into the office. "I remember that guy," the manager there told them. "Really old, and kinda out of it."

"What room is he in?" Jim asked.

"He's not here anymore," the manager said. "You should talk to the guy in twenty-three. He knew Max real well."

They went to room twenty-three and knocked on the door. An old bald guy answered.

"Sid Weisman?" Jim asked.

"Who wants to know?" the old guy asked with a scowl.

"Don't you remember us, Sid?" Dusty Bob asked. "*Dead Man in South Dakota?*"

"He didn't write *Dead Man in South Dakota*," Jim interrupted. "Sid Weisman wrote *Dead Man's Hand*."

"No, Jim. That was Abe Fingerhut," Dusty Bob said. "Sid wrote *Dead Man in South Dakota*."

"Gabriel Levinson wrote *Dead Man in South Dakota*," Jim insisted.

"I beg to differ with you, partner," Dusty Bob said.

"No, I'm sure it was Gabriel Levinson," Jim said. "I remember, because I dated his sister, Delilah, a few times – you remember her, the girl with thick coke-bottle glasses an' buck teeth –"

"That was *Sid Weisman's* sister," Dusty Bob said.

"No, it wasn't," Jim said emphatically. "Sid Weisman's sister was the girl with the weak chin and underbite. I only went out with her once, because she drank too much tequila and got sick all over the seat of my brand-new Oldsmobile."

"No, it was Gabriel Levinson's sister who couldn't hold her liquor," Dusty Bob declared. "An' she got sick on the seat of your *Pontiac*."

"I ought to know what car the girl got sick in, Bob."

"Well, I ought to know who wrote *Dead Man in South Dakota*, Jim."

"Well, let's ask Sid," Jim said. "Sid, was your sister able to hold her liquor?"

"Well enough, I suppose," Sid said.

"Well, was your sister's name Delilah, or Mary?" Dusty Bob asked.

"My sister's name is Miriam," Sid replied.

"Now Miriam was a gal who _could_ hold her liquor, as I recall!" Jim said. "How is good ol' Miriam these days, any-hoo?"

"Oh, she married a guy who owns a million restaurants and hotels in Europe," Sid replied. "They live in a castle in France."

"Oh – ain't that somethin', though?" Jim said.

"Sid, we're lookin' for Max Hoffman," Dusty Bob blurted out.

"Max Hoffman…let's see…" Sid said, thinking.

"Feller in the office said Max stayed here a spell," Dusty Bob said.

"Oh – _that_ Max Hoffman!"

"Do you know where he moved to?" Jim asked.

"It got to where Max really couldn't take care of himself anymore," Sid said. "He had to go into a retirement home for writers."

"Thanks, Sid," Jim said. "It was nice seein' you again."

"You, too," Sid said. "One thing though: who the hell _are_ you guys?"

They went to the Writer's Guild and found out Max was living in the Writer's Guild Home for Retired Members, just down the street. They walked into the retirement home and looked around. It was a sad, lonely place: a bunch of aging, depressed writers sitting around waiting to die.

"Let's go," Dusty Bob said, disgusted.

"No, look – there he is, over there," Jim said.

"This was a bad idea, Jim," Dusty Bob said. "This place reminds me of _death_."

"Look, partner: if this works, you'll have more time with Olivia," Jim said. "Now think of that, an' come on!"

They approached Max slowly. Some of the old-timers were playing cards or checkers. Others were just wandering around listlessly or staring out windows. Max was sitting in a chair watching Woody Woodpecker cartoons on TV. He wore brown corduroy pants with obvious adult diapers underneath, and suspenders over a yellow shirt. He had a shock of wild white hair, like Albert Einstein. Dusty Bob and Jim took seats on either side of him; he didn't seem to notice them at all.

"Hi there, Max," Jim said quietly. Max didn't respond. "You remember us, don't you?"

"Let's go, Jim," Dusty Bob said.

"Be still!" Jim said to Dusty Bob. "It's Jim Dupree an' Dusty Bob from the old days, Max. It's been a while, hasn't it? How've you been?"

"Fine."

"So, you remember us?"

"No."

Jim leaned back behind Max and said, "Say somethin' to Max, Bob."

Dusty Bob cleared his throat. "We need you to do some re-writes."

"Re-writes?" Max said blankly.

"That's right," Dusty Bob said. "On *Rendezvous in Reno*. It's one of your screenplays – remember?"

"Screen-plays?"

"He's missin' a few pickles from his barrel," Dusty Bob said to Jim.

"It'll just take some time for him to remember, that's all," Jim said.

"I don't got that much time left," Dusty Bob pointed out.

"Oh, you'll outlive us all!" Jim scoffed.

"But what do we do about *him*?" Dusty Bob asked. "He don't even know who he *is*."

"At night, they take the roof off this building, and you can see all the beautiful stars," Max said. "I like Woody Woodpecker..."

"Well, what do we do now, Jim?"

"Let's get him outta this place," Jim said.

"What? Why?"

"Well, we cain't work with him *here*."

"Won't they come after us?" Dusty Bob worried.

"Look at him, Bob," Jim said. "Why would they want him back? We'd be doin' them a favor. Hell, they probably won't even *miss* 'im."

"I don't know, partner..."

"Do you like chocolate sodas, Max?" Jim asked.

"Oh, yes," Max said.

"Schwab's is right around the corner," Jim said. "C'mon – let's go get one."

"Right now?" Max asked.

"Why not?"

"Tonight is Salisbury steak," Max said. "I never miss Salisbury steak."

"We'll have you back for dinner," Jim said. "C'mon – let's go."

"I don't know about this, Jim," Dusty Bob said. "Isn't this kidnappin'?"

"It ain't kidnappin'," Jim said. "We're just goin' out for chocolate sodas."

They got up and walked Max out of the retirement home without anyone noticing.

"See?" Jim said. "Easy as pie."

At Schwab's, they sat at the counter and ordered chocolate sodas. Dusty Bob kept glancing nervously at the booth in the back – *their* booth – but Olivia wasn't there.

Max took a few sips of his soda, then looked at both of them knowingly. "Dusty Bob – Jim! How are you boys doing?"

"Fine, Max," Jim said. "Just fine."

"Well, it's been a long time, boys," Max said happily. "You know, I'll never forget that time we were working on *Rendezvous in Reno*. You remember that picture, Dusty Bob? We were on the set and you boys felt like having a little fun with the Jewish kid from Brooklyn who'd never ridden a horse before. So you saddle up three horses for a ride, only you leave the cinches on _my_ saddle loose so halfway through the ride I start slipping sideways on the horse, until I'm all the way *under* him. 'Fellas – help!' I cried, and all you two had to say was 'Hold on real tight, Max! It's a long way back!' Oh, you two got me real good, that time!" His memory seemed sharp and his eyes were clear as crystal now.

"Yeah, I reckon we did, at that," Jim agreed.

"Say, Dusty Bob," Max said. "How's Olivia?"

"Olivia's dead, Max," Dusty Bob replied.

"Oh, I'm sorry to hear about that." Then Max's eyes went blank, and all the life drained out of his countenance. "Finish that soda, Harold," he barked at Dusty Bob. "We've got to get home for dinner! Your mother's making her Salisbury steak!"

"Who's Harold?" Dusty Bob asked.

"His _son_," Jim reminded him.

"Oh," Dusty Bob said. "His mind slips in an' out of gear like an old Model T, doesn't it?"

Then he glanced over and saw *her* in the booth. "Jim. She's _here_." He watched as Olivia stood up and walked to the door. She stopped momentarily, turned to look at Dusty Bob, then walked outside. "I think she wants us to follow her."

They got up and walked outside. Dusty Bob saw her down the street. "See her, Jim?"

"No, I don't, Bob."

Dusty Bob followed Olivia, and Jim and Max followed him. They walked several blocks. Olivia crossed the street and walked another block. They followed. She ducked into a pawn shop, and they followed. Inside, Dusty Bob lost her.

"Why, I _saw_ her come in here." They walked through the shop looking for her. It was cluttered with an eclectic assortment of junk and yesteryear's treasures.

"Wait – where did Max go?" Jim asked suddenly. "Max!" Now they were looking for _him_. The shop seemed much larger on the inside than it had from the street. Then they heard a typewriter clacking, and followed the sound. There was Max – typing away on an old machine.

"There's no paper in it, Max," Dusty Bob said. Max ignored him.

It was a 1932 Olivetti. It was beat-up and well-used.

"He sure seems to like this typewriter," Jim said. "Hold on a second, partner." He stopped Max from typing. He turned the typewriter over and looked at the bottom. A chill went up his spine.

"Look at _this_," he said to Dusty Bob seriously. Dusty Bob looked. MAX HOFFMAN was engraved in the metal.

"Well, I'll be…" was all Dusty Bob could say.

They paid three dollars for the typewriter and left the pawnshop.

"Don't you see, Jim," Dusty Bob said excitedly. "She _knew_. He needs to use his own typewriter – the one he wrote _Rendezvous_ on back then – to do the re-writes."

"I see it all, partner."

The next morning, Dusty Bob and Jim woke up to find Max gone. The envelope with Dusty Bob's movie money was also missing. Alvin picked them up and drove them all around Hollywood, but there was no sign of Max.

They went back to the retirement home, but he wasn't there. Then they went to Harold's apartment and told him they found his father living in a retirement home and then he took off with Dusty Bob's money.

"He's a slippery fella," Dusty Bob observed.

"Hey, whatever he does – I'm not responsible," Harold said, still in the same undershirt and boxers. His undershirt had more ketchup and mustard stains on it than before. "You're the ones who took him out of that home and unleashed him on the public – not me."

"Where do you think he would've gone with all that money?" Dusty Bob asked.

"I have no idea," Harold replied defensively. "And if you think you're getting any money from _me_, you're crazy –"

"Don't worry yourself," Dusty Bob said. "I'm not holdin' you accountable for that."

They decided to go back to their motel in case he came back while they were out looking for him. He wasn't there.

But they got a call from Haze MacAffrey. "You still lookin' for Max Hoffman? Well, he's sittin' at my bar right now."

Dusty Bob told him to keep Max there until they arrived. "No matter what – don't let him leave!"

When they got to Haze's bar, Max was gone. "Look, I don't have no legs," Haze said. "I couldn't stop him."

"Did he say where he was goin'?" Jim asked.

"No. But he had a racing form in his shirt pocket," Haze said.

They drove to Hollywood Park and described Max to every bookmaker in every betting window. Finally, a guy said, "Yeah, the guy who looks like Albert Einstein. He placed a bet on a nag that surprised everyone – and he won BIG. Made a ton of money."

"Do you know where he went?" Dusty Bob asked in anticipation.

"I called a cab for him," the bookmaker said. "He said he wanted to go to the Balboa Gardens Motel."

They drove straight to the Balboa Gardens and knocked on Sid Weisman's door.

"Is Max here?" Jim demanded when Sid answered.

"You just missed him," Sid said. "He just paid me back some money he owed me. He only owed me fifty, but he gave me a hundred. He said he'd come into a lot of money lately, and the rest was interest."

"Where did he go next?" Dusty Bob asked anxiously.

"He mentioned going to see an old girlfriend," Sid said. "Lola...Oly...Oily-something –"

"Lola Olanola?" Jim asked.

"Yeah, I think that was it," Sid said. "She runs a massage parlor on La Cienega."

"I think I know the place," Jim said.

Lola's massage parlor was in a seedy storefront on La Cienega Avenue, among a bunch of tattoo parlors, adult theaters, and dive bars. Lola Olanola was sixty-three, four-foot-two, a hundred and seventy pounds, with a tall rat's nest hairdo. Lola specialized in massages with live mammals, which was considered not only questionable, but barely legal in the state of California at that time. She was eating a huge wedge of chocolate cake single-handed when they walked in.

"Don't tell me," she said, smiling with chocolate frosting covering her green teeth. "You're here for the Ferret Ecstasy, aren't you?"

"The what?" Dusty Bob asked, immediately sorry he did.

She opened a door and showed them a naked fat guy lying face-down, moaning, with live ferrets running up and down his back.

"God, _no_," Dusty Bob blurted out, turning away in horror. "Close the door – _please_..."

"Actually, we're looking for Max Hoffman," Jim said.

"Oh, Max was just here," Lola said. "He had the Wombat Special." Dusty Bob winced. "Don't worry, honey – they've been de-clawed."

"Do you know where he went next?" Jim asked.

"Oh, he said he was in the mood for some raw Vietnamese eel."

As they turned to leave, Lola asked, "Would you like to take a badger home with you? I rent 'em by the day!"

Dusty Bob knew there was only one place that served raw Vietnamese eel: Ed Minh's place, in Venice. It was a dirty dive. Rats gnawed at and fought over pieces of discarded eel on the floor. They walked in and were greeted by Ed Minh himself.

"Dusty Bob! Jim Dupree! It's been a long time, fellas!" Ed was half Swedish and half Vietnamese. He had blond hair and Asian features. "What brings you two back here?"

"We're looking for Max Hoffman," Dusty Bob said. "You seen him lately?"

"I see him right now," Ed said, pointing to a barrel in the back where Max was sitting at it like a table. They walked back to him and stood over him, half expecting him to bolt. He was enjoying a raw eel in *kabayaki* sauce and a bottle of *saki*.

"Ah, Dusty Bob and Jim!" he said affectionately. "Please – join me, boys!"

They pulled mismatched chairs up to the barrel and had a seat.

"You know, I was just reading how scientists believe our bodies are made of the same matter as the stars," Max said, referring to an open magazine on the barrel table.

"You don't say," Dusty Bob said.

"It's true! They say the whole universe started with a great big explosion. Would you like some raw eel?"

"Uh, no thank you, Max," Dusty Bob replied. "I think your dinner just twitched."

"That's the best way to eat eel – still half alive and kicking!"

"Where's my money, Max?" Dusty Bob asked impatiently. "Do you have it?"

"Not exactly on me," Max said. "But it's *safe*."

"Well – where is it?"

"I gave it to Mr. Birdseye."

Max finished his eel and took them to a Chinese laundry on Fairfax. He presented a claim stub to the attendant, who took them to an office in the back.

"You will wait patiently until Mr. Birdseye makes eye contact," the attendant said, ushering them into the office.

Mr. Birdseye was a small, extremely thin man in his eighties. He was nattily-dressed, with a smartly-pressed and folded mustard-colored handkerchief in his navy blazer pocket. He sat behind an expansive desk in a dark, modern, well-appointed office. Three dour-looking Korean men in dark suits and sunglasses sat side by side on a small sofa against the wall, silently smoking cigarettes and watching them. Important-looking men in business suits were always coming in and out through a series of side doors, whispering things into Mr. Birdseye's ear every few minutes. Then he would nod slightly, and they would leave.

There was imported Italian *pizzicato* and espresso on a mahogany sideboard. A woman in fashionable office apparel that could have been purchased in a member's only upscale boutique in Milan brought seven or eight European newspapers in and spread them out on his desk, then left. One minute Mr. Birdseye got a call and spoke to the caller in Finnish. The next minute, he had a heated, almost violent argument with another caller in Mandarin Chinese, using the unmistakable dialect of the Shanxi province. He spoke very politely to the next caller in fluent Portuguese. When his flurry of phone calls was over, Mr. Birdseye looked up and made explicit and direct eye contact with Dusty Bob.

"We're sorry to disturb you, sir, but my name's Dusty Bob, an' we think you might have somethin' of ours."

"And what might that be, my good sir?"

"Well, Max here told us that he gave you some money that belongs to us."

"People don't 'give me money,'" Mr. Birdseye politely corrected him. "People entrust their assets to me for a pre-determined period of time."

Without interrupting the flow of conversation, a nurse came in and took Mr. Birdseye's blood pressure, then gave him two pills to swallow – a blue one and a green one.

"Well, it was a mistake, an' we'd like our money back now, if it's all the same to you," Dusty Bob said. "See, sometimes ol' Max just ain't hisself."

"I'm sorry, but I can't just give you the money back," Mr. Birdseye said. "I'm afraid it's just not that simple, Mr. Bob."

There was a long pause. The Korean men in the dark suits smoked and watched the interaction with great interest.

"Well, why not?" Dusty Bob finally asked.

"Because giving you the money back before the OFI – the Optimal Fruition Interval – would involve phone calls to Shanghai and Lisbon, possibly even Bangkok and Amsterdam. It would require rash communications across numerous international time zones, hasty midnight and early morning telegrams to several foreign banks, embassies, and international trade regulatory agencies – not to mention a host of accusations, denials, recriminations, charges and counter-charges, and countless lawsuits and internecine legal maneuvers. In short, sir – it simply cannot be done."

"Well, how long will it take to get our money back?" Dusty Bob asked.

Mr. Birdseye snapped his fingers and an assistant rushed to his side. They exchanged a series of anxious whispers into each others' ears for a while, then Mr. Birdseye gestured for the assistant to leave the office. He did so, and a moment later an almost identical assistant entered and exchanged another flurry of rapid-fire whispers with Mr. Birdseye.

When they finished, Mr. Birdseye opened a desk drawer and pulled out a huge leather-bound book. He skimmed through pages until he found the one he was looking for, and ran a boney finger down the page. He slammed the book closed and did some quick calculations on a scratch pad. He showed the calculations to the assistant, who pointed out a minor error. Mr. Birdseye corrected it and showed the assistant again. The assistant nodded. Mr. Birdseye put the scratch pad down and looked at Dusty Bob.

"About three hours."

They waited in Mr. Birdseye's office for three hours. More assistants came in and whispered in his ear from time to time. More phone calls, with Mr. Birdseye speaking a dazzling number of foreign languages impeccably. All the while, the Korean men just smoked and watched.

Finally, another assistant came in and whispered something in Mr. Birdseye's ear.

"Well, gentlemen. I have just been notified by Brussels that the transaction has been completed, and everything has gone according to plan." Mr. Birdseye made a gesture to the assistant. The assistant walked to a painting of a ship on the wall, took it down, opened a wall safe, and took out several bundles of cash.

"After my cut, plus the Helsinki fees, the Vatican tax, and the commission to the Saudis, the rest is all yours." Mr. Birdseye slid the bundles across his desk to them.

"Well, thanks a heap," Dusty Bob said, scooping them up.

"And gentlemen," Mr. Birdseye said ominously. "You must speak of this to no one. Otherwise, I shall be forced to involve the *Taiwanese*."

When they got back into Alvin's car, Dusty Bob counted the money. "In my hasty estimation, there is upwards of ten thousand dollars here!"

"That Mr. Birdseye's a miracle-worker, all right," Jim declared.

That night, they tied Max to the rolling bed so he couldn't escape again. He continued to vacillate between periods of dementia and senility, and rare moments of lucidity.

During Max's worst moments on the bus ride back to Arizona, they tied him to his seat with ropes to keep him from escaping or harassing passengers. The bus driver pulled over and came back to tell them they couldn't do that.

"The Greyhound Corporation has strict rules against tying passengers to the seats with ropes," he informed them, as if it were a common occurrence.

Dusty Bob showed the driver a badge and told him Max was a dangerous escaped mental patient and they needed to bind him in order to ensure the safety of the passengers.

The bus driver bought it and went back to the front of the bus. A few passengers around them heard the exchange, and nobody complained about the ropes again.

"Where'd you get that badge?" Jim asked.

"Kern County made me honorary sheriff in 1934," Dusty Bob smiled.

Even when he was bound, Max was a handful. He told the passengers that Dusty Bob was his son, Harold, who had been brainwashed into kidnapping him by Jim, who was really a spy for the Vatican. "The Pope is cultivating a race of zombies for slave labor," he told the passengers. "He's replaced Chiang Kai-shek's head with a radio receiver and programmed him to lobotomize President Eisenhower!"

"Hush up now, Max!" Dusty Bob told him. "Don't pay no mind to ol' Max, folks. The lid on his cracker barrel's a might loose, is all."

"The Jesuits have taken me aboard their spacecraft and probed my body cavities. They need a specimen to take back with them when they return to their planet, Zorad, after the Third Apocalypse."

"I told you to hush up, now," Dusty Bob said.

"Please untie me, Harold!" Max begged Dusty Bob. "I promise I won't eat pork anymore! How can you do this to your own father?"

People were turning to look.

"The North Koreans turned me into a woman, on the Pope's orders," Max said. "Why do they do his bidding? Is it for those little wafers? He wants to control the world's supply of Ovaltine! J. Edgar Hoover ate my ham sandwich! Richard Nixon showed me his nipples! Howard Hughs wants my spleen. He's taking the best parts from everyone so he can live forever! Teddy Roosevelt told me he had feelings for me – and I reciprocated in kind! I saw Eleanor Roosevelt chopping wood in the forest without a shirt! I flew the Spirit of St. Louis to Mars and back! Howard Hughs took all the credit! Ask Joe Louis – he was my co-pilot. I invented the atom bomb and toothpaste!

The rings of Saturn are made of Spam and cigarette butts and everyone's missing socks!"

The driver pulled the bus over and came back again. "Look, I'm getting a lot of complaints about your friend here. You're gonna have to get him to stop talking."

"How am I supposed to do that?" Dusty Bob asked.

"I don't know, just DO IT!" the driver said. "Or I'll have to kick you all off."

Dusty Bob gagged Max with a handkerchief, which seemed to keep him quiet enough. But there were other problems, like food stops and changing Max's adult diapers. Neither Dusty Bob nor Jim relished this duty, so they decided to switch off to make it fair. But whenever Max was untied, he could slip away in a second.

In Barstow, Max escaped and was found eating twenty pounds of baloney in a supermarket.

In Kingman, he got away again. He stole an older woman's suitcase and put on her wig and one of her dresses and tried to buy a train ticket to Norway with empty chewing gum wrappers and pocket string.

In Flagstaff, he broke into a woman's apartment and got undressed. When she came home, she found him wearing her nightgown while taking a bubble bath, and called the police.

Chapter 19

When they got back to Memory Ranch, Debra Lynn had had her baby – a boy. She named him Hamlet.

"Debra Lynn told us she didn't have any people to go to, so we let her stay on," Kitty informed Dusty Bob. "She's handy in the kitchen and really helpful to Sally. Besides, I thought it would be nice for Siggy to know his brother from a different mother, and have someone to play with."

"Well, I reckon you done the Christian thing, Sweetheart," Dusty Bob agreed.

Dusty Bob and Jim installed Max in a guest cabin and told Blanch he was an old friend from the Hollywood days who wasn't well and needed a place to stay until he died. She bought it. Jim and Sally set him up with his old typewriter and started working with him to write a new scene for *Rendezvous in Reno* in which Olivia could warn Dusty Bob about Blanch.

"It's tricky," Max confided in one of his lucid moments. "Anything we try to add has to fit with the plot and make sense with the story. We can't just mention a new character with no background in the middle of the picture – it would break up the stream-lined flow of the narrative."

"Then we'll go back to the beginning and write Blanch into the story from the start," Jim suggested. Max agreed it might work, but it was slow-going. For one thing, each day they had to reintroduce themselves to Max and explain what they wanted him to do because he had forgotten overnight. And, he was only lucid a few hours each day. To make things even more complicated, they had to keep everything they were doing from Dusty Bob and Blanch.

Progress was slow.

A few mornings after their return from L.A., Trooper Torres showed up at his usual coffee time and announced that he had to see Blanch right away.

"She's wanted for questioning by the FBI," Trooper Torres informed them officiously. "It's a big fraud case out in California involving that used car guy, Ed Munley. They say she might have stolen that fancy car of hers."

"Not Blanch," Dusty Bob said.

"I'm supposed to take her into Holbrook this morning," Trooper Torres continued. "Two FBI men from Phoenix wanna talk to her."

They went to Blanch's cabin and knocked on the door. There was no answer.

"Her car's gone," Jim observed. Dusty Bob opened the door with a master key. The place was empty – all Blanch's things were gone. And Dickie was, too.

"Oh, Lord, no," Dusty Bob moaned.

"Take it easy, partner," Jim said. "Believe me: it's better this way."

"You don't understand, Jim," Dusty Bob said, turning white as milk. "I gave her all the California money, to build the new tradin' post."

"All of it?" Jim asked.

"Yep," Dusty Bob said. "Every penny. It's all gone."

"Well, why on earth did you go an' do a thing like that for?" Jim demanded.

"I trusted her, Jim," Dusty Bob admitted, glassy-eyed. "I trusted her…" Dusty Bob looked faint. Jim and Trooper Torres carried him to the diner porch and plopped him in his chair. He sagged.

"Is it true, Jim? Did Blanch and Dickie run off with all the money?"

"I'm afraid so, Bob."

"And Dickie's not really her brother, is he?"

"No, Bob," Jim said gently.

"I'm fadin', Jim," Dusty Bob said weakly. "All the life's drainin' outta me."

"Now, you'll be fine, Bob," Jim assured him. "Just take a deep breath."

"I'll get him some water," Trooper Torres said, dashing into the diner.

"I'm fadin'," Dusty Bob repeated, slumping horribly in the chair. He reached out feebly and took Jim's hand. "You've been a good friend, Jim. Just like my brother."

"Aw, stop it now," Jim said, trying not to sound afraid.

"Whatever hand life dealt us, we played it together," Dusty Bob said. "An' before I go, I just wanna let you know how much your loyal companionship has meant to me."

"You're not gonna die, Bob," Jim said, trying to believe it himself. Dusty Bob _did_ look pretty bad – pale and clammy, eyes closed, voice weak.

Trooper Torres came out of the diner with a glass of water, followed by Sally.

"Here you go," Trooper Torres said, holding the glass up to Dusty Bob's lips and letting him drink.

"Much obliged," Dusty Bob croaked.

"He's faking," Sally said, glaring down at him contemptuously.

"T'would that I were, Devil Woman," Dusty Bob said weakly. "I would not leave this mortal coil in such a hasty manner, but I fear such matters are beyond my selfish desires. No, I leave you now unwillingly, a hankerin' for more life, but resigned to my fate, knowing there is work left to be done –"

"That's right," Jim said. "You can't go yet, Bob. We've gotta get this place in shape for the interstate – all those tourists – comin' to see *you*."

Dusty Bob rallied almost imperceptibly, then sunk back into his death funk. Kitty exited the diner and knelt next to him. "Daddy – what's wrong?"

"Oh, my lovely daughter," Dusty Bob lamented. "I wish I'd had the chance to know you better in this life – but no, it was not to be. An' little Siggy – my grandson – to watch him grow into the man I know he will someday be, would've been my greatest joy. But I must leave you now, my darlin'. Don't be sad – don't be sad…"

"But Daddy," Kitty protested. "You can't leave us so soon!"

"I'm afraid I must," Dusty Bob replied bravely. "After this last, great setback, I feel my heart growin' fainter with every breath…"

"Well, get on with it already!" Sally urged.

"But, what will we do?" Kitty asked.

"You an' Siggy will get this place," Dusty Bob assured her. "Everything I have…I wish it was more…if I'd only been a better steward of the Good Lord's gifts…"

"Oh, I don't want anything from you, Daddy," Kitty cried. "I just want you to stay!"

"Thank you, dear, but it's *time*," Dusty Bob said stoically. He got real quiet and still. His eyes closed. There was a look of eternal rest and peace upon his rugged countenance.

"Is he breathing?" Jim asked.

Trooper Torres felt his wrist. "He's still got a pulse."

Jim leaned in close. "Bob! Are you still in there?"

Dusty Bob stirred slightly. He half-opened his left eye. "I think I'm feelin' a might better now…"

He took a few sips of water, and seemed much revived.

"How do you feel now?" Jim asked.

"Well, the old ticker's keepin' better time now," Dusty Bob said, the color returning to his face.

"So you're not dyin' now?" Kitty asked hopefully.

Dusty Bob sat up straighter and looked at all the faces around him with renewed vigor. "You know, I reckon that ol' Grim Reaper decided to take a rain check, after all!"

Later that day, Jim discovered the mysterious glowing box with the eerie green light emanating from its cracks was also missing.

"After I got it from Old Mr. Young, I called the university to see if that professor feller wanted it, but they told me he'd never come back after they took him to Washington, D.C." he told Dusty Bob. "So I just put it in the junk room behind the kitchen, an' now it's gone."

"Maybe Blanch an' Dickie took it," Dusty Bob suggested.

"I reckon we'll never know," Jim said.

After Dusty Bob's near-death experience, things seemed to take a turn for the better around the place. For starters, Bud Silverman sent a check for five hundred dollars for *Dry River* ticket sales. It was accompanied by a note stating that Bud had secured the legal copyright to the film for Dusty Bob, had taken possession of the original prints, and was distributing the film nationwide. More checks were to follow.

Secondly, a gigantic Lincoln Continental arrived bearing a tall, barrel-chested man dressed in a business suit, bolo tie, shiny cowboy boots, and a two-hundred-dollar Stetson hat. Jonas Tiberius (J.T.) Cash was a Phoenix real estate developer who'd made a fortune building shopping centers, apartment buildings, and suburban housing tracts. He now had his sights set on the tourist trade via the new interstate system.

"I'll get right to the point, Bob," J.T. said bluntly. "I wanna buy your place here and build an all-purpose tourist center for the new interstate. I see a truck stop with restaurants and gift shops. I see a hotel with an Olympic-sized swimmin' pool and tennis courts. I see a country club with a PGA-grade golf course. Now, I know what you're thinkin': 'Why can't *I* build all that stuff,' right? Well, you could – *maybe*. Maybe you could get a million-dollar loan from a bank.   Maybe you could find the architects, contractors, and construction companies of a level required for such an audacious project. But it would be hard for you to pull off, right? But not for me.   With my assets, connections, experience, and know-how, it would be a breeze. No, my friend – your selling this place to me would be the easiest way to do it, all-around."

"But Memory Ranch ain't for sale," Dusty Bob told him.

J.T. Cash took a check out of his blazer pocket and unfolded it. "How does forty thousand dollars sound?"

Dusty Bob took the check and looked it over. "I reckon it sounds mighty fine," he said.

"You sold the *ranch*?" Jim exclaimed when Dusty Bob told him about it later. "I thought this place meant more to you than all the money in the world!" Everyone gathered around to hear the news.

"That was before the new interstate come along an' changed everything," Dusty Bob explained. "This is a once-in-a-lifetime deal, so I took it."

"But where will we go?" Kitty wanted to know.

"Don't worry, Darlin'," Dusty Bob assured her. "With this much money, we can go *anywhere*."

"What about the rest of us?" Sally demanded.

"It's enough to take care of everybody," Dusty Bob said. "I'm not throwin' no one to the wolves – not even *you*. Maybe we'll find another place somewheres, an' start up a real workin' ranch again. Or retire to Mexico, or Florida. I don't rightly know what yet, but it's enough to do whatever we decide!"

"I don't know, Bob," Jim shook his head. "Somethin' just don't sound right…"

"Well, it sure sounds right to me," Dusty Bob said, a little perturbed. "For once I wish you'd just up an' be glad for good news, Jim. This is the biggest thing that's ever happened to us! This J.T. Cash feller's a big Phoenix real estate mogul – he's got the vision to see what this place could <u>really</u> be, an' none of us have that kinda vision. An' he's also got plenty of *wampum*," he held up the check. "An' we got some of it, right here – an' I, for one, am celebratin' the good fortune for a change!"

"Maybe we could find another place – just like Memory Ranch," Kitty said enthusiastically.

"It won't be the same," Jim said sullenly.

"Well, you can pout all you want, Jim, but we got enough money here to make it anything we want," Dusty Bob said cheerfully. "Not many people ever get a second chance like this one!"

Dusty Bob decided they'd close down in a week's time. He had a sign made that said, *Last week of memories at the ranch, folks!* And put it up by the highway. Every family that stopped by was regaled with an extra helping of stories, memories, and songs from Dusty Bob's past. The proceedings became something of a ritualistic, week-long goodbye, each day closer to the end becoming more bittersweet than the last.

"Won't you miss it, Daddy?" Kitty asked.

"I reckon so," Dusty Bob said. "But this money is your future, girl – you an' Siggy's – an' I'd trade anything in the world to give you that. Even this tired ol' ranch."

Two days before the planned shut-down, Trooper Torres showed up with some news. "The interstate route has been moved fifteen miles to the south because the Indians won't let it go through their sacred burial grounds," he told Dusty Bob and Jim.

"Fifteen miles?" Dusty Bob asked. "<u>South</u>?"

"You sure?" Jim asked.

"Positive," Trooper Torres said. "We just heard this morning."

"Fifteen miles ain't that far," Dusty Bob scoffed. "Folks'll still need a restaurant an' a room for the night. Mr. Cash will still wanna build his hotel here, right? He can put a sign at the interstate: *Only fifteen miles north...*" It wasn't sounding very convincing. "Right, Jim? Folks'll be willin' to drive fifteen miles, won't they? It's not that far..." His voice was beginning to sound desperate.

Dusty Bob and Jim got into the pickup and drove to the bank in Holbrook. They presented the check to the teller, whose eyes almost popped out of their sockets when he read the amount.

"Oh, my...you'll have to wait here while we make a few phone calls, I'm afraid," the teller said, taking the check straight to the bank manager. They waited at the window while the manager made a flurry of phone calls.

"He'll still want the land, right, Jim?" Dusty Bob asked blankly. "He'll still want to build his hotel, right?"

Jim didn't have an answer. A few minutes later, the bank manager brought the check back.

"I'm afraid I have some bad news," he said. "A stop payment order was placed on this check a few hours ago. Mr. Cash's bank won't honor it."

"What does that mean?" Dusty Bob asked hopefully. "Do we get our money?"

"I'm afraid not," the manager said. "As a matter of fact, Mr. Cash's bank has instructed us to destroy the check immediately." He tore the check in half in front of them. Dusty Bob winced.

"Now see here, mister – that's forty thousand dollars right there," Dusty Bob blurted out in shock. "That's *our* money – Mr. Cash gave me that check – for my place – for the *interstate* –"

The manager continued to tear the check into itty-bitty pieces.

"C'mon, partner," Jim pulled Dusty Bob away gently. "It's all over. Let's go."

All the way back to the ranch, Dusty Bob was silent.

"You all right, Bob?" Jim asked. Dusty Bob gave no answer. Jim had seldom seen him so deflated.

When they got back, Dusty Bob slowly got out of the truck and walked with a disturbing determination to the work shed and found a can of gasoline. He brought the can of gasoline over to the diner and began pouring gas around the base of the diner and onto the porch.

"Bob – what're you doing?" Jim asked.

Dusty Bob stopped a moment and turned to Jim. "I'm going to burn the place down," he said calmly, then went back to his work.

Sally came out onto the porch and watched Dusty Bob slosh the gas around without a word.

"Sally – get the young 'uns outta there, NOW!" Jim shouted.

Sally shook her head, and went back inside to get the others.

"Bob – your grandson's in there!" Jim said. Dusty Bob didn't seem to hear him.

"It's nothin' but bad luck an' heartache," he kept repeating as he soaked the old wooden porch. Kitty and Debra Lynn came outside holding their babies and watched Dusty Bob in bewilderment.

"Daddy, please – STOP!" Kitty cried out, but he didn't hear her.

"Man works his whole life, for what?" Dusty Bob asked himself. "For nothin', that's what."

"What's wrong with him?" Kitty asked Jim, turning little Siggy's head away from his grandfather.

"The interstate got moved," Jim replied. "The check didn't go through. The deal's off."

Kitty turned to her father. "That's okay, Daddy – we get to stay here now. This is our home."

Dusty Bob had set the can down and was now calmly rolling a cigarette.

"Did you hear me, Daddy? We'll stay here – we'll make a go of it without the interstate!"

"He can't hear you, Darlin'," Jim said. "Somethin's broke inside his head."

Sally appeared just inside the screen door.

"Sally – get outta there!" Jim shouted.

"I'm not comin' out," Sally said calmly. "He'll have to burn me down with the place."

"Don't think I won't do it, Devil Woman," Dusty Bob laughed coldly, lighting the cigarette.

"Come out of there, now!" Jim called to Sally.

"Go ahead," Sally said to Dusty Bob. "Burn it down, White Man."

"Leave her be, Jim," Dusty Bob said. "She knows what she's doin'." He took a few puffs on the cigarette, and held it over the porch.

"You people are insane!" Debra Lynn exclaimed.

Dusty Bob dangled the cigarette over the gasoline-soaked porch. Sally glared at him defiantly through the rusty screen door. "What're you waiting for?"

"Daddy – where will me an' Siggy go?" Kitty pleaded. "Where will Debra Lynn an' Hamlet go? This is our _home_."

Still, the cigarette dangled. Still, Sally wouldn't budge. Everyone held their breath.

Then, a station wagon with luggage tied to the roof pulled off the highway and parked in front of the diner. Doors flung open and kids piled out, rambunctiously kinetic after a long drive. Giggling, they ran over to the corral to see the horses. "Look – horseback riding!" one of them shouted. "Yippee!"

The parents climbed out of the car and stretched. "Can we ride the horses, Dad?" one of the children called out.

"Let's get something to eat first, kids," their father said. "You can ride the horses after lunch."

Dusty Bob was as still as a statue, arm extended, cigarette dangling in the air. Jim looked at him, making eye contact.

"Guests, Bob," he said gently, cocking his head toward the family.

Dusty Bob still didn't move. He looked at Jim with recognition, then at the family. He looked at Kitty and Siggy, and Debra Lynn and Hamlet, then back at the family, still not moving.

"Bob..." Jim said.

"Well, what's everybody just standin' around for?" he asked, switching on the folksy Dusty Bob persona. "Let's get some burgers on the grill for these hungry folks!" He dropped the cigarette in the dirt and ground it out with his boot. Sally rolled her eyes and went into the kitchen to fire up the grill.

"Where you folks from, anyhow?" Dusty Bob asked in his friendliest voice. "Sacramento? St. Louis? Say, if I can guess the city, you get a free meal!"

Chapter 20

With Blanch out of the picture and no longer a threat, Jim and Sally switched their focus with Max, working with him instead to write new scenes to prolong Dusty Bob's time with Olivia. Through painstaking trial and error, they discovered that every new scene Max wrote on the ancient Olivetti appeared in the film when Dusty Bob played it. And each new scene was clear, vibrant, and unfaded – as if it had been filmed yesterday.

In the few lucid hours he enjoyed each day, Max actually wrote some wonderful new scenes for the not-so-young lovers – Dusty Bob and Olivia. In one scene, Olivia's character, Kate, baked an apple pie for Dusty Bob's character, Jake Matson. She took it to his office and proudly presented it to him, but his reaction was strangely subdued.

"Well, what's the matter?" Kate asked, confused.

"I reckon I'm not hungry," Jake replied evasively.

"Nonsense," Kate said, cutting him a big slice. "There you go – give it a try!"

Jake picked at the pie and tried to change the subject. "Lovely weather we're havin' for this time of year, ain't it?"

"Aren't you going to try it?"

Jake nibbled at a corner of the slice, without enthusiasm. "Mmm. Sure is good…"

"Well, you hardly had a bite!" Kate said, upset now. "What's the matter with it? Is it no good?"

"No, Kate – I'm sure it's mighty tasty –"

"I knew it!" she said, grabbing the pie out of his hand and throwing it into a waste paper basket. "Why am I kidding myself? I'm no baker –"

"I'm sure it's real good pie, Kate."

"But you didn't even taste it!"

"I know, but that don't mean it ain't good."

"Well, why didn't you eat any, then?"

"Well, I, umm…"

"It's no good, isn't it?"

"No, that's not it," Jake hemmed. "You see, it's just that…ever since I was a boy…Oh, darn it, I just don't like apples!"

"Well, who doesn't like *apples*?" Kate demanded in disbelief.

"I reckon me..."

It was a cute scene, but it wasn't quite fiction. It happened that way, more or less, when Olivia tried to bake an apple pie for Dusty Bob early in their relationship.

In another new scene, Kate confronted Jake about his drifting past.

"You're the sheriff of this town now," she told him. "The people have put their faith in you. Responsibility comes with that badge, mister. So, I need to know, before we take this relationship any further: what, exactly, are your intentions, Jake? Are you going to be a _real_ sheriff and stand up to my father and all his hired men, or are you going to run away like all the times before when things got tough?"

"This time it's different," Jake replied.

"Oh? What's different this time?"

"This time I got a reason to stay."

"A reason? You mean, justice?"

"Justice is only part of it," Jake said. "A man's gotta have more than justice to make life tolerable. Justice don't keep you warm at night. Justice don't make you wanna do what's right. Justice don't make a man feel like a man. Only a woman's love can do that. You make me feel like a man, Kate. So I'll stay. That's right – I'll stay an' take on your father an' all his henchmen – I'll take on all the cattle barons in Nevada, if I have to. But I need you by my side, Kate. I love you, an' I never wanna lose you!"

Then, they kissed passionately.

This was Dusty Bob's favorite new scene with Olivia, and he replayed it night after night.

"But even the new scenes are beginning to fade," he confided to Jim one day.

"Then we'll just have Max write you some more," Jim replied. Then he coughed.

"Well, I reckon even ol' Max Hoffman won't live forever," Dusty Bob predicted gloomily.

"You've always been a glass-half-full kinda man," Jim said. "Just enjoy each day while you can, Bob." Then he coughed some more.

"You all right, partner?" Dusty Bob asked.

"Just the dust around this place," Jim said.

"Never bothered you before," Dusty Bob observed.

"Why don't you just mind your own business?" Jim snapped. "I'm _fine_."

*   *   *

As the weeks passed, things settled into a kind of easy, familiar routine on Memory Ranch. Kitty still doted on Trooper Torres, but he still pined for Sally, who still pined for Jim, who, in turn, still pined for Lucia.

"Seems everyone around here loves the wrong person," Jim told Dusty Bob one day. "Things would work out a whole lot better if folks wasn't so particular."

"I reckon love's a powerful riddle, all right." Dusty Bob agreed.

"Well, I'm beginnin' to think Memory Ranch is a place where love can never be satisfied," Jim opined.

As if to prove the point, Howie showed up the very next day. He was a tow truck driver who wore a red bandana around his neck and an Australian bush hat with one side pinned up. Howie also had a false leg, his ill-fated appendage having been amputated after a rattlesnake bite on a childhood camping trip.

Howie wanted to see Kitty.

"Who is he?" Dusty Bob asked.

"This is Howie," Kitty replied casually. "He's Vince's brother. And Siggy's father."

"I thought you said Vince was Siggy's father," Dusty Bob said, confused.

"I told Vince that to protect Howie," Kitty explained. "Because Howie was engaged to get married to Agnes."

"The wedding's off now," Howie said cheerfully.

"Why?" Kitty asked.

"Because Vince came back to Albuquerque an' I caught the two of 'em carryin' on," Howie replied.

"Vincent Archuleta!" Kitty said, shaking her head in disapproval.

"But everything's all right," Howie insisted. "_We_ can get married now!"

Kitty was stunned. She wanted to talk to Howie privately, so everyone gave them their space. They talked animatedly for over an hour. Then Kitty gathered everyone together to make an announcement.

241

"I'm getting married!"

"You sure about this, Sweetheart?" Dusty Bob asked.

"Yes," Kitty replied. "Howie's not like Vince at all. He treats me real good. He says he wants to be a father to Siggy."

"But what about Trooper Torres?" Jim asked.

"I'll never love another man with the intensity and devotion I feel for Trooper Torres," Kitty admitted, with Howie standing right next to her. "But it's unrequited. Trooper Torres is so in love with Sally that he is blind to my very public and unabashed feelings for him. On the other hand, Howie is right here, laying all his cards on the table, and while my feelings for him will never match my feelings for Trooper Torres, I think he will be a faithful husband and a suitable father for Siggy."

Howie, smiling, seemed completely okay with her speech.

"Well, if that's the way you feel, honey, I'll be more than proud to walk you down the aisle," Dusty Bob said.

The hastily-arranged nuptials occurred two days later at a small, cheap wedding chapel in Holbrook. Sally and Debra Lynn were Kitty's bridesmaids. Trooper Torres graciously agreed to serve as best man, and Dusty Bob walked the bride down the aisle, as he had promised. The bride wore a well-worn thrift store gown, but both Dusty Bob and Howie thought she looked beautiful.

Everything was going according to plan until the happy couple were about to exchange vows, when the chapel doors burst open and a five-foot-ten woman in overalls, a backwards baseball cap, and combat boots stomped in. She was built like a longshoreman and didn't look happy.

"Agnes!" Howie gulped. "What are _you_ doing here?"

"So, you thought you could run off and get married without me knowin', did you?" Agnes growled. "You thought I'd never find you, did you? Well, here I am, Bub!"

"What – what do you want?" Howie asked, visibly shaken.

"What do I _want_?" Agnes repeated, striding confidently down the aisle toward the bridal couple. "Don't you remember all that sweet pillow-talk, honey? I want the honeymoon in Carson City you promised me. I want the double-wide in the best trailer park in Albuquerque you promised me. AND I WANT THAT WHIRLPOOL WASHING MACHINE YOU PROMISED ME!"

"Well, feelin's change, Agnes, an' I'm marryin' Kitty now."

"Oh, we're marryin' *Kitty* now, are we? Listen to me, you little worm: you took away my happiness. You took away my dreams. You took away my future. Now I'm going to take something from *you*!"

She reached out and grabbed his ankle with her meaty red mitts. She twisted several times, and tore his false leg right off. The fabric of his cheap pants gave way easily.

"I've got your leg, and I'm not giving it back!" she sang as she skipped back up the aisle toward the doors. Outside, she hopped into a waiting car and drove off, waving the leg out the window as she screeched away.

Everyone stood in stunned horror.

"I'm not going to let this spoil our special day," Howie told Kitty, hopping on one leg. "I love you, baby!"

"I like you an awful lot too, Howie," Kitty replied politely – and then they exchanged their vows like nothing had ever happened.

The next morning, the local paper carried the headline: *Jilted Lover Makes Off With Groom's Leg*. The story even got picked up by the Phoenix newspapers.

Despite the rough start, within a week Kitty was pregnant again and Howie drove his tow truck into Holbrook to be fitted for a new leg. Crossing the street to the doctor's office on crutches, he was run down and killed instantly by a drunk, manic-depressive, out of work orthopedic shoe salesman who had stolen a truck full of pies. Reginald Deems had moved to Arizona from Melton Mowbray, England – known internationally as the Town of Pies – where he was wanted in connection with the Great Pie Heist of 1948. In Arizona, he had taken to drinking, gambling, and chronic unemployment, but never lost his taste for stolen pie.

Mr. Deems fled the scene and, with no witnesses to the event except a legally-blind traffic cop, was never brought to justice for his crimes.

"That pie thief did you a favor," Sally later told Kitty. "Your husband was a very stupid man. He wouldn't have been able to make you happy."

Sadly, Kitty found it hard to disagree.

Chapter 21

As time moved lazily along at Memory Ranch, Debra Lynn began to come out of her shell and come into her own. She became more confident and creative in the kitchen, updating the diner menu to include Caesar Salad and Chicken a la King. It was a talent few knew she possessed – including herself – a skill which challenged some of the palates around the place, but unequivocally pleased others.

One day an odd little man with features like a cat and very large, doleful eyes came through and found his way into the diner. Not expecting to see much more than meatloaf and chili with beans due to the pedestrian nature of the place, he was pleasantly surprised when he took a look at the menu.

"Beef Wellington – *here*?" he asked, his already large eyes growing in circumference. He ordered the dish and nibbled gingerly on a saltine while he waited with great expectation. When the dish came, he ate a few bites and put the bent fork down decisively.

"You must introduce me to this chef," he said with a directness that took Sally aback, given his diminutive stature and overall genteel demeanor. Sally went into the kitchen and told Debra Lynn a diner wanted to speak with her. Thinking she'd done something terribly wrong, Debra Lynn emerged from the kitchen with slumped shoulders and bowed head, as if submitting in advance to the tongue-lashing that was certain to come.

"You – you're the chef?" the man asked in astonishment when he saw the slender, young, pony-tailed girl come out.

"Yes, sir," Debra Lynn said sheepishly.

"And you made *this*?" the man asked, indicating the Beef Wellington on his plate.

"Yes, sir," Debra Lynn repeated. "Is – is there something wrong with it, sir?"

"Wrong with it? Of course not, my dear," the man smiled. "Why, it's simply wonderful! Tell me: are you formally-trained? You have such a command of the seasonings!"

"No, sir. I just sorta follow the recipe, but I make a few changes to make it more the way I like."

"I can see that," the man concurred. "Why, this is the most distinctive Beef Wellington I've ever tasted." He told Debra Lynn he owned restaurants in Phoenix, Denver, and Las Vegas, and couldn't find enough good chefs to keep them all going. He offered her a job and a five-hundred -dollar cash advance on the spot.

So Debra Lynn packed up little Hamlet and her few belongings and moved to Las Vegas, where she did very well in the restaurant business – so well, in fact, that she was able to open her own restaurant twelve years later.

Around the same time, Trooper Torres had an epiphany about Sally: he could never marry her because she was already married to her peripatetic husband. Besides, he knew she would never stop loving Jim. So, he humbly asked Dusty Bob if he could marry Kitty.

"Well, if she'll have you, I reckon she couldn't do no better," Dusty Bob replied.

Trooper Torres and Kitty, still pregnant with Howie's child, got married quietly before a justice of the peace in Holbrook. They moved into the little white adobe house because Lucia moved her cult to San Diego, California, to take advantage of the favorably mild weather and the abundance of UFO sightings there. It made a cozy little home for Trooper Torres, Kitty, and Siggy, and Trooper Torres fully intended to raise both children just as if they were his own.

Trooper Torres dropped Kitty and Siggy off at the ranch every morning when he came for his coffee. From now on, though, Kitty insisted on making his coffee – without chili pepper – and Trooper Torres slowly acquired a taste for her less-spicy brew. Siggy, for his part, continued to be cooed over and spoiled by both Dusty Bob and Sally.

In fact, everything at Memory Ranch seemed to hum along rather pleasantly – except for Jim, whose coughing fits had increased in frequency and intensity to the point where Dusty Bob and Sally were growing quite alarmed. When he began coughing up blood and trying – unsuccessfully – to hide it from the others, Dusty Bob put his foot down and drove him to the hospital in Holbrook.

The emergency room doctor looked alarmed when he saw Jim and heard the deep rattle of his cough. "You really should have brought him in sooner," he told Dusty Bob.

"I tried, but he's an ornery ol' mule," Dusty Bob replied.

They admitted him and began running tests immediately. Dusty Bob stayed with him a few hours, but Jim asked him to go home.

"I'm fine, Bob," he insisted. "This is nothin', partner. You go on home to the ranch an' take care of things. I'll be good as new before you know it."

Dusty Bob drove back to the ranch, but he came back to Holbrook to visit Jim about every other day. But despite Jim's declarations that he'd be fine, he looked weaker and thinner each visit. And he was coughing more.

"You don't look so hot, *amigo*," Dusty Bob commented one time. "What does the doctor say?"

"Aww, you know doctors," Jim groused, sitting up in bed with tubes running out of his arms and nose. "These quacks don't know what the hell they're talkin' about. I'm feelin' better already!"

"You don't look better."

"I need to get outta here, Bob. I can't afford these hospital bills."

"Don't you worry, I'll take care of that," Dusty Bob said. "Them checks from Bud Silverman is comin' pretty regular, now."

"If I ever get outta here, I'll pay you back."

"Well, Sally wanted me to bring you this pie," Dusty Bob said, setting it on a table next to Jim's bed. "It's cherry, your favorite."

"Aww, I cain't taste nothin' with these tubes runnin' in my nose an' down my throat, anyway," Jim complained, pushing the pie away from him.

"Well, you should eat somethin', partner," Dusty Bob said. "You're lookin' a might thin."

"I'm not hungry," Jim said, looking out the window. "You go on home now – I don't want you lettin' the place go to hell on account of me. I said I'd be fine." Then he had such a strong coughing spell that the nurse had to come in and ask Dusty Bob to leave.

The next time Dusty Bob came, Jim looked even worse.

"What the hell you want?" he asked in a raspy voice.

"Sally wanted me to drop off this chili n' beans she made for you," Dusty Bob answered.

"I ain't hungry," Jim barked. "Look, I don't want you comin' around here no more, Bob. It ain't no good, now." He wouldn't look at his old friend. He was emaciated now – Dusty Bob knew he felt ashamed of the way he looked.

"I don't want you getting' lonesome, is all," Dusty Bob said.

"I ain't lonesome," Jim insisted. "I ain't lonesome, I ain't hungry, an' I don't want you comin' around no more. Just get on, now…"

"I'm not leavin' you, Jim. Not like this."

"Well, this is the best you're gonna see me," Jim said bitterly. "Doctor said there's nothin' they can do. It's just a matter of time…"

"Well, why'd you let it go for so long, then?"

"It wouldn't have made no difference," Jim replied. "I'm not gonna be fine, Bob. I'm dyin'. The doctors know it, an' now I know it. An' it's gonna be sooner rather than later."

"Jim…I…"

"Shut your damn pie-hole," Jim said. "I don't want your sympathy. You really wanna do somethin' for me? Get me outta here. Right now. Let's go – I don't wanna die in here, Bob. Not in this dreary, God-forsaken place."

"Where would we go?"

"Take me to that little ridge over-lookin' Lucia's house. That's where I wanna spend eternity."

"But Kitty an' Siggy an' Trooper Torres live there now," Dusty Bob reminded him.

"I don't care," Jim said. "That was Lucia's house. That's where I wanna be."

"I don't know, Jim. What will the doctor say?"

"We won't tell 'im. Just help me get dressed an' get me the hell outta this damn morgue."

"Let's just stop an' think about this, now," Dusty Bob hedged.

"I'd be much obliged if you'd be the one to plant me in the ground," Jim said. "It's my last wish."

"That's a mighty big thing to ask."

"I'd do for you, an' you know it."

"You don't want me to..?"

"You won't have to. It's just gonna happen. I can feel it. I don't want no fuss, Bob. Just put me in the ground by Lucia's place, an' be done with it."

They pulled all the tubes out of him and Dusty Bob helped him get dressed and pull his boots on. Jim put on his old cowboy hat and sighed with satisfaction. "That's much better, partner."

With Jim leaning against Dusty Bob, they were able to sneak out of the hospital when the nurse at the front desk took a smoke break. They shuffled outside and got into the pickup truck without being seen. Dusty Bob drove out to the little adobe house and parked on the ridge overlooking it.

Dusty Bob shut the engine off and waited. It was late afternoon and the sun was going down in the west. The tall, silent *saguaros* cast their long, black shadows across the chalky desert floor, like grotesquely deformed actors frozen on a stage. Dusty Bob looked over at Jim – he was fading with the sun.

"Oh, Jim – you cain't just go off an' leave me all alone like this," Dusty Bob lamented.

"Typical," Jim smiled. "It's always about you, isn't it? I'm the one dyin' here."

"Who's gonna give the kiddies their horseback rides, then?"

"You're just gonna have to put the whiskey bottle down for a minute an' get up off your duff an' pick up the slack around the place for a change," Jim said, his voice hoarse and his breathing labored.

"Well, who do you want your things to go to?" Dusty Bob asked.

"I want Lucia to have 'em, but she probably wouldn't take 'em. So give 'em to Sally."

"What about Lucia's paintings?"

"Sell 'em an' start a college fund for the young 'uns."

There was a long pause. The sun was just about to go down now.

"Well, if you're gonna do it, hurry up an' be done with it," Dusty Bob said, fighting back tears. "I got things I gotta tend to."

"Why don't you stop bein' so damn pushy an' let the Grim Reaper do his job for once?"

"That bastard can go straight to hell, as far as I'm concerned." Dusty Bob spat out the window for emphasis.

"I want a smoke," Jim said.

"Do you think that's a good idear, partner?"

"What's it gonna do – kill me?"

Dusty Bob rolled Jim a cigarette and lit it for him.

"Ah…" Jim sighed. "One for the road, so to speak." He had a long coughing spell, coughing up a lot of blood into a rag, then recovered. "It won't be long now, partner."

The sun was down now, leaving the desert bathed in a purple glow.

"I don't want you to go, Jim." Jim reached over and gave Dusty Bob's hand a weak squeeze. He didn't say anything. A few moments later, he was gone. His last words, or breaths, really, were, "She never knew…" as he looked down at Lucia's little house.

Dusty Bob got out of the truck and stood numbly in the twilight a moment.

"I was the one who was supposed to go first," he said out loud. "Now what am I supposed to do?" Then he reached for a shovel in the bed and buried his friend on that little ridge overlooking the house of his one true love.

"He was hard-headed an' stubborn as a mule," Dusty Bob told the others when he got back to the ranch and gave them the news. "He once told me, 'Don't worry about dyin', worry about _livin'_.'"

Dusty Bob was lost without Jim – especially at sunup when it was time for cigarettes and coffee on the porch. But the one who took it the hardest was Sally. She started going down to Resurrection Creek, where the two of them used to skinny dip, every evening when the sun went down to sit on the bank and think about Jim.

One evening after supper, Dusty Bob followed her down to the creek and sat down beside her.

"We agreed to meet here if anything ever happened to one of us," Sally explained. "He's here right now."

"Oh, Sally – I'm so sorry," Dusty Bob said. "I know you miss him somethin' awful. I do, too."

Sally was quiet a long time. "I feel like I fought you for him my whole life," she finally said quietly. "You won. You had him – you an' Lucia. I never did. But I'm tired of hating. Jim's free now, an' I don't hate you anymore."

Dusty Bob didn't say anything.

That night, he spooled up _Rendezvous in Reno_ for possibly the five hundredth time. It was the customary midnight showing, with all of Max's new scenes, but something was different this time. Olivia appeared in the room during the saloon dance scene and they did their waltz as usual. After the dance, Olivia lingered longer than normal. She looked very sad, as if she had something to tell him.

"That was the best dance yet," she said quietly.

"You're breaking the script," he said.

"I know," she said. "Our time together has come to an end, and now I must go."

"Do you have to?"

"Yes. This dream was only meant for a brief time. Now you must return to the waking world."

"But, I've just lost Jim, and now you – I can't lose you again."

"Take a look around you," she said comfortingly. "You still have so much."

"Goodbye, my love."

"We'll be together soon," she said. She kissed him gently and disappeared into the shadows. He wiped his eyes dry, put the film back into its metal canister for the last time, and put the canister back into the old trunk of memories in the storage room.

*   *   *

The loss of Jim and Olivia's bittersweet farewell kept everyone on Memory Ranch good and somber for a spell. There was a general sense that a generation was quietly passing away, but the proliferation of life all around them buoyed their spirits somewhat.

Kitty had her baby, and it was a girl. She named her Lily Rose. Sally said Lily had a heart murmur that sounded just like the beating of hummingbird wings. "She is going to be a very loving, free spirit," Sally predicted.

On the porch, Dusty Bob bounced young Siggy on his knee. "I'll teach you to ride n' rope like a real cowboy soon," he told his grandson contentedly. "You'll make a fine cow-puncher. An' someday, this place'll be all yours!"

Later that night, Dusty Bob asked Sally if she knew the day he would die.

"What you want to know *that* for?" she demanded.

"Because, I wanna know if I can keep my promise to Siggy or not."

Sally wrote something down on a piece of scratch paper and handed it to him. Dusty Bob read it, then folded it in half and stuffed it into his shirt pocket.

"Fine, then," he said with satisfaction. "I'll be able to keep my promise."

They never spoke of it again, but, in reality, Sally didn't really know when Dusty Bob was going to die. She just picked a random date and wrote it down.

Sometime around this time, Max Hoffman escaped and wandered the desert for several days. Then he found the glowing wooden box abandoned on the ground by Blanch and Dickie. He looked down at it a while, then picked it up and walked off into the desert with it under his arm.

No one even noticed he was gone.